DR OFF-LIMITS

BY
ROBIN GIANNA

FROM FLING
TO FOREVER

BY
AVRIL TREMAYNE

MILLS &
BOON

After completing a degree in journalism, working in the advertising industry, then becoming a stay-at-home mum, **Robin Gianna** had what she calls her mid-life awakening. She decided she wanted to write the romance novels she'd loved since her teens, and embarked on that quest by joining RWA, Central Ohio Fiction Writers, and working hard at learning the craft.

She loves sharing the journey with her characters, helping them through obstacles and problems to find their own happily-ever-afters. When not writing, Robin likes to cr̶ in her kitchen, dig in the dirt, and enjoy life with̶ tolerant husband, three great kids, drooling bulldog̶ grouchy Siamese cat.

To learn more about her work visit her website: www.robingianna.com

Avril Tremayne read *Jane Eyre* as a teenager and has been hooked on tales of passion and romance ever since. An opportunistic insomniac, she has been a lifelong crazy-mad reader, but she took the scenic route to becoming a writer— via gigs as diverse as shoe salesgirl, hot cross bun packer, teacher, and public relations executive. She has spent a good chunk of her life travelling, and has more favourite destinations than should be strictly allowable.

Avril is happily settled in her hometown of Sydney, Australia, where her husband and daughter try to keep her out of trouble—not always successfully. When she's not writing or reading she can generally be found eating although she does *not* cook!

Check out her website: www.avriltremayne.com or follow her on Twitter: @AvrilTremayne and Facebook: www.facebook.com/avril.tremayne

FROM FLING TO FOREVER
is Avril Tremayne's debut book
for Mills & Boon® Medical Romance™!

FLIRTING WITH
DR OFF-LIMITS

BY
ROBIN GIANNA

Published in Great Britain 2014
by Mills & Boon, an imprint of Harlequin (UK) Limited,
Eton House, 18-24 Paradise Road, Richmond, Surrey, TW9 1SR

© 2014 Robin Gianakopoulos

ISBN: 978-0-263-90794-0

Harlequin (UK) Limited's policy is to use papers that are natural, renewable and recyclable products and made from wood grown in sustainable forests. The logging and manufacturing processes conform to the legal environmental regulations of the country of origin.

Printed and bound in Spain
by Blackprint CPI, Barcelona

Dear Reader

Have you ever been tempted by something you know might not be the wisest choice for you? That second piece of chocolate cake, or a few extra Lottery tickets for that big jackpot, or maybe an item you want to buy but can't afford?

My heroine in this book, Katy Pappas, hero-worshipped her older brother's best friend Alec Armstrong. Until he disappointed her—twice—and she wrote him off. Now that she's graduated from medical school Katy has taken a job as a student intern at a hospital in beautiful San Diego, California. The same hospital where her brother and Alec both work as surgeons. As she begins to see the Alec she once believed him to be Katy finds herself drawn to him again. Except he's her teacher, and a relationship between them is strictly forbidden. Should she give in to temptation, risking her heart to a man with a past? A man who also happens to be completely off-limits?

Alec Armstrong made a mistake in his life he's determined not to repeat. Until Katy shows up and turns that conviction upside down. Risking his heart isn't the problem for Alec—but risking both their careers most definitely is!

I hope you enjoy Alec and Katy's story. Drop me a line through my website, www.robingianna.com, or on my Robin Gianna Facebook page. I'd love to hear from you!

Robin

Dedication

This one's for you, Meta, as you well know!

Whether I just need your great advice or
I'm seriously panicking, you're always there for me.
I can't thank you enough for that. You're the best! xoxo

Acknowledgements

A huge thank you to my agent, Cori Deyoe
of Three Seas Literary Agency, for pulling me from the
fires with this one. I so appreciate your tremendous help
and steadfast encouragement.

Another big thank you to my editor, Laurie Johnson, for
the wonderful suggestions to pull this book together, and
for your patience and support. I truly appreciate it.

Recent titles by Robin Gianna:

THE LAST TEMPTATION OF DR DALTON
CHANGED BY HIS SON'S SMILE

**These books are also available in eBook format
from www.millsandboon.co.uk**

Praise for
Robin Gianna:

'If you're looking for a story sweet but exciting,
characters loving but cautious, a fan of Medicals or
looking for a story to try to see if you like the medical
genre, CHANGED BY HIS SON'S SMILE is the story
for you! I would never have guessed Robin
is a debut author: the story flowed brilliantly,
the dialogue was believable and I was
thoroughly engaged in the medical dramas.'
—*Contemporary Romance Reviews*

CHAPTER ONE

KATHERINE PAPPAS HOPED with all her heart that she'd been abducted by aliens. And that an extraterrestrial scientific experiment had sucked her brain dry.

After all, she'd much rather believe that the blankness of her mind throughout the night had been due to interplanetary interference and not because she'd just plain forgotten everything she'd ever learned in medical school. Exactly three weeks after she'd graduated. With a new job as a first-year intern at the same well-respected hospital as her hotshot surgeon brother.

Katy sucked in a calming breath. *You know this stuff. Just quit with the nerves and do the job you've been dreaming of doing forever.* She moved into a corner so no one, hopefully, would notice her until she felt ready to head to the first patient's room for morning rounds. After wiping her sweaty hands on her scrubs, she began to organize cards on each patient she'd be seeing that morning.

The shrill sound of her phone made her nearly jump out of her skin, and her stomach somehow both sank and knotted as she answered. The words that had been so wonderful to say just a week ago seemed to stick in her throat and choke her. "Dr. Pappas."

"Paging Dr. Katherine Pappas, world's best surgical

intern on her way to becoming world's best family practice physician. Is she available?"

Hearing the voice of her closest friend in med school, Rachel Egan, made Katy relax and even conjure a small grin. "Dr. Pappas is available, except more likely she's on her way to becoming the first intern booted out of Oceancrest Community Hospital only hours after arriving."

"Uh-oh," Rachel said. "Bad night on call?"

"The nurses are probably referring to me as Dr. Dolittle. As in do very little." She sighed. "All night when they asked me questions, the right answer seemed to take a minute to percolate in my brain. I was sure I could do this, but now I'm worried."

"You're being ridiculous. Who had a straight four-point GPA in both undergrad and med school, like any human can do that? Who got the Alpha Omega Alpha award when we graduated? You're brilliant, Katy, and you're the only one who doesn't realize it."

"Then why doesn't the perfect answer pop instantly into my 'brilliant' brain?"

"Because we're nervous newbies, that's why. We crossed that med-school finish line, and all of a sudden we have the word 'Doctor' in front of our names and have to answer to it. Who wouldn't be scared? I know I am."

"Really? You are?" Rachel had always been the calm and confident student, the one who'd earned smiles and praise from professors and attending physicians for her cool and collected demeanor. In stark contrast to Katy's often ruffled one.

"Heck, yes, I am! I wish we'd ended up training at the same hospital. Maybe we'd both feel less freaked out if we had each other to lean on."

"I know. But you're happy to be back in your hometown, and I'm thrilled to be in San Diego. Plus I think it's good that I moved in with Nick. He's going through a hard time right now."

"Still pretty depressed about his divorce, huh?"

"Actually, the divorce isn't final yet. But, yeah, he's very glum compared to his usual self." Katy didn't know what had gone wrong in her brother's marriage, but it was sad that, after just a year, it hadn't worked out. She wished she could blame his wife, Meredith, except Katy had always liked her a lot—and, as the saying went, it took two to tango. Whatever their problems, both of them had probably contributed to them.

"It'll be good for him to have you there, I'm sure, though I hope nobody gossips about favoritism since you're his sister."

Favoritism? Katy hadn't even thought about that, and hopefully no one else would either.

"So, tell me—"

Katy's hospital call system buzzed and her belly tightened. "Gotta go, Rachel." She punched the button and swallowed hard before she tried to talk. "Dr. Pappas."

"Mrs. Patterson's potassium is at three point zero, and I need to know what you want me to do."

Okay, so that was low. She should order a potassium IV—probably four mil. No, wait. Maybe she should give it orally? A nervous laugh bubbled up in her throat as she wondered how the nurse would react if she prescribed a banana to bring up the patient's potassium.

She swallowed. "You know, I'll have to call you right back."

"Are you serious?" the nurse said in an annoyed and condescending tone. "Fine. I'll be waiting."

"Okay." Katy's face burned as she turned off her phone and wiped her hands, which were somehow sweaty and icy cold at the same time, on her scrubs again. She fumbled in her pocket for her Scut Monkey book. Rachel made fun of her that she infinitely preferred using it over trying to look things up on the internet. But her little book had helped her more than once, and she was determined to get this right.

Katy gnawed her lip and studied the little book. Based on the patient's age, weight, and kidney function, it looked like she was right. Four ml potassium to drink would be the safest, most effective approach. Okay, good. As she tried to call the nurse back she dropped her phone on the hard floor, sending the plastic cover soaring across the room.

She groaned as she grabbed up the phone, relieved to see it was still working. Klutzy Katy. Why had she been plagued with some pitiful clumsiness gene, and why did it get worse when she was nervous? Graceful under fire she was not.

She called the nurses' station, surprised that a different nurse answered to take the oral potassium order. How many staff worked in this hospital? The number must be mind-boggling.

Right, time to get to rounds!

The patient card on the top of her pile read "Angela Roberts, Room 1073." She went to knock on the door, pausing to inhale a deep breath. This was it! Seeing her very first patient in person as a real doctor! Yes, she'd inherited all of them from the resident who'd already seen them, but still. The thought was nerve-racking but thrilling, too, and a big, spontaneous smile came on her face.

"Hello, Mrs. Roberts. I'm Dr. Pappas, your intern. How are you feeling?"

"I'm all right, dear. Wishing they could figure out my spells so I can get the gall-bladder surgery over with."

"We're working hard to figure that out." She warmed her stethoscope against her palm before examining the woman. "We're in the process of ruling out things like seizures or transient ischemic attacks, which are little mini-strokes."

"Strokes? I'm sure I would know if I'd had a stroke, dear."

"TIAs are so tiny you might not notice." Katy smiled, her chest a little buoyant as she thought about this puzzle they were solving.

"Well," Mrs. Roberts said, waving her hand, "I trust Dr. Armstrong to know what he's doing. Whatever he figures out is right, I'm sure. He's a lovely man."

Katy felt her smile slip and she forced it back up, at the same time avoiding rolling her eyes. "No doubt Dr. Armstrong is an excellent surgeon."

And excellent at other things, too. Like giving fake excuses for not being with someone—breaking hearts in the process—then turning around and doing exactly that with someone else. Like having inappropriate hospital affairs that got other people fired. Fooling everyone who used to think he was wonderful in every way.

The old embarrassment and anger filled her chest again when she thought of how many years she'd hero-worshipped the man who didn't deserve it.

"And handsome! So good looking, like a doctor on TV. I'm sure a young thing like you can hardly resist a handsome surgeon like Dr. Armstrong."

"He's my superior here at the hospital, Mrs. Roberts." Long ago, she'd agreed. She'd thought everything about him gorgeous—his football-player physique, his warm amber eyes, his thick dark hair. Funny and smart, with a teasing grin that was irresistible.

But no more. A man had to be beautiful on the inside as well as the outside to appeal to her. Not that she appealed to him anyway, which he'd made abundantly clear.

"I'm feeling a little tired." The woman snuggled down

into her bed as Katy continued her examination. "Can you come back later?"

"I'm almost done for now, Mrs. Roberts. May I pull your sheet down a little? I just want to take a listen to your belly."

Katy glanced up when she didn't respond and was startled to see that her head had lolled to one side of the pillow, her mouth slack and her eyes closed. Had she fallen asleep, just like that?

"Mrs. Roberts?" Katy's heart sped up and she spoke louder, shaking the woman's shoulder. "Mrs. Roberts?"

The monitor the patient was hooked up to began to screech and Katy looked at the screen. Her oxygen level was dangerously low, but there was no change in her heart rate. That couldn't be right, could it? Quickly, she rubbed her knuckles against Mrs. Roberts's sternum.

Nothing. No response. Katy put shaky fingers against the woman's carotid artery. Her pulse was so slow and faint Katy knew this was beyond serious. Heart pounding in her ears now, she leaped up and smacked the red code button on the wall then ran back to the bedside.

"Okay, Katy, you've got this," she said out loud to herself as her mind spun through the advanced cardiac life support protocol she'd finished during orientation just yesterday. "It's as easy as ABC, right? Airway, breathing, circulation."

Her own breath seriously short and choppy, she shoved the pillows from the bed to get Mrs. Roberts lying flat and lifted her chin to open her airway. The woman's chest still barely moved.

Damn it! Katy knew she had to get a bag valve mask on her immediately, then noticed the EKG wires had been disconnected, probably when she'd gone to the bathroom. Stay calm here, you know what to do, she reminded herself, sucking in a deep breath to keep from fainting along with Mrs. Roberts.

Fumbling with the equipment, she managed to stay focused as two nurses ran into the room. "We need to get her back on the monitor. I need to bag her. Can you get me a bag valve mask? And another IV." She could practically smell their alarm and forced down her own. *Do not panic, Katy. This woman's life could depend on you.*

The loud sound of a cart rumbling down the hall and into the room made Katy sag in relief. The cavalry had arrived.

"Give me the patient's history," a guy said, as he moved from the crash cart to the head of the bed, quickly getting a bag on Mrs. Roberts to provide the oxygen she desperately needed. He was probably from the ICU team, but Katy wasn't about to waste time asking questions.

"Patient is eighty-two, with cholecystitis, her surgery is on hold until she's medically cleared by Cardiology." Katy gulped as she stared at the still-unresponsive Mrs. Roberts and forged on. "She was talking to me and just kind of collapsed. She has fainting spells and we're trying to figure out why."

She stared at the monitor as the ICU guy attached the last EKG lead. Involuntarily, Katy let out a little stressed cry when she saw the heart rate was alarmingly slow at only thirty-five beats per minute. "Sinus bradycardia," she said. "Atropine point five milligrams and we need pads for transcutaneous pacing."

Had all that really come right out of her mouth? No time to give herself a pat on the back as the ICU guy barked to the nurse, "Get Cardiology on the line. You, Doctor, get her paced as I intubate."

Katy blinked and a touch of panic welled in her chest that she resolutely tamped down. He'd just called her

"Doctor". She was part of this team, which would hopefully save this woman's life. Concentrating intently on getting the pads placed amid a flurry of activity by the nurses, she didn't even notice the tall, broad form that came to stand next to her.

"I'll take over now," a familiar deep voice said. "Good job, Dr. Pappas."

Alec Armstrong brushed past her as she moved to one side, allowing him to deliver the electricity to Mrs. Roberts's heart. Katy stood there, stunned, her hands now shaking like a tambourine. Beyond glad it wasn't her trying to get the pacing finished and giving orders to the nurses.

Which wasn't the right attitude, she scolded herself, since she wanted to be a doctor—was a doctor. But, dang it, how many newbies had to deal with their very first patient coding on them?

She watched Alec work, and couldn't help but notice how different he was, and yet somehow the same as when she'd known him years ago. As a boy and teen, he'd practically lived in their house as Nick's best friend. While he'd been as fun and adventurous as anybody she'd known, he'd always become calm and focused when there had been an important task at hand, his eyes intent, just like they were now. His hands moved swiftly and efficiently, as they had during all the crazy science experiments they'd done together. All the times he and Nick had worked on projects with her, teasing about her endless quest to learn new things and solve weird problems.

Her hero-worship of Alec was over. But the moment that thought came into her head, as she watched him work, she knew it wasn't true. How could she not admire how capably he dealt with a critical situation? But she didn't have to like him as a person to admire how good he was as a doctor and doubtless as a surgeon.

In a short time the frantic flurry of activity was over and the ICU guy began to wheel Mrs. Roberts from the room. As he left, he said over his shoulder, "I'll dictate my procedure note. You got the code note?"

"I've got it," Katy and Alec said at the same time. Their eyes met, his the amused, warm amber she remembered so well, and she felt her face flush. How could she have thought the guy was talking to her when attending surgeon extraordinaire Alec Armstrong had taken over?

"So, Katy-Did." His lips curved as he folded his arms across his chest. "What the hell did you do to my patient to make her code like that?"

"Please call me Katherine or Katy. I'm not a kid anymore," she said with dignity. Which he should know after her ill-advised behavior at her brother James's wedding five years ago. Her cheeks burned hotter at the memory.

"Fine, Dr. Katherine Pappas." His smile broadened, showing his white teeth. "How did you almost kill her?"

"I didn't almost kill her, and you know it. I didn't do anything." Katy's voice rose to practically a squeak on the last word and she cleared her throat, forcing herself to sound somewhat professional. "I was talking with her and giving her an exam, and she just fainted. I think she probably has sick sinus syndrome, which is why she's sometimes fine and other times faints."

"Do you, now?" He laughed. Actually laughed, and Katy felt her face heat again, but this time in annoyance.

"Yes, I do. I may be a total newbie, but I'm allowed to give my opinion, aren't I? Isn't it part of my training to form an opinion, even if it's wrong?"

"It is. And you are. Right, I mean, not wrong. And why am I not surprised that on your first day you've figured out this woman's likely diagnosis?" He stepped closer, touching his fingertip to her forehead and giving it a few little taps. "Some things never change, and one of them is that amazing, analytical brain of yours."

Some things never changed? Wasn't that the unfortunate truth? In spite of him making clear he had no interest in her as a woman, in spite of everything she knew about the kind of man he was, being so close to Alec made her breath a little short, which irritated her even more. How was it possible that the deepest corners of her brain still clung to the youthful crush she used to have? But being on Dr. Playboy's teaching service for the next month would most definitely squelch the final remnants of that for good. She was sure of it.

His fingertip slipped to her temple then dropped away. "Teaching rounds begin in an hour. Not too many people get to brag about dealing with a code on their very first day." That crooked grin stayed on his mouth as he gave her a little wink. "You did great. Welcome to Oceancrest, Katy-Did."

He turned and walked from the room, and she found herself staring at his back. Noticing that his thick dark hair was slightly longer than the last time she'd seen him. Noticing how unbelievably great his butt looked in those scrubs, how his shoulders filled every inch of the green fabric.

Noticing how horribly unkempt she herself looked at that moment. She looked down at her own wrinkled scrubs before she glanced in Mrs. Roberts's bathroom mirror at circles under her eyes the size of an IV bag. Ridiculously messy hair that had been finger-combed at best and now looked like it had been tamed by an eggbeater. Sleeping in the on-call room—if you could call the few hours her eyes had been closed sleeping—did not exactly lend itself to looking pulled together and rested.

She sighed and ran her fingers through her hair. Why

did it have to be that the first time Alec saw her at the hospital, she looked like a wreck?

And why did she care, anyway? The man was a player through and through.

Never would Alec have guessed he'd someday have Katy Pappas on his surgical teaching service. The cute but clumsy little girl who'd bugged the hell out of him and her brother Nick when they'd been young, tagging along on their adventures and asking nonstop questions, for some reason believing they'd know the answers.

The worshipful gaze of her blue eyes had always made his chest puff up a little with pride. Despite how much he and Nick had complained about her hanging out with them, he'd always secretly liked it when she had. That someone had thought he was smart and worthy of that kind of adulation had felt damned good, since it had been in very short supply in his own home.

The nonstop criticism his father had doled out had made Alec want to live up—or down—to his father's expectations of him. He'd worked as hard at partying as he had at football, and probably the only reason he hadn't gone down in flames had been because he'd had the steady support of the Pappas family, and Dr. George Pappas in particular.

After he and Nick had headed off to college and medical school, he hadn't seen the Pappas clan again until five years ago at a family wedding. Gobsmacked that Katy, awkwardly geeky child and studious teenager, had morphed into a drop-dead gorgeous twenty-one-year-old woman, he remembered standing stock-still, staring at her in disbelief. Shocked that he'd found her attractive in a way that was *not* at all brotherly.

He'd been even more shocked when, standing in a quiet corner at the reception, a champagne-tipsy Katy had grabbed his face between her hands and pressed her mouth to his. A mouth so warm and soft and delectable that every synapse in his brain had short-circuited and he'd found himself kissing her back. Their lips had parted and tongues had danced as he'd sunk deeply into the mind-boggling pleasure of it.

Then sanity had returned and he'd practically pushed her away, horrified. No way could he have anything like that with Katy Pappas, little sister of his best friend. She was totally off-limits. Period.

He'd tried to make a joke of it. Katy, however, hadn't thought it was remotely amusing when he'd told her he didn't feel that way about her, and that it would be all wrong if he did.

If she'd been pressed closer against him, she would have known part of that statement was a lie. But appropriate? Hell, no.

He sighed. From that moment on his friendship with Katy had been pretty much over. She'd been cool at other family functions since then. Aloof, even.

Alec had shoved down his feelings of disappointment that she was no longer the Katy who'd thought he was great. Hell, after the mess he'd made of some things in his life, he shouldn't expect anyone to feel that way.

Then he'd walked into the coding patient's room and seen her, wrinkled, messy, and nervous. Beautifully messy and nervous, yes, but so much like the Katy he'd once known he hadn't been able to help but want that old friendship back.

And just like the old Katy, in the midst of all the chaos she'd still shown what a brainiac she was. That she was good at figuring out what to do in any circumstances, despite being brand new at the art and science of doctoring.

Maybe it was absurd, pathetic even, but he wanted to

see again the Katy who used to like and admire him, who had tolerated and even enjoyed his teasing.

Alec remembered well the feel of her lips against his. But a woman like her no doubt had so many boyfriends that a little kiss five years ago would have been completely forgotten.

CHAPTER TWO

As ALEC STRODE down the hall, he could see the residents and interns waiting for him at the end of it, but his gaze stuck fast on Katy.

She'd changed into street clothes and a lab coat, and had obviously found a minute to brush her hair, which was no longer in a tangle but instead covered her shoulders in lustrous waves. He remembered that thick hair of hers always falling into her eyes and face as they'd studied things together, and he'd gotten into the habit of tucking its softness behind her ears so she'd been able to see whatever he and Nick had been showing her.

Her hands waving around as she spoke—another thing that was such a part of who she was—Katy was talking intently to the young man next to her, a frown creasing her brows, which made Alec smile. If he had to guess, she was regaling the other new intern with details about some condition or patient she was wondering about, because that brain of hers never rested.

"Good morning, everyone. I'm Dr. Alec Armstrong, as most of you know." He forced his attention from Katy to look at the young man she was speaking with. "You must be Michael Coffman, one of our new interns. We're glad you're here. Please tell us about yourself."

"I'm going into general surgery, planning to specialize in urology."

"Excellent. Our other intern here is Katy Pappas." He smiled at her, but she just gave a small nod in return. "Tell us about your intended specialty."

"I'm going into family practice medicine. I really enjoyed working with all kinds of people during med school." She looked at the group around her and her expression warmed. "Older folks and little ones and everybody in between. Figuring out what their medical problems are, when sometimes it can be a bit of a mystery, fascinates me. Knowing I'm helping individuals and families alike. I'm going to love doing that kind of work."

She spoke fast, her blue eyes now sparkling with the enthusiasm he remembered from their childhood whenever she had been tackling a puzzle or been deep into a science project, and his own smile grew.

"I'm glad you've discovered your calling. Figuring that out is sometimes the hardest part of medical school." He found himself wanting to keep looking at her, wanting to hear her speak and see her smile, but he made himself turn to the rest of the group.

"So let's continue our introductions. This is our fifth-year surgical resident, Elizabeth Stark, who performed some of the surgeries on the patients we'll see this morning. You met our second-year surgical resident, Todd Eiterman, this morning on work rounds."

Alec finished the spiel he always gave new interns, hoping they actually listened. "Beyond the nuts and bolts of diagnosis and surgery I want to teach you how to talk to people, to ask questions and listen carefully to the answers, which is the only way to truly learn their histories. Conclude what you think the working diagnosis might be then order tests based on those conclusions."

"Excuse me, Dr. Armstrong, but last month Dr. Hillen-brand said the opposite, so I'm confused," Todd, the second-year resident, said with a frown. "I thought we were to order tests then, based on those tests, come up with a working diagnosis."

"Technology is an amazing thing, Todd. But it can't replace hands-on doctoring, which is the single most important thing I want you to learn on my rotation." Alec studied the expressions on the faces before him. Smug understanding from Elizabeth, who'd heard it more times from him than she wanted to, he was sure, and also liked to play suck-up to the doctor evaluating her. Skepticism from Todd. Bewilderment and confusion from Michael. And avid concentration and focus from Katy's big blue eyes, which made him wish he could pin a gold star on her before rounds had even begun.

The thought sent his gaze to the lapels of her coat and the V of smooth, golden skin showing above her silky blouse, and he quickly shifted his attention to Todd. She was his student, damn it. And perhaps someday again his friend. But thinking of her as a very attractive woman? An absolute no-no.

"We'll be seeing patients who had surgery the past couple of days," he continued, keeping his eyes off Katy. "But first we'll see Mrs. Patterson, on whom tests were run yesterday. I know you've made your work rounds, so a lot of what I'm going to say will be a repeat of what you already know."

Alec led the way toward Helen Patterson's room with the group of students following behind. Katy was closest to him, and her light, fresh scent seemed to waft to him, around him, pleasing his nostrils so much he picked up the pace to put another foot or so between them.

What kind of doctor was distracted by someone's sex

appeal while in the middle of work? Not the kind of doctor he demanded he be, that was for sure. Not the kind of doctor he'd been at one time, long ago when he'd been younger and stupid.

"Dr. Pappas, will you tell me about this patient from your work rounds this morning?"

"This is Mrs. Helen Patterson, and she has been in a rehabilitation nursing facility for one week, post-op after surgery for a broken hip," Katy said. "She was admitted here yesterday for abdominal pain and referred to the surgery service. She had low blood pressure and her lactate was elevated."

Katy licked her lips nervously, and Alec yanked his gaze away from them. He tried to simply listen and not notice the serious blue of her eyes as she spoke. "We ordered a CT scan of her belly, and there was no evidence of perforation in the bowel or appendicitis. We observed her overnight, gave her IV fluids and pain meds and she has spontaneously improved. We've determined that she has a mild case of ischemic colitis. She had a normal breakfast, and her physical exam is normal, so she can be released today."

Her expression was both pleased and slightly anxious, and Alec hoped he wouldn't have to remind her about the low potassium he'd read about in Mrs. Patterson's chart, and that the repeat potassium was still slightly low. "And?"

"And her potassium was low this morning, but I gave orders that brought it up."

"Except that those orders were all wrong, Dr. Pappas," Elizabeth said. She had on her usual superior smirk that Alec had tried, with limited success, to get her to tone down when talking to less-experienced students. "You gave her forty mils to drink, which is way too much to give orally. How did you expect someone to drink that amount?

I can only imagine how nasty it tasted to poor Mrs. Patterson. No surprise that she vomited it up and had to be given some intravenously to replace it."

Katy's smile froze, and all color seeped from her face, then surged back to fill her light olive skin with a deep rose flush. "What...? I... Oh. Oh, no! I didn't order forty mil. I ordered four ml!"

"Really?" Elizabeth raised her eyebrows. "Nurses sometimes mishear an order, but it's still your responsibility—"

To Alec's shock, Katy turned and tore into the patient's room, and he quickly followed. What in the world was she doing?

She slid to the side of the patient's bed and reached for the woman's hand. Katy's expression was the absolute picture of remorse. "Helen, I didn't know it was my fault you got sick to your stomach this morning. I feel terrible! I guess the nurse misheard me and gave you way too much to drink. That's why you vomited. I'm so, so sorry."

Alec was torn between being impressed that she instantly took responsibility for what technically wasn't her mistake, and concern that the patient might get angry and let loose on her. He stood next to Katy, placed his hand on her back to let her know he was there to support her. "It's unfortunate that orders get confused sometimes, Mrs. Patterson. You're feeling okay now, though, aren't you?"

"Yes, it was just an upset stomach. Don't be angry with dear, lovely Dr. Pappas, now. She's such a good doctor. Everyone makes mistakes once in a while."

Dear, lovely Dr. Pappas? Alec smiled in relief. Obviously, the woman liked Katy and wasn't going to create a stink about the error. He glanced at the residents standing at the end of the bed and almost laughed at the variety of expressions on their faces. Michael was wide-eyed, Todd scowling, and Elizabeth fuming. Having been raked over the proverbial coals often during their training, the two more experienced doctors had obviously been hoping for the same for Katy.

"I'm glad you're feeling better." He looked at Katy and, luckily, she understood that he wanted her to stop holding the woman's hand and stand next to him in a more professional manner.

"Helen, as you can see, I have some interns and residents here with me this morning. Is it all right if they stay while we talk?"

"Of course, that's fine."

"Thank you." He proceeded to ask her questions and explain tests that were run, while palpating her abdomen and listening to her heart and lungs. In the midst of it she held up her hand and interrupted.

"Wait a minute." Helen frowned at him. "First, why don't you warm up that stethoscope before you press it on my skin, like Dr. Pappas always does? That thing is cold!" She shifted her attention to Katy. "And why is he asking me the same things you asked me already, dear? Don't you two talk to each other?"

Katy laughed a little, and glanced at him with a smile in her eyes that felt like old times, making him smile, too. "It's just how it's done when we're being taught by the attending physician, Helen. I know it's kind of annoying but Dr. Armstrong is an amazing surgeon. I promise you're in good hands."

How absurd that her words, which were just to reassure the patient, made him almost feel like puffing up his chest just like the teen Alec who'd always appreciated her faith in him. Helen nodded and waved her hand. "Fine. Carry on."

"I appreciate the endorsement, Dr. Pappas." Alec could hear warmth creeping into his voice as he spoke and concentrated on cooling it. On sounding professional and impartial.

Katherine Pappas was his best friend's little sister and his own student. He had to make sure no one thought they saw any kind of favoritism in the way he interacted with her.

The term "bone-tired" took on a whole new meaning after all-night call with minimal sleep followed by a long day of rounding and scut work. Katy thought she'd worked long and hard in med school, but that had been a veritable party compared to this.

As she stepped through the front door into Nick's living room, he emerged from the kitchen. "Katy-Did, you're finally home! You look beat."

"Now, there's a surprise. I'm sure I look every bit as hot, sweaty, and wrinkled as I feel."

"Living hot, sweaty, and wrinkled is an intern's existence pretty much. Sometimes it's a general surgeon's existence, too." Nick grinned. "I knew you'd be exhausted, so I'm fixing dinner. You don't have to do a thing."

"Aw, you're the sweetest big brother anyone could ever have." She gave him a quick hug, hoping she didn't smell too bad. "What are we eating?"

"Steaks from the grill, baked potatoes, veggies. To celebrate your first day, and because you probably need iron and protein after practically twenty-four hours of work. How did it go, rounding with Alec?"

"He's a good teacher, of course. I'm sure I'll learn a lot from him." She dropped into a chair in Nick's living room because she thought her legs just might give out if she was on her feet another minute. "But you know how I feel about him personally."

"Katy." Her brother's smile faded. "Alec is a good guy,

and I regret that I ever told you what happened. Yes, he went through a hellion stage when there was too much partying and too many of the wrong kinds of women in his life, but that was a long time ago. You need to cut him some slack."

"Why? He's not the person I thought he was. I'm allowed to be bothered by that, aren't I?"

"You thought he was cool and smart and cared about other people. You liked him because he treated you great. And that's exactly who he is, along with older and wiser than he was back then. Hell, I'm still working on the older and wiser part."

"Don't worry, I'm not going to be unpleasant or anything. I just don't want to be friends with him again, that's all."

"Well, that's too bad. Just remember he's still my friend. And a partner in my practice." He frowned at her for a moment then sighed. "You never really knew that Alec's dad was always putting him down, and I think that's part of why he acted out some back then. But for a long time now he's worked hard to gain respect. It's important to him. While he never did get it from his dad, he has it in spades from everyone here."

"I'm sure he's a good doctor, so of course people respect him."

"It's more than that, but I'm not going to waste my breath trying to convince you." He turned toward the kitchen. "I'm going to get the steaks on the grill and play with the dogs out in the yard. I'll let you know when it's ready."

He disappeared, and she stayed slumped in the chair, closing her eyes. Which made ignoring the mess of stuff she'd left lying around the room, still packed and unorganized, much easier. She knew she should work on it right now since Nick was being so sweet about letting her live with him for a while, but she also knew he was happy to let her rest a moment.

Much as he'd teased her over the years, Nick had been good to her, too. All six of the Pappas kids were, in fact, close, which Katy was more than thankful for. As an only child, she knew Alec had never had a sibling that he fought with sometimes but who also always had his back, and she knew that had been a big part of why he'd been at their house so much. Her mother had welcomed him, and her dad had adored and mentored him.

Which was why learning of his unethical and distasteful behavior had cut Katy to her very core. Not only that, Alec's parents had shoved what he'd done under a rug then wrapped it up with a nice tidy bow while someone else had paid the price.

Ah, who was she kidding? It hadn't been just his mistake and the aftermath that remained stuck as a sharp barb in her soul. It was that he'd done it all practically right after she'd boldly kissed him and he'd pushed her away. Told her it wouldn't be "appropriate." Which obviously had just been another way of saying, *I think of you as a little sister, not a woman*, since "appropriate" clearly hadn't entered his mind before the scandal.

Her chest burned in embarrassment and disgust but at the same time she couldn't deny that the man was an impressive doctor and teacher. And, yes, even more ridiculously good looking than he'd been years ago. Today, in Mrs. Patterson's room, as they'd smiled together at the woman's comments, she had to admit it had felt nice. A little like old times, and thoughts of his past had momentarily faded from her brain until she'd sternly reminded herself.

She was smart enough to take advantage of his intelligence and experience and learn what she could from him, just as she had long ago. But as far as a friendship happening between them again? Never.

The doorbell rang and, still collapsed in the chair, she nearly groaned. The last thing she wanted to do was talk to anyone. Maybe if she ignored it, whoever it was would go away.

The bell rang again and with a resigned sigh she shoved herself from the chair and forced herself to open the door.

To her shock, Alec stood there, looking annoyingly handsome in jeans and a yellow polo shirt that showed off his broad shoulders. Sunglasses covered his eyes. The evening sun gleamed in his dark hair and his admittedly attractive lips were curved in a smile that no doubt had women flocking around him like seagulls. And yet again she looked like she'd been through the heavy-duty wash cycle and hung out to dry.

What was Alec doing here?

"Hello, Dr. Armstrong. What can I do for you?"

His dark eyebrows rose as he slipped off his sunglasses. "Oh, so formal. What happened to the old 'Hi Alec, come on in' you used to greet me with?"

How was she supposed to answer that? She wanted to say that had been back when she'd been young and naive and worn rose-colored glasses, but there was no point in going there. "I wasn't sure if I should call you Alec, as you're an attending and I'm a student."

"It's fine for you to call me Alec when we're not in the hospital. Unless you particularly like guys in scrubs and want to call me 'Doctor.'" The teasing grin he gave her was downright dazzling, and she turned away from its power, opening the door fully as she doubted he'd stopped by just to say hello then leave.

"Funny. Though perhaps you're saying that because I

know that you particularly like women in scrubs. Or, even more, in nothing at all."

Crap, had she actually just said that? Her cheeks burned and she couldn't figure out what part of the room to focus on, because she sure as heck wasn't going to look at him now. She quickly walked over to the pile of stuff she'd pulled out of a box and left on the sofa yesterday.

"Katy Pappas, I'm shocked that you—"

"Sorry the place is a bit of a mess," she interrupted, the deeply amused rumble of his voice making her blush all over again. She did not want to hear whatever he'd been about to say in response to her extremely ill-advised comment. She grabbed up her things and shoved them back in the box. "I haven't had time to put away all my stuff yet."

"Don't worry, I saw the housekeeping police are busy a few blocks away. I think you're safe until tomorrow."

His voice still held laughter and she focused on the box. Not. Going. To look at him. "As you can see, I haven't had a chance to change my clothes. Excuse me while—"

Excited woofs drowned out her words as Nick's two yellow Labrador retrievers bounded through the house to greet Alec, slamming against Katy and nearly knocking her off her feet. "Whoa!" she yelped, her tired legs not quite balancing the way they should. Before she tumbled to the floor Alec lunged to grab her and hold her upright, flattening her tight against him.

Her hands slapped up against his muscular shoulders as the feel of his firm chest against her breasts, his strong arms around her sent her breathing haywire. Their eyes met, and the grin faded from his, replaced by what looked like a slightly confused frown.

The seconds ticked by and both stood motionless, oddly frozen, until Katy grabbed what wits she had left. She pushed against his shoulders and stepped back as his arms dropped to his sides, but their gazes remained locked. The tingling of her nerves and the imprint of his body that she could still feel against her own must be some sort of "muscle memory" thing, from the years she'd written in her journal about how much she wanted to be held close by Alec.

"I see you still have a little clumsiness problem."

Her gaze moved from the oddly disturbing eye contact to his lips, which disturbed her in a different way. She looked down at the dogs for a distraction. "I don't think being knocked into by these crazy pups of his makes me clumsy," she said, hoping she didn't sound as breathless as she felt. The dogs wagged their tails and rubbed against her for attention, leaving dog hair all over her black skirt. As if she wasn't already enough of a mess. "Nick can't have much company—they've acted like this every time someone comes to the door. If they hadn't been outside, we would have been mauled the second you came in."

"They're still young and rambunctious." He looked oddly serious, considering his teasing of just a moment ago. "And in case you don't remember, your dogs pretty much all acted this way at your family's house. I remember your mutt, Buddy, chewing up one of my shoes that I'd left at the door."

She looked up at him as she scratched the dogs' heads. "You had to put up with a lot at our house, didn't you? Utter chaos, with six crazy kids and badly behaved dogs."

"I think the term would be bedlam." The smile was back on his face, and why she was pleased to see it again she wasn't sure. "But I enjoyed every minute of the time I spent with Nick. And you. And the rest of your family, of course."

"You two sitting out there, socializing, with your feet

up?" Nick's voice called from the kitchen. "Katy has the night off, but you don't, Alec. I need a hand here."

"Coming in a sec. Just realized I left the wine I brought in the car." His index finger reached out to give her nose a gentle flick, a soft stroke from between her brows to its tip as he'd done more times than she could possibly count, but the expression in his eyes seemed different than in the past. Hotter, more intimate, somehow, and her heart stupidly sped up in response.

Thankfully, he turned and went back out the door, and Katy sucked in a breath. She would not allow her old, youthful crush to muscle its way in and crowd out her older, smarter self. No way, no how.

She moved toward the kitchen, resolutely passing by the hallway to her bedroom with barely a longing glance. She hadn't planned to do anything more than wash her hands for dinner and refused to give in to her sudden urge to clean up a little and change her clothes. Maybe it would even be a good thing, she thought as she shook her head at herself, if Alec noticed she didn't exactly smell perfume fresh.

"Why didn't you tell me you'd invited Alec for dinner?" she asked Nick in a whisper, even though she hadn't heard the man come back into the house.

"Because he's my best friend, and I didn't realize until tonight that you still felt such animosity toward him." Her brother glanced at her before he turned his attention back to the dinner. "Which I frankly hope you'll get over."

"No animosity. As I told you, I just don't want to be friends with him anymore." And her darned shortness of breath and flippity heart and awareness of his hunkiness quotient was far different from feelings of friendship anyway, dang it. Which made it even more important that they not be together anywhere but at work until her smart brain prevailed over her not-so-smart one. "But obviously, since he's my instructor for the month, I'm perfectly fine with spending work time with him. I just would've appreciated a heads-up."

"Okay. Hey, Katy-Did." Nick turned to her, the evil big-brother smile on his face she was more than used to. "Alec's coming over for dinner."

She rolled her eyes. "Thanks for telling me. If I'd known it wasn't just the two of us, I wouldn't have dressed up in my nicest clothes."

As Nick chuckled in response, Alec's voice filled the kitchen, followed by his tall, broad form. "You look good in whatever you're wearing, Katy."

She looked up at his eyes that were all golden and warm again, accompanied by a beautiful smile that seemed absurdly sincere, since she knew she couldn't look much more of a wreck if she tried. Why did the darned man have to have the kind of charm that made it all too easy to overlook his not-charming characteristics?

"Thank you." She busied herself with getting the food together, despite both men's protests that she was supposed to be off duty. In short order, they were sitting at the small table, holding crystal glasses and lit, to her touched surprise, with candles.

"To Dr. Katherine Pappas," Nick said, holding up his glass of red wine. "Congratulations on finishing med school with honors and for living through your first day as an intern."

"Cheers to that," Alec said, his focus so entirely on her it was unnerving. "We always knew you were special, and you've proved it over and over again."

Special? And here she'd thought it had been her domain to think of Alec that way when they'd been young. "Thank you. And here's hoping I don't do anything stupid to embarrass you in rounds over the next month."

"You could never do anything to embarrass me, Katy, and that's a fact. I'm more than sure you're going to make me look good."

As if he needed her to make him look good.

They all sipped their drinks, and Katy wasn't sure if it was the wine slipping down her throat that made her chest feel so warm or something else. Something like Alec talking about the faith he had in her, as he had so many times in the past.

Despite it being just the three of them, their meal together brought a welcome feeling of normalcy. Almost like the years hadn't passed and Alec was just hanging out with the Pappas clan for dinner. Except those times would never come again. Her and Nick's father was gone, and Alec was not the knight in shining armor she'd painted him to be.

"I was called in to help with a rough surgery today," Nick said. "Bob Rollins had a teen girl with a torsion in her ovary, and when he opened her up she was a total mess. Had to bring in another gynecologist and me to dive in there with him to identify and try to save her entire reproductive system. So remember, Katy, don't be surprised if some surgeries turn out to be completely different than you expect." He gave her a pointed look. "Just like people."

It didn't take a genius to know what he was saying. "I'll remember."

Nick turned to Alec. "What time is your flight next weekend?"

"For the wedding? Nine a.m., I think."

"You were able to take time off even though you're doing teaching rounds?" Katy hoped she didn't sound as dismayed as she felt, but she wasn't excited about trying to keep her distance from him at another family event.

"You bet." A grin slowly creased his cheeks. "Maybe you can help me with my marginal Greek dancing skills."

She stared into his amused eyes then shook her head. Holding his hand in more ways than one? There had been a time when she'd have loved to. "You fake it well, Alec. You don't need anyone's help with that."

CHAPTER THREE

ALEC WONDERED WHY Katy's expression had become strained, just as he still wondered why she seemed so cool toward him. Surely she wasn't still upset about their little kiss from five years ago?

Then there'd be a brief moment when she was more like the old Katy he used to know. He couldn't deny that he wanted to see more of that Katy, who used to think he was great. Why did he miss her former adulation when he was no longer the troubled kid he used to be?

"Are your parents coming to the wedding?" Nick asked.

"I doubt it. They're both still in Russia while Dad teaches how to do his valve-replacement technique there." And he'd be just as glad to not have his father there, grilling him on his life and telling him his surgical work wasn't as important as a cardiologist's.

"I figured you'd have to work," Katy said, "so I hadn't even thought about you coming."

And didn't that make his ego feel great? Though the way she'd been toward him the past times he'd seen her at family get-togethers had shown she no longer thought of him much, period. "Are you really going to make me fake again that I can Greek-dance?" Alec asked, which earned him a small smile from her.

"Nick's the master dancer. He can teach you."

"Never did me much good in the past." It was pretty obvious Katy didn't want to teach him, which gave him a twinge of disappointment. He remembered well the times he'd watched her lead the dancing, mesmerized by her movements and her joyful smile. "What time are you two flying out?"

"Nick has us leaving at some crazy time, like six a.m.," Katy said with a scowl. "As though I'm not already getting zero sleep."

"Think of your lack of sleep as a rite of passage. Kind of like hazing in a fraternity," Nick said with a grin.

"Mr. Empathy, as usual," she said, punching her brother none too gently on the arm. Nick raised both fists, jabbing them in the air back at her.

"Okay, you two." Alec shook his head but at the same time he had to chuckle. Some things never changed. And when it came to the Pappas family, not changing was the best thing in the world, as far as Alec was concerned. "Truthfully, though, the more hours you're in the hospital, Katy, the more you're exposed to all different kinds of cases that are invaluable for learning. The time schedules aren't just for torture."

"I know, I know. I'll try to remember that in the midst of my zombie state tomorrow. I doubt we interns will even be able to stay awake for the after-work welcome dinner with the teaching staff," she said. Her tone might be grumbling, but those blue eyes of hers were lit with the enthusiasm and wonder he'd seen in them, and had always enjoyed, forever. She turned her beautifully lethal gaze on Nick. "Does it sound silly to say I'm really excited to be one of…of you now? A real doctor, like Dad?"

George Pappas. Alec's chest grew a little heavy, thinking of the man who'd been more of a father to him than his own. Knowing how hard it had been on every one of the man's family when he'd died. And on himself too, despite not being a real member of the Pappas tribe.

"Your dad would be proud of you." He reached for her soft hand and squeezed it. "He was proud of each one of you, but I think he had a special place in his heart for his youngest."

Tears filled her eyes, and he kicked himself. The last thing he wanted to do was make her sad. Then she smiled through the tears, and the jab of guilt eased.

"Thank you. I know I don't have much experience yet—that I have a crazy amount to learn. But I think you're right. I think he would be proud that I'm at least trying."

Trying? The Katy Pappas he knew never tried. She worked until she accomplished whatever damned goal she'd set for herself, from the most simple to the most difficult.

"There's no question about that, Katy," Nick said, his voice a little rough. "Here's another toast to you for always making him proud."

"To you, Katy." Alec raised his glass to hers. Maybe it was because she couldn't see too well through the tears in her eyes, but for whatever reason, as she tried to clink her glass to his, she completely missed. And managed to toss most of her glass of wine straight onto his lap.

"Oh! I'm so sorry, Alec!" Katy leaped from her seat, grabbing her napkin to dab vigorously at the wine staining the bottom of his shirt, moving down to dab even harder at the biggest pool of liquid in a place he didn't want her dabbing.

Or maybe he did, because seeing her hands on his groin, feeling them pressing against him, shortened his breath, stepped up the beat of his heart and invited an instant physical response he couldn't control.

"Let me handle it, Katy," he said, firmly grabbing her

wrist before she could feel exactly what was happening to him and embarrass them both.

"But the stain is setting, and— Oh!" Suddenly her motions stilled and her widening eyes met his. Obviously, his body's response to her hands all over him was plenty clear.

"Yeah. 'Oh.'" What else could he say? Except maybe, *Touch me some more, please.*

"Katy, having you around sure livens things up." Laughing, Nick headed to the kitchen. "I'll get a wet towel."

"I'm…sorry. Really sorry. So, so sorry." Her face was nearly as red as the wine, and she stood staring at him as though she was frozen.

"It's okay. Really." He should be sorry, too. Sorry that she felt embarrassed, sorry that his clothes might be ruined, and sorry that his body had responded the way it had. In spite of all that, though, he found he didn't feel sorry at all. In fact, his primary feeling at the moment was wishing the two of them were alone so he could strip off his wet clothes and see if that led anywhere good.

As soon as the thought came, the heat that had surged throughout his body was quickly replaced by ice, and he wanted to pummel some sense into himself. Not only was Katy Nick's little sister, she was his student, damn it. He absolutely could not think of her in that way, ever, despite the fact that, right now, he clearly was. But that was not acceptable. Not under any circumstances, but especially while he was her superior at the hospital.

He'd already tried to blow up his own career with that kind of mistake, and had succeeded all too well in blowing up someone else's. The last thing he wanted was to lose the respect he'd tried so hard to regain since his stupidity of the past.

And risking Katy's career and reputation with the same kind of stupidity? Never.

* * *

Had she really rubbed her hands all around and pressed down on Alec's privates?

Katy walked down the hospital corridor, face burning as she thought about the reality that, yes, she sure had. Even worse, she now knew something she hadn't before. Which was that he apparently became aroused easily and was more than well endowed.

Long ago, she'd fantasized about—well—all of that. But she knew last night's impressive reaction had had nothing to do with her. Lots of men might respond that way to any woman fondling them, inadvertently or not. And since Alec had gone through girlfriends in high school like a patient with a bad cold went through tissues, she shouldn't be surprised he was one of them.

What was a surprise had been her own reaction. That in addition to feeling beyond embarrassed, she'd also found herself fascinated by the swelling beneath those jeans of his. As though she was some innocent kid and not a grown woman. She was quite sure Alec's swelling—and what a ridiculous way for her, a doctor, to be thinking of his erection—was no more impressive than any other man's. Well, she wasn't sure, but she no longer had any desire to find out. Did. Not.

For the tenth time that morning she shoved down thoughts of any and all of Alec's body parts and headed to her next patient's room. "Good morning, Helen!" Katy stepped to Mrs. Patterson's bedside and patted her thin shoulder. "Ready to go home?"

"I wish I could. But I'm heading back to rehab at the nursing home until I'm stronger."

"I know. But you're going to be out of there before you know it." She took her stethoscope from her neck and pressed the bell to her palm to warm it before she placed it against the woman's chest. "Do you have someone to help take care of you when you're home?"

"My daughter's coming for a bit after I'm home. Today, though, my son is taking me back to rehab."

"That's good." The woman didn't look too excited about that, but who would be? "I know it's not much fun doing rehab, but knowing it's going to make you independent again makes it worth it."

"I don't mind it, really. The nurses and physical therapists are lovely. But all this has been very depressing." Helen sighed. "Until I broke my hip, I was pretty strong and walked my little dogs every day. Now I feel just awful with this stomach pain. It's enough to make me want to move on to heaven to be with my Albert."

The sadness and frustration on the poor woman's face squeezed Katy's heart. She wrapped her arm around Helen's shoulders to give her a hug. "I can imagine how hard it is to feel weak and not well when you're used to being up and about. But your tests don't show any problems, so I bet you're going to be feeling good again soon. Hang in there."

A tall, skinny man with long hair knocked on the doorjamb, which surprised Katy. It couldn't be any later than seven a.m. "Can I come in?"

"Hello, Jeffrey." Helen shifted her gaze from the man to Katy. "Dr. Pappas, this is my son. Jeffrey, this is Dr. Pappas. She's been taking good care of me."

"Thanks for that," Jeffrey said, then came to stand between Katy and his mother, rather rudely. "Mom, I need a little cash to fix my car. Can you front me a loan? I brought your checkbook."

"I just gave you money for your car last week." Helen frowned, but took the checkbook he handed her.

"I know, but there's something else wrong now, so I've been driving yours. I'll pay you back soon."

"This has to be the last time. My medical bills are adding up." Helen scribbled out a check. "Please remember I need you to pick me up whenever I'm released today."

"Okay. Call me." He dropped a quick kiss on her forehead and headed out the door. Katy couldn't believe he hadn't even asked his sweet mother how she was feeling.

She squeezed Mrs. Patterson's hand one more time. "If I don't see you again before you're released, I hope you're back to walking your pups very soon."

Katy left the room and looked at her patient notes. Next was a seven-year-old boy named David, who'd had a complication when his appendix had ruptured. Alec had done the surgery nearly a week before Katy had arrived, but the poor child still had a drain in his belly.

About to knock quietly on David's door in case he was still asleep, she was surprised to hear the deep rumble of a man's voice. Then was even more surprised to see Alec in scrubs, sitting on the side of the boy's bed. What was he doing, seeing a patient so early?

She shoved aside the discomfort that again heated her cheeks. She had to see the man every day, for heaven's sake, and he'd probably forgotten all about the little fondling incident. "Good morning, Dr. Armstrong. You're an early bird today."

"I wanted to stop in and see our star patient before I start morning surgery." He stood and smiled down at David. "The drain's looking good, buddy. We just might be able to take it out in a day or two."

"I can't wait!" David grinned, showing a missing tooth. "But I'm feeling lots better, Dr. Armstrong. Thanks for the car stuff you brought me. Will you come back and see me later?"

"I'll try, David." He tousled the boy's hair and turned

to leave, and his sweet expression and the warmth in his eyes made Katy's breath catch in her throat.

Had she ever seen him around children before? Except back when she'd been a child? She couldn't remember, but it seemed he was pretty good with them. His surgery schedule was so heavy she couldn't imagine he'd be able to come back to see the child later, not to mention that the welcome dinner was tonight, but it was nice of him to tell the boy he'd try.

"I've checked David out, so you don't need to, Dr. Pappas." They moved to the shadow of the doorway where he paused. "What patient are you seeing next?"

They stood so close together she could smell his aftershave, see a tiny spot next to his lips that he'd missed when shaving, feel the heat of his body near hers. Unwittingly, her thoughts turned to touching him the night before, and she started to feel overly warm. From embarrassment, of course.

"Mr. Lyons in 2215."

"Better watch out you don't spill anything on him. Mr. Lyons can be quite a character."

Lord, she'd hoped he wouldn't mention it again. Even in the low light of the room she could see the amused glint in his eyes. His lips tipped up into a slow smile, and she found herself staring at his mouth. Swallowing, she took a step away from him so she could breathe. "Can we please just forget about that? You know I sometimes have a clumsiness problem."

"I'll try to forget about it. But you know what, Dr. Pappas? I'm pretty sure that's not going to happen."

He left the room and she sucked in a breath. Their exchange had smacked dangerously of flirting, and she shouldn't let that happen. Also shouldn't enjoy it, but she'd be lying to herself if she claimed she hadn't.

About to head to her next patient's room, Katy realized she'd been so distracted she hadn't thought to ask Alec to sign Mr. Lyons' release papers. What was wrong with her? Work had to be her number-one focus, dang it.

She hurried down the hall to catch Alec, wishing their last conversation hadn't been about her grabbing his privates. His tall figure stood by an elevator, and she stepped up her pace. "Dr. Armstrong!"

He turned to her, and his gaze swept her slowly from head to toe. Feeling a little breathless from hurrying, she stopped next to him. "I forgot to ask you to sign Mr. Lyons' release papers."

She looked up at him, his eyes meeting hers for a long moment before he reached for the papers. "And I forgot to ask you if you're excited about helping with some surgeries in a few days. I've put you first on the list."

"Is that an honor, or is it because you want me in and out of there before I kill someone?"

"We try not to let interns kill anybody. It's against hospital policy."

So were some other things he hadn't worried about in the past. But, of course, he was joking. "I confess I'm not excited. But I'm sure it will be an interesting experience."

"It will be. Especially for you, Miss Science. Weren't you always the one conducting various weird experiments on the kitchen counter until your mom yelled at you?"

"Is this your way of calling me a geek? I—" Her phone beeped a text message and she looked at it then frowned. This couldn't be right.

"What is it?"

"The nurse says Mrs. Levitz is having a panic attack. Shortness of breath, chest pain, and a fast heartbeat."

"She's the one who had her gall bladder removed by Nick yesterday, right?" Alec asked, his teasing expression instantly replaced by calm professionalism. "Her chart said she's prone to panic attacks. Prescribe lorazepam and see how she does."

Katy frowned up at Alec. "I don't know. I left her only a short time ago and she was fine. Looking forward to being discharged. I just don't see her having a panic attack right now."

"Since she has a history of them, most likely that's what it is. You'll see this more often than you would guess." His eyes were thoughtful, seeming to study her. "But sometimes it's important to listen to your instincts. Go see her. Let Nick know your conclusion and what your thoughts are on what needs to be done."

"Okay. I will. Thanks." She turned and her chest felt suddenly buoyant. How could it not when Alec had basically just told her he had faith in her to figure it out? She had a ridiculous impulse to look over her shoulder to see if he still stood there and was surprised that he was. Not just standing there but holding the elevator door open with his eyes still on her.

Something about his expression made her heart thump a little, and she realized she was failing miserably in keeping her former crush from rearing its ugly head. Also failing in re-erecting the cool wall she'd been so good at keeping between them before she'd started working there.

"Hello, Mrs. Levitz," she said as she walked into the patient's room. "I hear you're feeling upset."

"I don't know what's wrong." The poor woman was breathing hard and wringing her hands. The brown eyes staring up at Katy were filled with fear. "My chest hurts. I don't feel good. I'm scared."

"Okay, let's take a look," Katy said in a soothing voice as she took her pulse. No doubt about it, Mrs. Levitz was behaving completely differently than she had been only an hour earlier. But why? A panic attack seemed unlikely, despite her chart saying she was prone to them, since she certainly hadn't been worried about going home. Quite the opposite. But something was going on, there was no doubt about that.

"Did something upset or worry you, Mrs. Levitz?"

"No. No. I just started feeling bad all of a sudden."

"Her chart says she often has panic attacks," the nurse said in a low voice as she reset the monitor that had been screeching at the patient's elevated pulse.

"I know," Katy murmured. "But that just doesn't seem right to me, after speaking with her earlier." Think, Katy. What could be going on here that's not obvious? Chest pain, shortness of breath, and elevated heart rate were, indeed, consistent with a panic attack. But as she peered at the monitor next to the bed she noted that Mrs. Levitz's oxygen level was low, too. And a panic attack wouldn't cause that.

With tension rising in her own chest, she pulled out her little medical book and studied it. Thought back to the cases she'd had in med school. Then she nearly shouted *Eureka* as the answer struck her.

Pulmonary embolism. Unusual, but not impossible after gall-bladder surgery, and it would account for every symptom the woman was experiencing. It was a post-op complication she knew every surgeon dreaded. It also had to be diagnosed and addressed immediately.

"I want a CT scan run on Mrs. Levitz," she said to the nurse, adrenaline surging through her. *"Stat."*

CHAPTER FOUR

KATY STOOD IN the park by Mission Bay and breathed in the tangy sea air. This was exactly why she'd wanted to train in San Diego. The beautiful sandy beaches with tall, swaying palms, the emerald-green grass, the deep blue of the water were all utterly breathtaking. Why choose to work in a cold, gray, rainy place when you could be here?

All kinds of people mingled and chatted at this welcome party for students and staff, but she felt like she'd been talking nonstop all day and enjoyed having a little moment of quiet.

A server stopped next to her with a tray of champagne, and she swiped the last of the sand from her hands and took a glass. Hopefully no one had noticed her sneak down to the beach to dig in the sand and see what creatures lived in there. She'd found little gray crabs of all sizes, and the moment she did she found herself ridiculously looking at the crowd to see if Alec had arrived so she could show him.

Hadn't she decided to stay cool and as distant as possible? To keep their relationship strictly professional as student and teacher?

But the crab discovery had instantly taken her back to all their adventuring days together. To how he'd never made fun of her experiments and discoveries, and in fact had seemed to enjoy them as much as she had. She'd been shocked at the disappointment she'd felt when he was nowhere in sight.

How strange that she still had this ingrained habit of looking to him now that he was back in her life, so to speak. She knew it for what it was, though, which gave her complete power to control it.

She moved closer to the crowd, figuring she should socialize a bit and maybe learn something in the process.

"I had so much pizza last night I'm not going to do justice to the food here," a nurse said to the group of women she was standing with.

"I know." A different woman chuckled. "Dr. Armstrong bought enough to feed an army, which was really sweet of him. Just because we all worked so late on the emergency perforated ulcer didn't mean he had to spring for dinner for everyone."

"He always does that when we work late. I just love him. If I wasn't married, I'd have his babies."

The group of women laughed and Katy moved on, not wanting to be an eavesdropper. She'd heard women swooning over the hunky surgeon before—but the fact that he bought pizza after a long day? She'd probably want to have his babies too.

No. Wrong thought. All wrong.

As though drawn by some magnetic force, her eyes lifted to the opposite edge of the party, and there stood Alec. Looking even better in casual dress clothes than he did in scrubs—which seemed nearly impossible, since he looked incredible in them—his hair fluttered across his forehead as he spoke with the woman standing next to him.

The woman stepped closer until they were nearly touching. There was nothing professional or distant about their body language as she rested her hand on his biceps, and the woman had a clear, come-hither look on her attractive face. The face of fifth-year resident Elizabeth Stark.

Katy's gut squeezed and her hand tightened on the stem of her glass. Here it was, right in her face. A cold reminder of who exactly Alec Armstrong was in addition to the good-with-children, pizza-bringing surgeon the nurses adored. Why she'd kept her distance from him until working together had made that impossible.

The image bothered her far more than it should have, considering she'd known all about his player reputation of the past, which clearly was also part of his present. Just as she was thrashing herself for feeling illogically disturbed, Alec stepped back from Elizabeth. His lips flatlined from the cordial smile there a moment ago, and a frown creased his brow.

Then he walked away, leaving Elizabeth staring after him.

Had they had some kind of tiff? Or was it because Alec wasn't like that any more, as Nick had insisted? The thought lightened the weight in her chest. Maybe she'd held onto her disappointment in him for too long. Maybe it was time to let that go, to see the more mature Alec. The man who still had so many of the appealing qualities of his youth.

Surely she was more mature, too. Mature enough to put behind her old crush and hurt at his rejection and accept him as a friend again.

Alec tried not to stare at Katy, making anyone who might notice wonder why, but he couldn't seem to stop his gaze from traveling back to her. The fragrant breeze coming from the bay fluttered the floral dress she wore, which was significantly shorter than her conservative hospital clothes. He knew he damn well shouldn't but he couldn't resist letting his gaze slowly drop from her appealing face down the length of her body. To her breasts, which were completely covered by a neckline that went all the way up to her collarbone but were still all too well outlined by the filmy fabric.

He'd thought, more than once, that no woman looked better in scrubs than Katy. But watching her now, with the wind outlining her body and the evening sun giving her hair a golden glow, he realized she looked even more spectacular outside the hospital.

Smart, sweet, and gorgeous were one damned lethal combination.

When he'd first found out Katy would be coming to Oceancrest as an intern, he'd been pleased, thinking it would be a good chance to renew the friendship she hadn't seemed to want to continue. Never would he have dreamed he'd have so much trouble keeping himself from looking at her every curve, trouble keeping firmly in mind that she was a student and Nick's little sister.

Hell, who was he kidding? After the way he'd responded to her kiss long ago, he should have known. Shouldn't have been surprised at the stirring of attraction he'd felt the second he'd seen her that first day in the coding patient's room. More than a stirring when she'd wiped the wine from his body. Now every time he saw Katy he saw a special woman there was no denying he wanted more than friendship with.

This inconvenient attraction—hell, unacceptable attraction—was a problem he wasn't sure how to deal with.

"Alec." Nick came to stand next to him and he was glad for a reason to stop watching Katy. "You missed the speeches. Which I'm sure you're real sad about."

"Yeah. Not. After hearing the CEO give the same

speech at every welcome gathering, I may be forced to write a new one for him myself."

Nick turned his head to the crowd of people mingling in the park then turned back to Alec. "What—or should I say, who—are you looking at?"

"Uh, nobody in particular. Just seeing who's here." Was it that obvious his gaze kept returning to Katy? Of all the many people he didn't want to notice that, number one was Nick.

"I saw one person here who's already singled you out. Elizabeth Stark," Nick said. "Tell me you aren't going to fall for her coming on to you."

"Why would you even ask me that? Since when are you my father?" Alec frowned at Nick as they walked up the slope of grass. Hadn't he tried his damnedest to make sure he never got involved with any woman at the hospital? To make sure he and his reputation were stainless now? "You know, it was five years ago. At a different hospital. In a different capacity. I think the chief medical officer is the only person here who even knows about it."

"I know that mess is in the past. You're the one who still avoids any woman within a ten-mile radius of the hospital."

"Then why are you on my case about Elizabeth? Who, for the record, I have zero interest in."

"Because Elizabeth is a student, who's made it clear she has more than zero interest in you." Nick stared at him like he'd grown two heads. "Which you sure as hell know is different than just someone working in the hospital."

No one knew that better than Alec. His gaze caught on Katy again, and his stomach twisted. Good to be reminded that he couldn't think of her the way he kept thinking of her. That he couldn't look at her smooth skin and imagine touching it, couldn't think about tangling his fingers in her soft hair, couldn't want to cover her sweetly smiling lips with his own.

Alec gritted his teeth and forced his attention back to Nick as they headed to the food table. "Don't worry. I'll never cross that line again."

Nick nodded, the conversation obviously over, thankfully. "How about that sister of mine?"

Alec's heart nearly stopped. Surely Nick hadn't noticed... Ah, hell. "What about her?"

"She's been saving lives all by herself."

"Saving lives?" The tightness in Alec's chest slid away. "What did she do?"

"You didn't hear?" Nick grinned at him. "One of my patients. Post-op gall bladder, with anxiety disorder. Everybody assumed she just needed a dose of lorazepam to calm her down, but Katy figured out what was really wrong."

Alec remembered Katy talking with him about the patient earlier. "So, what was wrong?"

"I guess Katy just had a gut feeling about it not being a panic attack, despite the woman's history. Ordered a CT scan and found pulmonary emboli. Got her into the ICU, got a heparin drip going and—bam! Alive and well." Nick looked as pleased as if he'd been the one who'd figured out the problem, though, of course, the woman was his patient, too. "Gotta say, I'm pretty proud of her. I don't think too many first-year interns would have thought of that, especially knowing about the patient's anxiety disorder."

"You've got that right." Alec felt a peculiar pride welling up within his chest, which seemed ridiculous. It wasn't as though his teaching had helped her figure it out. And she was Nick's sister, not his. "I've already seen that Katy has good instincts when it comes to patients. Great bedside manner and rapport, too. The only thing she lacks sometimes is self-confidence, so this is bound to give her that."

And wasn't that the truth? He couldn't think of anything lacking in the woman, including the sex appeal that just oozed from her without her even being aware of it.

His gaze slipped back to where she'd been and saw she was headed their way. A good chance to congratulate her on her great job with Mrs. Levitz, then mingle with others to keep his distance.

"Hey, Nick! Alec. How can you two stand not to be out here every day? This place is beautiful!" Strands of her silky hair feathered across her face in the breeze, and her slim fingers shoved them aside as she smiled at him.

"It is beautiful. And I'm out here every day I can be. My condo is just across the bay."

"Is it really? I'll bet your view is amazing."

"It is. I could take you sailing or kayaking some time, if you want." Sailing with her sounded great to Alec. Also sounded like a hell of a bad idea, and he quickly changed the subject. "I hear congratulations are in order."

"Congratulations? For what?"

"I know you probably have many things to be congratulated on today." He had to smile at her questioning look. Did she really not know what a great job she'd done? "But I'm referring to figuring out that Mrs. Levitz wasn't having an anxiety attack. Most docs—and especially interns—might not have gotten the diagnosis until it was too late."

"I'm sure that's not true." Pink filled her cheeks, and he realized he loved to see her blush, for some reason. How many women blushed like that these days? "You would have figured it out."

"Probably. Hopefully. But too often we look at the first thing that comes to mind and assume it's the correct thing. With her history of panic attacks, no one could have blamed you for treating her for that and not even considering another possibility. Hell, didn't I tell you to give her lorazepam to see if that did the trick?"

"Yes. But you hadn't seen her as recently as I had."

"I'll bet that in med school you heard about looking for the zebra when everyone else is looking for the horse. That's what you did. You found the zebra no one was looking for, and I'm proud of you. You should be proud of yourself."

"Thank you. I guess I am."

They smiled at one another as the breeze whipped a thick strand of hair onto her face, and he nearly reached to slip it from her eyes and tuck it behind her ear. Nearly leaned forward to kiss her on the cheek. Just her cheek, in celebration, as he would have long ago when they'd been young.

Who was he kidding? He wanted to start on her cheek and work his way over to that smiling mouth.

"I'm proud of you too, Katy," Nick said.

Damn. He'd practically forgotten Nick was there. Alec shifted his attention from the temptation of her lips and noticed she had sand all over her dress.

"You been rolling on the beach?"

"Rolling on the beach?" Her gaze followed his. "Oops. I thought I'd wiped it off. I was digging in the sand to see what was down in there."

He had to chuckle. Typical Katy. "And what did you find?"

"I'm not sure. Can I show you? You might know what they are."

There it was again. That absurd puffing-up-his-chest feeling, as though it meant something that she thought he'd know the answer to a simple question about crustaceans. "You're not pulling a joke on me are you? Have you dug a hole and covered it with palm fronds so I'll fall in?"

"As if I'd spend party time digging a hole big enough to trap you in." She laughed. "You're suspicious because those are the kinds of pranks you and Nick liked to pull."

"Thanks for the reminder. I'll have to think up a good way to prank you for old times' sake," Nick said with a grin. "I'm going to catch up with a few other folks here. You're checking on patients after this, aren't you, Katy? I'll see you when you get home."

"Okay," she said to Nick, but her eyes were on Alec. "Come on. They're down here."

They walked across a long stretch of grass and down a small hill to the water, leaving behind the party guest chatter. He was struck with an absurd desire to wrap his arm around her shoulders or to twine her fingers within his. Maybe it wasn't all that crazy, though—when they'd been young he'd often given her a brotherly hug.

Nothing brotherly about what he was feeling now, though, damn it. What he felt was hot and insistent and getting more and more difficult to tamp down.

"See all these little holes in the wet sand?" She pointed as the gentle waves receded, leaving bubbly holes behind. "I saw sandpipers and black-bellied plovers poking in their beaks. So I dug down and found some funny-looking gray crabs, some tiny and some as big as a spoon. Do you know what they are?"

"I'm afraid I don't. Folks here just call them sand crabs. And why am I not surprised you know the names of the birds, Miss Science?" Just like when she'd been little, she was curious about everything and because of that had an amazing, encyclopedic brain. He had to smile. That curiosity was going to make her a fine doctor one day.

"Are any bigger than the ones I described?"

"I confess I haven't paid that much attention." He crouched down and she crouched along with him, steadying herself by grasping the back of his arm, her knee bumping against his. They'd explored things this same way long ago, and it felt natural, right, to have her hold on to him that way. "Let's dig up some more to find out."

He scooped into the sand and she scooped and dug along with him, finally pulling out a handful of the grayish crabs in all sizes. "Looks like that's about the biggest one," he said, holding up a fat one. "They do look pretty tasty, don't they? If you're a bird, that is. Sandpipers and... what kind?"

"Black-bellied plovers. Willets, too." She looked up at him and laughed, her blue eyes sparkling. Her face was so close he could feel her breath brush his lips warmly. Teasing him without knowing. Tormenting him. When all he wanted was to press his own lips to her smiling ones.

"I wish I'd brought a bucket to put some in. I'd like to take a few home."

"For what? To keep as pets? Give to the dogs to play with?"

"No, to study, silly." Her teeth flashed white in the wide smile she gave him. "Don't you remember how we'd do that back at home all the time with beetles and locusts and things?"

"I remember." How could he be feeling this sensual pull towards her when they were talking about crabs and beetles and science? Because it was Katy, and that had always been a part of who she was. Because watching her lips move, watching her speak made him think of how he'd felt when she'd kissed him long ago. How it would feel to kiss her now, which was all he wanted to do.

He turned to place the crabs back into the hole they'd dug, to somehow take his mind away from this nearly overwhelming desire to lower her to the sand and kiss her and touch her, and to hell with the consequences.

Their hands touched, her fingers sliding against his as she tucked the crabs into the hole and covered them with sand. About to stand and end the torture of being so close to her, she clapped the wet sand from her hands and lost her balance. Rocked into him, shoulder to shoulder. Crouched on the balls of his feet, Alec wasn't prepared for the impact and promptly fell backward onto his rear, his elbow in the sand holding him half-upright, with Katy falling practically into his lap. One sandy hand slapped against his collarbone, the other grabbed his shoulder.

"Oh! Sorry!" Katy stared down at him, and he thought he saw more in her expression than just apology. He thought he saw a flicker of something in her darkened eyes. Something that was hot and intangible and irresistible and that hung, suspended, between them. Something he'd been feeling all damned day. All damned week.

Without thought, his heart beating fast, Alec wrapped one arm around her. An instinctive movement that brought her against him, her breasts against his chest. Her hair fell in a curtain around her face and tickled his cheeks. He watched her lips part in surprise, breathed in the scent of her that tormented him every time she was near. His sandy hand began to slowly slip up her back to cup her nape, to bring the mouth he'd wanted to kiss all day to his.

The sound of someone laughing poured over his mindless, surging libido like a full bucket of iced water, and he jerked up, nearly tossing Katy into the sand. He stared in horror at her, all too aware of what had just about happened. With a student. With everyone at the hospital just a stone's throw away.

How many times had he vowed to never again make a foolish mistake that could jeopardize his career? Or, damn it, hers, too, which was even more important. He fought for calm in the midst of his self-disgust. "Sorry. I...didn't do a good job of catching you, did I?"

"I'm the one who's sorry. It was my fault. I lost my balance." Her expression was serious, that little frown creasing her brow again, and Alec figured it was probably in reaction to his own expression. He could only imagine what it was. He heaved in a breath, then stood and stretched his sandy hand to hers to help her up. Despite his anger at himself, the feel of her hand within his as he tugged her to her feet still sent that not-allowed zing, which he kept feeling when he touched her, all the way up his arm, and never mind that grit rubbed between their palms, masking her skin's usual softness.

Standing close, she still stared up at him, her blue eyes now wide. Questioning. Did she know how she affected him? She had to, considering she'd been practically lying on him a moment ago.

"Dr. Armstrong I don't think I've had the pleasure of meeting your intern."

Alec swung toward the voice that spoke from directly behind him, and felt like a second, even icier bucket of water had been dumped on his brainless head when he saw who stood there. The only person in the hospital besides Nick who knew about the scandal he'd been involved in long ago. The person responsible for ensuring doctors in the hospital were held to a strict code of ethics.

"Hello, Margaret." He struggled to sound calm and normal. "This is Dr. Katherine Pappas. Katy, meet Oceancrest's Chief Medical Officer, Dr. Margaret Sanders."

CHAPTER FIVE

NEARLY FINISHED WITH checking on patients for the night, Katy stretched her tired muscles and flexed her fingers. Which reminded her of how Alec's grip on her hand earlier, when he'd helped her up from the sand, had become downright vise-like after he'd turned to speak with the CMO. Then how he'd dropped it like it had been a red-hot coal...

And of course she knew why. The woman had likely seen Katy practically sprawled on top of Alec after she'd lost her balance. Might even have seen the way Katy knew she'd been looking at him, which had been with serious thoughts of kissing the man until he couldn't breathe. Alec had probably seen it, too. And since he knew better than anybody the potential consequences of inappropriate conduct between a supervisor and student, he'd practically left divots in the grass after he'd introduced them and taken off.

She smacked the side of her head. Clearly, there was something wrong with her. What kind of woman would kiss a guy again after he'd pushed her away and said he wasn't interested the last time? Only a woman who enjoyed rejection, and apparently she was that woman. A woman who also enjoyed flirting with danger, since that kind of relationship with Alec could jeopardize her own fledgling career anyway.

She looked at her patient list and headed to David's

room. Poor little guy had been in the hospital for quite awhile, and she hoped Alec would be able to remove the child's drain soon.

As she approached the room, she heard a man's voice speaking in an almost melodic voice and stopped short of the door. This time she knew who the voice belonged to. Alec.

He'd actually come back to the hospital after the welcome party? After getting here by at least seven a.m. this morning, since that was when she'd seen him in this very room? She may be a newbie, but she'd spent a lot of time in hospitals during medical school and couldn't remember seeing any surgeon do such a thing unless there was an emergency.

He'd told David he'd try to come back, and obviously he'd meant it. Amazed, she couldn't resist peeking inside, even though she knew it was tantamount to spying. Her heart melted into a gooey little puddle at the sight of Alec sitting on the side of the boy's bed, a picture book in his hand with race cars on the front, reading out loud. David stared raptly at the pages, though his eyelids were drooping a bit.

Oh. My. She was supposed to try fighting her attraction to this man? This man who'd always included her in his and Nick's adventures? This man who was now this caring doctor who took the time to keep his word to this child when he could be home with his feet up?

The answer was, yes, she had to, for all the reasons she'd been thinking about just five minutes earlier.

She moved into the room. "Sorry to interrupt. Just wanted to see if you need anything from me."

Alec looked up and his eyes met hers for a long moment. Something about the expression in his eyes sent her heart thumping harder and made her think of exactly what she needed and wanted from him, even though she shouldn't and couldn't, and how come she seemed unable to keep that firmly in her mind?

"Dr. Pappas. Thanks, but I think David's all set. And ready to sleep, from the looks of it." He stood and pulled the covers up to the child's chin. "Sleep tight, buddy. I'll see you in the morning."

"Night, Dr. Armstrong. Thanks for my book."

Katy followed Alec out the door, where they stood silently. Awkwardly.

"Look, I just have to say I'm sorry I fell on you on the beach." Getting it out there was the best way to clear the air. "I could tell you were embarrassed that Dr. Sanders saw me sort of on top of you."

"I wasn't embarrassed. Don't worry about it." His serious expression said something other than his words, but she wasn't sure exactly what. Concern for her? Guilt?

"Well, anyway. Sorry." She cleared her throat. "I can't believe you came back to see David, and even read him a book. That's a lot more patient care than most surgeons offer."

"I had to come back to see a patient in the ER, so I was here anyway. And most docs would read a book if a kid asked."

"Still, that was really sweet of you."

"Sweet? I'm a lot of things, but sweet isn't one of them."

Oh, yes it was. He was. When he wanted to be. "What about the time I had chicken pox and you smuggled me bubble gum? You stuffed it inside a teddy bear and brought it to me...remember? Or the time I jumped on Nick's skateboard after he told me not to and then fell and skinned up my knees? While he yelled at me, you ran inside and got first-aid stuff."

His face relaxed into a grin. "That wasn't sweet. I just

used you as a guinea pig. Was practicing for someday when I became a doctor."

"I hope you've gotten better at it," she teased, glad to replace the awkwardness with their familiar banter. "You put so much ointment on my legs the bandages wouldn't stick. So you wrapped me with gauze and tape until I looked like a mummy."

He laughed. His cheeks, dark with five-o'clock shadow, creased and his eyes twinkled, and despite her prior stern talks to herself, her heart swelled a little in response.

"But you were a very cute mummy." Still smiling, he ran his finger slowly down her nose and her breath grew short at the touch. "I remember—"

Alec's phone rang, and she moved away discreetly to give him some privacy while he answered it. Wondering, since it was so late, if it was a woman he dated. Feeling ridiculously, stupidly jealous at the thought, she wanted to thrash herself all over again.

"We have a blunt trauma cardiac arrest in the ER," he said, moving toward her as he shoved his phone in his pocket. "Stab wound to the chest. I need to do an emergency thoracotomy." He grasped her arm, his hand slipping down to hers as he strode so fast down the hall she had to run beside him. "This is something you'll probably never have a chance to see again."

"Do I have to?" Okay, she knew she sounded like a little kid who didn't want to clean her room. But she wasn't going to be a surgeon, and knew the procedure was only done on someone in an extremely life-threatening situation. Wouldn't she just get in the way?

"Yes, you have to." His intense expression gave way to a quick grin. "I'm your teacher this month and I say so. Believe me, you'll be glad you came along."

He pushed open the stairwell door and released her

hand to jog down the steps. "Don't trip," he said over his shoulder. "The stairs are faster than the elevator, and I need to get in there. You can join me when you're scrubbed."

"What, you think I can't keep up with you? You and Nick never succeeded in ditching me in the past."

She could hear his chuckle as he widened the distance between them. "Keep up with me? Sweetheart, you've always been ten steps ahead. See you down there."

Sweetheart? Her breath caught, and it wasn't from hurrying down the stairs. Never, in all the years she'd known him, had he called her that. She shouldn't read anything into it, but the word warmed her heart anyway.

He disappeared through the door to the ER, and she hurried to get ready, nervous but excited, too. An emergency thoracotomy was a rare and difficult procedure, and she knew it was lucky that she'd actually get to see it.

Nothing could have prepared her for the chaos in the OR. It seemed like a dozen people were moving everywhere. Equipment beeped. Tense but controlled voices talked over one another. The patient lay on the gurney as someone steadily performed cardiac compressions on his chest. Alec stood beside a young doctor, who was slicing through the patient's skin from his sternum down between his ribs.

"All the way down to the shoulder, Jason. All the way," Alec said, his voice authoritative but calm. He turned to someone next to him. "We need a bigger knife."

She stood there, taking in the astonishing scene, feeling the sense of urgency in the air, hanging back to stay out of everyone's way. In moments, someone handed another knife to Alec and he stepped close to the patient. "Good job, Jason. I'll take over now. Somebody get the blunt-tipped scissors."

Alec sliced deeper between the ribs, then reached for

the scissors and began to cut rapidly, roughly, through the man's flesh and cartilage in a way only a supremely confident and experienced doctor could. Multiple hands reached to hold open the ribs as Alec hacked open the man's body. "Where's the rib spreader? I need it right now."

He lifted his gaze to take the spreader being handed to him, and for a brief moment his intense eyes met hers across the room. He maneuvered the spreader between the ribs and cranked it to widen the opening. And all of it had been done in about one minute.

Part of Katy wished she could see better exactly what was happening, and part of her wasn't sure she wanted to.

"Dr. Pappas, I need you to assist me," Alec said, without looking up.

She gulped and headed to the other side of the patient, listening to the urgent voices of the nurses and residents as they worked, seeing the ragged flesh around the now wide opening in the man's chest, the blood being suctioned out, the hands still performing steady cardiac compression as Alec finished positioning the spreader.

She felt a little hot and swayed ever so slightly on her feet. Do not faint and take people's attention from this man who might be dying, you fool, she scolded herself as she took a deep breath. She forced herself to move close to Alec. "What do you need me to do, Dr. Armstrong?"

"Hold the clamp in place. I want you to see how I snip then manually spread the pericardium to expose the heart."

Lord, why did he want her to see that? But she knew the answer. Because Alec had shown her so many crazy things over the years, and knew she'd benefit as a doctor to see first-hand how this was done.

Heart pounding, she slid her gloved fingers around the edges of the bloodied spreader and tried to hold it steady as Alec reached into the man's chest cavity.

He made a tiny incision in the pericardium then tugged the membrane apart with his fingers to expose the heart. He then grasped that vital organ in his hand and began to gently massage it. In moments the man's heart was moving, beating, pumping on its own right in front of her eyes, and it was the most amazing thing she'd ever seen.

"Oh, my God!" she exclaimed, looking up at Alec, whose eyebrows were lowered over his supremely focused eyes as he worked. "It worked! He's got cardiac activity!"

Alec nodded. "Somebody get me sutures to repair this small cut in the heart. Mammary artery is bleeding. I need a clamp for that. May have to cross-plant the aorta, too."

The flurry of activity continued as Alec, unbelievably calm, gave orders, repaired the cut in the man's heart, and worked to address the other issues for another hour and a half or so. Katy kept looking at Alec, wondering if he was tiring. Heck, her arms were numb and she was just standing there! But his posture and focused expression never changed.

Finally, it was over. The patient's vital signs were within acceptable range. He was moved to the ICU as everyone beamed, slapped each other on the back and chattered in relief, congratulating each other and Alec.

He stripped off his gloves and yanked down his mask, a broad smile on his face. "Great teamwork, everyone. You all made Oceancrest proud tonight."

"Awesome job, Dr. Armstrong," one of the nurses said. "I'll be honest, I didn't think he was going to make it until you got here."

"I wasn't sure either. But an amazing staff and a little luck made it all work out."

As everyone made their way out of the OR, Alec turned to Katy, his finger moving her hair from her eyes to tuck it behind her ear. "So was I right? Are you glad you were in here to see this?"

She looked at his smile and the crinkles at the corners of his tired eyes. Moved her gaze around the now empty room. Empty except for the blood spattered all over the floor and the instruments and tubing and sponges strewn everywhere, looking like a war zone of sorts. Which it had been. An epic battle to save that man's life.

It was an experience she'd never forget. And the most unforgettable part had been seeing Alec in action under extreme stress.

"Yes. I'm glad I was here."

"You did great. Held the clamp steady and didn't faint on me. I'm proud of you."

"I confess I did feel a little faint for a minute."

"But you controlled it. That's what's important. Besides, Miss Science wouldn't want to miss one of the coolest surgeries there is."

His eyes, full of admiration, met hers, and she could picture the little pit-pat her heart was doing in her own chest since she'd just seen, incredibly, that man's heart pumping inside his.

Alec may have made a big mistake in the past, but she could no longer deny that today he was pretty much the total package. Uber-talented. Generous and appreciative of his staff. Beyond caring for his patients.

"Thank you for including me." As he always had. "It was an incredible experience."

"We make a good team." He moved closer, cupped her face in his palms, his eyes focused as intently on her now as they'd been on his work.

To her shock, his mouth lowered to hers in a light touch, at first soft and warm, then firmer, hotter, and she found herself wrapping her arms around his neck, sinking into the incredible, delicious sensation of kissing him. Of him kissing her.

Her heart beat hard and her breath grew short, and just as she was about to open her mouth in invitation to a deeper exploration, he pulled away. His eyes now the darkest she'd ever seen them, his chest rose and fell in a deep breath.

"Congratulations on getting through it like the superstar you are," he said, his voice rough. "Tomorrow's rounds won't be as exciting as tonight's surgery but I promise to make it as good as it can be."

Staring after him as he walked out the door, she lifted her fingers slowly to her lips, wondering why he'd kissed her. And thinking about what she'd really like for him to make as good as it could be.

CHAPTER SIX

CONSIDERING HER LACK of sleep all week, it was hard to believe anything could have kept Katy awake. But she'd found herself wound up after the exhilaration of watching Alec perform that amazing surgery. Not to mention the feel of his lips had still been imprinted on hers, questions swirling through her mind. She hadn't gotten to sleep until the wee hours of the night, and by the following afternoon even constant hits of coffee couldn't keep her from dragging.

She tried to come up with how many hours she'd slept the past couple of days, but finally decided it didn't matter. All she knew was that she was so tired her vision was starting to blur.

About to check on another patient on the floor, her call system buzzed.

"Dr. Pappas."

"Becky from ER here. We have a fifteen-year-old girl with abdominal pain and want Surgery to check her out, rule out any surgical necessity, and sign off on her."

As she headed to the ER, she realized her hands weren't sweaty and she knew exactly what to do when she got there. Interview the patient, give her a physical exam, order blood work then check the results. She'd come pretty far the past week, and the thought managed to perk her up a bit.

A resident was stepping out of the patient's room when Katy got there. "Anything I should know before I talk with her?"

He shrugged and shook his head. "Tenderness in the belly, but it seems unremarkable. I ordered blood work, CBC and urinalysis. Should be able to look at results soon."

"Okay. Good." A young teen lay on the gurney and a well-groomed woman sat in a chair next to her. "Hi, I'm Dr. Pappas. You must be Emma." She smiled at the girl then turned to the woman. "Are you a relative?"

"I'm Emma's mother. Barbara Brooks."

"It's nice to meet you both." Thank heavens the girl didn't look like she was in acute pain or at death's door. "I hear you're having some tummy pain. Want to tell me about it?"

"It just…hurts kind of right here." Emma pointed to her belly button.

"Okay, let me see." She snapped on gloves and gave her a general physical exam, noting no pain in the right or left quadrants. Probably not gall bladder or appendicitis. "Have you had any vomiting? Does it hurt when you go to the bathroom?"

"No. I did throw up a few times, but just in the morning."

"All right." She glanced at the mother and then back at Emma. "Do you have a boyfriend? Are you sexually active?"

"No! I don't have a boyfriend."

Barbara nodded in agreement. "No boyfriend so far, I'm happy to say. She's too young for that."

"Okay." She studied the girl's face and couldn't tell if

she was fibbing or not. "Mrs. Brooks, would you mind if I speak to Emma alone?"

The woman bristled visibly. "I most certainly do mind. She needs me here to support her, and I want to hear everything that's discussed."

Katy inclined her head, wondering how she'd get a chance to talk to Emma privately. For now, she'd check the girl's blood work and see if the ER resident had ordered a pregnancy test. "I'm going to check what your blood work shows, but try not to worry." She patted the girl's arm and smiled at her, hoping to soothe the worried look from her brown eyes. "I bet this is just some tummy bug that's got hold of you. Back in a minute."

Katy dodged the nurses and techs, as well as the EMTs that were wheeling in new patients they'd brought in by ambulance, as she made her way to the computers.

"Dr. Pappas?" The ER resident stopped her in the hallway. "I need you to see another patient, Samuel Green in Room 26, and evaluate for surgery. Possible bowel obstruction. Evaluate and report back to me."

"I'll see him as soon as I check the test results for the patient with abdominal pain and I get my report to you about that." Whew! The ER was a crazy place, and she felt glad again that she'd decided to go into family practice medicine, where she could take time to get to know her patients.

Emma's blood work and urinalysis were normal, with no sign of infection, so Katy felt satisfied to report that she didn't have any condition requiring surgery. No pregnancy test on file, though.

She found the busy ER resident and reported her findings. "She's clear to have the medical intern take a look at her now, except for one thing."

He didn't look up from the computer files. "What?"

"There wasn't a pregnancy test ordered. Do you want me to order it?"

He shook his head and headed down the hall, speaking over his shoulder. "I'll have the medical intern do it."

She nodded and moved to see the next patient, studying the papers in her hand, when her head ran smack into Alec Armstrong's hard sternum as he strode down the emergency department corridor.

"Oh!" She stared up at Alec as his hands grasped her arms to steady her. He shook his head, and her gaze got stuck on the curve of his lips, which sent her breathing a little haywire as she thought of the way he'd kissed her last night. "I'm so sorry. I should have been watching where I was going."

"Walking in a busy hospital while staring downward is asking for trouble," he said, a touch of amusement in his voice. His hands still held her arms, warm and steady, even though she was no longer in danger of toppling over, which seemed to be a common problem when she was around him. As was her heart rate zooming and her mouth going a little dry.

"I know. I guess I can't chew gum and talk at the same time."

"There's no gum chewing allowed in the hospital." He grinned and released one of her arms, holding out his palm. "Spit it out before I have to give you detention."

"What, now you're Mrs. Smith from Highland High School?"

"She probably never gave perfect Miss Katy Pappas detention, but she slapped Nick and me with plenty." He leaned closer, his eyes mischievous, his voice low. "Maybe I should keep you after class to sharpen my pencils."

"Sharpen your pencils? That would be a cakewalk compared to being in charge of washing every test tube and

Petri dish, like you and Nick always had me do. Which never occurred to me was completely unfair."

He laughed. "You were so much better at it than we were, you probably would have done them over again anyway." A nurse headed their way, and Alec dropped his hand from her arm. "I was called down here to talk about the teen patient you saw. Did you—?"

"Dr. Armstrong." A nurse stepped up to them, standing close. She glanced over her shoulder then looked back at Alec again. "I know Dr. Platt called you down because your intern didn't order a pregnancy test for the patient." She leaned closer to Alec, waving a piece of paper and giving him a conspiratorial smile. "Just wanted you to know I got it ordered. And also wanted you to know that Dr. Platt didn't spend more than one minute with the girl and left the history and physical completely to surgery. So if he gives you grief about it, you have some ammo to throw back."

"Thanks, Ruth." Alec smiled and, to Katy's astonishment, gave the woman a little wink. "What would I do if you didn't have my back down here?"

Ruth beamed. "What would we do if we didn't have you to deal with some of the other docs around here?" She handed him the paper and winked back. "Good luck."

He looked at the paper and his lips twisted before he turned to Katy. "Okay, teaching moment here. Whenever—"

"Well, it looks like our little helpers don't know what the hell they're doing, doesn't it, Dr. Armstrong?" A short man whose name tag said Dr. Edward Platt strode up to them, with the ER resident Katy had talked to walking behind him. The younger man's expression bore a strong resemblance to a dog who had his tail firmly tucked between his legs. "Both my resident and your intern apparently don't know that any adolescent female who walks through these doors is assumed to be pregnant until we know otherwise."

"I was just about to discuss the case with Dr. Pappas," Alec said in a surprisingly cool voice. Cooler than Katy could remember ever hearing him speak.

"So let's discuss it together," Dr. Platt said with a smirk that hovered between nasty and self-satisfied. "Why didn't you order a pregnancy test, Dr. Pappas? Do you have any idea the liability to this hospital, and to me personally, if we ran radiological tests on a pregnant woman because we were too lazy and careless to check?"

"I..." Katy swallowed, hands sweating, heart pounding, completely taken aback at the hostility on the man's face. She glanced at the resident. Should she say he'd told her he'd take care of ordering the test? "I asked the patient if she was sexually active, and she said no. However, I did—"

"Well, it's another miracle of immaculate conception." He threw up his hands and the condescending expression on his face made Katy literally quake in her shoes. "Was her mother in the room? Did you shoo her out before you asked? Anybody with half a brain knows a teenager isn't going to tell the truth about something like that when Mommy or Daddy are around."

"Actually, Dr. Platt, I am aware that—"

Alec took a step forward so that he was in front of Katy, and she had an urge to slip all the way behind him to hide. She made herself stay put, but was grateful for the slight protection and distance from the man throwing figurative darts at her. "It's certainly true that not ordering the test is a serious mistake. A mistake both these doctors will make only once in their careers, and that day seems to be today. Luckily, we have great staff who ordered the test before anyone else even saw the girl."

"What if we aren't so lucky next time? I don't want a

lawsuit on my hands or my ass raked over the coals be-cause of these two being inept."

"Dr. Pappas is far from inept. She is excellent with patients and did a stellar job assisting me just last night in an emergency surgery." Alec's cool tone had grown harder, flintier, as had his eyes. Those tiger eyes, defending Katy as he'd done so many times in her life. "Maybe this wouldn't have happened if you'd done any kind of history and physical on the girl yourself. If you'd spent any time with the patient before either of them did."

"That's why we have the residents and interns." Dr. Platt's face flushed as his eyes narrowed at Alec. "That's their job."

"Well, that's where you and I differ. I think it's my job." He met the man's gaze, his expression steely. "The residents are my backup, not the other way around. Now, if you'll excuse me, I'd like to speak with my intern about this alone."

Alec turned and walked away. Katy followed, im-mensely glad to get away from the angry Dr. Platt. Alec may be upset with her, too, but she knew he wouldn't flay her skin from her body and leave her bleeding, figura-tively speaking.

Silently, she followed him down the corridor and through to another longer, empty corridor. She started to wonder if maybe they were going somewhere private enough that he could flay her after all. Or spank her, she thought, nearly laughing nervously as she thought of his earlier teasing. Except there wasn't anything funny about her messing up with the test.

He finally stopped short of the swinging double doors that led to Radiology and turned to her, his expression thoughtful. But not annoyed or disappointed, thank heavens.

"All right, Katy-Did. Fess up. What happened with the test?"

She inhaled a breath, glad it was Alec she was ratting the ER resident out to. But it didn't make her blameless. "I asked the resident if he wanted me to do it, but he said he'd handle it. I'm sorry, I realize I should have done it anyway. That was a mistake."

Her extreme lack of sleep must be making her embarrassingly overemotional, because just seconds ago she'd wanted to laugh and now, out of the blue, a lump formed in her throat, and to her horror tears stung her eyes.

Since when was she a wimpy, teary girl of an intern just because she'd made an error and someone had yelled at her? She wanted to be strong and tough and capable and the awful awareness that she was none of those things at that moment sent the tears spilling over. Quickly, she turned away, swiping her fingers against her cheeks. No way could she let herself be all weepy and weak like this.

She squared her shoulders and took a deep breath. "I'm…I'm sorry."

He grasped her arms and turned her toward him. His gaze had softened and his hands moved up to cup her face. His thumbs feathered across her cheeks, wiping away her tears with a gentle touch. "Hey, what's all this?"

"I just…feel stupid. I hate making mistakes." As she struggled to control her frustration with herself, she found herself staring at the fine lines at the corners of his eyes, at the thickness of his lashes, just before he gathered her into his arms and folded her against his chest.

His embrace was beyond comforting. His chest, wide and warm and firm, was the absolutely perfect place to lay her tired head. The sound and feel of his steady heartbeat against her cheek, the arms holding her close, and the heady scent of him in her nose had her wrapping her own arms around his back without even considering that she shouldn't.

"Hate to break it to you, but you're human, Katherine Pappas. And humans make mistakes. As for being stupid? Now, that's about the only thing I've ever heard you say that is stupid." His voice rumbled through her, warm and amused, as his wide palm held her cheek to his heart and his lips grazed the top of her forehead. "Being an intern is tough. There's a lot to learn and you thought someone else was going to do it. Now you know it's better to just take care of those details yourself. Remember this is a teaching hospital, and my job is to teach you. Every day that you're working, I'm here to help. I'm here in whatever way you need me to be."

Any way she needed him to be? She lifted her head and looked into his eyes, no longer the flinty tiger eye they'd been in the ER but now golden amber, looking at her with an expression she couldn't quite interpret. An expression that felt more than just comforting. And as she stared into them, she imagined that a hot flicker touched his gaze. His chest rose and fell against hers as his arms tightened around her.

"Thank you," she whispered, her breath short, oh, so aware of how closely they held one another. How good it felt. "I'm sorry to be a crybaby. I'm just really tired, that's all."

"You, a crybaby?" He pressed his smiling lips to one damp cheek, lingered, then kissed the other. "You were the toughest little girl in the world, and now you're one tough intern. Who dove into a thoracotomy without blinking an eye?"

With his breath feathering across her face, her lips, an overwhelming urge to lift up onto her toes and press her mouth to his was nearly impossible to ignore. Thinking about that, and how amazing it had felt last night, sent her back to all the years she'd dreamed of kissing him when she had been a teenager and he a young man.

And to the moment five years ago when she'd kissed him and he'd quickly given her the brush-off, saying anything but friendship between them would be all wrong.

It would be even less right today.

The memory of that humiliating moment had her lowering her arms and she began to step back at the same moment his face lowered an inch and his lips touched hers.

Her eyes slid closed as she savored the sweet sensation. Had he kissed her last night in congratulation? Was he kissing her now in comfort? As his mouth moved slowly, gently, on hers, she didn't care why. She just wanted to feel.

The radiology doors swung open and Alec's head snapped up before his arms dropped and he quickly stepped back. As someone wheeled a gurney into the hallway, a gust of air through the doorway cooled all the warmth she'd felt just a moment ago.

"I'll stop back into the ER after you work up your next patient," he said in a stiff, professional tone. "Sounds to me like he will be a surgical candidate, but we'll confirm that after you run some tests." Abruptly, he turned and strode back down the long hall.

Katy watched him. Couldn't help but notice how his wide shoulders filled out his green scrubs, his tight butt in those loose pants still somehow so unbelievably sexy she couldn't stop looking at it. Then wanted to smack herself.

Her focus had to be on becoming the best doctor she could be. The kind of doctor her father had been—confident, kind, respected and admired. She couldn't allow anything, even delicious Alec Armstrong, to interfere with that goal.

* * *

"That would be great, Barney. Thanks. I owe you." Alec turned off his cell, sucked in a breath of relief, and strode down the hospital corridor to check a patient's chart as tension eased from his chest.

Unbelievable that, after all he'd been through five years ago, he'd nearly been caught holding his student intern close against him, murmuring words in her ear and kissing her. Right there in the hallway outside Radiology.

How could he have let himself kiss her in the OR last night? Was he out of his mind? Apparently the answer was a resounding yes.

Something about Katy simply reached inside him. Something that made him want to be there for her, comfort her when she was distressed and not believing in herself. Something that made him forget their student–teacher relationship, forget that she was his best friend and partner's little sister, forget she was completely off-limits for any kind of relationship other than those that came with a little distance.

He'd fought those feelings for the past week, and definitely wasn't doing a good job of it. He'd been so pumped after the successful thoracotomy, so impressed with the way Katy had hung in there, he'd found himself kissing her before he'd known he was going to. And when her beautiful eyes had filled with tears, he'd had only one thought in his head, which had been to hold her close. Once she'd been in his arms, kissing her again had seemed like the most natural thing in the world.

The final realization that he was in serious trouble had come when, as he'd been comforting Katy, he'd spied a roomful of empty gurneys and could think of only one thing. Which had been sweeping up his intern to lie down on one of those beds with him on top of her, making love together until she'd forgotten everything but the feel of him buried inside her.

Damn it. What the hell was wrong with him? Before tongues began to wag, before anything bad could happen to her reputation and career, he realized he had to take himself off the teaching service for the rest of the month. Not an easy thing to accomplish, since every one of the general surgeons had crazy schedules.

Barney Boswell, though, had been willing to switch. Take over for him now, and having Alec do teaching rounds in August. Barney had actually been happy to, since he had a second kid heading to college and wanted to be involved in helping her move in, which would require taking a few extra days off.

So now all Alec had to do was come up with some excuse for why he'd switched with Barney, something convincing and not suspicious. Get through tomorrow, when he and Katy were scheduled to go to the free clinic together. Then after that somehow steer as clear as humanly possible from Katy Pappas.

"How's Katy doing, Alec?"

He looked up to see Nick had just walked out of a patient's room. Apparently not talking about Katy was going to be nearly as challenging as not thinking about her. But he couldn't mind giving her the praise she deserved.

"She's incredible. Did she tell you about the emergency thoracotomy? For a woman who's going into family practice, she was tough as nails through the whole thing."

"I can't believe you got her to go in with you. Good for her. I hear she's good with patients, too."

"She is. Unlike you, who has such a lousy bedside manner you probably should have been an anesthesiologist instead of a surgeon. Though at least your patients are asleep half the time you're around them."

Nick chuckled, probably because this was something he'd been razzed about more than once, not only from Alec but other hospital workers. His ex, too, and Alec wondered if his lack of empathy about her problems had contributed to their marital difficulties.

"Yeah, yeah. Having a touchy-feely bedside manner isn't as important to my patients as my excellent surgical skills. Which even you, Dr. Golden Hands, must acknowledge I have." He grinned. "I really just wanted to ask if there was anything I could do to help her."

"Starting tomorrow, you'll have to ask Barney, because he's taking over teaching rounds this month."

"You're kidding. Why?"

"He wanted off next month's rounds so he could move his daughter into her college dorm. So we switched." Which was true, except it had been Alec who'd initiated it.

Nick frowned. "Barney's a good guy, but you're a better teacher. I'd hoped—"

"Hello, Doctors. Doing anything fun after work?" Alec's fifth-year resident, Elizabeth, stepped over to put away a chart, smiling at Alec the way she often did, and it was a smile that made him feel distinctly uncomfortable. It was the smile of a woman trying to use her sex appeal to ingratiate herself with her superior.

While it didn't happen often, it did happen occasionally. Alec knew it was tough going for a woman wanting to be a surgeon, and it wasn't unusual for them to feel like they had to work harder to get respect. To be either hard-nosed and aggressive or use their feminine wiles to get ahead. He wished Elizabeth wasn't one of them, and he also wished he could just come out and tell her the way she was coming across. But that would open a can of worms he absolutely did not want to open.

"We have a couple of tough cases this afternoon, Elizabeth," Alec said, keeping the conversation on work. "Are you ready?"

"I'm always ready." The smile she gave made the double entendre more than obvious.

"Dr. Stark," Nick said, his tone and eyes cold, "Dr. Armstrong and I were having a private conversation, if you don't mind."

"Oh. Sorry." She looked both disconcerted and annoyed. "I'll see you in surgery later, Alec, er, Dr. Armstrong."

When she was out of hearing range Nick looked around before speaking. "That woman is getting more obvious every day with her come-ons to you. You need to talk to her about it. The last thing you need is rumors about you and a student to start up. It could dredge up your past and jeopardize your job."

Wasn't that the truth? The thought sent a cold chill running down his spine. He'd worked too hard to earn the respect of his peers. To put behind the lack of respect he'd unfortunately managed to earn five years ago.

The rumors he was worried most about had to do with his attraction to Nick's sister. And the thought of damaging her reputation was a hell of a lot worse than any thoughts of damaging his own. "Don't worry. I steer as clear of Elizabeth as possible. On the occasions I'm at the Flat-Foot Tavern and she shows up for a drink, I leave as soon as I can."

He knew it would take a Herculean effort to stay strictly professional with Katy tomorrow at the clinic, but he had to do it. And if Katy showed up at the bar for after hours "liver rounds," he'd have to somehow make sure he treated her just like any other member of the gang.

CHAPTER SEVEN

KATY TRIED TO keep her eyes on the road and thoughts on what she might learn at the free clinic, but found her gaze drifting more than once to Alec. To his attractive profile and the broadness of his shoulders in a dress shirt and tie instead of his usual scrubs. He swung his car into the lot of a strip mall and parked the car. Katy turned to him in surprise.

"This is where the free clinic is?"

"Yep. It's central to a lot of low-income neighborhoods, and easy to access by bus, too," Alec said. "You already know we have a sizable indigent population here also, and this location serves them well."

He led the way into the clinic, which had a modest but tidy waiting room, and through to a common room, with doors to exam rooms. "This is where the nurses take patients' vital signs, weigh them, and get general histories," Alec said, as he put down his bag then picked up some charts. "There are four exam rooms off it."

"What do you usually do here?" she asked, as she looked around the small space.

"Various stuff. Hernia repair, skin biopsies, chronic wound care, things like that."

"How often do you come? Do all the doctors at Oceancrest work here sometimes?"

"No. It's on a volunteer basis. Nick and I come about once a month. We both think it's important to give to the community, and plenty of other docs do too, but not all of them."

Having already met a lot of doctors at the hospital, she could guess which ones might not. Then again, that would make her judgmental, and she knew from experience you couldn't always judge a book by its cover.

Alec being the most difficult book of all to read.

One minute he was the teasing Alec she used to know, then the new Alec who looked at her the way she used to dream he would. A new Alec who had kissed her twice now, and while she couldn't deny she had enjoyed it she wasn't sure exactly how it made her feel. Well, other than turned on, that was.

He'd turned her down flat five years ago when she'd kissed him. So could his kissing her now be all about the conquest and nothing more? Or was she reading something into it that wasn't there at all? That it really had been just his way of congratulating or comforting her? No matter what it was, Katy scolded herself, she had to stop wondering. While years ago a relationship between them wouldn't have been off-limits, as he'd stated at the time, now it most definitely was.

"Since you're going into family practice, why don't you see Miss Kraft first? She's twenty-four years old with possible cellulitis of the arm. She's already had her vitals taken and is waiting in room two," Alec said, as he looked at the chart, all business. Which was good. "I'm going to do a follow-up with a patient who is post-gall-bladder removal. Shouldn't take me long, then I'll join you."

"All right." She took the chart and knocked on the door of the exam room before going in.

A young, attractive woman sat there in a sleeveless

dress, and even from across the room the redness of her arm was obvious. Katy introduced herself then sat next to her. "Can I take a look at your arm? Tell me what happened."

"It's been real red and hurting for a few weeks now. I went to the ER at Oceancrest and they prescribed me antibiotics, but they haven't helped."

Katy gave her a physical exam, and the woman's arm was hot to the touch. The redness ran from her forearm all the way up to her biceps. "Did you fall down? Did you have some kind of skin injury?"

"No. I don't think so. I don't know how it got like this."

Katy looked at her arm a few more minutes, asked a couple more questions, then decided to look at the records from the hospital. Excusing herself, she went into the hallway to the computer and saw that it was her nemesis, Dr. Platt, who'd seen the woman. The antibiotic he'd prescribed was clearly not the right one, and Katy couldn't help but feel a little smug.

Alec came out of the exam room he'd been in and stood next to her, looking at the computer screen along with her. "What do you think, Dr. Pappas?"

"Patient has cellulitis, and our Dr. Platt prescribed cephalexin. It seems clear it's MRSA and that she needs tetracycline."

"Slow down there, Katy-Did." His eyes crinkled at the corners. "How do you think she got the MRSA? Did she fall? Have a pimple that got infected?"

"She says she didn't fall, and doesn't know why she has it."

"Okay, then, Miss Science. What did I say on your very first day? Why do you think she has it? It has to have come from something."

Katy stared up into his smiling eyes and heard loud

and clear what he was saying. What he was teaching her. That she'd taken the cellulitis diagnosis at face value, had been pleased with herself, thinking she was smarter than Platt, and hadn't looked any further for a real diagnosis.

"I hate it when you're right," she said, and warmed at the grin he gave her in response. "I wasn't careful enough getting the patient's history. I don't yet have a real diagnosis, do I?"

"Bingo." His hand reached to cup her cheek, his thumb briefly stroking before he dropped it. "You're close to your gold star for the day, Dr. Pappas. Let's go talk to her together."

Alec sat on the stool next to the patient. Katy found herself studying the way he smiled at the woman, reassuring and warm. He asked a few questions and examined her infected arm then the other, though she resisted briefly. Looking more closely now, she could see a few tiny track marks on the skin of both arms, and shook her head at herself. How could she have missed them? Because she hadn't looked carefully enough, but she would never make that same mistake again.

"I hope you know that all we want is to help you, Miss Kraft. And we can't do that unless we're honest with one another. Can we be honest here?" The sincerity in his eyes as he spoke squeezed Katy's chest. Never could she remember hearing a surgeon speak with such understanding to a patient with addiction. With such compassion.

The patient stared at him a moment before her face crumpled and she began to cry. Katy reached for her hand, her own throat closing. "I don't know how it started," the woman said, sobbing. "I just thought it would be a one-time thing. My old boyfriend asked me to give it a try. But then I started shooting up more. And now I don't know how to stop."

"All right. I want you to know you're not alone in this."
He reached to squeeze her shoulder. "Dr. Pappas and I are
going to get your arm fixed up. I can feel a clot in your
vein that's causing the infection and needs to be taken out.
After that, there are people here who can help you with
your addiction. Okay?"

"Okay." The patient sniffed and wiped her eyes with
the tissue Katy handed her. "Thank you. Thank you for
helping me."

Katy watched Alec give the woman a local anesthetic
then make an incision in her arm to access the vein and
remove the infected clot. Her attention kept going from his
talented hands to his face as he worked. His dark lashes
fanning his cheekbones, his lips pressing together, his eyebrows twitching as he cut and stitched.

Her heart stuttered as she watched him. What a beautiful man. How could she ever have thought he was beautiful on only the outside and not the inside too?

After tying off the vein, he showed her how to drain
off the surrounding pus, then wrapped the wound and prescribed tetracycline. Once they were finished, he spoke to
the nurse and social worker who took over.

"You were wonderful with her, Alec." Katy looked up
at him and wanted to cup his cheek with her hand, as he'd
done to her. Wanted to wrap her arms around him to show
him how much she admired what he'd done. Who he was.

"So were you. I'm glad you were here today. This is the
kind of patient you might get in your practice. To look at her,
you wouldn't guess she's a heroin addict. But there are more
functional addicts out there than you would ever guess."

"I'm glad, too. Especially since you schooled me."

He laughed. "Schooled you? That sounds kind of negative."

"Not negative at all. You taught me again to not assume

the correct diagnosis is the first thing that comes to mind. To look beyond that for a cause. I knew it, but promptly forgot it when it seemed obvious. You reminded me about looking for the zebra instead of the horse."

He touched his finger to her brow and tapped a few times before tracing it slowly down her nose. "If you can remember that, and I know you will, Dr. Pappas, you're going to be the best doctor at Oceancrest."

She lifted her hand to grasp his. Stared into his warm, smiling eyes, lowered her gaze to the curve of his lips, and knew she was right back to where she'd been all those years ago when she'd written about him in her journal. To when she'd kissed him at her brother's wedding.

But this time it was different. She was different. She was older and wiser and she no longer saw him through the filter of rose-colored glasses. Now she saw him for who he was. A man who was flawed like anyone else, who was capable of making mistakes. A man who was smart and funny and beyond talented, and who cared deeply enough about others to volunteer at a free clinic and take care of anyone who needed his understanding expertise.

A man she so wanted to know more deeply and intimately. Could there be any possibility of that happening, without risking her career in the process?

CHAPTER EIGHT

ALEC STOOD AT the edge of the crowded ballroom, watching the bride and groom dance their first dance together as husband and wife, their big extended family smiling and clapping.

Funny how being around the entire Pappas clan just felt right. The years he'd spent at their house, having lively conversations and disagreements over dinners, intervening in various sibling squabbles, going on day trips crammed into their van, had been some of his happiest childhood memories.

Even now, he felt the tiniest pang that he was, in truth, an outsider, looking in. Still wished, as his childhood self had, that his own family was as close and caring as the Pappas family. That he had a real brother or sister to argue with and be close to. A parent that respected him, believed in him.

The meal had been served, the cake cut, and traditional Greek pastries filled a long table. Earlier, as Elena Pappas had walked down the aisle of the Greek Orthodox church, on Nick's arm, he'd known everyone acutely felt the absence of the bride's father and were doubtless feeling it again at that moment. The wise and gentle man whose dry sense of humor had often found just the right quip to bring strife in the house to a halt and bring on laughter instead.

He thought of how cool Katy had been to him at the past two family weddings. Even at her father's funeral. It had bothered him. A lot. He'd wished he could go back in time and react to Katy's kiss differently. How, exactly, he wasn't sure, since it had shocked the hell out of him as much as his own reaction had. But at least their friendship seemed back on track.

Friendship? Back on track? The smoldering attraction he felt for her now was nothing like friendship and a whole lot like admiration and desire.

She'd constantly impressed him all week. Then working with her at the clinic, she'd made a typical young doctor mistake. But instead of bashing herself about it, or making excuses, she'd quickly realized her error, backtracked, and listened, which too many students didn't do. When she'd looked up at him, telling him how great he was, he'd realized no one had ever made him feel the way she did. Appreciated and admired, and he'd wanted her to know he felt the same way about her. Had nearly gathered her up in his arms for another kiss, but had forced himself to keep his hands off.

His eyes had been on Katy through the whole wedding. The woman was attractive as hell in anything she wore, including scrubs. But today she looked like an angel from heaven, though as soon as the thought came, he rolled his eyes at himself. How corny could he be? Yet that was exactly what she made him think of.

The bridesmaids wore dresses that were a dark purple and strapless, showing off the smoothness of Katy's shoulders and the golden skin above her breasts where a strand of pearls lay. Her thick hair was piled on her head, with wispy tendrils around her face and down her neck, and the sapphire of her eyes was as intensely blue as the stained-glass windows of the church had been.

As she'd followed the newlywed couple back down the aisle, her gaze had caught his, and her smile had somehow ratcheted even higher, seeming to reach right into his chest to squeeze his heart. To reach out and grab him by the throat. And he was damned if, as he'd watched her disappear through the doors, he hadn't thought of someday when she had her own wedding, and of how incredibly beautiful she would look. He felt a deep stab of envy for whoever the lucky guy would be. Knew that might be the first Pappas wedding he wouldn't attend.

He brought his thoughts back to the present and noticed that Katy had moved onto the dance floor with a groomsman. All he wanted to do was watch her, look at her. Ask her to dance with him next. Which was not a good idea, even outside the hospital. He had to find ways to keep his distance, not look for excuses to hold her close.

He forced himself to look away from Katy and glance around the ballroom to see who he might know. A number of attractive women stood in groups, laughing and smiling and openly flirting with the men standing with them. At any other wedding reception Alec might have been interested in meeting some of them. Maybe even enjoy a brief fling for a night or the weekend. But as he turned back to watch Katy dancing, as the music drew to a close and another man approached her, he knew he wouldn't find one other woman he'd rather spend time with than her.

He turned away, no longer wanting to see her in someone else's arms.

A soft hand closed loosely around his wrist, and his heart gave a little stutter when he saw Katy's sweet face smiling up at him.

"I haven't had a chance to talk to you all day," she said. "Wasn't it a beautiful wedding?"

"Beautiful." And watching her had been the most beautiful part of it, her every emotion sending shadows and joy across her face as she'd stood at the front of the church.

"I love Elena's dress. Though I guess men don't care about things like that."

Not unless the dress was wrapped around a smart, gorgeous, adorable woman. Then unwrapped off her. "Your dress is nice too. In fact, you look...very nice." And wasn't that a clumsy comment? But he couldn't tell her what he was really thinking and feeling.

"Thank you." Her smile seemed genuinely pleased, as though it had been a great compliment instead of the lame one he knew it was. It was just like Katy. A woman who was always herself and didn't fish for compliments or play coy with anyone.

"I can't believe I'm the last single sibling in the family," she said, smiling, before sadness flickered in her eyes. "Well, if you don't count Nick, who isn't technically single yet. I'm still hoping something good will happen there."

"You never know." Though Alec had his doubts that anything positive would emerge from the current cinders of that marriage.

"I haven't had any dessert yet. Want to check out the table? I heard Aunt Sophie brought her—"

"Come on, Katy!" Her cousin grabbed Katy's hand and yanked her toward the mass quickly forming on the dance floor. The band had apparently taken a break, and Greek music began blasting from speakers flanking the floor. "It's your favorite!"

Katy sent Alec a laughing shrug and shouted, "Come with us!" before she joined the circle that snaked around the floor. He had to smile. He'd been dragged to participate a number of times in his life the same way Katy had been just now, and while he'd never learned the steps of various dances to be particularly proficient at them, he could usually muddle along and fake it.

Unlike Nick, who was the real deal when it came to Greek dancing. As the line of dancers gyrated, he led the group, hand in the air holding a kerchief, his graceful turns seemingly effortless. And he supposed it was effortless for Nick, since the man had learned them literally at his father's knee and practiced for years.

His attention slid from Nick to Katy again. She, too, knew Greek dancing like she could do it in her sleep. Watching her as she held hands with those on either side of her, as she stepped in and out in one of the intricate patterns, it struck him how amazingly graceful she was.

Klutzy Katy? Not this woman. Not the woman who, with a wide, encouraging smile, helped the guest to her left whose hand she held, a guest who was even less adept at Greek dancing than he was. This wedding was a break from the extreme fatigue of an intern, and she simply radiated energy.

Had he ever really watched her like this? Ever noticed her proud posture and delicate footsteps as she danced? Ever noticed how slim and shapely her ankles were as she gave little kicks and circled the room in the strappy high heels she wore?

Entranced, he watched her approach his side of the floor. To his surprise, she dropped her cousin's hand and grabbed his as she swept by, and he had no choice but to join the controlled chaos on the dance floor.

"*Opa!*" She grinned, any resemblance to studious Katy completely gone, replaced by this vibrant and exciting woman. Her hand was warm, nearly hot, as it clutched his. "You remember this one—it's the syrtos, one of the easiest," she said encouragingly, slightly breathless. Damned if it wasn't obvious that the tables had turned, and she'd become the teacher to the student. And what had changed her mind about that, when she'd been so clearly unwilling before? "One, two, three, four, five, six, seven, back, then again."

"I've only done this a couple of times at your family's weddings, remember?"

"Surely a brilliant surgeon can do a little Greek dance," she said in a teasing voice. "Just follow my footsteps and you'll do fine."

He tried his best to follow her lead, shaking his head as he messed up, yet feeling exhilarated, too, her hand clutched in his, her blue eyes laughing. The music pounded across the floor for what seemed like forever, and he felt his tension fade away, replaced by the simple pleasure of dancing with her. Finally, the music stopped, and everyone moved from the floor, catching their breath as the band returned to play popular dance music.

"Whew! That was a workout. But you did great!" Katy turned to him, her face flushed and dewy from exertion. Without warning, she flung her arms around his neck and gave him a smacking kiss on the lips.

Shocked, he stared into her laughing blue eyes and couldn't resist wrapping his arms around her, just like he had long ago. Unlike in the past, though, their embrace created a cyclone of emotion in his chest that threatened to burst out. The same emotion he'd felt both times he'd kissed her at the hospital. Emotion that nearly had him kissing her again right there in front of everyone at the reception.

He folded her close against his chest, savoring the moment. Let his lips touch her temple, slip to her soft cheek and linger there, before he forced himself to loosen his arms. To step back and shove his hands in his pockets before he did something he'd regret. Like grab her hand and pull her to his room and beg her to make love with him the rest of the night.

Her eyes had closed and she slowly opened them, her gaze holding his, and he wasn't sure what he saw within that beautiful blue. He just knew he wanted to keep looking there.

"YiaYia brought her famous kourambiethes. How about we get a few?"

"Sounds good." He knew he should find an excuse not to. But all he wanted was to spend a few more minutes with her. And what was the harm after all? They weren't at the hospital, around eyes that might judge them for talking together.

He let his hand rest against her back, touching her soft skin where the dress dipped low. They walked to the dessert table where the powdered-sugar-covered cookies were nestled in fluted paper cups.

"I'm betting you'll eat two," Katy said, as she put several on a plate.

"And I'm betting the extra one is really for you. As I recall, you had the biggest sweet tooth of the family."

"I admit nothing. I'm a doctor, so of course I only eat healthy foods." She grinned at him and grasped his hand, and damned if it didn't feel absolutely right for their palms to be pressed together.

Katy led them to a darkened corner of the ballroom and slipped the plate of cookies onto a tall, empty table. Her slender fingers picked up one of the cookies and held it to his mouth. "Remember not to do what you did last time you ate these," she said. The teasing tone had returned to her voice, her eyes twinkling with mischief.

God, he loved this Katy—the fun and relaxed woman who, outside the hospital work setting, couldn't be more adorable.

"What did I do last time I had these? Something stupid?"

"Not stupid. A rookie mistake. Inhaling while eating one, then the powered sugar makes you choke like crazy."

"Ah, yes, it's coming back to me." He grinned, remembering her teenage fists pounding on his back when the sugar had stuck in his lungs. "You almost injured my kidneys, whomping on my back like you did. It wasn't like I needed the Heimlich maneuver. What exactly did you think it would accomplish to assault me like that?"

"I guess it was silly." He liked her smile, both guilty and amused. "All us kids did that to one another whenever it happened, though there's clearly no medical reason for it. Maybe it was just an excuse to pound on one another. Sorry."

"Never be sorry." He couldn't resist running his finger down her cute nose. "Pretend to be confident, no matter what, and people will believe you are."

"Is this the secret to your success?" she asked, taking a bite of the cookie.

"I'm not sure I should share my secrets with you." In fact, he knew he shouldn't. The secret about his past that weighed on his present. That made it imperative he not think about Katy the way he couldn't stop thinking about her.

But as he stood close to her like this, seeing her lips covered with powdered sugar, he wanted more than anything to cover her mouth with his once more. To taste the sweetness of her along with the sweetness of the cookie.

Her gaze dropped to his lips, as though she'd read his mind, and her fingertip lifted to stroke her bottom lip. To lick the crumb of almonds and sugar there. His breath grew short, his pulse kicked into a different rhythm at that seductively tempting mouth. At the way she looked at him. He was no inexperienced kid. And damn if her eyes didn't hold the same intense heat and want that tilted his world sideways.

As though drawn by some unseen force, his head lowered and his mouth touched hers. His tongue slipped lightly across her lower lip, tasting the sugary sweetness there. His hand on her back drew her close as they shared an excruciatingly slow, soft, mind-blowing kiss. Her fingers slipped up his chest to the sides of his neck, and he heard a low, throaty groan, not sure if it came from her or from him. The sound had him pulling her closer, sent him deepening the kiss, until the band striking up a loud tune cut through his sensual fog.

It was all he could do to loosen his hold, to pull his mouth from hers, to leave the seductively sweet taste of sugar and of Katy. Panting slightly, they stared into one another's eyes for a long moment until Katy breathed, "Wow."

"Yeah. Wow." And wow was an understatement. But what, exactly, was he supposed to do now? Unlike the last time they'd kissed at a wedding, he was the one who'd started it. Along with the two others he hadn't been able to resist at the hospital. But she'd been so upset five years ago when he'd told her anything between them would be all wrong, how was he supposed to deal with the reality that it truly was?

"Who knew a kourambiethes kiss could be so incredible?" Katy said, her eyes heated but smiling, too, and he huffed out a breath of relief.

"How many kourambiethes kisses have you had in your life?"

"Ah, that's for you to wonder. You're not the only one who isn't sure they should share their secrets."

He smiled and shook his head. How the hell was he supposed to resist her teasing smile and beautiful eyes and incredibly sexy lips?

He would because he had to. Any sexual relationship between them—and God knew he wanted that more than he wanted his next breath—was strictly against hospital policy. Hurting her reputation or her career was something he couldn't risk, no matter how much he wanted her.

He shoved his hands into his pockets and cleared his throat. "I'm going to find your Uncle Constantine. Haven't seen him for years, since he couldn't make it to Nick's wedding."

"Before you go, will you dance with me, Alec?" The band had struck up a slow, dreamy tune and Katy licked the last of the sugar from her lips. Her eyes, now, oh, so serious, held his. Eyes he kept getting lost in when he let himself forget.

"I've already Greek-danced until my feet hurt." Until her hand had felt like it belonged in his. Until her brilliant smile had filled his soul to overflowing.

Her hand slipped from his arm to his wrist and, without thinking, he slid his hand out of his pocket. Her fingers, slim and still warm, captured his. "Please? Just one dance? I promise not to bother you the rest of the night."

Bother him? If she meant bother as in torture him with dreams of her naked in his arms and in his bed, he was sure she'd be doing exactly that for the rest of the night.

He moved toward the swaying couples on the floor, still holding her hand in his, anticipating the pleasure and torture it would be to dance with her. To let the scent of her warm perfume surround him, let his hand drift from her waist to the soft, exposed skin of her back, let the loose tendrils of her silky hair tickle his face.

"Alec! We thought you'd probably be here."

Alec turned and froze. Shocked to see his elegant

mother and sophisticated-looking father standing there, holding glasses of champagne in their hands. "Mom. Dad. I thought you were in Russia."

"Just got back this morning, which is why we didn't make the ceremony. Staying home a short time before we head back," his father said.

"We spotted you over in the corner with your...friend. Can you introduce us?" His mother's eyebrows were slightly raised as she looked at Katy, an intrigued expression on her face.

Alec realized with sudden, sickening clarity that he was holding Katy's hand, tucked closely against him. And he remembered extremely well the long, intense kiss they'd shared.

Dropping her hand like he'd been bitten by a snake, he turned to look at Katy. That small frown he'd become accustomed to seeing dove between her brows again as her eyes scanned his face, and he wondered what the hell his expression looked like. He swallowed hard before he addressed his parents. "You remember Katy. Katherine Pappas. Nick's sister."

"Nick's baby sister? Why, I wouldn't have recognized you!" His mother shook Katy's hand. "What are you doing these days?"

"I just graduated from medical school and am interning at Oceancrest Medical Center."

"Interning at Oceancrest?" Charles Armstrong narrowed his gaze at his son, and Alec's gut clenched. He knew exactly what was coming next. "Are you an idiot, Alec? Cuddling up and dancing with a student from your hospital? Don't you ever learn?"

Alec set his jaw. Years of experience had taught him not to respond to his father's insults, and he certainly wouldn't react the way he wanted to. Not in the middle of a damned wedding reception. "Contrary to what you've always believed, I'm not an idiot. And what I do is my own business."

"Then don't be expecting me to bail you out again. I mean it."

"I never asked you to do that. Would never ask. And for what it's worth, Katy is like a sister to me." Which was a damned lie. Except he knew he had to double his efforts to remind himself that was all there could be between them. "If you'll excuse me, Katy and I were about to go talk with her Uncle Connie."

He turned and didn't even look to see if Katy was coming along or not. Hopefully not, because the last thing either of them needed was more speculation about their relationship. Then he realized she hadn't followed him at all…that she'd found someone else to dance with.

CHAPTER NINE

HER SHIFT THANKFULLY over after twelve hours, Katy headed to the changing room, grateful to put on real clothes for what seemed like the first time all week. She felt physically and mentally exhausted. Emotionally, too. Today was the anniversary of her father's death. It was the one day of the year she allowed herself to mourn and be sad. The distance between her and Alec added to the heaviness in her chest.

The heaviness had been weighing there since the wedding. Just as the two of them had been about to dance, after they'd shared a kiss so sweet she'd nearly melted to the floor, he'd yanked his hand from hers like she was a leper. Told his parents he thought of her as a sister, and the words had felt like he'd jammed his fist in her solar plexus.

The man had kissed her three times, damn it. Wouldn't any woman think that meant he wasn't thinking of her as a "sister"? Player or no player, she had to believe Alec didn't kiss every woman he met before turning as cold as the proverbial cucumber and running away. Then again, history had shown she was very capable of deluding herself when it came to Alec Armstrong.

It had been a week since Dr. Boswell had taken over Alec's teaching rounds. Except for her current weariness, Katy felt like she was really finding her sea legs and not drowning in the hospital undertow. Dr. Boswell had proved to be a good teacher on rounds. Not as good as Alec, of course. But also not as distractingly attractive either.

She figured that had to be a good thing. Her goal was to learn how to be an excellent doctor, and being sidetracked as she noticed other things instead was a hindrance to that.

Noticed, for example, Alec's amazing bedside manner that engendered trust from even the most difficult patient. Diverted from listening to what patients had to say as he touched them with his long, beautifully shaped surgeon's hands. Engrossed by the vision of how incredibly sexy he looked in his green scrubs, his muscular chest and athletic tush filling them out in a way that would make any woman practically swoon.

She yanked off her scrub top and pulled on her sundress, thinking of how wonderful Alec had looked in his suit and tie at the wedding, how adorable he'd been, trying to Greek-dance. He'd seemed so much like the Alec she'd been getting to know again, teasing and fun and natural, and the memory of their kiss at the hospital had made her insides all warm and gooey. She'd felt a little Cinderella-like in her beautiful dress, dancing and eating with an oh-so-handsome prince then kissing him until she'd been breathless.

Then he'd just walked away, their planned dance apparently forgotten. Angry for deluding herself, she'd found someone else to dance with.

But then she'd seen him standing there, watching her. And the look on his face, a peculiar combination of fierceness and defeat and something she couldn't quite figure out, had brought back a small, budding hope that maybe she hadn't been wrong about him wanting her the way she wanted him.

With that tiny hope had come a tentative conviction. If presented with another opportunity to kiss him, she wasn't going to regret and wonder. She planned to be bold. To find out what might or might not be there between them.

She huffed out a long sigh. The unfortunate part of that plan was that she rarely saw Alec now. And today, of all the three-hundred-sixty-five days in the year, she would have loved to have his understanding support beside her. His presence would be a comfort, she knew, because it always had been.

Tears clogged her throat and she quickly swallowed to banish them. This year, the painful loss seemed even worse than it did most years. Her dad's absence at the wedding had left a sad emptiness in everyone's heart on an otherwise very happy day.

Nick understood a little. After all, it wasn't the best day of the year for him either. For some reason, though, they both seemed to want to handle it in their own ways. Separately, not together.

The door swung open and Elizabeth walked in and quickly stripped, throwing on her clothes like she was in a hurry. The fifth-year resident had seemed to thaw a little toward Katy, becoming nearly friendly since Dr. Boswell had taken over the teaching rounds. Katy didn't know what had motivated the change but was glad of it.

"You coming over to the Flat-Foot Tavern for liver rounds?" Elizabeth asked as she pulled a beaded shirt over her head.

"Liver rounds?"

"Yeah. Those of us off duty and not on call drink until our livers complain." Elizabeth grinned. "There'll be cute guys there from other services you might not have met yet. It's a fun break after a long week, and a good way to get to know people out of the hospital."

"I don't think I'm really in the mood to socialize."

"Suit yourself." Elizabeth shrugged. "But I'm heading over if you end up changing your mind."

Katy thought about her plan for the night. Which was to go to Nick's house and look through old family photo albums. Laugh and cry, then put them away for another year. Is that what her dad would want her to do?

No. He'd be so proud of her for getting through these first weeks of her internship, and even having a few successes. He'd want her to celebrate that. Make new friends. Maybe Alec would even be there, and her spirits would be lifted just by being with him, the way they'd always been.

"You know what? Mind's changed. I'm in."

Alec finished up the last of the paperwork on his desk, glad that this hell of a long day was finally over. He closed his eyes and let his head drop back against his chair, disgusted with himself that he'd had the gall to think he'd had a bad day. This latest news about a patient he'd liked and cared about, a patient whose family he'd become close with, was a painful blow. And he knew that, as painful as the sad prognosis for this man was for Alec, it was nothing compared to how it affected the man's wife and children.

His own unpleasant day had started with a phone call from his father in the morning, before his parents had left to go back to Russia for another week or two. The man had felt a need to ream Alec out yet again for his lack of good judgment and general failings as a doctor and human being.

Then Margaret Sanders had stopped by his office to talk about which fifth-year residents he would recommend being offered a permanent position. Talking with Margaret had made him think about nearly kissing Katy on the beach, which the CMO would have seen all too clearly if he had. Then thought about the times he had kissed her, and how much he wanted to do it again. Starting with her mouth and working his way down every inch of her beautiful body.

Damn it, he knew he couldn't act on this intense, nagging desire for her, but didn't need a constant reminder of that reality.

Or maybe the truth was he did need it. Should, in fact, welcome it. He couldn't ever make the same mistake again, no matter how much he wanted to. He could not risk Katy's reputation. Her future. And since he couldn't, avoiding her as much as possible was the least torturous solution to the attraction that felt inescapable.

He'd felt terrible after he'd walked away from her at the wedding. Then a different emotion—jealousy—had stabbed even deeper when she'd just moved on to dance with someone else. Though he sure couldn't blame her for that, since he couldn't be with her the way he wanted to be.

The deep breath he pulled into his lungs didn't calm the disquiet he felt. What he needed was a long run to clear his mind before the sun set. He knew running wasn't going to push the tragic news about his patient from his mind. Definitely wouldn't erase thoughts of Katy. Not thinking about her had proved impossible, but it had gotten slightly easier since he no longer saw her every day on teaching rounds.

Damn it, though, he missed her. Missed seeing her warm bedside manner. Missed seeing that little crease in her forehead as she pondered a problem. Missed seeing the desire in her eyes that mirrored his own, making not kissing her impossible.

He nearly groaned when his phone rang in his pocket, wondering how he'd get through another surgery in his current state of mind, until he remembered he wasn't on call tonight. He looked at it, relieved to see it was Nick. "What's up?"

"I need you to do a favor for me. Are you able to go to the Flat-Foot Tavern tonight?"

He stared at his phone. Nick's favor was to go to a bar? "Why?"

"Katy's there with the crew. I'd hoped to join her and keep her out of trouble, but I just got called in for an emergency surgery and can't."

"Why do you need to keep her out of trouble?" Of all the people he knew, Alec couldn't imagine Katy whooping it up and getting drunk and out of control.

"Today's the anniversary of Dad's passing. It sure as hell doesn't feel like he's been gone four years, does it?" Nick sighed in his ear. "You know how tough that was on all of us, but especially Katy. She was his baby, you know?"

"I know." His chest compressed in sympathy for the whole family, but he had a bad feeling he knew where this conversation was going. "What exactly are you asking me to do?"

"Katy usually stays home on this day and, basically, mourns. I expected to find her here, going through old family memorabilia, so I was surprised when she wasn't. Then she called and told me she was going to the bar. She's not a big drinker, and it doesn't take much for her to get looped. I'm afraid tonight might be the night she has a bit too much. To forget. And I can't be there to make sure she gets home okay."

Hell. "All right. I'll go."

"Thanks, Alec. I appreciate it."

A peculiar sensation rolled around in his chest. A strange combination of trepidation and anticipation at spending time with Katy, of being there for her. Thinking how much it would mean to him to be with her tonight as much as she might need him around.

He glanced at his watch. Just after nine. Surely it was

too early for her to already be tipsy. Except liver rounds usually started around seven, so who knew?

He stacked the papers he'd signed, put them in his outbox and stood, ready to head out the door. Until he realized he needed a quick shower and to change into street clothes. And never mind that half the people at the Flat-Foot would be there straight after work, wearing scrubs.

Twenty minutes later he headed outside and across the street to the tavern as the sun dipped beneath the horizon. Even with the low light inside the bar, his gaze was instantly drawn to her. Katy.

He hadn't seen her for days, and he let himself stand there a moment to absorb the sight of her. Her hair gleaming, her smile surprisingly wide for a woman who was supposed to be feeling sad today. Laughing and bright-eyed and clinking a glass with some intern he hadn't met yet.

He remembered her trying to clink her glass with his, dumping her wine in his lap, and touching him until he'd nearly exploded. Good thing he'd arrived to make sure she didn't have the same effect on the young guy, and never mind that it shouldn't be any of his business.

He weaved through the crowded tables, the thump of the bass music seeming to pound a primal rhythm into his body. He pulled up a chair next to Todd Eiterman, the second-year surgical resident. Close to Katy, but not so close as to raise eyebrows. Though eyebrows were raised anyway, since he didn't make a habit of doing liver rounds with the residents.

"Any lives saved today?" he asked, to make small talk, looking around the table of hardworking young doctors relaxing after a long week. Hoping no one saw him looking particularly closely at Katy, trying to see if she'd been drinking much. Trying not to think about how good it would feel to drape his arm across her shoulders. To feel her soft skin beneath his hand that was exposed by the spaghetti-strapped sundress she wore.

"Every day, Dr. Armstrong. Every day." Elizabeth smiled coyly and lifted her glass of wine.

Alec didn't have a glass to lift, so he simply gave her a return half-smile. "Good. Cheers."

"Here, Alec. I mean Dr. Armstrong. Toast with this— I'm going to get another one." Katy held her glass out to him. Her mostly empty glass, and what had been inside it, he wasn't sure. Margarita? Daiquiri?

He didn't want her drink, but he also didn't want her to be drinking it either. It was more than obvious from the over-brightness of her eyes and the slight slur to her words that she'd already had plenty. He felt an urge to sweep her up and out of there before she embarrassed herself, but forced himself to be patient. To wait for the right moment when it wouldn't seem like a big deal.

He held up the glass. "Cheers, everyone. You're all doing a great job."

The cheer was loudly chorused, and he took a sip to be polite. Margarita, and a strong one, at that. How many had she had?

He looked at Katy again, but her face was turned to Elizabeth next to her. Within the loud beat of the music in the bar, he couldn't hear her words, so he just let himself study her profile. Her cute little nose and generous lips. Her slender hands fingering the necklace slipping down between the hint of her breasts that peeked from the top of her dress. He found his breath growing short, wished he could replace her hand with his own to stroke that delicate skin. Then figuratively smacked himself for the thought.

Damn. He took a swig of her drink, grimaced a little since he didn't particularly like margaritas, and pretty much emptied the already nearly empty glass. He answered questions and engaged in chitchat while half his mind wondered how he was going to discreetly get her out of there without anyone noticing.

Katy stood, clearly wobbly on her feet, and picked up her purse as she turned, likely to go to the restroom. This was his chance to talk with her alone and get her home. The waitress stopped at the table, and Katy sent Alec a wide smile. "Alec, let me buy you a drink. I'm having another one."

Like hell she was. Time to scrap the idea of being discreet. "I can't stay. And unfortunately you can't either because your brother asked me to drive you home."

"I don't need a driver. I have my car here."

"Except you're not driving it."

"Says who? Besides, I'm not ready to leave."

Alec nearly laughed at the look she gave him, which could only be described as a death glare, coupled with a deep frown. Apparently the normally sweet and apologetic Katy had another side that was unleashed after a few drinks. Or, he considered, she might still be ticked about the way he'd left her at the dance floor.

"I'll make sure she gets home, Dr. Armstrong," Todd said.

He looked at the young man, who seemed sober enough. But he'd promised Nick he'd see her safely home. At that moment Katy turned and stalked—if you could call her wobbly gait stalking—to the restroom, and Alec exhaled in relief. This was his chance.

"Thanks, Todd. That would be great. I'll see you all later." He headed toward the door then pivoted back toward the restroom. Out of the corner of his eye he saw one person was still watching him. Elizabeth.

Damn it. Caught.

No matter. He was going to get Katy out of there without a scene, text Todd that he'd driven her after all and fulfill his duty.

Duty? Who was he kidding? This had nothing to do with duty and everything to do with the surge of protective instinct he was feeling. That, for whatever reason, he'd always felt toward Katy.

After what seemed like an eternity the door to the women's restroom finally swung open. She tripped over her heel and stumbled into him, grasping his arms as he steadied her against his chest.

"Oh! Sorry." Her big blue eyes blinked up at him, and that scowl settled on her face again. "Oh. It's you. Why do you and Nick seem to think I need taking care of? I don't need a babysitter. I'm a big girl now. I can take care of myself."

"I know you can. But you've had too much to drink to drive, and I think you know that."

She stared up at him, now with just that tiny frown between her brows that was such a cute part of who she was. Did she know her fingers moved on the skin of his arms, caressingly, tantalizingly, as they stood so close to one another in the dark, narrow hallway? His hands tightened on her shoulders, and he forced himself to loosen them.

"Okay." Her breasts rose and fell in a deep sigh. "I know I shouldn't drive. But I…I don't want to go home. Not just yet."

"Fine. We'll go somewhere else." How could he insist he take her home when her eyes looked so clouded and sad, when her lips trembled ever so slightly? He needed to take her mind off the pain of losing her dad. Off the stress of work. Off anything but simple pleasures.

He shoved down thoughts of the kind of pleasure he'd really like to offer her, and decided on where he could take her. Somewhere sure to bring the smile to her face that he needed to see again. "Let's go to my place and take a walk along the bay to clear our heads."

"That sounds good." Already the clouds in her eyes were fleeing, and Alec's heart felt a little lighter as he led her out the side door of the tavern.

Moonlight lit the lapping water of the bay as he swung his car into the driveway of his condo. Katy had been uncharacteristically quiet the entire ride. He turned the ignition off and looked at her, so close in the seat next to him. The sadness that was back in her eyes knocked the air from his chest.

"Come on. Something's happening soon I want you to see. Something that will make you smile."

"I don't feel much like smiling today."

"I know. To be honest, I don't either. But maybe we can find a reason to smile together." He walked to her side of the car and opened the door, reaching for her soft hand. "It's a little chilly, so wear your sweater." She'd need the light warmth, and it would be good to see less of her smooth skin that tempted him to touch it.

He led her down to the bike path that circled the bay, holding her hand because she was still a little unsteady on her feet. And because it just felt right to twine his fingers with hers. It would've seemed oddly distant to just walk side by side with her, when both of them could use the warmth and comfort of that small connection. After all, it wasn't as though some spy from the hospital was watching.

The simple act of strolling with her, the crisp night air in his lungs, the moon hanging in the starry sky, all seemed to clear his mind of everything that had weighed him down that day. He looked at Katy and hoped she felt a little of that, too. "I'm sorry about your dad. I know him being gone is hard on all of you."

"Things like a family wedding are a sad reminder, you

know?" She looked up at him, and even through the darkness he could see the shadows in her eyes, a misting of tears that clutched at his heart. "He would've loved to live long enough to see a first grandchild and be a wonderful *papou*. He would've loved to see Elena married. He would've been so happy to see me graduate from med school. It…it really breaks my heart he never got to do any of those things."

He stopped walking to cup her cheek with his free hand. Wipe away the single tear that had escaped her brimming eyes and squeezed his heart. "I know. Life isn't fair, is it?"

She shook her head. "No. It definitely isn't. He gave me this necklace to remind me to always go after what I wanted. I wear it every day and can feel him with me."

Her eyes held wistful sadness as she fingered the necklace. Alec wanted to offer her comfort, to hold her, kiss her, until there was only happiness in their sapphire depths. But he couldn't. He could only offer words. "Your dad was proud of all of his kids, but I think you were special to him. You shared his love of puzzles and mysteries. I remember how much he got a kick out of the backward solutions you came up with when everyone else only thought forward."

"He did, didn't he?" The smile that touched her lips was small, but it was a start. "So tell me why you don't feel much like smiling today either."

Should he tell her? He rarely shared when he was upset about a patient. But she'd shared with him, so it was only fair that he open a little of himself up to her, too.

"A few years ago, I had a patient with colon cancer. I got to know him well, and his family, too. He's just a great person, as is his wife. They have three of the cutest kids." He sucked in a breath, thinking how they'd all been sure the worst health problems were over for the man. "I performed a hemicolectomy on him, then he had a course of chemotherapy, and he's been doing well until this week when he started having stomach pain. Today we found out the cancer has spread to his liver." He could still see the man's wife's tears, the way they'd clutched each other when he'd had to tell them the bad news. And damn if that wasn't the absolute hardest part of his job.

"I'm sorry." It was her turn to squeeze his hand, and he was surprised that telling her, and having her listen, felt good. "I haven't had to go through that yet, but I know I will have to help patients deal with bad news when I'm in a family practice. I hope I do okay."

"You don't have to hope. You have a wonderful way with patients. I've seen it firsthand and have had quite a few people tell me, too."

"Really?" This time a real smile touched her face, which made him smile, too. "That's good to hear. Thank you."

The first boom sounded in the air, and Katy stopped walking. "What was that?"

"What I brought you out here to see. What I said would make you smile."

More loud booms, and then red, green and white sparkles lit the night sky.

"Fireworks?"

"From the adventure park. You can see them across the bay."

"Oh! They're beautiful!"

He watched her face and was filled with a feeling of triumph when he saw her eyes light almost as brightly as the fireworks. As her smile grew wider she gasped with delight. And damned if the soft sound, the expression of pleasure on her face, didn't make him wonder how she would look, how she would sound, as he buried his nose in her soft neck and buried himself in her beautiful body.

He shouldn't think those kinds of forbidden thoughts,

but he just couldn't escape the fierce desire for her that had become a constant, intense ache.

He turned, not wanting to look at her. Not wanting to see her shining eyes and lush lips and her curves hidden beneath her dress that kept giving him these insane thoughts. Thoughts that gnawed at him. Thoughts of taking her to his condo and stripping off her clothes and making love with her all night.

No. He had to suppress it. And since he didn't seem to be able to accomplish that out here with the bright, silvery moonlight touching her hair and skin and smile, he had to end the evening and take her home. He took a few steps away, back toward the car.

"Nick will be wondering where you are." His voice came out gruff, hoarse, but it was the best he could do. "And I have an early morning tomorrow." It wasn't true. In fact, he had the day off. But a little lie was nothing if it helped him get her home before he did something he'd regret. That they'd both regret.

"Alec."

He looked back at her and, to his shock, she was right there. Inches away. His breath backed up in his lungs at the expression on her face.

It wasn't sad any more, or worried or studious or any of the things he was used to seeing on her lovely face. It was determined. And sensual. A combination that both excited and alarmed him.

"Yes?" he asked, wary, his heart beating harder, the excitement and alarm growing as she closed the small gap between them.

In answer, she rose up on her toes, wrapped her arms around his neck and pressed her mouth to his.

CHAPTER TEN

ALEC STOOD THERE motionless, as though he were a statue, as she kissed him. He didn't pull away, but didn't participate either. She'd known he'd be surprised, but she'd had to taste him. Had to kiss him one more time.

His lips were so warm, so soft. She ran her tongue across the seam of them, and was rewarded as he opened them slightly, as his tongue touched hers, and she drank in the taste of him.

His hands closed around her shoulders, tightened, and with a strange, strangled sound in his throat he seemed to give in. Tilted his head and opened his mouth over hers. Brought her body tightly against his. It felt so right, so wonderful, to be pressed so closely to his heart she could feel the pounding of it against her breasts.

His stiff form loosened, molded to hers, hip to hip and thigh to thigh. His hands left her shoulders to wrap around her back, his fingers digging slightly into her flesh as his mouth devoured hers. As though he was starving for her in exactly the same way she'd been starving for him.

Yes. Yes. Yes. The mantra broke through the fogginess of her brain. Each kiss before this had gotten longer, sweeter. Now they were sharing the kind of passion she'd dreamed of. She arched up, kissing him more boldly now, letting her fingers thread into his soft hair, the thick waves curving around her fingers, holding onto her. Her holding on to him.

Abruptly, his arms dropped from her back, his hands grasped her shoulders again, and he set her away from him. His chest heaved in deep breaths. Her stomach tightened as it became clear, even through the darkness, that his expression wasn't smiling and sensual. It was very serious.

"Katy. I'm sorry. I shouldn't have kissed you in the hospital and again at the wedding. I shouldn't have kissed you now."

"It's not for you to be sorry." She tilted her chin at him, refusing to let him take the blame. Trying to push down the regret she, too, felt. Not regret for the kiss. Regret that he wouldn't allow himself to be with her the way she so wanted him to be. "I kissed you, not the other way around."

"This time, maybe. But that still makes it three to one." His serious expression gave way to a glimmer of a smile.

"Actually, it's three to two, counting the time I kissed you five years ago."

"Okay, Miss Math. Though I didn't think you liked to remember that kiss too much."

"I don't. Do you have any idea how embarrassed I felt when you turned me down flat and ran away like a dog being chased by a cat?"

"I'm sorry. I was most definitely a dog that night." He lifted his hand to her hair, blowing in the breeze, and tucked it behind her ear. His fingers slowly continued down to stroke her cheekbone. "But I think you know now it wasn't because I wasn't attracted to you. Which, to my astonishment, I was that day."

"And now?"

"Now I'm beyond attracted to you." Even in the darkness she could see his eyes grow serious again as he cupped her face in his hand. "But I can't do anything about it."

"Why?"

"You know why. You're a student and I'm an attending physician. Your teacher. It's not ethical."

"You're not my teacher any more. Dr. Boswell is."

"It doesn't matter. People love to talk—you know that. I couldn't bear to have you gossiped about, maybe even have your career jeopardized. Nick and I even worried about people calling favoritism just because you're his sister. Believe me, I know how it can be. We can't do this, no matter how much I want to."

"How much do you want to?" she asked. Wondering if it could possibly be as much as she did.

"You want a demonstration?" His eyes glinted. "Something you can quantify, Miss Science? Then here it is." He pulled her tightly against him, angled his mouth to hers, and kissed her hard. Fiercely and possessively and without reserve. A kiss that most definitely beat out all their prior kisses tenfold. A kiss that sent her heart racing and hot tingles surging through every nerve and was everything she'd dreamed for years and years that kissing him would be.

Katy clutched his shirt with her hands. A moan formed in her throat as his hot mouth explored hers so deeply and thoroughly that her knees wobbled beneath her. Then nearly stumbled as he released her and backed away. A chill replaced the warmth that had spread across her body on every inch they'd touched each other.

"Does that give you something to measure?" The dark eyes that stared at her glittered with a passion that shortened her breath even more. "I want you, Katy. I think about you all day long. Wondering if I'm going to run into you in some patient's room or the hallway or the lunchroom. I look for you, even though I tell myself not to. Even though

I've tried hard not to. I want you, but we can't do this. I won't be responsible for damaging your career."

"No one has to know. No one will know."

"A dangerous assumption to make."

He grasped her hand and began to walk back toward his car, so quickly that she stumbled in her heels and he slowed down. "I'm taking you home now."

He'd told her he wanted her. Thought of her all day long. Just as she did him. But the huge problem keeping them apart couldn't be ignored, and she knew it. She didn't want her career damaged any more than he did. How could she be the doctor her father had been if she let her personal life cloud her judgment? A secret affair with a man who was technically her boss was not something her father would have wanted for her—even if that man was Alec. And she understood why he didn't want to go through that again either.

As they'd both said earlier, life wasn't fair. And that reality felt like a brick on her heart.

"Can I see your apartment before you take me home? Maybe have a quick cup of coffee?" She wasn't quite ready to say goodbye. Knew a cup of coffee wouldn't really make a difference but grasped at any reason to spend just a few more minutes with him.

He looked down at her, his expression now unreadable. "You want coffee?"

"Yes. Please."

He looked at her a long moment, so long she nearly fidgeted beneath his gaze, before he finally led her into his condo. Floor-to-ceiling windows looked over the starlit bay from his living room, which was furnished with modern pieces in clean, sleek lines. They moved into a spacious kitchen with gleaming appliances and a huge island with bar stools on one side. "Have a seat at the counter. You'll see there's a plate of kourambiethes your *yiayia* insisted I bring home with me."

Mmm...kourambiethes. Instantly, she remembered the powdered sugar on his lips as it had been at the wedding, and knew she'd never again eat one again without thinking of him.

He had one of those single-cup coffee-brewing machines, and placed a steaming cup in front of her before brewing one for himself. She looked at his strong back, his shoulders broad in the blue polo shirt he wore tucked into the waistband of jeans. Watched his long, surgeon's fingers nimbly work the machine.

Why couldn't she feel those talented fingers, just once, touching her everywhere? Feel his skin and muscles under her own hands? Knowing he wanted her the way she wanted him but that they couldn't let it happen made her chest ache even more than when he'd rejected her five years ago.

Welcoming the distraction of hot coffee with a sweet cookie, she picked up one of the kourambiethes and handed it to Alec, then took one for herself. She took a bite then realized he was looking at her mouth. Watching her eat, his eyelids low, his eyes dark. She ran her tongue slowly across her sugary lip, deliberately tempting him. What could be wrong with one last, sweet kiss?

Still staring at her, he took a bite of cookie, and his chest lifted as he drew a breath.

Suddenly he began to choke. Lord, it was the powdered sugar! She jumped off the stool and ran to the other side of the counter, pounding on his back with her fists as his body was wracked by a violent cough.

"Ow, damn it, stop!" His eyes watered as he choked and coughed and finally got his breathing under control. He turned and grabbed her wrists. "Geez, Katy! Didn't we already talk about the medical necessity for this? Or are you just mad and trying to kill me?"

"Trying to kill you, I guess. Haven't you heard about hell and the fury of a woman scorned? But if you kiss me, I'll spare you."

One more kiss. Was that so much to want? She pressed her hands, her wrists still imprisoned in his hands, against his chest. His heart beat hard against her palms. Harder than it should have been just from his choking episode. As hard as hers currently pounded in her own chest.

"Katy." His eyes were dark and hot. His voice low and rough. "It's nearly impossible for me to resist kissing you as it is. Now you have to add a threat of bodily harm?"

"Just trying to even up the score. Which is currently four to two." She leaned up to press her mouth to his, softly, slowly, not wanting to be accused of assaulting him again. Just wanting to taste him. Wanting him to feel what was between them.

His warm lips moved with hers for a long moment until he broke the kiss. "Does everything have to be a competition with you? How about letting me win this? Leave it at three to four?"

"I don't think so. I'm liking this kissing contest a lot." She kissed him again, and he tasted beyond wonderful, a spicy hint of coffee mixed with sugar and him.

He pulled his mouth from hers, his hands tighter on her wrists now. Tension emanated from him, and heat, too. His eyes glittered, most definitely a wild, tiger-eye color as he stared at her, and she could see very clearly that his need was every bit as powerful as her own. "So now we're even. Are you happy?"

"Yes. I'm happy. But I could be happier." She pulled her wrist loose from his hold and grasped his hand. Brought his palm to her breast and held it there. His fingers tightened, his thumb sweeping across her nipple, and it felt so wonderful she gasped.

"Damn it, you don't play fair," he said in a low growl, still stroking her breast.

"All's fair in love and war." She used her free hand to tug part of his shirt from his pants, slipping her fingers beneath until she could feel him tremble.

"Is this love or war?" His hot breath slipped across her cheeks as his lips caressed her face.

"Maybe a little of both."

"Yeah." The word came out on a groan as he released her other wrist, wrapped his arm around her back and kissed her. No longer teasing and soft. This was a real kiss, deep and hot and nearly desperate, and she sank into it as one hand caressed her breast, the other sliding down to squeeze her bottom.

"Katy." The word came against her lips as he kissed her, delved deeply again, their tongues dancing together as he claimed her mouth for his own. The countertop pressed into her lower back as he molded his body to hers. She wound her arms around his neck and held on, feeling the tension in the muscles of his shoulders, in the tautness of his body. Her knees felt so weak she thought she just might slither to the floor.

"Katy," he said again, his voice ragged, his eyes dark. He gave her a small smile as he imperceptibly shook his head. "I'm going to hell for this, you know." Then he kissed her again.

A feeling of relief swept through her as she realized they'd both finally, finally surrendered to the force that was clearly bigger than both of them. His kiss was filled with passion and sweetness but no regret. Only want.

She brought her hands to his waist, tugging his shirt

loose to feel his skin, his body. His muscles shivered beneath her palms as she stroked under his shirt.

He responded by pulling the straps of her dress off her shoulders, tugging more until it hung at her waist and her lacy bra was all that covered her breasts. With his agile fingers, he quickly flicked the clasp and slid it, too, from her arms.

"I've fantasized for more hours than you can imagine how your breasts look." His voice was hoarse as he looked at her. "Do you know how beautiful you are?"

"What I know is that I don't know exactly how beautiful you are," she said. She wanted to see him, look at him the way he was looking at her. She pulled his shirt up and off. Her breath caught at the width of his shoulders, at the muscled strength of his chest, at the fine layer of dark hair covering it. She smoothed her hands up and over all of it, loving the feel of him against her palms. Wanting the feel of all of him against all of her.

He grabbed a cookie from the plate on the counter, his eyes gleaming. "Promise not to bruise me again if I choke?"

"I— Oh…!"

All thought of how she was going to respond left her brain when he rubbed the cookie slowly across and around one nipple, then the other, his mouth following to lick and suck the sugar left behind. The feel of his lips and tongue were so magical and wildly erotic she could barely breathe. She tangled her fingers in his thick hair, held him to her, and moaned.

With his mouth still on her breasts, he pulled her dress the rest of the way down her body until she stood there wearing only her panties. He sank to his knees, his mouth continuing down, circling her navel. Moving lower until his lips and tongue pressed against the damp front of her underwear. She moaned again, melting for him.

Perhaps he sensed that her legs were about to crumple beneath the erotic invasion of his mouth, because he suddenly stood. His long, warm fingers grasped her bottom and lifted her to his waist before he began moving from the kitchen. She wrapped her legs around his hips and clung to his neck, kissing him, still able to taste a little of the sugar on his tongue.

"You taste unbearably sweet," he whispered between kisses. "Even without the sugar." He carried her into a bedroom, and her heart pounded so loudly in her ears it was like a drumbeat. Finally. Finally. But he passed the big bed and moved to a sliding glass door.

"Where are we going?" Surely he wasn't going to go all noble now after he'd made her crazy with wanting him. "I'm thinking a bed is a good idea. Like now."

"Who knew you could be so impatient?" He grinned as he shoved open the door and stepped into the breezy night, onto a covered, private balcony accessed only from the bedroom. "Ever since you came to San Diego I've thought of you out here with me. Thought of how you would look, naked on the cushions of this chaise lounge with the breeze in your hair and the moonlight in your eyes."

He gently lowered her to the chaise and the bay breeze did tease across her nakedness, sensuous and wonderful, and she wanted him to feel the same thing. Needed him naked—now.

"You, too." She sat up and grasped the belt of his jeans, undid the buckle. "I want to see your body in the moonlight."

"Your wish is my command." His eyes crinkled at the corners, but in their depths was the same deep longing and desire that had filled her from the moment he'd kissed her on the bay. From the moment she'd first seen him again.

He stripped off his jeans, socks and underwear in a hurry, then settled his torso between her legs. Licked along the inside of her thigh as he pulled the last bit of her clothing down and off. Kissed his way up her body as his hands gently stroked her legs, opening them, as he settled himself in between to nuzzle her neck and nip her earlobe.

"Too bad the fireworks are over," he said against the hollow of her throat. "We could have heard and seen them from here."

"I'm willing to bet we're going to make some fireworks of our own." There was no doubt about that as her body was already consumed by an intensely sparkling heat she'd never known existed.

He chuckled against her neck. "I won't take that bet, because my goal is to make you explode."

He kissed her again as his fingers found her core, touched her, caressed her, as her own fingers explored his smooth contours. His face, his shoulders, his tight buttocks, his back. Clasped him in her hand until both of them were gasping into one another's mouths, their bodies moving, skin against skin.

She'd dreamed of this for so long. Wanted this so long. Part of her wanted to savor every second, to draw out their lovemaking all night. But the part of her that wanted him beyond anything she'd ever experienced couldn't wait. She wrapped her legs around his hips, drew him in to join with her. They moved together, creating an instant rhythm of perfection between them, giving and taking until the moment couldn't be held off any longer. Her climax making her cry out, he covered her mouth with his, absorbing the sound as they both fell.

* * *

Alec lay propped on his elbow in his bed and watched
Katy sleep, listening to her breathe as she lay on her back
next to him. He gazed at her sweet face in repose, her
eyelashes resting on her cheeks. At her motionless body,
positioned as a sleeping fairy-tale princess would be, her
hands one on top of the other resting on her belly, her beautiful hair in a thick halo of waves around her head. Deep
in the kind of sleep only someone who'd been without it
too long could have.

The breeze from his ceiling fan lifted strands of her
hair, and he gently stroked them from her eyes and tucked
them behind her ears. His chest filled and his gut tightened
with too many swirling emotions.

Pleasure. Regret. Worry. Joy.

He shouldn't have let it happen. Hadn't been able to
keep it from happening.

He let his finger trace her eyebrow, slip down her nose,
touch her beautiful lips. Her face twitched in response,
and he had to smile. She was a woman of contrasts, like
no one he'd met before. So smart, someone who thought
deeply and carefully, who took her job seriously, and yet
who could be almost childlike at times in a charming and
adorable way.

Katy. He'd never have dreamed when she'd tagged along
after Nick and him all those years ago that he'd be lying
in bed with her, sated, happy, content. He should get up.
Leave her to get her much-needed rest as he went for a
run, fixed some breakfast for both of them. Then take her
home and hope to hell her brother had no clue why she'd
really spent the night at his home.

All this was dangerous. So potentially damaging to
both their careers. But as he looked at her, he knew he
couldn't walk away and end it now. He wanted to spend

the day with her. Wanted to spend more time learning how her interesting mind worked. Wanted to explore the world through her eyes, which had always seen things a little differently than most.

He wasn't her teacher any more. And, yes, he knew it was a damned lame excuse for not breaking it off right now, before it had barely started. He wished he was strong enough, but he wasn't.

He could only hope and pray they wouldn't both regret heading down the path in front of them. The all-too-thrilling path that was also scary as hell.

CHAPTER ELEVEN

"Hi, Dr. Boswell. Dr. Armstrong." Could anyone tell her heart thumped absurdly fast as she tried to stand nonchalantly in the doctors' lounge by their lunch table? How hard it was to suppress a secret smile as she looked at Alec's handsome face? How hard it was to not reach out and smooth his slightly messy hair from his forehead?

"Hello, Dr. Pappas." The smile Alec gave back to her probably seemed normal enough to anyone watching. But Katy could see the glint deep in their amber depths that showed he was feeling exactly as she was. Still remembering their incredible and beautiful time together three nights ago. "Are you giving Dr. Boswell any trouble?"

"I'm trying not to. I don't think I've made any mistakes for at least a few hours."

"I think it's actually been an entire day." Dr. Boswell chuckled. "In truth, Alec, our student is doing a stellar job. She's the kind of intern who makes teaching rounds a pleasure."

"She is indeed." That glint in his eyes grew a little hotter as their eyes met, which made Katy feel short of breath. He must have realized how he was looking at her as he seemed to quickly school his face into bland professionalism and turned back to Dr. Boswell. "I hope the interns

I get next month work as hard as she and Michael Coffman have been."

Elizabeth Stark stopped next to her as she stood at the men's table, holding an empty lunch tray, her gaze a little cold as it slid over Katy, which surprised her. A slight chill of anxiety slid down her spine. Elizabeth had been so much friendlier the past week. Had the woman somehow picked up on the vibe between Alec and her?

Elizabeth shifted her attention to the two surgeons. "Dr. Boswell, are you still planning for me to do the appendectomy this afternoon?"

The man nodded. "Should be a cakewalk for you by now, Dr. Stark. I'm impressed with the skills you've shown me so far. You're just about ready to go off on your own."

"Thank you." She inclined her head in acknowledgement of the compliment as her face relaxed a bit into a pleased smile. Katy knew Elizabeth put tremendous pressure on herself to achieve in the surgical arena, which was still primarily a man's world. Another reason Katy was more than happy that she'd chosen family practice for her future.

Elizabeth turned to Katy. "When you're done with lunch, come find me. I have a few patients I need you to see."

"Okay. I won't be long." She wanted one more quick look at Alec. Wanted to be the recipient of another smile that lit his eyes. But knew she couldn't linger and possibly raise any red flags, so she looked at Dr. Boswell instead. "I'll be here if you need me. Otherwise I'll see you for rounds in the morning."

Katy moved to a table at the back of the room and faced the wall so she wouldn't be tempted to stare at Alec. After their amazing night and day together, she'd found it a little hard to concentrate when she'd first come back to work.

Thankfully, she'd gotten back into the groove soon enough and was so busy working umpteen hours she didn't have time to think about anything but her patients.

Still, when she did have a free moment her mind instantly drifted to her wonderful day off. A day off that had seemed like far more than twenty-four hours. Probably, she thought, hoping the dreamy smile on her face wasn't obvious to the entire lunchroom, because she'd spent the day with Alec. A day filled with delicious lovemaking, laughter, and fun.

Kayaking on the bay, then lovemaking at Alec's place. Lunch by the ocean on Mission Beach, a little swimming, then back to his condo to make love. Sailing on Alec's small sailboat then making love again.

Could any day possibly have been any more perfect?

With a smile on her face she just plain couldn't suppress, she finished up her lunch. Alec had already left, and when she felt a twinge of disappointment sternly reminded herself that was a good thing. She contacted Elizabeth on the hospital call system to find out where she needed to be next.

"Twentieth floor. I have to be somewhere else in a few minutes, so I need you to get here quickly," Elizabeth responded. Was it Katy's imagination that her voice was a tad curt?

She hurried to the floor and found Elizabeth going over some charts. "What do you need from me?"

"That patient you tried to assassinate with potassium a couple weeks ago?" Elizabeth barely glanced up from the charts. "Like a boomerang, she's back again."

"Mrs. Patterson?" Katy frowned. "Why?"

"She actually was here a few days back when you were off work. Typical granny problems, but the nursing home sent her in anyway. She still had lactic acidosis, and the diagnosis was again ischemic colitis."

"So why is she back today?"

Elizabeth rolled her eyes. "Same old. Lactic acidosis again. In my opinion, she just has the dwindles and is depressed and nervous. Then the nursing home gets nervous, too, and sends her back. I remembered she liked you, so why don't you do her workup, see if you can reassure her before we send her back to the home?"

"Okay. I'll be glad to. Thanks." Katy took the chart and headed toward Mrs. Patterson's room. When she got there she stopped abruptly in the doorway, staring for a moment, shocked at what she saw.

"Helen?" She hurried to the woman's bedside. The woman looked astonishingly ill. Nothing at all like the energetic, chatty woman she'd been just weeks ago. How could she have lost so much weight in such a short period of time? She'd been the tiniest thing, anyway, when she'd been here before. Now she was practically skin and bones. She reached for the woman's hand. "Tell me what's going on."

"Who are you?" Her eyes had a hollow look to them as she peered at Katy, with none of the friendliness and vitality that had sparkled in them before.

Her words jerked Katy's heart. Was the woman delirious? "It's me, Katy Pappas. The intern. I took care of you the first time you came in. Just a couple weeks ago."

Helen stared at her, then gave a tiny nod. "Oh, yes. I remember."

Katy warmed her stethoscope, then listened to the woman's lungs and heart and took her pulse. "Tell me why you're here. How you're feeling."

"My stomach hurts so much. I can't eat. I don't sleep

well." Her thin hand rested on Katy's. "I think it's my time. I think I'm dying."

"Not if I can help it." Katy pressed her lips together. This didn't sound like a normal post-op problem. Or simply ischemic colitis. Before her hip surgery Helen had been a very active, healthy woman. What could possibly be going on? "I'm going to check some things and see what we can figure out. Hang in there." She squeezed the poor woman's shoulder and headed to the computers to look at Helen's lab results. And hoped and prayed there would be one little thing that would shed light on this peculiar mystery.

Katy closeted herself in one of the hospital computer labs where she'd have some quiet to study and think. She pulled up all Helen Patterson's records. Her hip surgery. Tests done at that time and during her next admissions. She turned to the mnemonic used for studying the anion gap of metabolic acidosis—MUDPILES.

Ruling out several of the various causes for acidosis in the MUDPILES mnemonic was fairly easy, but still didn't give her an answer. Then she called on the training her dad had given her. The puzzle master. The ultimate mystery-solver.

Define the goal. The topic. What did she already know on the subject? Set aside the first, most obvious solutions and keep an open mind. Place the facts in a pattern she could understand and evaluate.

She stared at all the information on the computer, gnawing her lip. Think, Katy, think.

It almost seemed as though the type on the screen grew crisper, brighter, practically leaping out at her. The answer was right there. But what a crazy answer it was! Would anybody believe it? Who should she try to convince first?

Nobody. The first thing she had to do was prove her hunch, her conviction, through a blood test.

Sucking in a fortifying breath, she ordered the test and asked for the results to be determined STAT. Then managed to distract herself by seeing other patients, but checked every few minutes to see if the tests were done, practically jumping for joy when the results came in. Then stared in both triumph and disbelief.

Katy's heard thumped and her adrenaline flowed. She remembered Alec reminding her to look for the zebra while everyone else was looking for the horse. And, man, this zebra was a big one.

She turned from the computer, hands a little sweaty. She'd start with Alec. He'd advise her what to do and what steps had to be taken.

After what was only ten or so minutes but seemed like hours, Katy was able to find out where he was. And what could possibly make the elevators so painfully slow? Rushing through the corridors, she finally found Alec about to enter a patient's room and ran up to him.

"Dr. Armstrong! I need to speak with you right away."

A frown formed between his brows as he looked at her then quickly glanced up and down the hall. He took a step back and spoke in a low voice. "Dr. Pappas. As you know, Dr. Boswell is covering teaching rounds now. You need to address any questions to him."

"No. I know." She gulped. Obviously, he thought she was here for personal reasons and was worried about hospital gossip. Didn't he know she fully understood they had to keep their distance here? "I have a very peculiar situation with a patient and I need to talk with you about it. Have you advise me, because we may have to get the police involved."

His expression turned to one of surprise. "All right. What's going on?"

"You remember Helen Patterson? The patient who

accidentally got too much oral potassium on my first night on call?"

"Yes. I remember."

"She's been back two more times for ischemic colitis, which seemed a little strange to me. Then when I went to see her I couldn't believe how different she was, really sick-looking and a little confused."

He stared at her intently. "Go on."

"I set aside the most obvious answers then did some critical thinking. I saw there was one thing that hadn't been checked because normally there wouldn't be a reason to. So I ordered the test. It's confirmed. Her ethylene glycol levels are through the roof."

"What? How is that possible? She's been living in a nursing home."

"Here's the crazy part. Are you ready?" She prayed he'd believe her hypothesis. "I believe her son is poisoning her with antifreeze. He needs money—I know he's been borrowing plenty from her, and she told him she wouldn't give him any more. I know it seems…unbelievable, but my gut tells me it's true and the lab results support it."

He studied her, his eyes thoughtful, then gave a nod. "I would have to agree that there doesn't seem to be any other way that her ethylene glycol levels would be high. I'll speak with Barney and the CMO. The hospital has specific protocol for situations like this, and the police will be contacted to investigate. Meanwhile, we'll get started treating her."

A huge breath of relief left her lungs. "Thank you for believing me. For not dismissing the idea because I'm a lowly intern."

A slow smile spread across his face, touched his eyes which grew warm and admiring. He reached out to cup her face in his hands. "Lowly intern? You, Dr. Pappas, are a superstar. Have I told you lately how much you amaze me?"

Without thinking, she pressed her own palm against the back of his hand. "Me, amazing? Not as amazing as you, Dr. Armstrong, surgeon extraordinaire."

A chuckle rumbled in his chest, and their gazes stayed locked on one another's. Memories of their night and day together hummed in the air between them, and both moved forward, their lips meeting for the briefest connection until a voice jolted them apart.

"What…the hell?" Nick was in the hallway, practically right next to where they stood, and Alec's hands fell to his sides as he took a step back. Nick stared then moved in, just inches away. His voice was quiet but filled with a confusion and anger Katy had rarely heard from him. "Are you kidding me?"

Alec's lips were pressed into a thin line, but he regarded Nick steadily. "Katy has come up with an impressive diagnosis for a patient, but wasn't sure anyone would believe her. She came to talk with me about it first."

Nick looked behind them before speaking again in a near whisper. "I may be as dense as my soon-to-be ex-wife claims, but I'm not totally stupid. The excuse you gave for Katy staying with you…" He shook his head, his eyes narrowed. His chest lifted in a deep breath as he glanced down the hallway again. "We'll talk about this later. My office. Tonight."

Katy's stomach churned. How had they let their guard down and allowed themselves even one second of anything smacking of a personal relationship between them while they were here? And a kiss more than smacked of that. It screamed it. Alec's expression had hardened to stone, and her heart sank at the worry and remorse in his eyes.

"Nick, I don't get what you're upset about." Could she

play the innocent, clueless Katy and convince him he hadn't seen what he thought he had?

"You—"

"Alec, I need to speak with you."

They all turned to see Barney Boswell walking toward them. His expression was as grim as Nick's, and Katy's heart about stopped. Dear God, had he seen, too? And if so, what would happen?

"Yes?" Alec's voice was even, but his stony expression hadn't changed.

"I've received…bad news." The man rubbed his hand across his face. "My mother has passed away, and I need to help my brother with all the arrangements. I'm leaving in the morning, so you'll have to take over teaching rounds again."

CHAPTER TWELVE

ALEC PACED IN his office, wondering how the hell to handle this latest problem. His gut churned at what a mess it all was—what a mess he'd allowed it to become.

After his magical night and day with Katy he'd wanted more of them. Hadn't wanted it to end. Had convinced himself they could be discreet and completely professional in the hospital. With him no longer doing the teaching rounds, he'd been sure it wouldn't be too difficult to keep their distance by day and be together when their schedules allowed it at night.

That plan had now gone up in flames. How could he possibly justify what had been wrong to begin with if he had to take over the teaching rounds again?

He'd also clearly been kidding himself about their ability to be discreet. After only moments in the hallway with Katy, looking into the intense blue of her eyes as she'd spoken, listening to her impressive detective work on Helen Patterson's illness, he'd forgotten every damned thing except how amazing she was.

He dropped down into his desk chair, wanting to think about all this for a minute before he went to Nick's office, and closed his eyes. They'd been beyond lucky that the only person who'd seen him holding her face in his hands and kissing her had been Nick. And while that brought

another dimension into the equation, at least Nick wasn't
going to run to the CMO and report a suspicion that a
teacher and senior staff member was hitting on a student.
Or, at least, he didn't think so, unless Nick thought he'd
be protecting his sister if he did.

"So what do you have to say for yourself?"

Alec opened his eyes and saw Nick standing in the
doorway, arms folded across his chest, looking almost as
angry as he had when he'd first seen them in the hall.

"Do you realize how much you sound like my father
right now?"

"Apparently someone damn well has to." Nick came
in and perched on the edge of the chair opposite Alec. "I
still can't believe what I saw today. How the hell long has
this been going on?"

Should he tell him? Or flat-out lie and try to make him
believe it had been a friendly, congratulatory kiss?

Alec didn't like either option, but knew he couldn't lie
to Nick. "What's going on is that, from the minute I saw
Katy again, I haven't been able to stop thinking about her.
About her beauty and brains and how damned all-around
incredible she is. And, yeah, I knew it was all wrong but
couldn't stop it. No matter how hard I tried." He leaned
his elbows on his desk and braced himself for the censure
he deserved. "When I found out she felt the same way, I
couldn't fight it anymore."

"Hell, Alec." Nick stood and paced across the room.
"First of all I'm having a hard time wrapping my brain
around you and my little sister being…you know…what-
ever it is you are."

"I know." He couldn't believe it either. But he didn't
have to believe it for his attraction, his obsession with her
to have consumed him anyway.

"To think, I was worried people would whisper favoritism because she's my sister. Which thankfully hasn't happened." Nick shook his head. "And I don't even have to say the rest of it, do I? I absolutely can't believe you've done this after all you went through before. You just can't go there. Period. It's bad for you, and it's bad for her. It's just plain bad."

"I know. You think I don't know that?" Alec clenched his fists, wanting to pound on something. "I—"

"It's only bad if you choose to decide it is," a quiet voice said from the doorway.

Both men looked at Katy. Alec's stupid, confused heart felt like it somehow squeezed and swelled at the same time. She stood there in green scrubs that were wrinkled and had some sort of orange stain beneath her breast. Her blue eyes had shadows smudging them and the hair he so loved to touch was pulled back into a messy ponytail that had numerous loose strands sticking out of it...and still she was the most beautiful thing he'd ever seen.

Nick walked over to her. "You two can't do this. A student having a relationship with an attending just isn't done."

"Really? Just isn't done? I've met several couples in this hospital who had exactly that kind of professional relationship before they had a personal one." Her eyes turned to blue steel as she stood toe to toe with Nick, and in spite of the whole damned situation Alec had to smile. This amazing woman standing in front of him was as tough as nails.

"Doesn't make it right. Doesn't make it ethical, and it doesn't mean the hospital won't boot both of you out of here on your asses. You know what happened five years ago when Alec made exactly this same kind of stupid mistake. It blows my mind that he's doing it again. To you, of all people! I won't let you make the same kind of mistake and have your reputation ruined, or worse."

Katy knew what had happened back then? Alec's chest tightened, because he knew everything Nick said was true. Risking her reputation was all kinds of wrong. Except their relationship felt so damned right.

Katy wrapped her arms around her brother's waist and leaned up to kiss him on the cheek. "I keep reminding you I'm a big girl. Alec and I will figure this out, and I promise you—no tears, no matter what."

Nick's face softened slightly as he looked down at his sister. "I love you, Katy, but the last thing you need is to get fired because of misconduct." He turned and pointed his finger at Alec, his eyes fierce. "This is my little sister you're messing with here, and you'd better end this now before she gets hurt."

He stormed out and Alec and Katy were left to just look at one another. Since simply looking at her made him feel alive in a way he hadn't felt in a long time—hell, had never felt—he didn't know what to do.

She took a few steps closer, surprisingly hesitant steps, considering her firm response to her brother a few minutes earlier.

"So, now what?" she asked quietly, her eyes searching his. "We've both known all along this might happen."

He stood and walked to her, wrapping her in his arms. She laid her head against his chest and he pressed his cheek to her silky hair.

If only there was a solution that would still allow him to hold the softness of her body to his, still tangle his fingers in her hair, still kiss her lush lips whether they were covered with sweet sugar or just savor the sweetness of them alone. A solution where he could enjoy her inquisitive and quirky mind and find ways to make her smile and laugh, which he'd just recently discovered was the best part of any day.

"I didn't know you knew about what happened five years ago," he said.

"I don't know much. Just that you were involved with a teacher of yours when you were a resident, and she ended up getting fired."

Realization dawned. "Is that why you'd been so chilly to me for so long after the wedding when you kissed me? I thought you were just mad about that."

"Hey, wouldn't you be upset, too? I kissed you and you turned me down flat, saying anything between us wouldn't be appropriate. Then ran right out and had a fling with your teacher just months later. I wanted to hit you." She smiled. "But I know now that's not at all who you are."

"It's who I was then."

"We all learn and grow, don't we?" She stroked his cheek with her hand. "So tell me the whole story."

"I was young and careless. Probably tried to live up to my dad's poor opinion of me." He sighed. "She was only a few years older than I was. But still my teacher and superior. She came on to me and I thought, Why the hell not? Then found out why not."

"What happened?"

"The university and hospital ethics board had a fit. Wanted to boot me out of the residency program." He didn't want to confess the worst part of it, but knew he had to. "My father was furious with me besmirching the Armstrong name that just happens to grace the cardiology wing of that hospital after his revolutionary valve-transplant discovery. He swept my dirty deeds under the rug, while making sure she got fired."

"Did you love her?"

The blue eyes looking up at him had gotten so serious he actually smiled, despite everything. "Hell, no. I barely knew her. From then on I never dated anyone in the hospitals I worked in."

"Then why get involved with me?"

"You're not really asking me that, are you?" He loved the way her brows were drawn together, at the way she seemed to be studying him, trying to figure out what he was thinking. And good luck to her with that, because his mind sure ping-ponged back and forth from moment to moment on how to deal with his feelings and hers and the damned professional risks.

"Yes, I am asking. And you'd better give me an honest answer."

"Because I couldn't resist, Katy-Did. Because I'm crazy about you. So crazy it seemed worth the risk to your reputation and mine too. Even though Nick is right. Risking yours makes me a selfish bastard."

"I knew about your past and the potential consequences but decided I wanted to be with you anyway. And it's still a risk I'm willing to take, if you are."

Her arms tightened around him and squeezed his heart. What should he do here? Could he really walk away from her on the slim chance someone found out and reported it? Could he make himself say goodbye?

His stomach churned, and that sensation made him realize that it wasn't just the thought of damaging her career that had made it feel that way all afternoon. It had been the thought of ending things before they'd even begun to explore what was happening between them.

"I'd never forgive myself if people started talking and it affected your job here."

"I'd never forgive you if you don't let us find out exactly what this is between us."

"I don't think I could stand never being forgiven by you. Having you turn all cold to me the past five years was hard enough." He realized the office door was open a crack, and released her to shove it closed. "I don't know what's right. But I do know that I can't just walk away from you. From this. Without finding out exactly what this is. Even though I know I damn well should." He wrapped his hands around her shoulders and drew her close again, breathing in the scent of her that tormented and teased him whenever she was near.

"Smart man." She smiled, flattening her palms against his chest, warming him. "I was hoping you wouldn't make me turn loose my woman-scorned fury on you."

He chuckled then kissed her cute nose, touched his lips to each soft cheek, to one beautiful eye then the other, before drawing back. "Tomorrow I have to take over teaching rounds again. My having a jones for an intern while being her teacher, supervisor and, in just over a week, giving her an evaluation grade, is completely unethical."

"This is not a news flash, Alec. We—"

"Shh. Let me finish before you unleash the scorned woman on me." He pressed his fingers to her lips, trailed them across her jaw to cup her cheek. "This is a complicated problem I feel requires some special problem-solving skills that a certain beautiful intern I know has in spades."

The irritation in her eyes faded to a smile. "Go on."

"So, I'm borrowing the technique you told me you used to figure out Mrs. Patterson's illness. I defined the goal. And that goal is to put back the sparkle and excitement that's been missing in my life by spending time with you. To kiss every inch of your body until you're in delirious ecstasy, then start all over again. Teach you how to sail, because you nearly got knocked into the water by the boom when we went last time."

"You know I have a clumsiness problem." Her warm hands slid up his chest to rest on each side of his neck. "I like your goals. Except there are three of them, and to truly solve a problem you have to concentrate on one."

"All right. The goal is to add excitement to my life by taking you out on my sailboat and kissing every inch of your body while we're on the water."

She laughed, her eyes now twinkling, and he nearly lost his train of thought while thinking about kissing her delectable body. "Next," he continued, before they never finished the conversation and he ended up making love to her on the floor, "I determined the facts, which is that no one can know about my kissing you all over or anything else that may come to mind."

"I can see you're very good at problem-solving. Did you learn this from my dad, too?" She reached up to nip his lips, nibble, lick, tease. He nearly dove into her mouth to give her a deep kiss and to hell with any and all conversation, but this had to come first.

"No. I learned from you." He kissed her softly, her sweet lips clinging to his. Her fingers slipped from his neck, slid into his hair as she pressed closely against him and he couldn't wait to finish the talking so they could move on to something infinitely more pleasurable.

"Final step is critical thinking." He lifted his hands to her cheeks and looked into the smiling eyes he could lose himself in. "I want you. You want me." Which made him the damned luckiest man on the planet. "We should try being together, not apart. But we have to get through the ten days you're my student being as cold as ice to one another in the hospital."

"That won't be easy for me, since what I'm feeling right now is very, very hot." She pressed her mouth to his chin, his jaw, his throat. "But I'll rise to the challenge."

She always rose to any challenge in front of her. Her mouth on his skin was making his body rise to a challenge, too, and he pulled an inch away before he lost control. "There are still some risks involved. But when you move off of the surgery rotation, it will be fairly easy to be discreet. And if people found out, at that point it would probably result in just a slap on the wrist, nothing more. What do you think?"

"I think your conclusion is most excellent. Just like you."

"Am I allowed to add another goal now?"

"Since you've concluded the last one, you may work on a new one."

He reached behind her and locked the door. "My goal is to enjoy our last few hours together before rounds tomorrow." He tugged her scrub top loose from her drawstring pants and wrapped his hands around her ribs, let them travel upward to cup her breasts, lightly thumbing her nipples.

A pleased gasp left her lips as she arched into him, but touching her wasn't enough. He wanted to see her, too. Moving his hands upward, he grasped her arms to push the cotton fabric up and off her.

"Are you sure no one will walk in?" She covered her breasts with her hands and glanced behind her.

"The door is locked. And this is the private office of a big, bad surgeon. No one will bother me."

"Big, bad surgeon?" She dropped her hands to cover his as they cupped her ribs again. "And here I didn't think you were egotistical."

"Don't be fooled. All surgeons are egotistical." He kissed the top of her breast then slid his mouth across the swell of it to kiss the other. "I love your pretty, lacy bra. And what's inside it. Every time I see you in your scrubs in the hospital, I can't believe how sexy you look in them. Even more now that I know what's under them."

"Scrubs are not sexy. Not on me, anyway. But on you? Most definitely." Her breathy laugh turned to a low moan as his mouth moved to her nipple beneath the lace. "However, having them off of you is sexier still."

She tugged his shirt over his head, which unfortunately required him to lift his mouth from her. Which he figured was a good opportunity to see more of her skin. All of it. He unclasped her bra and slid it down her arms to the floor. Then tucked his thumbs into her waistband and tugged until she kicked them off her ankles, along with her shoes and socks, yanking off his own clothes in short order.

He paused a moment to just look at her stunning nakedness. At the golden glow of the smooth skin that covered her delectable curves, the sensual smile on her lips, the blue eyes that looked at him with the same desire he felt that nearly overwhelmed him.

Breathless, he tugged her ponytail loose from the band holding it, let her silky hair slide over his hands. Holding her waist in his hands again, he moved backwards, bringing her with him, until he sat in his swivel chair. Let his hands slide to cup the smooth curves of her rear and brought her onto his lap.

"I've never made love in an office before." She straddled him, wrapping her arms around his neck, her hard nipples teasing and tickling his chest. "Is this how it's done?"

"I don't know. I've never made love in an office either. Though I've fantasized about you enough as I sat right here in this chair. And I'm more than excited to have that fantasy become real." He slipped his fingers between her legs, caressing her slick core until she gasped and sighed and pressed against him. She closed her eyes, and the little sounds that came from her beautiful lips made his pulse pound and his breath short. Watching her face as he touched her was beyond erotic, and he nearly plunged inside her that second.

But he didn't. He wanted the moment to last. Wanted to go slow, wanted to hear her sighs, wanted to look into her eyes and the bliss in their blue depths. The scent of her hair and her skin and her arousal nearly drove him mad, and he covered her mouth with his, needing that connection. Needing to taste her sweetness. Needing more of her. The kiss became deep, frenzied, until she lifted herself onto him and they moved together in a primal rhythm. Moved together with a growing need that nearly swamped him.

"Katy." He grasped her hips, trying to slow the moment down, to savor every single second of their joining, but as she tossed her head back, her glorious hair spilling across her shoulders she cried out his name, and he had no choice but to give in to the release, her name on his lips as they fused with hers.

CHAPTER THIRTEEN

THANK HEAVENS TEACHING rounds for the day were almost over, with Mrs. Patterson as their last patient. It was nearly impossible to listen to Alec speak without watching his mouth and remembering all the places on her body it had roamed. To look at his hands as he held a patient's wrist, or touched them in a physical exam without thinking of the places he'd touched her own body and how incredible he'd made her feel. To look at his eyes and remember how they had gazed at her nakedness with a hunger that had set her on fire.

Through sheer force of will she'd managed to make work her number-one focus.

"You look so much better, Helen!" Katy took in the woman's rosy color and bright eyes, and thought she might even have put on a pound or two.

"I certainly feel like a new woman." Helen reached out her hand and Katy clasped it in hers. "Dr. Armstrong here tells me it's all because you figured out what was... going on."

"She did indeed." His expression held warm admiration as he glanced at Katy. "Dr. Pappas is smart and thorough, and we're lucky to have her as an intern here, Mrs. Patterson."

"I know you are." She squeezed Katy's hand. "I want to

thank you for saving my life. It's not often someone gets a chance to say that. I know I wasn't far from being on the other side of the grass."

"You don't have to thank me. I'm just glad we were able to figure out what was making you ill." She couldn't imagine how beyond awful it must have made Helen feel to find out Jeffrey was poisoning her, and she didn't want to distress her by bringing it up.

"It's all hard to believe." Her eyes were sad. "A part of me feels bad for my son. That he would be so desperately in debt that he couldn't think of any other way."

Katy didn't reply. It was hard to feel sorry for someone who would do something so terrible to anyone, let alone his own mother.

"He wasn't trying to kill me, you know." The woman looked at them almost pleadingly, apparently hoping they'd believe her words. "He just thought I'd get sick enough that he'd have my power of attorney. Just long enough to get out of debt, then I'd be okay again. The judge will take into account his gambling problems, I think. I hope he can get over his addiction."

"Addictions are powerful things, Mrs. Patterson, but he's getting the help he needs," Alec said. "Meanwhile, I'd like you to focus on getting back to your old self and walking your dogs again."

Helen smiled. "I can't wait to have them jumping up in my lap. My daughter is bringing them down tomorrow, and I'll be so happy to be home and continuing my physical therapy there." She squeezed Katy's hand tight. "Thank you again, my dear. Oceancrest is very lucky to have you."

"Thank you, Helen. I'll be thinking of you with your pups."

They left the room and Alec paused in the hall to smile

at her. "It's got to make you feel great to see Mrs. Patterson so fit and ready to go home. Congratulations."

"Thank you."

"I hope you both remember this." Alec turned to Todd Eiterman and Michael Coffman. "Sometimes you have to look for the zebra when the first answer doesn't seem to make sense. I'll see you for rounds tomorrow."

He strode down the hall without a backward glance, with Todd following, and she quickly turned her attention to her schedule as she pulled it from her pocket.

"Must be nice to be teacher's pet," Michael said. His tone of voice was light but his expression wasn't.

"I'm not teacher's pet." Her stomach constricted a little, even though she knew he couldn't mean it in a personal way. "I just got lucky with the diagnosis, and I'm sure you will too some time."

"Yeah. I can only hope," he said. "Got more scut work to do. See you later."

She breathed a deep sigh of relief. Had she and Alec actually managed to always keep poker faces around one another the past week? Had not a single person noticed how their eyes sometimes met and clung, before they both quickly looked away? She hoped and prayed no one had. Thank heavens they wouldn't have to be under such a strain much longer.

Only four more days. Four more days of the stress of hiding how she felt about him while they rounded together. Though they'd still have to be discreet at the hospital when they did run into one another.

A smile spread across her face, and she hoped no one noticed that either. Because she knew it was a silly, lust-struck kind of smile that came every time she thought of their forced separation being over with. A smile from wondering what kind of quiet, behind-the-scenes relationship might blossom between them.

She shook her head to dispel all thoughts of Alec so she could concentrate on the work in front of her. Her next assignment was to give conscious sedation to a patient who required a special IV line that would be inserted into his neck vein. Just a few weeks ago she might have been a nervous wreck about doing it, and she felt a little proud at how far she'd come in such a short time.

Katy looked at the chart in her hand. Room 4280. Patient Richard Wynne. Elizabeth would be there to supervise as Katy performed the procedure.

She knocked on the doorjamb of the surgical intensive care room, then stepped inside with a smile. "Mr. Wynne? I'm Dr. Pappas. I'm here to insert the central IV line you need."

The man grimaced. "Sounds like it might hurt like hell."

"Don't worry." She came close and gave him what she hoped was a reassuring smile. "We'll be giving you an intravenous drug to make you drowsy. Technically, you'll be awake but you won't remember anything."

"I'll be awake but won't remember it afterward?"

"Strange, huh? But that's the way it works." She'd learned that patients didn't really have to know the details of how retrograde amnesia drugs worked, only that they did. She'd also learned not to tell patients she was a newbie at these procedures, unless they asked. Usually, they freaked out, and who could blame them? "I'll be assisted by Dr. Stark."

He nodded, seemingly satisfied. Katy cleaned up and put on a gown, mask, and gloves. The nurse brought all the necessary equipment, and Katy prepped the man's skin by sponging on a sterile soap solution. She and the nurse got the man draped to create a sterile field, his neck exposed by a hole in the fabric, and again Katy felt pretty darned proud how competent she'd become at all of it.

All systems go, she thought with satisfaction. She and the nurse sat there waiting quietly, Katy looking at her watch every few minutes. Where was Elizabeth? She should have been here twenty minutes ago. Katy tried calling her but got no answer.

"Is there some problem?" Mr. Wynne asked with a frown.

"I'm sorry, I'm not sure what the delay is." The man looked quite annoyed, which Katy could well understand. All draped and having to stay motionless, ready to get it over with, then lying there endlessly waiting. "Dr. Stark should be here any moment. I'll see if I can find her."

Katy looked up and down the hall, but there was no sign of Elizabeth. What should she do here?

"Something wrong, Dr. Pappas?"

Alec's deep voice seemed to rumble right into her chest, and her heart leaped as she looked up at him. His expression was carefully neutral as his eyes met hers, and she quickly schooled her own to look the same.

"As you likely recall, this patient is having extensive bowel surgery tomorrow, and we couldn't get a line placed in his arm. So I'm here to insert a central venous catheter in his neck, and Dr. Stark is supposed to supervise me. But she's not here and I can't find her."

Alec frowned and glanced into the room. "Obviously you have the patient ready. I assume you haven't given him sedation yet?"

"Not yet. I was waiting for Elizabeth."

"We need to just get this done. I'll supervise you."

Katy's heart did a little pit-pat in her chest as they walked together into the small room. She was all too aware of him as he stood just an inch away. Aware of the warmth of his body in the chilly room. Aware of his distinctive scent. Aware of his eyes lingering on her before turning to the patient.

She sucked in a breath and focused her attention on the procedure she had to perform, her hands sweating a little inside her gloves. Why did she suddenly feel so nervous about him watching her do this? She knew the answer. She was afraid she just might not do as good a job as he would expect her to, and she so wanted him to be impressed. Maybe that was vain and shallow, when she should be most concerned about the patient, but couldn't help the feeling.

She reminded herself she was a professional and needed to think and act like one. Not a nervous nellie newbie who had to cut into someone's skin in just a few minutes.

Alec moved a short distance away to scrub, gown, and mask himself before he came to stand beside her again. "Go ahead, Dr. Pappas. I'm here to assist you with anything you need," Alec said. Katy glanced up at him and while his face was mostly obscured by the mask, she could see the small smile in his eyes, see him give her a little encouraging nod, which instantly helped her relax.

"Okay." She stopped short of saying, *Here goes nothing*, figuring the patient wouldn't exactly be reassured by that. She drew the sedation into the syringe and injected it smoothly into Mr. Wynne's arm. Within seconds his eyelids drooped and it was obvious he was already under its effect. No matter how many times she saw it used, the speed with which the drug worked always amazed her.

The nurse handed her the small knife and Katy looked up at Alec, who gifted her with another smile from his eyes and another nod. Steeling herself, she turned to make the tiny incision in the man's neck. When she was finished, she carefully slid the central line, half the width of a pencil, through the skin and down into the patient's jugular vein.

When it was finally done, Katy realized she'd been holding her breath, and let it out in a whoosh. "All done, I think. Did I do okay?"

"Better than okay. You did great."

Alec's eyes now weren't just smiling, they were crinkled at the corners like she loved to see, and she grinned back. "Are you sure you don't want to be a surgeon?" he asked. "It just might be your calling after all."

"No thanks. But I do admit I've loved being on this service and learning all this cool stuff. Thanks for being a wonderful teacher."

"Thanks for being a wonderful student." He placed his palm between her shoulder blades and gave her a quick pat before he turned to take off his mask and gown.

"Excuse me, Dr. Armstrong."

Both Alec and Katy turned to see Elizabeth standing there. A very angry Elizabeth, whose fists were clenched and lips were pressed together into a thin line. Katy's heart flipped in alarm at her expression. Then reminded herself nothing inappropriate had happened. Alec had just given her the same kind of congratulatory shoulder pat she'd seen him give to all the interns and residents.

"Yes, Dr. Stark?" Alec's expression was cool, neutral, but Katy didn't think she was imagining the wariness in his eyes.

"With all due respect, sir, it was my job to supervise Dr. Pappas for this procedure. Why are you doing it?"

"Because you weren't here, and the patient had been ready for some time." Alec's voice was firm and authoritative. "When Dr. Pappas told me she'd been unable to locate you, I decided to supervise. There's no reason to keep a patient waiting unnecessarily when another physician gets delayed, is there?"

"My delay was unavoidable. Dr. Pappas should have waited for me instead of soliciting you to do my job."

"It was actually I who volunteered to supervise when I realized you'd been delayed." Alec regarded Elizabeth steadily, seemingly not affected by her surprising anger. "At no time did I think you not being here reflects on the quality of your work or your reliability, Dr. Stark, if that's what's worrying you. If you'd like to talk about this further, please come to my office later. Meanwhile, you may finish up with Dr. Pappas."

Without a backward glance Alec moved past Elizabeth and left the room.

With Alec gone, Elizabeth glanced at the nurse then turned to Katy. "May I speak with you privately?"

Katy trailed after her into the hallway, dismayed when Elizabeth turned and pointed her finger at her. "You. What a gunner you are." The resident's voice was shaking. "Always trying to make yourself look good and to hell with anybody else looking bad because of it."

"I don't know what you mean." Katy's stomach knotted. "I've just tried to learn and do my work on this rotation."

"That is such a load of bull. Every time I turn around you're talking to Dr. Armstrong about this or that, asking questions, trying to sound so smart. Trying to make everyone else look stupid. I wouldn't be surprised if you tried to get into Alec's pants just to win points from an attending. Don't think I haven't noticed the way you flirt with him. The way he looks at you."

Katy gasped and felt all the blood drain from her face. Had Elizabeth really noticed the vibe between them? Surely this must just be her lashing out at her because the woman put so much pressure on herself to succeed in a man's world.

"Elizabeth, I hope you don't really believe that of me. That I was trying to build myself up by putting other people down. And I'm certain Dr. Armstrong views me only as an intern who needs all the help I can get. I've seen how hard you work and what a good surgeon you are. I know it's tough to be a female surgeon, and I honestly wish the best for you."

To Katy's shock, Elizabeth's eyes filled with tears before she turned away. "Head on to your next assignment, please, and I'll finish with Mr. Wynne."

Should she try to talk out this shocking hostility from Elizabeth a little more? As she watched the woman remove Mr. Wynne's drape, she decided she'd leave it for now. Perhaps it was a conversation better suited to the tavern.

She headed to the next floor to see a patient, a cold chill running down her spine as she recalled Elizabeth's ugly words about trying to get into Alec's pants to win points and noticing the way he looked at her. Would Elizabeth ever suggest to someone else that Katy might have done that?

The chill spread to every inch of her body when she thought of the ugly turn gossip like that could take if her relationship with Alec became public.

"Thanks, everybody, for staying late and for doing such a great job. As always, you make Oceancrest one of the best hospitals around," Alec said to the medical staff as he finished his last surgery of one damned long day.

"Dr. Armstrong, can I speak with you real quickly? Privately?" a nurse asked.

"Of course." Alec stripped off his gloves and walked

out of the OR to the empty hallway, with the nurse following. "What's on your mind?"

"I really respect you, so I wanted you to know there's some talk going around."

His heart practically stopped before it sped up into a fast rhythm. "Talk?"

She leaned closer. "One of the residents was talking about Dr. Pappas being your favorite, and implying some things I'm sure you don't want implied."

"What kind of things?"

"Like she gets more attention from you because she's Nick Pappas's sister. Even worse, that she's been coming on to you to get a good evaluation."

Holy hell. His breath backed up into his lungs. "Is this… rumor all over the hospital, or confined to just a few people on the surgical service?"

"I don't really know. I've only heard it around surgery, but that's where I hang out most of the time. Anyway, I thought you'd want to know."

"Thank you. I do want to know. And for what it's worth, Dr. Pappas is a very upstanding intern, and my evaluation of her will be strictly professional."

She nodded. "Of course I know that, Dr. Armstrong. You're one of the most professional doctors at this hospital."

His chest compressed even tighter at her words. He moved on to the locker room and stripped out of his scrubs, feeling a little numb. His mind spun back to his interactions with Katy, and other than that brief kiss in the hallway that Nick had seen couldn't think of anything that would start the rumor mill going.

Except that he knew, damn it, the way he looked at her sometimes. Had caught himself giving her goo-goo eyes on a few occasions, but hadn't thought anyone had seen.

He could only hope and pray that the gossip was minor. Wasn't juicy enough to spread through the hospital or garner much interest. How could it be? From what the nurse had said, it was a minor comment that probably stemmed from jealousy at what a great job Katy was doing and nothing more.

Trying to relax his tense muscles and tamp down the nag of anxiety, Alec got dressed, glad the long day was over. Glad that what had seemed like the longest week ever was almost over. Just a few more days with the stress and pressure of being sure he didn't look at Katy or talk to her or smile at her in any way that might be misconstrued by observers.

Misconstrued? That was the crux of it, because there would be no misinterpretation to think his looks and smiles came from his all-too-vivid memories of making love with her, and thoughts of how he wanted more of it. More of her.

A nasty niggle of worry over this whole situation stayed stuck in his gut. A different, crappy feeling would definitely lodge there instead, though, if they decided the risk to both their careers was too big.

He picked up his shirt, realizing her addictive scent lingered on it. Realized it was the shirt he'd been wearing when they'd last made love. He lifted it to his nose and inhaled, and just that tiny memory of her stepped up his pulse and shortened his breath.

What a damned complicated situation. But surely they could keep their cool around one another for just a few more days until she was off the surgical rotation. After that the chances were good they'd barely see one another in the hospital and any germs of gossip would quickly die.

He'd call her to tell her what the nurse had said then double his efforts to keep his feelings hidden while they were at work.

CHAPTER FOURTEEN

"How much do you think they're paying this guy?" Nick whispered, leaning toward Alec. "I could put together a better lecture than this."

"Maybe. But then you'd alienate everyone in the room, because you wouldn't be able to resist throwing in a few opinions about how certain specialists are usually prima donnas."

"True." Nick chuckled, turning his attention back to the lectern.

The county-wide hospital meeting had been going on for hours, and Alec was glad this was the last speaker before lunch was served. Though, among the duds, there were always interesting presentations on new research and updates specific to general surgery and other surgical specialties. At their table sat doctors from three other medical centers, and it was always good to catch up with them, too.

Alec tried his best to not look across the room where Katy sat with other residents and interns, and was pleased he managed to accomplish that. Most of the time, anyway, until he occasionally caught his gaze sliding her way.

Apparently, he wasn't the only one ready for lunch as chatter broke out instantly when the presentation ended and food was served. He found himself wondering if Katy had ordered the fish or the chicken then shook his head at himself. Why the hell would that even cross his mind? The answer clearly was that she was on his mind, period, even when the subject was inane.

"Her name is Pappas," he heard a voice say at the next table, and he and Nick both paused their eating and turned their heads at the same time as the name caught their ears. A man was pointing across the room toward Katy's table. "I can't remember her first name."

"Kathy, maybe?" another voice said, then chuckled as he looked across the room in Katy's direction. "Yeah, I heard the same thing about her. But there are always a few of them, you know. She's pretty enough to tempt any attending into thinking with the wrong head."

He stared at Nick who stared back at him, and his heart thumped hard as an ice-cold chill swept through him. What the hell were they saying about Katy?

"Doesn't the CMO know what's going on?"

"I hear she's got all the docs wrapped around her little finger. Or maybe it's because she's got her legs wrapped around them," someone said, eliciting chuckles.

"She's the kind of doctor that gives the rest of us a bad name," a woman said. "Most of us don't have to sleep around to get a good evaluation. Though I admit there was one resident I knew who slept with every attending she worked with."

A man chuckled. "And what I want to know is why I wasn't ever lucky enough to have a female student like that."

As the entire table laughed, Alec had trouble swallowing the bite of food he'd stuck in his mouth when they'd first heard the chatter. After he got it down, it sat in his stomach like lead and he had trouble catching his breath.

He turned to look at Nick, who stared right back at him.

Nick's eyes were hard, his lips pressed tightly together, but he didn't say a word.

He didn't have to. Alec knew what Nick was thinking, and knew he was right. He also knew what had to happen next. And it had to happen in a way Katy couldn't argue with.

It was late in the afternoon when Katy made her way toward where she, Alec and Nick had arranged to meet up after the day conference. While the presentations had been interesting, she was more than glad it was over. After checking a few patients, she'd get to go home, put her feet up and have a leisurely evening with Nick and hopefully Alec, too.

Since her brother had been so disapproving of anything smacking of a relationship between her and Alec, the two of them had agreed to stay just friendly around each other while Nick was around. To let some time go by until she'd been off his teaching service for quite a while. Maybe by then Nick would see their relationship was important to both of them and that, hopefully, at that point it wouldn't jeopardize either of their careers.

She made her way through the crowd of people then headed out to the parking lot, spotting Nick next to the car, along with some woman. Alec was there, too, and seeing his smile made her heart swell. Quickly, she tamped it down, knowing her feelings would be written all over her face if she didn't.

Then realized Alec had his arm wrapped around the woman's shoulders. A very pretty woman, and his hold seemed more intimate than friendly. Her steps slowed as she stared then stopped completely as his arm slipped to the woman's waist, tightened around her to draw her close.

His handsome head dipped down and he kissed the woman on the cheek.

Then moved on to her mouth, lingering. Their lips separated an inch and held that position, almost nose to nose, before he pressed his lips to the woman's again for a long, long moment as she raised her palm to his face.

Katy felt like she couldn't breathe. What in the world…? Surely this wasn't what it looked like. It couldn't be.

She forced herself to start moving again, reassuring herself this had to be just a friend of his or something. But her gut knew that no two people who were just friends kissed the way she'd just seen them kiss.

As she approached them she was sure Alec would drop his arm from the woman's waist, but he didn't. Numbness began to seep through her body when she stopped to stand next to Nick.

"Hey, Katy," Alec said, smiling at her. Smiling as though there was nothing strange about his holding another woman close when he'd made love to Katy just days ago. "Did you learn a lot from the presentations?"

"Yes. They were interesting." She managed to say the words through a throat so tight it hurt. "Aren't you going to introduce me to your…friend?"

"Oh, sorry. This is Andrea Walton. She and I, and Nick too, were residents together." To Katy's disbelief, he actually gave the woman another lingering kiss on her forehead. "I didn't know she was working at Holland Memorial now, and was pretty excited to see her here today. Andrea, this is Nick's little sister, Katy."

Nick's little sister. Pretty excited to see Andrea. Katy felt woozy, but told herself she was making a mountain out of a molehill. Maybe Alec held and kissed all old friends who were female.

"It's nice to meet you, Katy. I hear you're an intern. Alec tells me you're a good student," Andrea said.

"Nice to meet you, too."

"Hey, listen," Alec said, "Andrea and I are going to head out and get some dinner before I take her sailing. Just like old times." Alec smiled at Andrea and damned if he didn't give her another kiss on the mouth right in front of Katy.

Suddenly, her numbness and shock began to give way to anger. Alec was going to give her an explanation for all this, and what it did or didn't mean, and he was going to do it right now.

"Can I speak with you privately for a second, Alec?"

"Sure." He finally dropped his arm from curving around Andrea and followed Katy a few yards away.

She turned to him, and didn't know what to think of the expression of apology and guilt on his face. "What's going on here? Who is Andrea?"

"I told you, she and I were residents together. She was also my girlfriend for awhile, as you probably figured out."

"Yeah, since I have that analytical brain and all." Her voice shook and she swallowed to control it. "Not that it would have been hard for anyone to figure out since you were kissing her right here in public."

"I was pretty crazy about her, but she got a job all the way across the country." He gave her a crooked, apologetic smile. "Listen, I know you're not going to like this. But, well, seeing her made me realize I never really got over her. And I want to see if we can have what we had before."

Katy swayed a little on her feet, unable to breathe. Was this really happening? "You want to date her."

"I do." He leaned closer, speaking low. "I'm sorry, but it was never a good idea for us to be involved to begin with, you know that. It's not good for your career, and I frankly don't want to risk my reputation again. I'm sure you understand. Andrea is my peer, which makes her perfect for me."

Perfect for him. "Alec, surely you don't mean this." The words were out of her mouth before she realized she was dangerously close to begging him to stay with her. And she'd never do that with any man.

"It's best for both of us, Katy. You know, you look a little tired." Alec patted her on the head and smiled like he was her uncle or something. "Why don't you go to bed early and get some sleep?"

While he took Andrea to dinner and out on his boat and made love with the woman, just like he'd done with her.

She didn't know how to respond to his words without screaming at him and beating him with her fists like she wanted to. Tears threatened to choke her, and she dragged in a shaky, shocked breath before turning away.

He stopped her with a hand on her shoulder then ran his finger from her forehead to her nose. "I hope we can still be friends."

Friends? Was he kidding? When he'd given her the brush-off long ago she'd been hurt. What she was feeling now after being foolish enough to sleep with a man with his kind of history was so far beyond hurt it was off the charts. "Thanks for the offer, but I don't want to be friends with you."

Somehow she managed to turn and get into the car before the tears began to fall.

CHAPTER FIFTEEN

KATY HAD BEEN too stunned to speak as she and Nick had driven back to the hospital to check on patients before they went home. Too busy swallowing back the tears and trying to wrap her brain around what had just happened.

As she talked with her patients and did her work, she felt like an automaton. Going through the motions in a state of utter numbness. Even when they grabbed a carry-out dinner to take home she didn't speak about it to Nick. Didn't know what to say.

By the next morning, though, her disbelief had morphed into an anger so intense, so deep she had to let some of it spill out. Had to get some answers. When she and Nick walked into the hospital together, she turned to him and spoke.

"Can you explain to me what happened yesterday?"

"I assume you're talking about Alec?" Nick's expression was grim. "No. But I can't say I'm sorry, Katy. I am sorry that you feel hurt. But Alec was never right for you anyway."

And wasn't that an understatement? Still, she needed some explanation for how one minute Alec had been making love with her and the next he was kissing another woman. Except, oh, wait. That's the kind of man he was.

"Did he date that woman a long time when you all were

residents? Was he…crazy in love with her or something?" Just the question made her chest hurt.

"They were close, I guess." His tone was strangely stiff and he wrapped his arm around her shoulders in a quick hug. "Listen, I know you feel bad right now. But it's for the best."

"Obviously." Her voice shook. "But you're the one who told me he wasn't the kind of guy I thought he was. A player. Why would you say that when you've known him forever? When you know exactly what he's really like?"

"He's my friend, regardless." Nick sighed. "I've got surgery scheduled and need to get to work. We can talk about this later but, honestly, I don't know what else there is to say."

She watched him head down the hallway, and fought back tears yet again. Then she squared her shoulders. She would not allow jerk-of-the-decade Alec to ruin even one day of her life. Somehow, some way, she'd have to get through rounding with him a couple more days. How, exactly, she didn't know. But she would not let him think for even one minute she was heartbroken.

Though at the moment that organ felt crushed into a million little pieces inside her chest.

She forced herself to march down the hall to meet the crew for morning rounds. When she saw Alec standing there talking to Elizabeth and Todd, her confidence wavered and a horrible feeling swept through her body. A peculiar tornado of fury and grief and humiliation, and the sensation was so overwhelming it was all she could do to keep going.

His eyes met hers for only the briefest moment before he turned away. Her throat closed at how gorgeous he looked on the outside. How could he have turned out to be so shallow on the inside? She wanted to scream at him but shoved her anger and pain down as best she could.

Becoming a good doctor was tremendously important to her. She couldn't believe she'd allowed herself to fall for him, especially after trying so hard to remain true to her goal of becoming a respected, admired doctor. The kind of doctor her father would have been proud of. From this moment on she'd give every ounce of her heart to her work.

"Congratulations on a great job today and all month long," Alec said to the young doctors standing with him, beyond thankful the last day of surgical teaching rounds was over with.

He'd known it would be difficult to work with Katy for a few more days after the scene he'd orchestrated with Andrea. But he hadn't begun to realize the depth of that difficulty.

It had been torture. Torture to look into her beautiful eyes and see only ice blue staring back at him. Torture to hear the disgust for him in her voice when she spoke. Torture to be close to her, to have her scent wrap around him, to want to touch the silkiness of her hair and skin and know he'd never again have that pleasure.

He thought it had been disturbing when she'd been chilly to him the past few years? That had been nothing compared to the deep freeze he knew she'd feel toward him forever, and had to wonder if what he'd done had been a terrible mistake.

"I'll be finishing your evaluations and turning them in to Dr. Sanders, who will give them to you this evening. Best of luck to all of you." One by one, he shook their hands. When he got to Katy's it felt as cold as the eyes that stared at him but still he didn't want to let it go.

He didn't have to. Katy yanked it from his after only the

briefest shake and turned away. He watched her walk down the hall with the others. Watched the slight sway of her hips, watched her lustrous hair swish across her shoulders.

Watched her walk out of his life.

With a painful hollow in his chest he went to his office to somehow work on the evaluations. But the papers kept blurring into images of Katy.

He knew he'd hurt her badly. Hearing those people saying such ugly things about her had sent him into protective overdrive, but he realized now that maybe he hadn't thought it through well enough.

Andrea had been his friend for years. She'd been around during the nasty scandal in his past, and had been nice enough to go along with his ploy to end it with Katy because she knew what it had been like for him. Katy had stubbornly insisted she wasn't worried about the risks to her reputation, and wouldn't have accepted it then either, he knew.

But had handling it that way been the right decision? Alec leaned back in his office chair and closed his eyes. At this point he supposed it didn't matter. It was over and done with.

Over and done with. Just like his relationship with Katy.

"Katy," he said out loud, just wanting to hear her name. She was smart and beautiful and wonderful and would be an incredible family practice doc someday, and he could not be the cause of others besmirching her name. No matter how much it hurt, and it hurt beyond anything he'd ever experienced, he'd stay away from her. For her sake, and for the sake of her future.

Hurting *her* that way, though, stabbed like a knife so deeply in his own heart he could barely stand the pain. He hoped she'd get over it soon and move on to someone else who wasn't her superior in the hospital. That thought twisted the knife even deeper, but he'd somehow endure it for her.

A knock on his door had him opening his eyes. "Come in."

Nick appeared and sat in the chair opposite, slumping back into it much like Alec was slumped in his. He had a thick sheaf of papers in his hands. "Guess what arrived today."

"What?"

"My divorce papers from my beloved wife's attorney." His voice was both bitter and pained. "I guess this is really happening."

"You thought it might not?"

"I hadn't admitted it even to myself. But getting these made me realize I thought it wouldn't. I thought maybe she'd change her mind."

"I'm sorry, Nick." What else was there to say?

"Me, too." His lips twisted as he looked at Alec. "We're two pretty pathetic jerks, aren't we?"

"Yeah." He was pathetic and most definitely a jerk.

"I'm going to say something, and you're going to be shocked as hell by it."

Alec raised his eyebrows. "Is this going to be some deep confession about your marriage or your private life? I'm not sure I want to know."

"No. But it's my nearly over marriage that's made me decide to say it." With his elbows on his knees, Nick leaned forward. "I was upset as hell about you and Katy, and even more upset when I heard those people talking about her. But seeing how sad and hurt she is now is upsetting me in a different way."

"Breakups hurt, Nick, as you well know. But we all eventually get over it and move on. Katy will, and you will, too." Though he wasn't too sure about himself.

"I do know. But I also know that sometimes when you really love someone you have to be willing to make a sacrifice. I wasn't willing to sacrifice what I thought was most important, which was my job at Oceancrest, and never mind that I worked so much it was one of the things that killed my marriage." He looked Alec in the eye. "Do you love my sister?"

Alec hadn't thought about putting his feelings into words. But as he sat there, nearly overwhelmed by the awful emptiness in his chest, he knew he did. "Yes. But it doesn't matter."

"It's the only thing that matters. That's what these papers made me realize today." He held them up. "It's probably too late to get Meredith back. But I am going to do something that, if I ever have a chance to fix things, will go a long way to help make that happen."

"I hope it's not that you're going to bomb the company that talked her into moving to New York."

"No." Nick gave him a glimmer of a smile. "I'm going to leave Oceancrest and start a private surgical practice so I can be in control of how many hours I work. And I'd like you to consider joining me."

A private surgical practice? Alec knew that usually meant more flexibility with the work schedule, and sometimes even more money, but he hadn't considered doing anything like that so early in his career. He'd been convinced he needed to establish the respect of everyone in the medical community first. Earn his father's respect first. "That alone would take a huge amount of time and effort to get going."

"I know. But then I'd be in charge of my own destiny. For a lot of reasons I've realized I want that." He stood up. "Think about it. And while you're doing that, think about one more thing. Which is that you love Katy and I know she loves you. I hate to see you both miserable the way I am about Meredith. If you join me, you'll be out of Oceancrest. Ethical problem solved."

Alec sat up straighter. Could that work? And would Katy ever forgive him for lying to her?

It was time to do some thinking. And the best place to do that was in the middle of Mission Bay.

CHAPTER SIXTEEN

KATY HAD NEVER been a person who wanted to drown her sorrows in alcohol, but she was about to make tonight the exception.

The residents and interns were extra-happy at the tavern happy hour, celebrating the end of the month's rounds before they moved on to the next rotation. Most were beaming at the good evaluations they'd received, though a few looked a little glum over their drinks. Katy felt more than glum, and never mind that Alec had given her the highest evaluation possible.

She should be proud and happy. Instead, she just felt relieved that she wouldn't have to work with Alec again. Wouldn't have to look at his amber eyes and handsome face and sexy body and picture him with Andrea, which made her feel so angry she wanted to hit something, and so hurt it gouged all the way to her soul.

She had to get over it. She'd known he was a player. A man who did as he pleased and twisted the rules to suit himself. Then she'd promptly forgotten all that when he'd kissed her. She'd let him wiggle inside her heart just like the worm he was until he'd dumped her like a hot potato when he'd tired of her.

She took a swig of her margarita to swallow down the bitterness filling her chest.

"What are you looking so mad about?" Elizabeth asked as she sat down beside her. "I am absolutely sure Dr. Armstrong gave you a great evaluation."

"Why are you so sure?" Probably because she thought what she'd said before. That Katy had dived into Alec's pants for good marks, and, boy, did she regret diving into them for a whole different reason.

"Honestly?" Elizabeth regarded her steadily. "Because you are one of the best interns I've ever worked with."

Katy stared at her in surprise. "Thank you. That's... nice of you to say."

"It's just the truth," Elizabeth said. "And I have another truth. A true confession about something I'm not proud of. Something you need to know."

Katy looked at her, wondering what she could be talking about.

"I was jealous of the way Alec looked at you, then it became pretty obvious there was something between you two. I think he's hot, but he never looked twice at me. I'm ashamed to admit this now but I said something to a couple other residents. Next thing I knew, a bunch of people were talking about you sleeping with him."

Katy gasped. "Are you kidding?"

"I wish I was." Elizabeth's lips twisted. "It's my fault, but I swear I never meant it to go any further than my few friends. I'm really sorry. Honest."

She looked at Elizabeth and realized she was telling the truth. That she did feel bad about it, and Katy had made enough mistakes in her own life that she wasn't going to judge Elizabeth too harshly for it. After all, it didn't really matter any more anyway. Alec had moved on.

"Thank you for telling me. Hopefully any more talk will die off since I won't be around him now."

"Won't you be? Anyone paying attention could tell he's crazy about you."

"No, he's not. He's got a girlfriend."

Elizabeth stared at her. "You're not his girlfriend?"

"Nope."

"You're just saying that because you're not supposed to be involved with an attending. Believe me, I was more than willing to be involved with him, and to heck with the rules." Elizabeth smiled. "I swear I'll never gossip about you again. But I have to tell you. I saw him kissing you in the hall."

Ah, damn. But again, it didn't really matter. But since Elizabeth knew, for some pathetic reason Katy wanted to unload on her. Maybe she'd feel better talking to another woman about it all.

"Okay. I thought we were involved. But when we were at the hospital meeting at the hotel he told me he didn't want to see me any more because he'd run into an old flame named Andrea Walton he hadn't known was in town." Just saying the woman's name made her stomach cramp. "She must work at a different hospital. And he kissed her right in front of me. The jerk."

To her surprise, Elizabeth burst out laughing. "Andrea Walton worked here for a while, so I can tell you she's not new to town. She's also married to a hunky cardiologist who happens to be a partner in her practice, and they have two cute little kids. I guarantee you they are not seeing one another. At least, not in a romantic sense."

Katy stared at her. Was there any way what she said could be true? And if so, why would Alec lie about it?

"I want to make it up to you for being catty and starting tongues wagging, so here's my advice," Elizabeth said, leaning in. "Ask Alec why he would lie to you, because he obviously did. I wouldn't be surprised if he heard the gossip about you and couldn't stand being the reason for it. If I were you, and I frankly wish I was, I'd be his girlfriend no matter what the hospital policy was on that. Go for it, girl."

Alec *had* been worried about her reputation and about any gossip. Was it at all possible that was why he'd broken up with her?

Maybe it wasn't. Maybe he really had moved on. But it was worth risking one more bash to her heart to find out for sure.

"Thanks, Elizabeth." Katy shoved her drink aside, grabbed her purse and headed out the door. Twenty minutes later she was pulling her car into the parking lot outside Alec's condo, her heart thumping nervously. What if Elizabeth was completely wrong? What if she banged on Alec's door and a half-naked Andrea opened it?

She gulped, but got out of the car anyway. She knew he'd still been at work just an hour ago, and did the math. Even if he'd left the second she'd been given her evaluation, which was unlikely, he would have gotten home only a short time ago.

In any case, she reminded herself sternly, whatever happened this evening would be good. If she found a naked Andrea there, she'd have that answer. If it was just Alec, she'd pay more careful attention to his expression and the tone of his voice if he rejected her again. After all, she'd known him most of her life and could read him pretty well. Or thought she could. Which brought her full circle to thinking she didn't really know him at all.

She shook her head at herself then squared her shoulders, about to head to his front door. Out of the corner of her eye she saw a distinctive sail coming from the center of the bay toward shore. The sail of Alec's boat, which was white with a cobalt-blue triangle in the top corner.

Lord, please do not have Andrea sailing with him and

kissing him, she prayed. Going through that again would be beyond torture.

She pulled off her shoes and walked along the sand toward the dock, reaching it just as he smoothly slid the boat in. Her heart pounding so loud in her ears it nearly drowned out the sound of the surf, Katy stepped onto the planks of the dock. Alec stood on the boat, his tanned arms reaching to tie a line to the dock post.

Her heart stuttered at how gorgeous he looked with his muscular legs wide apart on the rocking boat, his hair tossing in the wind, his chiseled features covered only slightly by his sunglasses. At least they could have this conversation alone, she thought as a breath of relief left her chest.

He looked up at her, and his hands and arms stilled in the middle of tying the line. She wished she could see the expression in his eyes behind the lenses of the sunglasses but had no idea what he was thinking. Hopefully it wasn't horror that she'd shown up on his doorstep.

"I'd like to talk to you, Alec," she said, summoning every ounce of bravery she could muster.

Without saying a word, he finished tethering the line and reached his hand out to her. She grasped it in hers and stepped onto the boat's deck.

Now that she was there, she felt utterly paralyzed. What, exactly, should she say? Have you had sex with Andrea yet? Were you being truthful, or were you lying? I love you, please don't leave me.

And wouldn't the last be beyond pathetic? But standing so close to him now, holding his hand and staring up at him, the words nearly fell from her mouth anyway, and she swallowed.

"I'm glad I found you here. I need to know if you really are involved with Andrea. I need to know if you really don't care for me. That you don't want to be with me. I want the truth."

Her chest felt both heavier and lighter now that she'd asked. Relieved that she'd managed to get the words out but scared to death to hear his response.

"The truth?" Alec took off his sunglasses, and the deep seriousness of his eyes closed her throat. "The truth is I'm an idiot."

"Right now, I can't disagree."

"I don't blame you." He nodded. "What would you say if I told you I lied to you? That I never had anything with Andrea, not in the past and sure as hell not today."

The giant weight on her chest lifted a little, but at the same time her lungs burned with anger. "I'd say you are a giant jerk to hurt me so badly. To make me suffer the way I've been suffering. Then I'd ask you why you lied."

"Ah, Katy." He dropped her hand, shoving his own through his hair. "I'm so sorry I lied. I'm sorry I made you suffer. If it means anything, I can tell you I'm pretty sure I've suffered even more than you."

The anger burned even hotter in her chest, realizing that he'd set up the whole scene with Andrea intentionally to hurt her and drive her away. Yet with the anger came hope that what he said next could bring them close again, instead of driving an even deeper and permanent wedge between them. "Why would you lie and tell me such a horrible thing if it wasn't true?"

"Because people had started to talk and say nasty things about you. I couldn't bear it. And my being the cause of it was even more unbearable." He lifted her chin with his hand to look into her eyes. "I knew if I told you we couldn't be together for that reason, you'd say it didn't matter. But it did matter, Katy. It mattered to me that people were telling ugly lies that could damage what should be a stellar reputation for a stellar intern. It mattered to me that it was my fault."

"And so you, almighty surgeon Alec Armstrong, thought you should play God and decide what's best for me? Lie to me and break my heart, all in the name of what's 'good' for me? I'm more than capable of deciding what's good for me. I can make my own decisions regarding my life and my future."

"I know. I'm sorry. I know I was wrong to lie to you in such a terrible way. It seemed like the best thing at the time, but since then I've thought about what that must have felt like. How much it would have destroyed me to have you do something like that to me. All I can do is tell you I'm sorry and beg you to forgive me. Will you?"

"I don't know. Give me a reason to forgive you."

"You want a reason?" He cupped her cheek in his hand then lowered his lips to hers in a soft, tender kiss. "I don't have a good enough reason for what I did. The only reason I can offer in asking for your forgiveness is that I'm crazy in love with you. So crazy it makes me do crazy things. I love you. And now I know I need you in my life no matter what it costs."

Her heart nearly burst with joy at his words. "I might forgive you if you promise to never worry about either of our reputations again."

"I do promise. I've come to realize that having a spotless reputation doesn't mean much unless you have the respect of the person you love." He gave her another soft kiss. "But I've decided to take a path that won't let tongues wag anyway. A path I considered in the past but rejected because I thought I needed everyone in the hospital to think I was great beforehand."

"What path are you talking about?"

"Nick and I are going to start a private surgical practice. It will take a lot of work, but the benefits will be worth it."

She frowned. Surely he wasn't doing something so extreme just so they wouldn't have to work together? "Why?"

"He wants more control over his schedule and his life, and I want the same thing. I'm not doing it just for us, Katy, I promise, though I would if I had to. But it does take that worry out of the equation."

"And no more playing God?"

He signed an X on his chest. "Cross my heart."

"Then I forgive you. And I love you too. So much."

He pulled her close and pressed his forehead to hers. "Thank you," he whispered. "For loving me back and forgiving my stupidity. What can I do to make it up to you?"

"I think we should get started on those goals we talked about." Just the thought made her breathless. "The one involving excitement and sailing and you kissing me all over."

"Goals are good things to have." A gleam filled his eyes and a slow smile curved his lips. "Must be fate that we're already on the boat, as I'm more than ready to get started on our first goal. Then work on a list of others that will take a long time to achieve."

"Any thoughts on new ones?"

"Yes. I know exactly what the first goal should be. Well, the first one after the other first one."

She had to laugh. "All right, what is it?"

"A big Greek wedding starring Dr. Katherine Pappas." He drew back an inch, and his gaze grew both serious and tender. "Will you marry me, Katy? I think maybe I loved you all those years ago when you were conducting weird science experiments, and insisting on helping Nick and me build a tree house, and even when you out-fished us with some special bait you'd come up with. But I'm absolutely sure I'm totally in love with you now, and I want to spend every day of the rest of my life with you."

Her heart swelled to bursting at his words, but before she could speak his lips touched hers with the sweetest of kisses.

The eyes gazing into hers weren't amber or tiger eye but gleamed like polished gold, precious and dazzling. "Will you marry me? Please, say yes."

"Yes." The easy answer barely squeezed past the lump in her throat. "Yes, I will, Alec Armstrong."

"Thank you." His arms wrapped around her and he caught her close against him. "How fast can a Greek wedding be pulled together?"

"Not very fast, but we'll see what we can do to expedite the process." She hugged him and whispered in his ear. "You do realize you'll have to practice Greek dancing."

"I might have to fake it. But one thing I'll never have to fake is how in love I am with you."

* * * * *

FROM FLING
TO FOREVER

BY
AVRIL TREMAYNE

Published in Great Britain 2014
by Mills & Boon, an imprint of Harlequin (UK) Limited,
Eton House, 18-24 Paradise Road, Richmond, Surrey, TW9 1SR

© 2014 Belinda de Rome

ISBN: 978-0-263-90794-0

Harlequin (UK) Limited's policy is to use papers that are natural,
renewable and recyclable products and made from wood grown in
sustainable forests. The logging and manufacturing processes conform
to the legal environmental regulations of the country of origin.

Printed and bound in Spain
by Blackprint CPI, Barcelona

Dear Reader

As a diehard romantic, I like the idea of a love so strong it feels as if it's written in the stars. And that's a concept I've enjoyed exploring in FROM FLING TO FOREVER.

Aaron and Ella have known enough heartbreak to have them setting very specific life paths for themselves. But when they meet at a wedding in Australia those paths are destined for the scrapheap—they just don't know it yet.

It takes a second encounter—in Cambodia—to ignite a scorching but unwanted passion between them as they work side by side at a children's hospital.

And a third—in England—for them to realise that the passion isn't going away, so they'd better get it out of their systems with a quick, hard fling before sailing into their separate futures.

But it seems fate isn't so crazy about the 'fling' part.

I hope you enjoy the ride as Ella and Aaron face some tense situations and the occasional emergency as they re-set their life paths from fling to forever.

Avril Tremayne

Dedication

This book is dedicated to my fellow writer PTG Man
and Dr John Sammut with many, many thanks
for the generous medical advice. Thanks also
to Dr John Lander and Dr Hynek Prochazka.
Any errors that snuck in despite their best efforts
are mine, all mine!

I would also like to acknowledge the amazing
Angkor Hospital for Children (AHC)—
a non-profit pediatric teaching hospital that
provides free quality care to impoverished children
in Siem Reap, Cambodia. All the characters, settings
and situations in FROM FLING TO FOREVER are
fictional—however, during the course of my research,
I learned so much from AHC, which has provided over
one million medical treatments, education to thousands
of Cambodian health workers, and prevention training
to thousands of families since it opened
in 1999. You can find out more about the hospital
at www.angkorhospital.org

CHAPTER ONE

WEDDINGS.

Ella Reynolds had nothing against them, but she certainly didn't belong at one. Not even this one.

But her sister, Tina, had insisted she not only attend but trick herself out as maid of honour in this damned uncomfortable satin gown in which there was *no* stretch. Add in the ridiculous high heels and hair twisted into a silly bun that was pinned so tightly against her scalp she could practically feel the headache negotiating where to lunge first.

And then there was the stalker. Just to top everything off.

She'd first felt his stare boring into her as she'd glided up the aisle ahead of her sister. And then throughout the wedding service, when all eyes should have been on the bride and groom. And ever since she'd walked into the reception.

Disconcerting. And definitely unwanted.

Especially since he had a little boy with him. Gorgeous, sparkly, darling little boy. Asian. Three or four years old. Exactly the type of child to mess with her already messed-up head.

Ella looked into her empty champagne glass, debating whether to slide over the legal limit. Not that she was driving, but she was always so careful when she was with her

family. Still... Tina, pregnant, glowing, deliriously happy,
was on the dance floor with her new husband Brand—and
not paying her any attention. Her parents were on the other
side of the room, catching up with Brand's family on this
rare visit to Sydney—and not paying her any attention.
She was alone at the bridal table, with *no one* paying her
any attention. Which was just fine with her. It was much
easier to hold it all together when you were left to yourself. To not let anyone see the horrible, unworthy envy of
Tina's pregnancy, Tina's *life*.

And—she swivelled around to look for a waiter—it
made it much easier to snag that extra champagne.

But a sound put paid to the champagne quest. A cleared
throat.

She twisted back in her chair. Looked up.

The stalker. *Uh-oh*.

'Hi,' he said.

'Hello.' Warily.

'So...you're Ella,' he said.

Oh, dear. *Inane* stalker. 'Yep. Sister of the bride.'

'Oh.' He looked surprised. And then, 'Sorry, the accent. I didn't realise...'

'I speak American, Tina speaks Australian. It does
throw people. Comes of having a parent from each country and getting to choose where you live. I live in LA. Tina
lives in Sydney. But it's still all English, you know.' Good
Lord—*this* was conversation?

He laughed. 'I'm not sure the British see it that way.'

Okay—so now what? Ella wondered.

If he thought she was going to be charmed by him, he
had another think coming. She *wasn't* going to be charmed.
And she was *not* in the market for a pick-up tonight. Not
that he wasn't attractive in a rough sort of way—the surfer-
blond hair, golden tan and bursting muscles that looked

completely out of place in a suit was a sexy combination. But she'd crossed the pick-up off her to-do list last night—and that had been a debacle, as usual. And even if she hadn't crossed it off the list, and it hadn't been a debacle, her sister's wedding was not the place for another attempt. Nowhere within a thousand *miles* of any of her relatives was the place.

'Do you mind if I sit and talk to you for a few minutes?' he asked, and smiled at her.

Yes, I do. 'Of course you can sit,' she said. Infinitesimal pause. 'And talk to me.'

'Great.' He pulled out a chair and sat. 'I think Brand warned you I wanted to pick your brains tonight.'

She frowned slightly. 'Brand?'

He smiled again. 'Um…your brother-in-law?'

'No-o-o, I don't think so.' Ella glanced over at Brand, who was carefully twirling her sister. 'I think he's had a few things on his mind. Marriage. Baby. Imminent move to London. New movie to make.'

Another smile. 'Right, let's start again and I'll introduce myself properly.'

Ella had to give the guy points for determination. Because he had to realise by now that if she really wanted to talk to him, she would have already tried to get his name out of him.

'I'm Aaron James,' he said.

Ella went blank for a moment, before the vague memory surfaced. 'Oh. Of course. The actor. Tina emailed me about a…a film?' She frowned slightly. 'Sorry, I remember now. About malaria.'

'Yes. A documentary. About the global struggle to eradicate the disease. Something I am very passionate about, because my son… Well, too much information, I guess. Not that documentaries are my usual line of work.' Smile, but looking a little frayed. 'Maybe you've heard of a television show called *Triage*? It's a medical drama. I'm in that.'

'So...' She frowned again. 'Is it the documentary or the TV show you want to talk to me about? If it's the TV show, I don't think I can help you—my experience in city hospital emergency rooms is limited. And I'm a nurse—you don't look like you'd be playing a nurse. You're playing a doctor, right?'

'Yes, but—'

'I'm flying home tomorrow, but I know a few doctors here in Sydney and I'm sure they'd be happy to talk to you.'

'No, that's not—'

'The numbers are in my phone,' Ella said, reaching for her purse. 'Do you have a pen? Or can you—?'

Aaron reached out and put his hand over hers on the tiny bronze purse. 'Ella.'

Her fingers flexed, once, before she could stop them.

'It's not about the show,' he said, releasing her hand. 'It's the documentary. We're looking at treatments, mosquito control measures, drug resistance, and what's being done to develop a vaccine. We'll be shooting in Cambodia primarily—in some of the hospitals where I believe you've worked. We're not starting for a month, but I thought I should take the chance to talk to you while you're in Sydney. I'd love to get your impression of the place.'

She said nothing. Noted that he was starting to look impatient—and annoyed.

'Brand told me you worked for Frontline Medical Aid,' he prompted.

She controlled the hitch in her breath. 'Yes, I've worked for them, and other medical aid agencies, in various countries, including Cambodia. But I'm not working with any agency at the moment. And I'll be based in Los Angeles for the next year or so.'

'And what's it like? I mean, not Los Angeles—I know what— Um. I mean, the aid work.'

Ella shifted in her seat. He was just not getting it. 'It has its highs and lows. Like any job.'

He was trying that charming smile again. 'Stupid question?'

'Look, it's just a job,' she said shortly. 'I do what every nurse does. Look after people when they're sick or hurt. Try to educate them about health. That's all there is to it.'

'Come on—you're doing a little more than that. The conditions. The diseases that we just don't see here. The refugee camps. The landmines. Kidnappings, even.'

Her heart slammed against her ribs. Bang-bang-bang. She looked down at her hands, saw the whitened knuckles and dropped them to her lap, out of Aaron's sight. She struggled for a moment, getting herself under control. Then forced herself to look straight back up and right at him.

'Yes, the conditions are not what most medical personnel are used to,' she said matter-of-factly. 'I've seen the damage landmines can do. Had children with AIDS, with malnutrition, die in my arms. There have been kidnappings involving my colleagues, murders even. This is rare, but…' She stopped, raised an eyebrow. 'Is that the sort of detail you're looking for?' She forced herself to keep looking directly into his eyes. 'But I imagine you'll be insulated from the worst of it. They won't let anything happen to you.'

'I'm not worried about that,' Aaron said, with a quick shake of his head. Then, suddenly, he relaxed back in his chair. 'And you don't want to talk about it.'

Eureka! 'It's fine, really,' she said, but her voice dripped with insincerity.

The little boy Ella had seen earlier exploded onto the

scene, throwing himself against Aaron's leg, before the conversation could proceed.

'Dad, look what Tina gave me.'

Dad. So, did he have an Asian wife? Or was the little boy adopted?

Aaron bent close to smell the small rose being offered to him.

'It's from her bunch of flowers,' the little boy said, blinking adorably.

'Beautiful.' Aaron turned laughing eyes to Ella. 'Ella, let me introduce my son, Kiri. Kiri, this is Tina's sister, Ella.'

Kiri. He was Cambodian, then. And he'd had malaria— that was Aaron's TMI moment. 'Nice to meet you Kiri,' Ella said, with a broad smile, then picked up her purse. 'Speaking of Tina and flowers, it must be time to throw the bouquet. I'd better go.'

She got to her feet. 'Goodbye Aaron. Good luck with the documentary. Goodbye Kiri.'

Well, that had been uncomfortable, Ella thought as she left the table, forcing herself to walk slowly. Calm, controlled, measured—the way she'd trained herself to walk in moments of stress.

Clearly, she had to start reading her sister's emails more carefully. She recalled, too late, that Tina's email had said Aaron was divorced; that he had an adopted son—although not that the boy was Cambodian, because *that* she would have remembered. She'd made a reference to the documentary. And there probably had been a mention of talking to him as a favour to Brand, although she really couldn't swear to it.

She just hadn't put all the pieces together and equated

them with the wedding, or she would have been better prepared for the confrontation.

Confrontation. Since when did a few innocent questions constitute a confrontation?

Ella couldn't stop a little squirm of shame. Aaron wasn't to know that the exact thing he wanted to talk about was the exact thing she couldn't bring herself to discuss with anyone. Nobody knew about Sann, the beautiful little Cambodian boy who'd died of malaria before she'd even been able to start the adoption process. Nobody knew about her relationship with Javier—her colleague and lover, kidnapped in Somalia and still missing. Nobody knew because she hadn't *wanted* anyone to know, or to worry about her. Hadn't wanted anyone to push her to talk about things, relive what she couldn't bear to relive.

So, no, Aaron wasn't to be blamed for asking what he thought were standard questions.

But he'd clearly sensed something was wrong with her. Because he'd gone from admiration—oh, yes, she could read admiration—to something akin to dislike, in almost record time. Something in those almost sleepy, silver-grey eyes had told her she just wasn't his kind of person.

Ella's head had started to throb. The damned pins.

Ah, well, one bouquet-toss and last group hug with her family and she could disappear. Back to her hotel. Throw down some aspirin. And raid the mini-bar, given she never had got that extra glass of champagne.

Yeah, like raiding the mini-bar has ever helped, her subconscious chimed in.

'Oh, shut up,' she muttered.

Well, that had been uncomfortable, Aaron thought as Ella Reynolds all but bolted from the table. Actually, she'd been walking slowly. Too slowly. Unnaturally slowly.

Or maybe he was just cross because of ego-dent. Because one woman in the room had no idea who he was. And didn't *care* who he was when she'd found out. Well, she was American—why *would* she know him? He wasn't a star over there.

Which wasn't the point anyway.

Because since when did he expect people to recognise him and drool?

Never!

But celebrity aside, to be looked at with such blank disinterest...it wasn't a look he was used to from women. Ella Reynolds hadn't been overwhelmed. Or deliberately *under*whelmed, as sometimes happened. She was just... hmm, was 'whelmed' a word? Whelmed. Depressing.

Ego, Aaron—so not *like you.*

Aaron swallowed a sigh as the guests started positioning themselves for the great bouquet toss. Ella was in the thick of it, smiling. Not looking in his direction—on purpose, or he'd eat the roses.

She was as beautiful as Tina had said. More so. Staggeringly so. With her honey-gold hair that even the uptight bun couldn't take the gloss off. The luminous, gold-toned skin. Smooth, wide forehead. Finely arched dusky gold eyebrows and wide-spaced purple-blue eyes with ridiculously thick dark lashes. Lush, wide, pouty mouth. No visible freckles. No blemishes. The body beneath the figure-hugging bronze satin she'd been poured into for the wedding was a miracle of perfect curves. Fabulous breasts—and silicone-free, if he were any judge. Which he was, after so many years in the business.

And the icing on the cake—the scent of her. Dark and musky and delicious.

Yep. Stunner.

But Tina had said that as well as being gorgeous her

sister was the best role model for women she could think of. Smart, dedicated to her work, committed to helping those less fortunate regardless of the personal danger she put herself in regularly.

Well, sorry, but on the basis of their conversation tonight he begged to differ. Ella Reynolds was no role model. There was something wrong with her. Something that seemed almost...dead. Her smile—that dazzling, white smile—didn't reach her eyes. Her eyes had been beautifully *empty*. It had been almost painful to sit near her.

Aaron felt a shiver snake down his spine.

On the bright side, he didn't feel that hot surge of desire—that bolt that had hit him square in the groin the moment she'd slid into the church—any more. Which was good. He didn't want to lust after her. He didn't have the time or energy or emotional availability to lust after anyone.

He turned to his beautiful son. 'Come on, Kiri—this part is fun to watch. But leave the bouquet-catching to the girls, huh?'

We're not going down that road again, bouquet or not, he added silently to himself.

CHAPTER TWO

ELLA HAD BEEN determined to spend a full year in Los Angeles.

But within a few weeks of touching down at LAX she'd been back at the airport and heading for Cambodia. There had been an outbreak of dengue fever, and someone had asked her to think about helping out, and she'd thought, *Why not?*

Because she just hadn't been feeling it at home. Whatever 'it' was. She hadn't felt right since Tina's wedding. Sort of restless and on edge. So she figured she needed more distraction. More work. More…something.

And volunteering at a children's hospital in mosquito heaven is just the sort of masochism that's right up your alley, isn't it, Ella?

So, here she was, on her least favourite day of the year—her birthday—in northwest Cambodia—and because it *was* her birthday she was in the bar of one of the best hotels in town instead of her usual cheap dive.

Her parents had called this morning to wish her happy birthday. Their present was an airfare to London and an order to use it the moment her time in Cambodia was up. It was framed in part as a favour to Tina: stay with her pregnant sister in her new home city and look after her health while Brand concentrated on the movie. But she knew Tina would have been given her own set of orders: get Ella to rest and for goodness' sake fatten her up—because her mother always freaked when she saw how thin and bedraggled Ella was after a stint in the developing world.

Tina's present to Ella was a goat. Or rather a goat in Ella's name, to be given to an impoverished community in India. Not every just-turned-twenty-seven-year-old's cup of tea, but so totally perfect for this one.

And in with the goat certificate had been a parcel with a note: 'Humour me and wear this.' 'This' was sinfully expensive French lingerie in gorgeous mint-green silk, which Ella could never have afforded. It felt like a crime wearing it under her flea-market gypsy skirt and bargain-basement singlet top. But it did kind of cheer her up. Maybe she'd have to develop an underwear fetish—although somehow she didn't think she'd find this kind of stuff digging around in the discount bins the way she usually shopped.

A small group of doctors and nurses had dragged her out tonight. They'd knocked back a few drinks, told tales about their life experiences and then eventually—inevitably—drifted off, one by one, intent on getting some rest ahead of another busy day.

But Ella wasn't due at the hospital until the afternoon, so she could sleep in. Which meant she could stay out. And she had met someone—as she always seemed to do in bars. So she'd waved the last of her friends off with a cheerful guarantee that she could look after herself.

Yes, she had met someone. Someone who might help make her feel alive for an hour or two. Keep the nightmares at bay, if she could bring herself to get past the come-on stage for once and end up in bed with him.

She felt a hand on her backside as she leaned across the pool table and took her shot. She missed the ball completely but looked back and smiled. Tom. British. Expat.

An…engineer, maybe? *Was* he an engineer? Well, who cared? Really, who cared?

He pulled her against him, her back against his chest. Arms circled her waist. Squeezed.

She laughed as he nipped at her earlobe, even though she couldn't quite stop a slight shudder of distaste. His breath was too hot, too…moist. He bit gently at her ear again.

Ella wasn't sure what made her look over at the entrance to the bar at that particular moment. But pool cue in one hand, caught against Tom's chest, with—she realised in one awful moment—one of the straps of her top hanging off her shoulder to reveal the beacon-green silk of her bra strap, she looked.

Aaron James.

He was standing still, looking immaculately clean in blue jeans and a tight white T-shirt, which suited him way more than the get-up he'd been wearing at the wedding. Very tough-guy gorgeous, with the impressive muscles and fallen-angel hair with those tousled, surfer-white streaks she remembered very well.

Actually, she was surprised she remembered so much!

He gave her one long, cool, head-to-toe inspection. One nod.

Ah, so he obviously remembered her too. She was pretty sure that was not a good thing.

Then he walked to the bar, ignoring her. *Hmm*. Definitely *not a good thing*.

Ella, who'd thought she'd given up blushing, blushed. Hastily she yanked the misbehaving strap back onto her shoulder.

With a wicked laugh, Tom the engineer nudged it back off.

'Don't,' she said, automatically reaching for it again.

Tom shrugged good-humouredly. 'Sorry. Didn't mean anything by it.'

For good measure, Ella pulled on the long-sleeved, light cotton cardigan she'd worn between her guesthouse accommodation and the hotel. She always dressed for modesty outside Western establishments, and that meant covering up.

And there were mosquitoes to ward off in any case.

And okay, yes, the sight of Aaron James had unnerved her. She admitted it! She was wearing a cardigan because Aaron James had looked at her in *that* way.

She tried to appear normal as the game progressed, but every now and then she would catch Aaron's gaze on her and she found it increasingly difficult to concentrate on the game or on Tom. Whenever she laughed, or when Tom let out a whoop of triumph at a well-played shot, she would feel Aaron looking at her. Just for a moment. His eyes on her, then off. When Tom went to the bar to buy a round. When she tripped over a chair, reaching for her drink. When Tom enveloped her from behind to give her help she didn't need with a shot.

It made her feel…dirty. Ashamed. Which was just not fair. She was single, adult, independent. So she wanted a few mindless hours of fun on her lonely birthday to take her mind off sickness and death—what was wrong with that?

But however she justified things to herself, she knew that tonight her plans had been derailed. All because of a pair of censorious silver eyes.

Censorious eyes that belonged to a friend of her sister. Very sobering, that—the last thing she needed was Aaron tattling to Tina about her.

It was probably just as well to abandon tonight's escapade. Her head was starting to ache and she felt overly hot.

Maybe she was coming down with something? She would be better off in bed. Her bed. Alone. As usual.

She put down her cue and smiled at Tom the engineer. Her head was pounding now. 'It's been fun, Tom, but I'm going to have to call it a night.'

'But it's still early. I thought we could—'

'No, really. It's time I went home. I'm tired, and I'm not feeling well.'

'Just one more drink,' Tom slurred, reaching for her arm.

She stepped back, out of his reach. 'I don't think so.'

Tom lunged for her and managed to get his arms around her.

He was very drunk, but Ella wasn't concerned. She'd been in these situations before and had always managed to extricate herself. Gently but firmly she started to prise Tom's arms from around her. He took this as an invitation to kiss her and landed his very wet lips on one side of her mouth.

Yeuch.

Tom murmured something about how beautiful she was. Ella, still working at unhooking his arms, was in the middle of thanking him for the compliment when he suddenly wasn't there. One moment she'd been disengaging herself from his enthusiastic embrace, and the next—air.

And then an Australian accent. 'You don't want to do that, mate.'

She blinked, focused, and saw that Aaron James was holding Tom in an embrace of his own, standing behind him with one arm around Tom's chest. How had he got from the bar to the pool table in a nanosecond?

'I'm fine,' Ella said. 'You can let him go.'

Aaron ignored her.

'I said I'm fine,' Ella insisted. 'I was handling it.'

'Yes, I could see that,' Aaron said darkly.

'I was,' Ella insisted, and stepped forward to pull futilely at Aaron's steel-band arm clamped across Tom's writhing torso.

Tom lunged at the same time, and Ella felt a crack across her lip. She tasted blood, staggered backwards, fell against the table and ended up on the floor.

And then everything swirled. Black spots. Nothing.

The first thing Ella noticed as her consciousness returned was the scent. Delicious. Clean and wild, like the beach in winter. She inhaled. Nuzzled her nose into it. Inhaled again. She wanted to taste it. Did it taste as good as it smelled? She opened her mouth, moved her lips, tongue. One small lick. Mmm. Good. Different from the smell but…good.

Then a sound. A sharp intake of breath.

She opened her eyes. Saw skin. Tanned skin. White next to it. She shook her head to clear it. Oh, that hurt. Pulled back a little, looked up. Aaron James. 'Oh,' she said. 'What happened?'

'That moron knocked you out.'

It came back at once. Tom. 'Not on purpose.'

'No, not on purpose.'

'Where is he?'

'Gone. Don't worry about him.'

'I'm not worried. He's a big boy. He can take care of himself.' Ella moved again, and realised she was half lolling against Aaron's thighs.

She started to ease away from him but he kept her there, one arm around her back, one crossing her waist to hold onto her from the front.

'Take it easy,' Aaron said.

A crowd of people had gathered around them. Ella felt

herself blush for the second time that night. Intolerable, but apparently uncontrollable. 'I don't feel well,' she said.

'I'm not surprised,' Aaron replied.

'I have to get home,' she said, but she stayed exactly where she was. She closed her eyes. The smell of him. It was him, that smell. That was…comforting. She didn't know why that was so. Didn't care why. It just was.

'All right, people, show's over,' Aaron said, and Ella realised he was telling their audience to get lost. He said something more specific to another man, who seemed to be in charge. She assumed he was pacifying the manager. She didn't care. She just wanted to close her eyes.

'Ella, your lip's bleeding. I'm staying here at the hotel. Come to my room, let me make sure you're all right, then I'll get you home. Or to the hospital.'

She opened her eyes. 'Not the hospital.' She didn't want anyone at the hospital to see her like this.

'Okay—then my room.'

She wanted to say she would find her *own* way home *immediately*, but when she opened her mouth the words 'All right' were what came out. She ran her tongue experimentally over her lip. *Ouch.* Why hadn't she noticed it was hurting? 'My head hurts more than my lip. Did I hit it when I fell?'

'No, I caught you. Let me…' He didn't bother finishing the sentence, instead running his fingers over her scalp. 'No, nothing. Come on. I'll help you stand.'

Aaron carefully eased Ella up. 'Lean on me,' he said softly, and Ella didn't need to be told twice. She felt awful.

As they made their way out of the bar, she noted a few people looking and whispering, but nobody she knew. 'I'm sorry about this,' she said to Aaron. 'Do you think anyone knows you? I mean, from the television show?'

'I'm not well known outside Australia. But it doesn't matter either way.'

'I don't want to embarrass you.'

'I'm not easily embarrassed. I've got stories that would curl your hair. It's inevitable, with three semi-wild younger sisters.'

'I was all right, you know,' she said. 'I can look after myself.'

'Can you?'

'Yes. I've been doing it a long time. And he was harmless. Tom.'

'Was he?'

'Yes. I could have managed. I *was* managing.'

'Were you?'

'Yes. And stop questioning me. It's annoying. And it's hurting my head.'

They were outside the bar now and Aaron stopped. 'Just one more,' he said, and turned her to face him. 'What on earth were you thinking?'

Ella was so stunned at the leashed fury in his voice she *couldn't* think, let alone speak.

He didn't seem to need an answer, though, because he just rolled right on. 'Drinking like a fish. Letting that clown slobber all over you!'

'He's not a clown, he's an engineer,' Ella said. And then, with the ghost of a smile, 'And fish don't drink beer.'

He looked like thunder.

Ella waited, curious about what he was going to hurl at her. But with a snort of disgust he simply took her arm again, started walking.

He didn't speak again until they were almost across the hotel lobby. 'I'm sorry. I guess I feel a little responsible for you, given my relationship with Brand and Tina.'

'That is just ridiculous——I already have a father. And

he happens to know I can look after myself. Anyway, why are you here?' Then, 'Oh, yeah, I remember. The documentary.' She grimaced. '*Should* I have known you'd be here now?'

'I have no idea. Anyway, you're supposed to be in LA.'

'I was in LA. But now— It was a sudden decision, to come here. So it looks like we've surprised each other.'

'Looks like it.'

Aaron guided Ella through a side door leading to the open air, and then along a tree-bordered path until they were in front of what looked like a miniature mansion. He *would* be in one of the presidential-style villas, of course. He didn't look very happy to have brought her there, though.

'How long will you be in town?' she asked, as he unlocked the door.

'Two weeks, give or take.'

'So, you'll be gone in two weeks. And I'll still be here, looking after myself. Like I've always done.' She was pleased with the matter-of-factness of her voice, because in reality she didn't feel matter-of-fact. She felt depressed. She blamed it on the birthday.

Birthdays: misery, with candles.

'Well, good for you, Ella,' he said, and there was a definite sneer in there. 'You're doing such a fine job of it my conscience will be crystal clear when I leave.'

Hello? Sarcasm? Really? Why?

Aaron drew her inside, through a tiled hallway and into a small living room. There was a light on but no sign of anyone.

'Is your son with you?' she asked. *Not that it's any of your business, Ella.*

'Yes, he's in bed.'

'So you've got a nanny? Or is your wife—?' *Um, not your business?*

'Ex-wife. Rebecca is in Sydney. And, yes, I have a nanny, whose name is Jenny. I don't make a habit of leaving my four-year-old son on his own in hotel rooms.'

Oh, dear, he really did *not* like her. And she was well on the way to actively disliking *him*. His attitude was a cross between grouchy father and irritated brother—without the familial affection that would only just make that bearable.

Aaron gestured for Ella to sit. 'Do you want something to drink?'

Ella sank onto the couch. 'Water, please.'

'Good choice,' Aaron said, making Ella wish she'd asked for whisky instead.

He went to the fridge, fished out a bottle of water, poured it into a glass and handed it to her. She didn't deign to thank him.

She rubbed her forehead as she drank.

He was watching her. 'Head still hurting?'

'Yes.'

'Had enough water?'

Ella nodded and Aaron took the glass out of her hand, sat next to her. He turned her so she was facing away from him. 'Here,' he said tetchily, and started kneading the back of her neck.

'Ahhh…' she breathed out. 'That feels good.'

'Like most actors, I've had a chequered career—massage therapy was one of my shorter-lived occupations but I remember a little,' Aaron said, sounding not at all soothing like a massage therapist.

'Where's the dolphin music?' she joked.

He didn't bother answering and she decided she would *not* speak again. She didn't see why she should make an effort to talk to him, given his snotty attitude. She swayed a little, and he pulled her closer to his chest, one hand kneading while he reached his other arm around in front of her, bracing his forearm against her collarbone to balance her.

She could smell him again. He smelled exquisite. So clean and fresh and...yum. The rhythmic movement of his fingers was soothing, even if it did nothing to ease the ache at the front of her skull. She could have stayed like that for hours.

Slowly, he finished the massage and she had to bite back a protest. He turned her to face him and looked at her lip. 'It's only a small tear. I have a first-aid kit in the bathroom.'

'How very *Triage* of you, Aaron.' He looked suitably unimpressed at that dig.

'Just some ice,' she said. 'That's all I need. And I can look after it myself. I'm a nurse, remember?'

But Aaron was already up and away.

He came back with a bowl of ice and the first-aid kit.

Ella peered into the kit and removed a square of gauze, then wrapped it around an ice cube. 'It's not serious and will heal quickly. Mouth injuries do. It's all about the blood supply.'

Not that Aaron seemed interested in that piece of medical information, because he just took the wrapped ice from her impatiently.

'I promise you I can do it myself,' Ella said.

'Hold still,' he insisted. He held the ice on her bottom lip, kept it pressed there for a minute.

'Open,' he ordered, and Ella automatically opened her mouth for him to inspect inside. 'Looks like you bit the inside of your lip.' He grabbed another square of gauze, wrapped it around another cube of ice and pressed it on the small wound.

He was looking intently at her mouth and Ella started

to feel uncomfortable. She could still smell that heavenly scent wafting up from his skin. Why couldn't he smell like stale sweat like everyone else in that bar? She blinked a few times, trying to clear her fuzzy head.

Her eyes fell on his T-shirt and she saw a smear of blood on the collar. Her blood. Her fingers reached out, touched it. His neck, too, had a tiny speck of her blood. Seemingly of their own volition her fingers travelled up, rubbing at the stain. And then she remembered how it had got there. Remembered in one clear flash how she had put her mouth there, on his skin. She felt a flare of arousal and sucked in a quick breath.

He had gone very still. He was watching her. Looking stunned.

CHAPTER THREE

'SORRY,' ELLA SAID. 'It's just… I—I bled on you.'

'Ella, I don't think it's a good idea for you to touch me.'

'Sorry,' Ella said again, jerking her fingers away.

Aaron promptly contradicted himself by taking the hand she'd pulled away and pressing it against his chest. He could actually *hear* his heart thudding. It was probably thumping against her palm like a drum. He didn't care. He wanted her hand on him. Wanted both her hands on him.

He could hear a clock ticking somewhere in the room, but except for that and his heart the silence was thick and heavy.

I don't even like her. He said that in his head, but something wasn't connecting his head to his groin, because just as the thought completed itself he tossed the gauze aside and reached for her other hand, brought it to his mouth, pressed his mouth there, kept it there.

Okay, so maybe you didn't have to like someone to want them.

He really, really hadn't expected to see her again. She was supposed to be in LA. Their 'relationship' should have begun and ended with one awkward conversation at a wedding.

And yet here he was. And here she was. And he had no idea what was going to happen next.

When he'd walked into that bar tonight and seen her with that idiot, he'd wanted to explode, drag her away, beat the guy senseless.

And he *never* lost his temper!

He'd been so shocked at his reaction he'd contemplated leaving the bar, going somewhere else—a different bar, for a walk, to bed, anything, anywhere else. But he hadn't.

He'd only been planning on having one drink anyway, just a post-flight beer. But nope. He'd stayed, sensing there was going to be trouble. She'd laughed too much, drunk too much, Tom the idiot engineer had fondled her too much. Something was going to give.

And something definitely had.

And of course he'd been there smack bang in the middle of it, like he couldn't get there fast enough.

And then his arms had been around her. And she'd snuggled against him. Her tongue on his neck. And he'd wanted her. Wanted her like he'd never wanted anyone in his life.

And it had made him furious.

Was making him furious now.

So why was he moving the hand he'd been holding to his mouth down to his chest, instead of letting it go?

His hands were only lightly covering hers now. She could break away if she wanted to. Bring him back to sanity. *Please.*

But she didn't break away.

Her hands moved up, over his chest to his collarbones then shoulders. Confident hands. Direct and sure.

He stifled a groan.

'You don't want me.' She breathed the words. 'You don't like me.' But her hands moved again, down to his deltoids, stopping there. Her fingers slid under the short sleeves of his T-shirt, stroked.

This time the groan escaped as his pulse leapt.

Ella moved closer to him, sighed as she surrounded him with her arms, rested the side of her face against his chest then simply waited.

He battled himself for a long moment. His hand hovered over her hair. He could see the tremor in his fingers. He closed his eyes so the sight of her wouldn't push him over the edge. That only intensified the sexy smell of her. Ella Reynolds. Tina's *sister*. 'I can't,' he said. 'I can't do this.' Was that his voice? That croak?

He waited, every nerve tingling. Didn't trust himself to move. If he moved, even a fraction…

Then he heard her sigh again; this time it signalled resignation, not surrender.

'No, of course not,' she said, and slowly disentangled herself until she was sitting safely, separately, beside him.

Whew. Catastrophe averted.

'A shame,' she said. Her voice was cool and so were her eyes as she reached out to skim her fingernail over his right arm, at the top of his biceps where the sleeve of his T-shirt had been pushed up just enough to reveal the lower edge of a black tattoo circlet. Her lips turned up in an approximation of a smile. 'Because I like tattoos. They're a real turn-on for me. Would have been fun.'

He stared at her, fighting the urge to drag her back against his chest, not quite believing the disdainful humour he could hear in her voice, see in her eyes. Wondering if he'd imagined the yielding softness only moments ago.

At Tina and Brand's wedding he'd sensed that there was something wrong with her. It had made him uncomfortable to be near her. Made him want to get away from her.

He had the same feeling now. Only this time he couldn't get away. He would be damned if he'd let Tina's sister stagger home drunk and disorderly, with a pounding head and a split lip. *Oh, yeah, that's the reason, is it? Tina?*

Ella shrugged—a dismissive, almost delicate gesture. 'But don't worry, I won't press you,' she said calmly. 'I've never had to beg for it in my life and I won't start now, tattoos or not.'

She stood suddenly and smiled—the dazzling smile that didn't reach her eyes. 'I'd better go,' she said.

'I'll take you home,' he said, ignoring the taunt of all those men she hadn't had to beg. None of his business.

'I'll walk.'

'I'll take you,' Aaron insisted.

Ella laughed. 'Okay, but I hope we're not going to drag some poor driver out of bed.'

'Where are you staying?'

'Close enough. I can walk there in under ten minutes.'

'Then we'll walk.'

'All right, then, lead on, Sir Galahad,' Ella said lightly, mockingly.

And that was *exactly* why he didn't like her.

Because she was just so unknowable. Contrary. Changeable. Ready to seduce him one moment and the next so cool. Poised. Amused. They made it to the street without him throttling her, which was one relief. Although he would have preferred a different relief—one for inside his jeans, because, heaven help him, it was painful down there. How the hell did she *do* that? Make him both want her and want to run a mile in the opposite direction?

Ella led off and Aaron fell into step beside her, conscious of her excruciatingly arousing perfume. The almost drugging combination of that scent, the damp heat, the sizzle and shout of the street stalls, the thumping music and wild shouts from the tourist bars, was so mesmerisingly exotic it felt almost like he was in another world. One where the normal rules, the checks and balances, didn't apply.

The minutes ticked by. A steady stream of motorbikes puttered past. A short line of tuk-tuks carrying chatty tourists. Jaunty music from a group of street musicians. Sounds fading as he and Ella walked further, further.

'Needless to say, tonight's escapade is not something Tina needs to hear about,' Ella said suddenly.

'Needless to say,' he agreed.

A tinkling laugh. 'Of course, you wouldn't want it getting back to your wife either. At least, not the latter part of the evening.'

'Ex-wife,' Aaron corrected her. He heard a dog barking in the distance. A mysterious rustle in the bushes near the road.

'Ah.' Ella's steps slowed, but only very briefly. 'But not really ex, I'm thinking, Sir Galahad.'

Aaron grabbed Ella's arm, pulling her to the side of a dirty puddle she was about to step into. 'It's complicated,' he said, when she looked at him.

She pulled free of the contact and started forward again.

'But definitely ex,' he added. And if she only knew the drug-fuelled hell Rebecca had put him through for the past three years, she would understand.

'Oh, dear, how inconvenient! An ex who's not really an ex. It must play havoc with your sex life.'

She laughed again, and his temper got the better of him.

The temper that he *never* lost.

'What is wrong with you?' he demanded, whirling her to face him.

She looked up at him, opened her mouth to say—

Well, who knew? Because before he could stop himself he'd slapped his mouth on hers in a devouring kiss.

Just what he *didn't* want to do.

And she had the audacity to kiss him back. More than that—her arms were around him, her hands under his T-shirt.

Then he tasted blood, remembered her lip. Horrified, he pulled back. 'I'm sorry,' he said.

She ran her tongue across her lower lip, raised her eyebrows. '*Definitely* would have been fun,' she said.

'I'm not looking for a relationship,' he said bluntly. And where had that come from? It seemed to suggest he *was* after *something*. But what? What was he after? Nothing—nothing from her.

It seemed to startle her, at least. 'Did I ask for one?'

'No.'

'That's a relief! Because I'm really only interested in casual sex. And on that note, how fortunate that we're here. Where I live. So we can say our goodbyes, and both pretend tonight didn't happen. No relationship. And, alas, no casual sex, because you're married. Oh, no, that's right, you're not. But no sex anyway.'

'I should have left you with the engineer.'

'Well, I would have seen a lot more action,' she said. She started forward and then stopped, raised her hand to her eyes.

'What is it?' Aaron asked.

'Nothing. A headache,' she answered. 'I'll be fine.'

'Goodbye, then,' he said, and turned to walk back to the hotel.

A lot more action! Ha! Aaron was quite sure if he ever let himself put his hands on Ella Reynolds she wouldn't be able to think about another man for a long time. Or walk straight either.

But he was not going to touch her, of course. *Not.*

* * *

Ella made her way to her room, cursing silently.

Her head was throbbing and her joints were aching and she longed to lapse into a thought-free coma. She'd just realised she'd contracted either malaria or dengue fever. She wasn't sure which, but either way it sucked.

But when she'd taken two paracetamol tablets and clambered into bed, praying for a mild dose of whatever it was, it wasn't the pain that made the tears come. It was shame. And regret. And a strange sense of loss.

Aaron James had wanted her. Ordinarily, a man wanting her would not cause Ella consternation. Lots of men had wanted her and she'd had no trouble resisting them.

But Aaron was different. He'd kissed her like he was pouring his strength, his soul into her. And yet he'd been able to fight whatever urge had been driving him.

Why? How?

She manhandled her pillow, trying to get it into a more head-cradling shape.

Not looking for a relationship—that's what he'd said. How galling! As though it were something she would be begging for on the basis of one kiss. All right, one *amazing* kiss, but—seriously! What a joke. A relationship? The one thing she *couldn't* have.

Ella sighed as her outrage morphed into something more distressing: self-loathing. Because she was a fraud and she knew it. A coward who used whatever was at her disposal to stop herself from confronting the wreck her life had become since Javier had been kidnapped in Somalia on her twenty-fifth birthday.

She'd been in limbo ever since. Feeling helpless, hopeless. Guilty that she was free and he was who-knew-where. In the year after his kidnapping she'd felt so lost and alone and powerless she'd thought a nervous breakdown had been on the cards.

And then she'd found Sann in a Cambodian orphanage, and life had beckoned to her again. Two years old, and hers. Or so she'd hoped. But he'd been taken too. He'd died, on her twenty-sixth birthday.

And now here she was on her twenty-*seventh* birthday. Still in limbo, with no idea of what had happened to Javier. Still grieving for Sann.

Panicking at the thought of seeing an Asian child with an adoptive parent.

Unable to entertain even the thought of a relationship with a man.

Pretending she was calm and in control when she was a basket case.

Her life had become a series of shambolic episodes. Too many drinks at the bar. Getting picked up by strange men, determined to see it through then backing out. *Always* backing out, like the worst kind of tease, because no matter how desperate she was to feel *something*, the guilt was always stronger. Coping, but only just, with endlessly sad thoughts during the day and debilitating dreams at night.

She knew that something in her was lost—but she just didn't know how to find it. She hid it from the people she cared about because she knew her grief would devastate them. She hid it from her colleagues because they didn't need the extra burden.

And she was just…stuck. Stuck on past heartbreaks. And it was starting to show.

No wonder Aaron James abhorred the idea of a 'relationship' with her.

Ella rubbed tiredly at her forehead. She closed her eyes, longing for sleep, but knowing the nightmares would come tonight.

* * *

Dr Seng slapped his hand on the desk and Aaron's wandering mind snapped back to him. 'So—we've talked about malaria. Now, a few facts about the hospital.'

Kiri had been whisked off to do some painting—one of his favourite pastimes—on arrival at the Children's Community Friendship Hospital, so Aaron could concentrate on this first meeting.

But he wasn't finding it easy.

He had a feeling... A picture of Ella here. Was this where she was working? He wasn't sure, but he kept expecting her to sashay past.

Dr Seng handed over an array of brochures. 'Pre-Pol Pot, there were more than five hundred doctors practising in Cambodia,' Dr Seng said. 'By the time the Khmer Rouge fled Cambodia in 1979 there were less than fifty. Can you imagine what it must have been like? Rebuilding an entire healthcare system from the ground up, with almost no money, no skills? Because that's what happened in Cambodia.'

Aaron knew the history—he'd made it his business to know, because of Kiri. But he could never come to terms with the brutal stupidity of the Khmer Rouge. 'No, I can't imagine it,' he said simply. 'And I'd say this hospital is something of a miracle.'

'Yes. We were started by philanthropists and we're kept going by donations—which is why we are so happy to be associated with your documentary: we need all the publicity we can get, to keep attracting money. It costs us less than twenty-five dollars to treat a child. Only fifty dollars to operate. Unheard of in your world. But, of course, we have so many to help.'

'But your patients pay nothing, right?'

'Correct. Our patients are from impoverished communities and are treated free, although they contribute if they can.'

'And your staff…?'

'In the early days the hospital relied on staff from overseas, but today we are almost exclusively Khmer. And we're a teaching hospital—we train healthcare workers from all over the country. That's a huge success story.'

'So you don't have any overseas staff here at the moment?'

'Actually, we do. Not paid staff—volunteers.'

'Doctors?'

'We have a group of doctors from Singapore coming in a few months' time to perform heart surgeries. And at the moment we have three nurses, all from America, helping out.'

'I was wondering if…' Aaron cleared his throat. 'If perhaps Ella Reynolds was working here?'

Dr Seng looked at him in surprise. 'Ella? Why, yes!'

Ahhhhh. Fate. It had a lot to answer for.

'I—I'm a friend. Of the family,' Aaron explained.

'Then I'm sorry to say you probably won't see her. She's not well. She won't be in for the whole week.'

Aaron knew he should be feeling relieved. He could have a nice easy week of filming, with no cutting comments, no tattoo come-ons, no amused eyebrow-raising.

But…what did 'not well' mean? Head cold? Sprained toe? Cancer? Liver failure? Amputation? 'Not well?'

'Dengue fever—we're in the middle of an outbreak, I'm afraid. Maybe a subject for your next documentary, given it's endemic in at least a hundred countries and infects up to a hundred million people a year.'

Alarm bells. 'But it doesn't kill you, right?'

'It certainly can,' the doctor said, too easily, clearly not understanding Aaron's need for reassurance.

Aaron swallowed. 'But…Ella…'

'Ella? No, no, no. She isn't going to die. The faster you're diagnosed and treated the better, and she diagnosed herself very quickly. It's more dangerous for children, which Ella is not. And much more dangerous if you've had it before, which Ella has not.'

Better. But not quite good enough. 'So is she in hospital?'

'Not necessary at this stage. There's no cure; you just have to nurse the symptoms— take painkillers, keep up the fluids, watch for signs of internal bleeding, which would mean it was dengue haemorrhagic fever—very serious! But Ella knows what she's doing, and she has a friend staying close by, one of the nurses. And I'll be monitoring her as well. A shame it hit her on her birthday.'

'Birthday?'

'Two days ago. Do you want me to get a message to her?'

'No, that's fine,' Aaron said hurriedly. 'Maybe I'll see her before I head home to Sydney.'

'Then let's collect Kiri and I'll have you both taken on a tour of our facilities.'

It quickly became clear that it was Kiri, not Aaron, who was the celebrity in the hospital. He seemed to fascinate people with his Cambodian Australian-ness, and he was equally fascinated in return. He got the hang of the *satu*—the graceful greeting where you placed your palms together and bowed your head—and looked utterly natural doing it. It soothed Aaron's conscience, which had been uneasy about bringing him.

They were taken to observe the frenetic outpatient department, which Aaron was stunned to learn saw more than five hundred patients a day in a kind of triage arrangement.

The low acuity unit, where he saw his first malaria patients, a sardine can's worth of dengue sufferers, and children with assorted other conditions, including TB, pneumonia, malnutrition, HIV/AIDS and meningitis.

The emergency room, where premature babies and critically ill children were treated for sepsis, severe asthma, and on and on and on.

Then the air-conditioned intensive care unit, which offered mechanical ventilation, blood gas analysis and inotropes—not that Aaron had a clue what that meant. It looked like the Starship *Enterprise* in contrast to the mats laid out for the overflow of dengue sufferers in the fan-cooled hospital corridors.

The tour wrapped up with a walk through the basic but well-used teaching rooms, some of which had been turned into makeshift wards to cope with the dengue rush.

And then, to Aaron's intense annoyance, his focus snapped straight back to Ella.

Tina and Brand would expect him to check on her, right?

And, okay, *he* wanted to make sure for himself that she was going to recover as quickly and easily as Dr Seng seemed to think.

One visit to ease his conscience, and he would put Ella Reynolds into his mental lockbox of almost-mistakes and double-padlock the thing.

And so, forty minutes after leaving the hospital, with Kiri safely in Jenny's care at the hotel, he found himself outside Ella's guesthouse, coercing her room number from one of the other boarders, and treading up the stairs.

CHAPTER FOUR

AARON FELT SUDDENLY guilty as he knocked. Ella would have to drag herself out of bed to open the door.

Well, why not add another layer of guilt to go with his jumble of feelings about that night at the bar?

The boorish way he'd behaved—when he was *never* boorish.

The way he'd assumed her headache was the result of booze, when she'd actually been coming down with dengue fever.

The door opened abruptly. A pretty brunette, wearing a nurse's uniform, stood there.

'Sorry, I thought this was Ella Reynolds's room,' Aaron said.

'It is.' She gave him the appreciative look he was used to receiving from women—women who weren't Ella Reynolds, anyway. 'She's in bed. Ill.'

'Yes, I know. I'm Aaron James. A…a friend. Of the family.'

'I'm Helen. I'm in the room next door, so I'm keeping an eye on her.'

'Nice to meet you.'

She gave him a curious look and he smiled at her, hoping he looked harmless.

'Hang on, and I'll check if she's up to a visit,' Helen said.

The door closed in his face, and he was left wondering whether it would open again.

What on earth was he doing here?

Within a minute Helen was back. 'She's just giving herself a tourniquet test, but come in. I'm heading to the hospital, so she's all yours.'

It was gloomy in the room. And quiet—which was why he could hear his heart racing, even though his heart had no business racing.

His eyes went first to the bed—small, with a mosquito net hanging from a hook in the ceiling, which had been shoved aside. Ella was very focused, staring at her arm, ignoring him. So Aaron looked around the room. Bedside table with a lamp, a framed photo. White walls. Small wardrobe. Suitcase against a wall. A door that he guessed opened to a bathroom, probably the size of a shoebox.

He heard a sound at the bed. Like a magnet, it drew him.

She was taking a blood-pressure cuff off her arm.

'I heard you were ill,' he said, as he reached the bedside. 'I'm sorry. That you're sick, I mean.'

'I'm not too happy about it myself.' She sounded both grim and amused, and Aaron had to admire the way she achieved that.

'Who told you I was sick?' she asked.

'The hospital. I'm filming there for the next week.'

She looked appalled at that news. 'Just one week, right?'

'Looks like it.'

She nodded. He imagined she was calculating the odds of having to see him at work. Flattering—not.

He cleared his throat. 'So what's a tourniquet test?'

'You use the blood-pressure machine—'

'Sphygmomanometer.'

'Well, aren't you clever, Dr *Triage*! Yes. Take your BP, keep the cuff blown up to halfway between the diastolic and systolic—the minimum and maximum pressure— wait a few minutes and check for petechiae—blood points in the skin.'

'And do you have them? Um…it? Petechiae?'

'Not enough. Less than ten per square inch.'

'Is that…is that bad?'

'It's good, actually.'

'Why?'

Audible sigh. 'It means I have classic dengue—not haemorrhagic. As good as it gets when every bone and joint in your body is aching and your head feels like it might explode through your eyeballs.'

'Is that how it feels?'

'Yes.'

Silence.

Aaron racked his brain. 'I thought you might want me to get a message to Tina.'

Her lips tightened. Which he took as a no.

'That would be no,' she confirmed.

A sheet covered the lower half of her body. She was wearing a red T-shirt. Her hair was piled on top of her head, held in place by a rubber band. Her face was flushed, a light sheen of sweat covering it. And despite the distinct lack of glamour, despite the tightened lips and warning eyes, she was the most beautiful woman he'd ever seen.

'Shouldn't you keep the net closed?' he asked, standing rigid beside the bed. Yep—just the sort of thing a man asked a nurse who specialised in tropical illnesses.

'Happy to, if you want to talk to me through it. Or you can swat the mosquitoes before they get to me.'

'Okay—I'll swat.'

She regarded him suspiciously. 'Why are you really here? To warn me I'll be seeing you at the hospital?'

'No, because it looks like you won't be. I just wanted to make sure you were all right. See if you needed anything.'

'Well, I'm all right, and I don't need anything. So thank you for coming but...' Her strength seemed to desert her then and she rolled flat onto her back in the bed, staring at the ceiling, saying nothing.

'I heard it was your birthday. That night.'

An eye roll, but otherwise no answer.

He came a half-step closer. 'If I'd known...'

Aaron mentally winced as she rolled her eyes again.

'What would you have done?' she asked. 'Baked me a cake?'

'Point taken.'

Trawling for a new topic of conversation, he picked up the photo from her bedside table. 'Funny—you and Tina sound nothing alike, and you look nothing alike.'

Silence, and then, grudgingly, 'I take after my father's side of the family. Tina's a genetic throwback.' She smiled suddenly, and Aaron felt his breath jam in his throat. She really was gorgeous when she smiled like that, with her eyes as well as her mouth—even if it was aimed into space and not at him.

He gestured to the photo. 'I wouldn't have picked you for a Disneyland kind of girl.'

'Who doesn't like Disneyland? As long as you remember it's not real, it's a blast.'

Aaron looked at her, disturbed by the harshness in her voice. Did she have to practise that cynicism or did it come naturally?

Ella raised herself on her elbow again. 'Look, forget Disneyland, and my birthday. I *do* need something from you. Only one thing.' She fixed him with a gimlet eye. 'Silence. You can't talk about that night, or about me being sick. Don't tell Tina. Don't tell Brand. My life here has nothing to do with them. In fact, don't talk to anyone about me.'

'Someone should know you've got dengue fever.'

'*You* know. That will have to do. But don't worry, it won't affect you unless I don't make it. And my advice then would be to head for the hills and forget you were ever in Cambodia, because my mother will probably kill you.' That glorious smile again—and, again, not directed at him, just at the thought. 'She never did like a bearer of bad tidings—quite medieval.'

'All the more reason to tell them now.'

Back to the eye roll. 'Except she's not really going to kill you and I'm not going to drop dead. Look...' Ella seemed to be finding the right words. 'They'll worry, and I don't want them worrying about something that can't be changed.'

'You shouldn't be on your own when you're ill.'

'I'm not. I'm surrounded by experts. I feel like I'm in an episode of your TV show, there are so many medical personnel traipsing in and out of this room.'

Aaron looked down at her.

'Don't look at me like that,' Ella said.

'Like what?' Aaron asked. But he was wincing internally because he kind of knew how he must be looking at her. And it was really inappropriate, given her state of health.

With an effort, she pushed herself back into a sitting position. 'Let me make this easy for you, Aaron. I am not, ever, going to have sex with you.'

Yep, she'd pegged the look all right.

'You have a child,' she continued. 'And a wife, ex-wife, whatever. And it's very clear that your...encumbrances... are important to you. And that's the way it *should* be. I understand it. I respect it. I even admire it. So let's just leave it. I was interested for one night, and now I'm not. You were interested, but not enough. Moment officially over. You can take a nice clear conscience home to Sydney, along with the film.'

'Ella—'

'I don't want to hear any more. And I really, truly, do not want to see you again. I don't want— Look, I don't want to get mixed up with a friend of my sister's. Especially a man with a kid.'

Okay, sentiments Aaron agreed with wholeheartedly. So he should just leave it at that. Run—don't walk—to the nearest exit. Good riddance. So he was kind of surprised to find his mouth opening and 'What's Kiri got to do with it?' coming out of it.

'It's just a…a thing with children. I get attached to them, and it can be painful when the inevitable goodbyes come around—there, something about me you didn't need to know.'

'But you're working at a children's hospital.'

'That's my business. But the bottom line is—I don't want to see Kiri. Ergo, I don't want to see you.' She stopped and her breath hitched painfully. 'Now, please…' Her voice had risen in tone and volume and she stopped. As he watched, she seemed to gather her emotions together. 'Please go,' she continued quietly. 'I'm sick and I'm tired and I— Just please go. All right?'

'All right. Message received loud and clear. Sex officially off the agenda. And have a nice life.'

'Thank you,' she said, and tugged the mosquito net closed.

Aaron left the room, closed the door and stood there.

Duty discharged. He was free to go. *Happy* to go.

But there was some weird dynamic at work, because

he couldn't seem to make his feet move. His overgrown sense of responsibility, he told himself.

He'd taken two steps when he heard the sob. Just one, as though it had been cut off. He could picture her holding her hands against her mouth to stop herself from making any tell-tale sound. He hovered, waiting.

But there was only silence.

Aaron waited another long moment.

There was something about her. Something that made him wonder if she was really as prickly as she seemed…

He shook his head. No, he wasn't going to wonder about Ella Reynolds. He'd done the decent thing and checked on her.

He was not interested in her further than that. Not. Interested.

He forced himself to walk away.

Ella had only been away from the hospital for eight lousy days.

How did one mortal male cause such a disturbance in so short a time? she wondered as she batted away what felt like the millionth question about Aaron James. The doctors and nurses, male and female, Khmer and the small sprinkling of Westerners, were uniformly goggle-eyed over him.

Knock yourselves out, would have been Ella's attitude; except that while she'd been laid low by the dengue, Aaron had let it slip to Helen—and therefore everyone!—that he was a close friend of Ella's film director brother-in-law. Which part of 'Don't talk to anyone about me' didn't he understand?

As a result, the whole, intrigued hospital expected her to be breathless with anticipation to learn what Aaron said, what Aaron did, where Aaron went. They expected Ella to marvel at the way he dropped in, no airs or graces, to talk to the staff; how he spoke to patients and their families with real interest and compassion, even when the cameras weren't rolling; the way he was always laughing at himself for getting ahead of his long-suffering translator.

He'd taken someone's temperature. Whoop-de-doo!

And had volunteered as a guinea pig when they'd been demonstrating the use of the rapid diagnostic test for malaria—yeah, so one tiny pinprick on his finger made him a hero?

And had cooked alongside a Cambodian father in the specially built facility attached to the hospital. Yee-ha!

And, and, and, *and*—give her a break.

All Ella wanted to do was work, without hearing his name. They'd had their moment, and it had passed. Thankfully he'd got the message and left her in peace once she'd laid out the situation. She allowed herself a quick stretch before moving onto the next child—a two-year-old darling named Maly. *Heart rate. Respiration rate. Blood pressure. Urine output. Adjust the drip.*

The small hospital was crowded now that the dengue fever outbreak was peaking. They were admitting twenty additional children a day, and she was run off her still-wobbly legs. In the midst of everything she should have been too busy to sense she was being watched...and yet she knew.

She turned. And saw him. Aaron's son, Kiri, beside him.

Wasn't the hospital filming supposed to be over? Why was he here?

'Ella,' Aaron said. No surprise. Just acknowledgement.

She ignored the slight flush she could feel creeping up from her throat. With a swallowed sigh she fixed on a smile and walked over to him. She would be cool. Professional. Civilised. She held out her hand. 'Hello, Aaron.'

He took it, but released it quickly.

'And *sua s'day*, Kiri,' she said, crouching in front of him. 'Do you know what that means?'

Kiri shook his head. Blinked.

'It means hello in Khmer. Do you remember me?'

Kiri nodded. '*Sua s'day*, Ella. Can I go and see her?' he asked, looking over, wide-eyed, at the little girl Ella had been with.

'Yes, you can. But she's not feeling very well. Do you think you can be careful and quiet?'

Kiri nodded solemnly and Ella gave him a confirming nod before standing again. She watched him walk over to Maly's bed before turning to reassure Aaron. 'She's not contagious. It's dengue fever and there's never been a case of person-to-person transmission.'

'Dr Seng said it deserved its own documentary. The symptoms can be like malaria, right? But it's a virus, not a parasite, and the mosquitoes aren't the same.'

Ella nodded. 'The dengue mosquito—' She broke off. 'You're really interested?'

'Why wouldn't I be?'

'I just…' She shrugged. 'Nothing. People can get bored with the medical lingo.'

'I won't be bored. So—the mosquitoes?'

'They're called *Aedes aegypti*, and they bite during the day. Malaria mosquitoes—*Anopheles*, but I'm sure you know that—get you at night, and I'm sure you know that too. It kind of sucks that the people here don't get a break! Anyway, *Aedes aegypti* like urban areas, and they breed in stagnant water—vases, old tyres, buckets, that kind of thing. If a mosquito bites someone with dengue, the virus will replicate inside it, and then the mosquito can transmit the virus to other people when it bites them.' Her gaze sharpened. 'You're taking precautions for Kiri, aren't you?'

'Oh, yes. It's been beaten it into me. Long sleeves, long pants. Insect repellent with DEET. And so on and so forth.'

'You too—long sleeves, I mean. Enough already with the T-shirts.'

'Yes, I know. I'm tempting fate.'

Silence.

He was looking at her in that weird way.

'So, the filming,' she said, uncomfortable. 'Is it going well?'

'We're behind schedule, but I don't mind because it's given me a chance to take Kiri to see Angkor Wat. And the place with the riverbed carvings. You know, the carvings of the genitalia.' He stopped suddenly. 'I—I mean, the…um…Hindu gods…you know…and the—the…ah… Kal…? Kab…?'

Ella bit the inside of her cheek. It surprised her that she could think he was cute. But he sort of was, in his sudden embarrassment over the word genitalia. 'Yes, I know all about genitalia. And it's Kbal Spean, you're talking about, and the Hindu God is Shiva. It's also called The River of a Thousand Lingas—which means a thousand stylised phalluses,' she said, and had to bite her cheek again as he ran a harassed hand into his hair.

'So, the filming?' she reminded him.

'Oh. Yeah. A few more days here and then the final bit involves visiting some of the villages near the Thai border and seeing how the malaria outreach programme works, with the volunteers screening, diagnosing and treating people in their communities.'

'I was out there a few years ago,' Ella said. 'Volunteers were acting as human mosquito bait. The mosquitoes would bite them, and the guys would scoop them into test tubes to be sent down to the lab in Phnom Penh for testing.'

'But wasn't that dangerous? I mean...*trying* to get bitten?'

'Well, certainly drastic. But all the volunteers were given a combination drug cocktail, which meant they didn't actually develop malaria.'

'So what was the point?'

'To verify whether the rapid treatment malaria programme that had been established there was managing to break the pathways of transmission between insects, parasites and humans. But you don't need to worry. That was then, this is now. And they won't be asking you to roll up your jeans and grab a test tube.'

'Would you have rolled up your jeans, Ella?'

'Yes.'

'And risked malaria?'

'I've had it. Twice, actually. Once in Somalia, once here.'

'Somalia?'

Uh-oh. She was not going there. 'Obviously, it didn't kill me, either time. But I've *seen* it kill. It kills one child every thirty seconds.' She could hear her voice tremble so she paused for a moment. When she could trust herself, she added, 'And I would do anything to help stop that.'

Aaron was frowning. Watching her. Making her feel uncomfortable. Again. 'But you're not— Sorry, it's none of my business, but Kiri isn't going with you up there, right?'

'No.' Aaron frowned. Opened his mouth. Closed it. Opened. Closed.

'Problem?' she prompted.

'No. But… Just…' Sigh.

'Just…?' she prompted again.

'Just—do you think I made a mistake, bringing him to Cambodia?' he asked. 'There were reasons I couldn't leave him at home. And I thought it would be good for him to stay connected to his birth country. But, like you, he's had malaria. Before the adoption.'

'Yes, I gathered that.'

'I'd never forgive myself if he got it again because I brought him with me.'

Ella blinked at him. She was surprised he would share that fear with her—they weren't exactly friends, after all—and felt a sudden emotional connection that was as undeniable as it was unsettling.

She wanted to touch him. Just his hand. She folded her arms so she couldn't. 'I agree that children adopted from overseas should connect with their heritage,' she said, ultra-professional. And then she couldn't help herself. She unfolded her arms, touched his shoulder. Very briefly. 'But, yes, we're a long way from Sydney, and the health risks are real.'

'So I shouldn't have brought him?'

'You said there were reasons for not leaving him behind—so how can I answer that? But, you know, these are diseases of poverty we're talking about. That's a horrible thing to acknowledge, but at least it can be a comfort to you. Because you know your son would have immediate attention, the *best* attention—and therefore the best outcome.'

He sighed. 'Yes, I see what you mean. It is horrible, and also comforting.'

'And it won't be long until you're back home. Meanwhile, keep taking those precautions, and if he exhibits any symptoms, at least you know what they are—just don't wait to get him to the hospital.'

She swayed slightly, and Aaron reached out to steady her.

'Sorry. Tired,' she said.

'You're still not fully recovered, are you?' he asked.

'I'm fine. And my shift has finished so I'm off home in a moment.'

Ella nodded in Kiri's direction. The little boy was gently stroking the back of Maly's hand. 'He's sweet.'

'Yes. He's an angel.'

'You're lucky,' Ella said. She heard the…thing in her voice. The wistfulness. She blinked hard. Cleared her throat. 'Excuse me, I need to— Excuse me.'

Ella felt Aaron's eyes on her as she left the ward.

Ella was doing that too-slow walk. Very controlled.

She'd lost her curves since the wedding. She'd been thin when he'd visited her a week ago, but after the dengue she was like a whippet.

But still almost painfully beautiful. Despite the messy ponytail. And the sexless pants and top combo that constituted her uniform.

And he still wanted her.

He'd been furious at how he'd strained for a sight of her every time he'd been at the hospital, even though he'd known she was out of action. Seriously, how pathetic could a man be?

He'd tried and tried to get her out of his head. No joy. There was just something…something under the prickly exterior.

Like the way she looked at Kiri when he'd repeated her Cambodian greeting. The expression on her face when she'd spoken about diseases of the poor. It was just so hard to reconcile all the pieces. To figure out that *something* about her.

He caught himself. Blocked the thought. Reminded himself that if there *was* something there, he didn't want it. One more week, and he would never have to see or think of her again. He could have his peace of mind back. His libido back under control.

He called Kiri over and they left the ward.

And she was there—up the corridor, crouching beside a little boy who was on one of the mattresses on the floor, her slender fingers on the pulse point of his wrist.

Arrrggghhh. This was *torture*. Why wasn't she on her way home like she was supposed to be, so he didn't have to see her smile into that little boy's eyes? Didn't have to see her sit back on her heels and close her eyes, exhausted?

And wonder just who she really was, this woman who was prickly and dismissive. Knowledgeable and professional. Who wouldn't think twice about letting mosquitoes bite her legs for research. Who looked at sick children with a tenderness that caused his chest to ache. Who made him feel gauche and insignificant.

Who made him suddenly and horribly aware of what it was like to crave something. Someone. It was so much more, so much *worse*, than purely physical need.

'Ow,' Kiri protested, and Aaron loosened his hold on Kiri's hand.

Ella looked up, saw them. Froze. Nodding briefly, she got to her feet and did that slow walk out.

This was not good, Aaron thought.

A few days and he would be out of her life.

Ella felt that if only she didn't have to converse with Aaron again, she would cope with those days.

But she hadn't banked on the *sight* of him being such

a distraction. Sauntering around like a doctor on regular rounds, poking his nose in everywhere without even the excuse of a camera. Not really coming near her, but always *there*.

It was somehow worse that he was keeping his distance, because it meant there was no purpose to the way she was perpetually waiting for him to show up.

Him and the boy, who reminded her so much of Sann.

It was painful to see Kiri, even from a distance. So painful she shouldn't want to see him, shouldn't want the ache it caused. Except that alongside the pain was this drenching, drowning need. She didn't bother asking why, accepting that it was a connection she couldn't explain, the way it had been with Sann.

On her fourth day back at work, after broken sleep full of wrenching nightmares, the last thing she needed was Aaron James, trailed by his cameraman, coming into the outpatient department just as a comatose, convulsing two-year-old boy was rushed up to her by his mother.

The look in Ella's eyes as she reached for the child must have been terrible because Aaron actually ran at her. He plucked the boy from his mother's arms. 'Come,' he said, and hurried through the hospital as though he'd worked there all his life, Ella and the little boy's mother hurrying after him.

This was a child. Maybe with malaria. And Aaron was helping her.

How was she supposed to keep her distance now?

CHAPTER FIVE

AARON SIGNALLED FOR the cameraman to start filming as what looked like a swarm of medical people converged on the tiny little boy in the ICU.

Ella was rattling off details as he was positioned in the bed—name Bourey, two years old, brought in by his mother after suffering intermittent fever and chills for two days. Unable to eat. Seizure on the way to the hospital. Unable to be roused. Severe pallor. Second seizure followed.

Hands, stethoscopes were all over the boy—pulling open his eyelids, taking his temperature. Checking heart rate, pulse and blood pressure. *Rash? No.* Feeling his abdomen.

I want a blood glucose now.

Into Bourey's tiny arm went a canula.

Blood was taken, and whisked away.

Intravenous diazepam as a slow bolus to control the seizures.

The doctor was listening intently to Bourey's breathing, which was deep and slow. The next moment the boy was intubated and hooked up to a respirator.

Every instruction was rapid-fire.

'Intravenous paracetamol for the fever.'

'Intravenous artesunate, stat, we won't wait for the blood films—we'll treat for falciparum malaria. Don't

think it's menigococcus but let's give IV benzylpenicillin.
We'll hold off on the lumbar puncture. I want no evidence
of focal neuro signs. What was his glucose?'

'Intravenous dextrose five per cent and normal saline
point nine per cent for the dehydration—but monitor his
urine output carefully; we don't want to overdo it and end
up with pulmonary oedema, and we need to check renal
function. And watch for haemoglobinuria. If the urine is
dark we'll need to cross-match.'

Overhead an assortment of bags; tubes drip, drip, drip-
ping.

How much stuff could the little guy's veins take?

A urinary catheter was added to Bourey's overloaded
body. Empty plastic bag draped over the side of the bed.

A plastic tube was measured, from the boy's nose to
his ear to his chest, lubricated, threaded up Bourey's nose,
taped in place.

'Aspirate the stomach contents.'

'Monitor temp, respiratory rate, pulse, blood pressure,
neuro obs every fifteen minutes.'

*Hypoglycaemia, metabolic acidosis, pulmonary oe-
dema, hypotensive shock. Watch the signs. Monitor. Check.
Observe.*

Aaron's head was spinning. His cameraman silent and
focused as he filmed.

And Ella—so calm, except for her eyes.

Aaron was willing her to look at him. And every time
she did, she seemed to relax. Just a slight breath, a soft-
ening in her face so subtle he could be imagining it, a
lessening of tension in her shoulders. Then her focus was
back to the boy.

The manic pace around Bourey finally eased and Aaron
saw Ella slip out of the ICU. Aaron signalled to his cameraman to stop filming and left the room.

They had enough to tell the story but they needed a face on camera.

He went in search of Dr Seng, wanting to check the sensitivity of the case and get suggestions for the best interviewee.

Dr Seng listened, nodded, contemplated. Undertook to talk to Bourey's family to ascertain their willingness to have the case featured. 'For the interview, I recommend Ella,' he said. 'She knows enough about malaria to write a textbook, and she is highly articulate.'

Aaron suspected the ultra-private Ella would rather eat a plate of tarantulas and was on the verge of suggesting perhaps a doctor when Ella walked past.

Dr Seng beckoned her over, asked for her participation and smiled genially at them before hurrying away.

Ella looked at Aaron coolly. 'Happy to help, of course,' she said.

They found a spot where they were out of the way of traffic but with a view through the ICU windows. The cameraman opted for handheld, to give a sense of intimacy.

Great—intimacy.

'Well?' she asked, clearly anxious to get it done.

'Don't you want to…?' He waved a hand at his hair. At his face.

'What's wrong with the way I look?'

'Nothing. It's just that most people—'

'What's more important, how my hair looks or that little boy?'

'Fine,' Aaron said. 'Tell me about the case.'

'This is a two-year-old child, suffering from cerebral falciparum malaria. Blood films showed parasitaemia—'

'Parasitaemia?'

'It means the number of parasites in his blood. His level is twenty-two per cent. That is high and very serious. Hence the IV artesunate—a particular drug we use for this strain—which we'll administer for twenty-four hours. After that, we'll switch to oral artemisinin-based combination therapy—ACT for short. It's the current drug regime for falciparum. We'll be monitoring his parasitaemia, and we'd expect to see the levels drop relatively quickly.'

She sounded smart and competent and in control.

'And if they don't drop?' Aaron asked.

Her forehead creased. 'Then we've got a problem. It will indicate drug resistance. This region is the first in the world to show signs of resistance to ACTs, which used to kill the parasites in forty-eight hours and now take up to ninety-six hours. It was the same for previous treatments like cloroquine, which is now practically useless—we're like the epicentre for drug resistance here.'

'How does it happen, the resistance?'

'People take just enough of the course to feel better. Or the medicines they buy over the counter are substandard, or counterfeit, with only a tiny fraction of the effective drug in it. Or they are sold only a fraction of the course. Often the writing on the packet is in a different language, so people don't know what they're selling, or buying. And here we have highly mobile workers crossing the borders—in and out of Thailand, for example. So resistant strains are carried in and out with them. The problem is there's no new miracle drug on the horizon, so if we don't address the resistance issue…' She held out her hands, shrugged. Perfection for the camera. 'Trouble. And if the resistance eventually gets exported to Africa—as history suggests it will—it will be catastrophic. Around three thousand children die of malaria every day in sub-Saharan Africa, which is why this is a critical issue.'

He waited. Letting the camera stay on her face, letting

the statistic sink in. 'Back to this particular case. What happens now?'

'Continuous clinical observation and measuring what's happening with his blood, his electrolytes. I could give you a range of medical jargon but basically this is a critically ill child. We hope his organs won't fail. We hope he doesn't suffer any lifelong mental disabilities from the pressure on his brain. But, first, we hope he survives.'

A forlorn hope, as it turned out.

One minute they had been working to save Bourey's life, preparing for a whole-blood transfusion to lower the concentration of parasites in Bourey's blood and treat his anaemia. The next, Ella was unhooking him from the medical paraphernalia that had defined his last hours.

She left the ICU and her eyes started to sting. She stopped, wiped a finger under one eye, looked down at it. Wet. She was crying. And what was left of the numbness—one year's worth of carefully manufactured numbness—simply fell away.

She heard something and looked up. She saw Aaron, and tried to pull herself together. But her body had started to shake, and she simply had no reserves of strength left to pretend everything was all right.

A sobbing sort of gasp escaped her, a millisecond before she could put her hand over her mouth to stop it. Her brain and her heart and her body seemed to be out of synch. Her limbs couldn't seem to do what she was urging them to do. So the horrible gasp was followed by a stumble as she tried to turn away. She didn't want Aaron to see her like this. Didn't want anybody to see her, but especially not Aaron. He knew her sister. He might tell her sister. Her sister couldn't know that she was utterly, utterly desolate.

'I'm fine,' she said, as she felt his hand on her shoulder, steadying her.

Aaron withdrew his hand. 'You don't look fine,' he said.

Ella shook her head, unable to speak. She took one unsteady step. Two. Stopped. The unreleased sobs were aching in her chest. Crushing and awful. She had to get out of the hospital.

She felt Aaron's hand on her shoulder again and found she couldn't move. Just couldn't force her feet in the direction she wanted to go.

Aaron put his arm around her, guiding her with quick, purposeful strides out of the hospital, into the suffocating heat, steering her towards and then behind a clump of thick foliage so they were out of sight.

Ella opened her mouth to tell him, again, that she was fine, but... 'I'm sorry,' she gasped instead. 'I can't— Like Sann. My Sann. Help me, help me.'

He pulled her into his arms and held on. 'I will. I will, Ella. Tell me how. Just tell me.'

'He died. He died. I c-c-couldn't stop it.'

Aaron hugged her close. Silence. He seemed to know there was nothing to say.

Ella didn't know how long she stood there, in Aaron James's arms, as the tears gradually slowed. It was comforting, to be held like this. No words. Just touch. She didn't move, even when the crying stopped.

Until he turned her face up to his. And there was something in his eyes, something serious and concerned.

A look that reminded her Aaron James could not be a shoulder to cry on. He was too...close, somehow. She didn't want anyone to be close to her. Couldn't risk it.

Ella wrenched herself out of his arms. Gave a small, self-conscious hunch of one shoulder. 'It shouldn't upset me any more, I know. But sometimes...' She shoved a lank lock of hair behind her ear. 'Usually you think if they had just got to us faster…they are so poor, you see, that they wait, and hope, and maybe try other things. Because it is expensive for them, the trip to the hospital, even though the treatment is free. But in this case I think…I think nothing would have made any difference… And I…I hate it when I can't make a difference.'

She rubbed her tired hands over her face. 'Usually when I feel like this I donate blood. It reminds me that things that cost me nothing can help someone. And because the hospital always needs so much blood. But I can't even do that now because it's too soon after the dengue. So I've got nothing. Useless.'

'I'll donate blood for you,' Aaron said immediately.

She tried to smile. 'You're doing something important already—the documentary. And I didn't mind doing that interview, you know. I'd do anything.'

She started to move away, but he put his hand on her arm, stopping her.

'So, Ella. Who's Sann?'

Ella felt her eyes start to fill again. Through sheer will power she stopped the tears from spilling out. He touched her, very gently, his hand on her hair, her cheek, and it melted something. 'He was the child I wanted to adopt,' she said. And somehow it was a relief to share this. 'Here in Cambodia. A patient, an orphan, two years old. I went home to find out what I had to do, and while I was gone he…he died. Malaria.'

'And you blame yourself,' he said softly. 'Because you weren't there. Because you couldn't save him. And I suppose you're working with children in Cambodia, which must torture you, as a kind of penance.'

'I don't know.' She covered her face in her hands for one long moment. Shuddered out a breath. 'Sorry—it's not something I talk about.' Her hands dropped and she looked at him, drained of all emotion. 'I'm asking you not to mention it to Tina. She never knew about Sann. And there's no point telling her. She doesn't need to know about this episode today either. Can I trust you not to say anything?'

'You can trust me. But, Ella, you're making a mistake. This is not the way to—'

'Thank you,' she said abruptly, not wanting to hear advice she couldn't bear to take. 'The rain...it's that time of the day. And I can feel it coming. Smell it.'

'So? What's new?'

'I'd better get back.'

'Wait,' he called.

But Ella was running for the hospital.

She reached the roof overhang as the heavens opened. Looked back at Aaron, who hadn't moved, hadn't taken even one step towards shelter. He didn't seem to care that the gushing water was plastering his clothes to his skin.

He was watching her with an intensity that scared her.

Ella shivered in the damp heat and then forced her eyes away.

The next day Helen told Ella that Aaron James had been in and donated blood.

For her. He'd done it for her.

But she looked at Helen as though she couldn't care less. The following day, when Helen reported that Aaron had left for his visit to the villages, same deal. But she was relieved.

She hoped Aaron would be so busy that any thought of her little breakdown would be wiped out of his mind.

Meanwhile, she would be trying to forget the way Aaron had looked at her—like he understood her, like he knew how broken she was. Trying to forget *him*.

There was only one problem with that: Kiri.

Because Kiri and Aaron came as a set.

And Ella couldn't stop thinking, worrying, about Kiri. Knowing that the cause was her distress over Bourey's death didn't change the fact that she had a sense of dread about Kiri's health that seemed tied to Aaron's absence.

Which just went to prove she was unhinged!

Kiri has a nanny to look after him. It's none of your business, Ella.

She repeated this mantra to herself over and over.

But the nagging fear kept tap-tapping at her nerves as she willed the time to pass quickly until Aaron could whisk his son home to safety.

When she heard Helen calling her name frantically two days after Aaron had left, her heart started jackhammering.

'What?' Ella asked, hurrying towards Helen. But she knew. *Knew.*

'It's Aaron James. Or rather his son. He's been taken to the Khmer International Hospital. Abdominal pains. Persistent fever. Retro-orbital pain. Vomiting. They suspect dengue fever.'

Ella felt the rush in her veins, the panic.

'They can't get hold of Aaron,' Helen said. 'So the nanny asked them to call us because she knows he's been filming here. I thought you should know straight away, because— Well, the family connection. Ella, what if something goes wrong and we can't reach Aaron?'

Ella didn't bother to answer. She simply ran.

Aaron had been unsettled during his time in the monsoonal rainforest.

Not that it hadn't been intriguing—the medical challenges the people faced.

And confronting—the history of the area, which had

been a Khmer Rouge stronghold, with regular sightings of people with missing limbs, courtesy of landmines, to prove it.

And humbling—that people so poor, so constantly ill, should face life with such stoic grace.

And beautiful, even with the daily downpours—with the lush, virgin forest moist enough to suck at you, and vegetation so thick you had the feeling that if you stood still for half an hour, vines would start growing over you, anchoring you to the boggy earth.

But!

His mobile phone was bothering him. He'd never been out of contact with Kiri before, but since day two, when they'd headed for the most remote villages that were nothing more than smatterings of bamboo huts on rickety stilts, he'd had trouble with his phone.

He found himself wishing he'd told Jenny to contact Ella if anything went wrong. But Jenny, not being psychic, would never guess that was what Aaron would want her to do—not when she'd never heard Ella's name come out of his mouth. Because he'd been so stupidly determined *not* to talk about Ella, in a misguided attempt to banish her from his head. And what an epic fail *that* had been, because she was still in his head. Worse than ever.

He'd hoped being away from the hospital would cure it. Not looking likely, though.

Every time he saw someone with a blown-off limb, or watched a health worker touch a malnourished child or check an HIV patient, he remembered Ella's words at the wedding reception. *I've seen the damage landmines can do. Had children with AIDS, with malnutrition, die in my arms.* He hadn't understood how she could sound so prosaic but now, seeing the endless stream of injuries, illness, poverty, he did.

And anything to do with malaria—well, how could he not think of her, and that searing grief?

The malaria screening process in the villages was simple, effective. Each person was registered in a book. *Ella, in the outpatient department, recording patient details.*

They were checked for symptoms—simple things like temperature, spleen enlargement. *Ella's hands touching children on the ward.*

Symptomatic people went on to the rapid diagnostic test. Fingertip wiped, dried. Squeeze the finger gently, jab quickly with a lancet. Wipe the first drop, collect another drop with a pipette. Drop it into the tiny well on the test strip. Add buffer in the designated spot. Wait fifteen minutes for the stripes to appear. *Ella, soothing children as their blood was siphoned off at the hospital.*

Aaron helped distribute insecticide-impregnated mosquito nets—a wonderfully simple method of protecting against malaria and given out free. *Ella, blocking him out so easily just by tugging her bed net closed.*

Arrrggghhh.

But relief was almost at hand. One last interview for the documentary and he would be heading back to Kiri. Jenny would have already packed for the trip home to Sydney. Ella would be out of his sight, out of his reach, out of his life once they left Cambodia.

Just one interview to go.

He listened closely as the village volunteer's comments were translated into English. There were three thousand volunteers throughout Cambodia, covering every village more than five kilometres from a health centre, with people's homes doubling as pop-up clinics. Medication was given free, and would be swallowed in front of the volunteers to make sure the entire course was taken. People diagnosed with malaria would not only have blood tested on day one but also on day three to assess the effectiveness of the drug treatment. *Ella, explaining drug resistance. Mentioning so casually that she'd had malaria twice.*

Half an hour later, with the filming wrapped up, they were in the jeep.

Twenty minutes after that his phone beeped. Beeped, beeped, beeped. Beeped.

He listened with the phone tight to one ear, fingers jammed in the other to block other sounds.

Felt the cold sweat of terror.

If he hadn't been sitting, his legs would have collapsed beneath him.

Kiri. Dengue haemorrhagic fever. His small, gentle, loving son was in pain and he wasn't there to look after him.

His fault. All his. He'd brought Kiri to Cambodia in the middle of an outbreak. Left him while he'd traipsed off to film in the boondocks, thinking that was the safer option.

He listened to the messages again. One after the other. Progress reports from the hospital—calm, matter-of-fact, professional, reassuring. Jenny—at first panicked, tearful. And then calmer each time, reassured by one of the nurses. Rebecca frantic but then, somehow, also calmer, mentioning an excellent nurse.

Three times he'd started to call the Children's Community Friendship Hospital to talk to Ella, wanting her advice, her reassurance, her skills to be focused on Kiri. Three times he'd stopped himself—he *had* expert advice, from Kiri's doctor and a tropical diseases specialist in Sydney he'd called.

And Ella had made it clear she wanted nothing to do with him.

And his son wasn't Ella's problem. Couldn't be her problem.

He wouldn't, couldn't let her mean that much.

* * *

The hospital where Kiri had been taken was like a five-star hotel compared with where Ella worked, and Kiri had his own room.

Ella knew the hospital had an excellent reputation; once she'd satisfied herself that Kiri was getting the care and attention he needed, she intended to slide into the background and leave everyone to it.

There was no reason for her to be the one palpating Kiri's abdomen to see if his liver was enlarged, while waiting to see if Kiri's blood test results supported the dengue diagnosis. Hmm, it was a little tender. But that wasn't a crisis and she didn't need to do anything *else* herself.

The blood tests came back, with the dengue virus detected. Plus a low white cell count, low platelets and high haematocrit—the measurement of the percentage of red blood cells to the total blood volume—which could indicate potential plasma leakage. Serious, but, as long as you knew what you were dealing with, treatable. He was still drinking, there were no signs of respiratory distress. So far, so good.

Hands off, Ella, leave it to the staff.

But… There was no problem in asking for a truckle to be set up for her in Kiri's room, was there? At her hospital, the kids' families always stayed with them for the duration.

So all right, she wasn't family, but his family wasn't here. And kids liked to have people they knew with them. And Ella knew Kiri. Plus, she was making it easier for his nanny to take a break.

She'd got Aaron's cell number from Jenny, and was constantly on the verge of calling him. Only the thought of how many panicked messages he already had waiting for him stopped her. And the tiny suspicion that Aaron would tell her she wasn't needed, which she didn't want to hear—and she hoped that didn't mean she was becoming obsessive about his son.

By the time she'd started haranguing the doctors for updated blood test results, double-checking the nurses' perfect records of Kiri's urine output, heart and respiratory rates, and blood pressure, taking over the task of sponging Kiri down to lower his fever and cajoling him into drinking water and juice to ensure he didn't get dehydrated, she realised she was a step *beyond* obsessive.

It wasn't like she didn't have enough to do at her own place of work, but she couldn't seem to stop herself standing watch over Kiri James like some kind of sentinel—even though dashing between two hospitals was running her ragged.

Kiri's fever subsided on his third day in hospital—but Ella knew better than to assume that meant he was better because often that heralded a critical period. The blood tests with the dropping platelet levels, sharply rising white cells and decreasing haematocrit certainly weren't indicating recovery.

And, suddenly, everything started to go wrong.

Kiri grew increasingly restless and stopped drinking, and Ella went into hyper-vigilant mode.

His breathing became too rapid. His pulse too fast. Even more worryingly, his urine output dropped down to practically nothing.

Ella checked his capillary refill time, pressing on the underside of Kiri's heel and timing how long it took to go from blanched to normal: more than six seconds, when it should only take three.

His abdomen was distended, which indicated ascites—an accumulation of fluid in the abdominal cavity. 'I'm just going to feel your tummy, Kiri,' she said, and pressed as gently as she could.

He cried out. 'Hurts, Ella.'

'I'm so sorry, darling,' she said, knowing they needed to quickly determine the severity of plasma leakage. 'You need some tests, I'm afraid, so I'm going to call your nurse.'

Ella spoke to the nurse, who raced for the doctor, who ordered an abdominal ultrasound to confirm the degree of ascites and a chest X-ray to determine pleural effusion, which would lead to respiratory distress.

'As you know, Ella,' the doctor explained, drawing her outside, 'a critical amount of plasma leakage will indicate he's going into shock, so we're moving Kiri to the ICU, where we can monitor him. We'll be starting him on intravenous rehydration. We'd expect a fairly rapid improvement, in which case we'll progressively reduce the IV fluids, or they could make the situation worse. No improvement and a significant decrease in haematocrit could suggest internal bleeding, and at that stage we'd look at a blood transfusion. But we're nowhere near that stage so no need to worry. I'll call his father now.'

'Aaron's phone's not working,' Ella said mechanically.

'It is now. He called to tell us he's on his way. I know you're a close friend of the family, so...'

But Ella had stopped listening. She nodded. Murmured a word here and there. Took nothing in.

The doctor patted her arm and left. The orderly would be arriving to take Kiri to ICU. This was it. Over. She wasn't needed any more. And she knew, really, that she had never been needed—the hospital had always had everything under control.

Ella braced herself and went to Kiri's bedside. 'Well,

young man,' she said cheerfully, 'you're going somewhere special—ICU.'

'I see you too.'

Ella felt such a rush of love, it almost choked her. 'Hmm. In a way that's exactly what it is. It's where the doctors can see you every minute, until nobody has to poke you in the tummy any more. Okay?'

'Are you coming?'

'No, darling. Someone better is coming. The best surprise. Can you guess who?'

Kiri's eyes lit up. 'Dad?'

'Yep,' she said, and leaned over to kiss him.

The door opened. The orderly. 'And they'll be putting a special tube into you here,' she said, touching his wrist. 'It's superhero juice, so you're going to look like Superman soon. Lucky you!'

A moment later Ella was alone, gathering her few possessions.

Back to reality, she told herself. Devoting her time to where it was really needed, rather than wasting it playing out some mother fantasy.

Ella felt the tears on her cheeks. Wiped them away. Pulled herself together.

Walked super-slowly out of the room.

Ella was the first person he saw.

Aaron was sweaty, frantic. Racing into the hospital. And there she was, exiting. Cool. Remote.

He stopped.

If Ella is here, Kiri will be all right. The thought darted into his head without permission. The relief was immediate, almost overwhelming.

A split second later it all fell into place: Ella was the nurse who had spoken to Rebecca. His two worlds colliding. Ex-wife and mother of his child connecting with the woman he wanted to sleep with.

No-go zone.

He reached Ella in three, unthinking strides. 'It was you, wasn't it?'

His sudden appearance before her startled her. But she looked at him steadily enough, with her wedding face on. 'What was me?'

'You spoke to Rebecca.'

'Yes. Jenny handed me the phone. I wasn't going to hang up on a worried parent. I had no *reason* to hang up on her.'

'What did you tell her?'

She raised an eyebrow at him. 'That you and I were having a torrid affair.'

She looked at him, waiting for something.

He looked back—blank.

'Seriously?' she demanded. '*Seriously?*' She shook her head in disgust. 'I told her what I knew about dengue fever, you idiot. That it was a complex illness, and things did go wrong—but that it was relatively simple to treat. I shared my own experience so that she understood. I said that early detection followed by admission to a good hospital almost guaranteed a positive outcome. I explained that, more than anything else, it was a matter of getting the fluid intake right and treating complications as they arose.'

'Oh. I—I don't—'

'I told her Kiri was handling everything bravely enough to break your heart, and that Jenny and I were taking shifts to make sure he had someone familiar with him at all times. I didn't ask her why she wasn't hotfooting it out here, despite the fact that her son was in a lot of pain, with his joints aching and his muscles screaming, and asking for her, for you, constantly.'

'I—'

'Not interested, Aaron.'

'But just—he's all right, isn't he? In ICU, right?'

A look. Dismissive. And then she did that slow walk away.

'Wait a minute!' he exploded.

But Ella only waved an imperious hand—not even bothering to turn around to do it—and kept to her path.

CHAPTER SIX

WELL…IT BOTHERED Aaron.

Ella's saunter off as though he wasn't even worth talking to.

Followed by Jenny's report of Ella's tireless care: that Ella had begged and badgered the staff and hadn't cared about anyone but his son; the fact that she of all people had been the only one capable of reassuring Rebecca.

He had to keep things simple.

But how simple could it be, when he *knew* Ella would be visiting Kiri—and that when she did, he would have to tell her that, all things considered, she would have to stay away from his son.

Two days. The day Kiri got out of ICU. That's how long it took her.

Aaron had left Kiri for fifteen minutes to grab something to eat, and she was there when he got back to Kiri's room, as though she'd timed it to coincide with his absence.

It wrenched him to see the look on Ella's face as she smoothed Kiri's spiky black hair back from his forehead. To experience again that strange combination of joy and terror that had hit him when he'd seen her coming out of the hospital.

He would *not* want her. He had enough on his plate.

And if Ella thought she got to pick and choose when their lives could intersect and when they couldn't—well, no! That was all. No.

She looked up. Defensive. Defiant. *Anxious?*

And he felt like he was being unfair.

And he was *never* unfair.

No wonder she made him so mad. She was changing his entire personality, and not for the better.

After a long, staring moment Ella turned back to Kiri. 'I'll see you a little later, Kiri. Okay?' And then she walked slowly away.

Kiri blinked at his father sleepily, then smiled. 'Where's Ella gone?'

'Back to her hospital. They need her there now. And you've got me.'

Kiri nodded.

He was out of danger, but he looked so tired. 'Are you okay, Kiri? What do you need?'

'Nothing. My head was hurting. And my tummy. And my legs. But Ella fixed me.'

'That's good. But I'm here now.'

'And I was hot. Ella cooled me down.'

'How did she do that?'

'With water and a towel.'

'I can do that for you, sport.'

'I'm not hot any more.' Kiri closed his eyes for a long moment, then blinked them open again and held out his skinny forearm, showing off the small sticking plaster. 'Look,' he said.

'You were on a drip, I know.'

'Superhero juice, Ella said.'

'To get you better.'

A few minutes more passed. 'Dad?'

'What is it, sport?'

'Where's Ella?'

Aaron bit back a sigh. 'She has a lot of people to look after. I'm back now. And Mum will be coming soon.'

'Mum's coming?'

'Yes, she'll be here soon.'

Kiri's eyes drifted shut.

The elation at knowing Kiri was out of danger was still with him. Even the prospect of calling Rebecca again to reinforce his demand that she get her butt on a plane didn't daunt him—although he hoped that, this time, Rebecca wouldn't be off her face.

Of course, breaking the other news to her—that he and Kiri would be heading to LA for his audition after Kiri's convalescence, and then straight on to London—might set off a whole new word of pain. He knew Rebecca was going to hate the confirmation that Aaron had landed both the audition and a plum role in Brand's film, because she resented every bit of career success that came his way.

He suspected she would try to guilt him into leaving Kiri in Sydney with her, just to punish him—for Kiri's illness and for the role in Brand's film—but that wasn't going to happen. Until Rebecca got herself clean, where he went, Kiri went.

So he would call Rebecca, get her travel arrangements under way so she could spend time with Kiri while he got his strength back, and tell her that London was all systems go.

Then he would have only two things to worry about: Kiri's convalescence; and figuring out how to forget Ella Reynolds and the way she had looked at his son.

Rebecca wasn't coming.

It was a shock that she would forego spending time with Kiri, knowing she wouldn't see him for months.

Aaron was trying to find the right words to say to Kiri and had been tiptoeing around the subject for a while.

The last thing he needed was Ella breezing in—triggering that aggravating, inexplicable and entirely inappropriate sense of relief.

Not that she spared Aaron as much as a look.

'You don't need to tell me how you are today,' she said to Kiri, leaning down to kiss his forehead. 'Because you look like a superhero. I guess you ate your dinner last night! And are you weeing? Oops—am I allowed to say that in front of Dad?'

Kiri giggled, and said, 'Yes,' and Ella gave his son that blinding smile that was so gut-churningly amazing.

She looked beautiful. Wearing a plain, white cotton dress and flat leather tie-up sandals, toting an oversized canvas bag—nothing special about any of it. But she was so…lovely.

She presented Kiri with a delicately carved wooden dragonfly she'd bought for him at the local market and showed him how to balance it on a fingertip.

Then Kiri asked her about the chicken game she'd told him about on a previous visit.

'Ah—you mean Chab Kon Kleng. Okay. Well they start by picking the strongest one—that would be you, Kiri—to be the hen.'

'But I'm a boy.'

'The rooster, then. And you're like your dad—you're going to defend your kids. And all your little chickens are hiding behind you, and the person who is the crow has to try and catch them, while everyone sings a special song. And, no, I'm not singing it. I'm a terrible singer, and my Khmer is not so good.'

'You asked me something about *ch'heu*. That's Khmer.'

'Yes—I was asking if you were in pain and forgot you were a little Aussie boy.'

'I'm Cambodian too.'

'Yes, you are. Lucky you,' Ella said softly.

Aaron was intrigued at this side of Ella. Sweet, animated, fun.

She glanced at him—finally—and he was surprised to see a faint blush creep into her cheeks.

She grabbed the chart from the end of Kiri's bed, scanning quickly. 'You will be out of here in no time if you keep this up.' Another one of those smiles. 'Anyway, I just wanted to call in and say hello today, but I'll stay longer next time.'

'Next time,' Kiri piped up, 'you'll see Mum. She's coming.'

'Hey—that's great,' she replied.

Aaron sucked in a quick, silent breath. Okay, this was the moment to tell Kiri that Rebecca wasn't coming, and to tell Ella that she wasn't welcome. 'Er…' *Brilliant start.*

Two pairs of eyes focused on him. Curious. Waiting.

Aaron perched on the side of Kiri's bed. 'Mate,' he said, 'I'm afraid Mum still can't leave home, so we're going to have to do without her.'

Kiri stared at him, taking in the news in his calm way.

'But she knows you're almost better, and so you'll forgive her,' Aaron continued. 'And I have to give you a kiss and hug from her—yuckerama.'

Kiri giggled then. 'You always kiss and hug me.'

'Then I guess I can squeeze in an extra when nobody's looking.'

'Okay.'

'Right,' Ella said cheerily. 'You'd better get yourself out of here, young man, so you can get home to Mom. You know what that means—eat, drink, do what the doctor tells you. Now, I'm sure you and Dad have lots to plan so I'll see you later.'

That smile at Kiri.

The usual smile—the one minus the eye glow—for him.

And she was gone before Aaron could gather his thoughts.

See you later? No, she would *not*.

With a quick 'Back soon' to Kiri, Aaron ran after her.

'Ella, wait.'

Ella stopped, stiffened, turned.

'Can we grab a coffee?'

Ella thought about saying no. She didn't want to feel that uncomfortable mix of guilt and attraction he seemed to bring out in her. But a 'no' would be an admission that he had some kind of power over her, and that would never do. So she nodded and walked beside him to the hospital café, and sat in silence until their coffee was on the table in front of them.

'I wanted to explain. About Rebecca.' He was stirring one sugar into his coffee about ten times longer than he needed to.

'No need,' she said.

'It's just she had an audition, and because Kiri was out of danger…'

She nodded. 'And he'd probably be ready to go home by the time she arrived anyway…'

Aaron looked morosely at the contents in his cup, and Ella felt an unwelcome stab of sympathy.

'Actually, the audition wasn't the main issue,' he said. 'I know the director. He would have held off for her.'

Ella waited while he gave his coffee another unnecessary stir.

'Has Tina told you about Rebecca?' he asked, looking across at her.

'Told me what?'

'About her drug problem?'

'Ah. No. I didn't know. I'm sorry.' That explained the not-really-divorced divorce; Sir Galahad wasn't the type to cut and run in an untenable situation.

'Things are…complicated,' he said. 'Very.'

'I'm sure.'

'It doesn't mean Rebecca isn't anxious about Kiri. I mean, she's his mother, and she loves him.'

'I understand. But he should recover quickly now. At this stage—the recovery phase—all those fluids that leaked out of his capillaries are simply being reabsorbed by his body. Like a wave—flooding, receding, balancing. But he'll be tired for a while. And there may be a rash. Red and itchy, with white centres. Don't freak out about it. Okay?'

Silence. Another stir of the coffee.

'Are you going to drink that, or are you just going to stir it to death?' Ella asked, and then it hit her: this was not really about Rebecca. 'Or…do you want to just tell me what this all has to do with me?'

Aaron looked at her. Kind of determined and apologetic at the same time. 'It's just…he's very attached to you. *Too* attached to you. I don't know how, in such a short time, but he is.'

'It's an occupational hazard for doctors and nurses.'

'No, Ella. It's you. And that makes things more complicated, given he won't be seeing you again once we leave the hospital. I—I don't want him to miss you.'

'Ahhh,' she said, and pushed her cup away. 'I see. Things are complicated, and he already has a mother, so stay away, Ella.'

'It's just the flip side of what you said to me—that you don't like saying goodbye to a child when a relationship goes south.'

'We don't have a relationship. And the fact you're a father didn't seem to bother you when you were kissing me, as long as we weren't *in* a "relationship".'

'Don't be naïve, Ella. It's one thing for us to have sex. It's another when there are two of us sitting together at my son's bedside.'

The hurt took her by surprise. 'So let me get this straight—you're happy to sleep with me, but you don't want me anywhere near your son?'

'We haven't slept together.'

'That's right—we haven't. And calm yourself, we won't. But the principle is still there: it would be *okay* for you to have sex with me, but because you *want* to have sex with me, it's *not* okay for me to be anywhere near your son. And don't throw back at me what I said about not wanting to get mixed up with a man with a kid—which would be my problem to deal with, not yours. Or tell me it's to protect him from the pain of missing me either. Because this is about *you*. This is because *you're* not comfortable around me. I'd go so far as to say you disapprove of me.'

'I don't know what to think of you.' He dragged a hand through his hair. 'One minute you're letting a drunk guy in a bar paw you and the next you're hovering like a guardian angel over sick kids. One minute you're a sarcastic pain in the butt, and the next you're crying like your heart's breaking. Do I approve of you? I don't even know. It's too hard to know you, Ella. Too hard.'

'And you're a saint by comparison, are you? No little flaws or contradictions in your character? So how do you explain your attraction to someone like me?'

'I don't explain it. I can't. That's the problem.' He

stopped, closed his eyes for a fraught moment. 'Look, I've got Rebecca to worry about. And Kiri to shield from all that's going on with her. That's why I told you I couldn't develop a relationship with you. To make it cl—'

'I told *you* I didn't want one. Or are you too arrogant to believe that?'

'Wake up, Ella. If Kiri has developed an affection for you, that means we're *in* a relationship. Which would be fine if I didn't—'

'Oh, shut up and stir your coffee! This is no grand passion we're having.' Ella was almost throbbing with rage, made worse by having to keep her voice low. A nice yelling match would have suited her right now but you didn't yell at people in Cambodia.

She leaned across the table. 'Understand this: I'm not interested in you. I'm not here, after having worked a very long day, to see you. I'm here to see Kiri, who was in this hospital parentless. No father. No mother. Just a nanny. And me. Holding his hand while they drew his blood for tests. Coaxing him to drink. Trying to calm him when he vomited, when his stomach was hurting and there was no relief for the pain. Knowing his head was splitting and that paracetamol couldn't help enough. So scared he'd start bleeding that I was beside myself because what the hell were we going to do if he needed a transfusion and you weren't here? How dare you tell me after that to stay away from him, like I'm out to seduce you and spoil your peace and wreck your family?'

She could feel the tears ready to burst, and dashed a hand across her eyes.

He opened his mouth.

'Just shut *up*,' she said furiously. 'You know, I'm not overly modest about my assets, but I somehow think a fine upstanding man like you could resist making mad passionate love to a bottom feeder like me in front of Kiri, so I suggest you just get over yourself and stop projecting.'

'Projecting?'

'Yes—your guilty feelings on me! I have enough guilt of my own to contend with without you adding a chunky piece of antique furniture to the bonfire. It's not my fault your wife is a drug addict. It's not my fault you got a divorce. It's not my fault your son got dengue fever. It's not my fault you find me attractive, or a distraction, or whatever. I am not the cause or the catalyst or the star of your documentary, and I didn't ask you to lurk around hospital corners, watching me.'

She stood, pushing her chair back violently. 'I'm no saint, but I'm not a monster either.'

She headed for the door at a cracking pace, Aaron scrambling to catch up with her.

He didn't reach her until she was outside, around the corner from the hospital entrance.

'Wait just a minute,' he said, and spun her to face him.

'This conversation is over. Leave me *alone*,' she said, and jerked free, turned to walk off.

His hand shot out, grabbed her arm, spun her back. 'Oh, no, you don't,' he said, and looked as furious as she felt. 'You are not running off and pretending I'm the only one with a problem. Go on, lie to me—tell me you don't want me to touch you.'

He wrenched her up onto her toes and smacked her into his chest. Looked at her for one fierce, burning moment, and then kissed her as though he couldn't help himself.

In a desperate kind of scramble, her back ended up against the wall and he was plastered against her. He took her face between his hands, kissed her, long and hard. 'Ella,' he whispered against her lips. 'Ella. I know it's insane but when you're near me I can't help myself. Can't.'

Ella was tugging his shirt from his jeans, her hands sliding up his chest. 'Just touch me. Touch me!'

His thighs nudged hers apart and he was there, hard against her. She strained against him, ready, so ready, so—

Phone. Ringing. His.

They pulled apart, breathing hard. Looked at each other. Aaron wrenched the phone from his pocket. Rebecca.

The phone rang. Rang. Rang. Rang. Stopped.

And still Ella and Aaron stared at each other.

Ella swallowed. 'No matter what you think of me—or what I think of myself right now, which isn't much—I don't want to make things difficult. For you, for Kiri. Or for me.' She smoothed her hands down her dress, making sure everything was in order. 'So you win. I'll stay away.'

'Maybe there's another way to—'

Ella cut him off. 'No. We've both got enough drama in our lives without making a fleeting attraction into a Shakespearean tragedy. I just…' Pause. Another swallow. 'I don't want him to think I don't care about him. Because he might think that, when I don't come back.'

Aaron pushed a lock of her hair behind her ear. It was a gentle gesture that had her ducking away. 'That's not helping,' she said.

'Don't think I don't know how lucky I am to have had you watching over Kiri. He knows and I know that you care about him. And I know how much, after Sann—'

'Don't you dare,' she hissed. 'I should never have told you. I regret it more than I can say. So we'll make a deal, shall we? I'll stay away and you don't ever, *ever* mention Sann again, not to anyone. I don't need or want you to feel sorry for me. I don't need or want *you*. So let's focus on a win-win. You go home. I'll go…wherever. And we'll forget we ever met.'

Ella walked away, but it was harder than it had ever been to slow her steps.

The sooner Aaron James was back in Sydney the better.

She was putting Sydney at number three thousand and one on her list of holiday destinations—right after Afghanistan.

CHAPTER SEVEN

'ELLA!'

Tina was staring at her. Surprised, delighted. 'Oh, come in. Come in! I'm so glad you're here. I was wondering when you'd use that ticket. Brand,' she called over her shoulder.

Ella cast appreciative eyes over the grand tiled entrance hall of her sister's Georgian townhouse. 'Nice one, Mrs. McIntyre,' she said.

Tina laughed. 'Yes, "nice".'

'So I'm thinking space isn't a problem.'

'We have *oodles* of it. In fact, we have other g—. Oh, here's Brand. Brand, Ella's here.'

'Yes, so I see. Welcome,' Brand said, pulling Tina backwards against his chest and circling her with his arms.

Ella looked at Brand's possessive hands on Tina's swollen belly. In about a month she would be an aunt. She was happy for her sister, happy she'd found such profound love. But looking at this burgeoning family made her heart ache with the memory of what she'd lost, what she might never have.

Not that Ella remembered the love between her and Javier being the deep, absorbing glow that Tina and Brand shared. It had been giddier. A rush of feeling captured in a handful of memories. That first dazzling sight of him

outside a makeshift hospital tent in Somalia. Their first
tentative kiss. The sticky clumsiness of the first and only
time they'd made love—the night before the malaria had
hit her; two nights before he was taken.

Would it have grown into the special bond Tina and
Brand had? Or burned itself out?

Standing in this hallway, she had never felt so unsure,
so…empty. And so envious she was ashamed of herself.
Maybe it had been a mistake to come. 'If you'll show me
where to dump my stuff, I'll get out of your hair for a
couple of hours.'

Tina looked dismayed. 'But I *want* you in my hair.'

'I'm catching up with someone.'

'Who? And where?'

Ella raised her eyebrows.

Tina made an exasperated sound. 'Oh, don't get all
frosty.'

Ella rolled her eyes. 'She's a nurse, living in Ham-
mersmith. We're meeting at a pub called the Hare and
something. Harp? Carp? Does it matter? Can I go? Please,
please, pretty please?'

Tina disentangled herself from her laughing husband's
arms. 'All right, you two, give it a rest,' she said. 'Brand—
show Ella her room. Then, Ella, go ahead and run away.
But I don't expect to have to ambush you every time I
want to talk to you.'

Ella kissed Tina's cheek. 'I promise to bore you rigid
with tales of saline drips and bandage supplies and oxygen masks. By the time I get to the bedpan stories, you'll
be begging me to go out.'

London in summer, what was there not to like? Aaron
thought as he bounded up the stairs to Brand's house with
Kiri on his back.

He went in search of Brand and Tina and found them in the kitchen, sitting at the table they used for informal family dining.

'Good news! We've found an apartment to rent,' he announced, swinging Kiri down to the floor.

Tina swooped on Kiri to kiss and tickle him, then settled him on the chair beside her with a glass of milk and a cookie. She bent an unhappy look on her husband. 'Why do all our house guests want to run away the minute they step foot in the place?'

'We've been underfoot for two weeks!' Aaron protested. 'And we're only moving down the street.'

'It's her sister,' Brand explained. 'Ella arrived today, stayed just long enough to drop her bag and ran off to some ill-named pub. Princess Tina is *not* amused.'

Aaron's heart stopped—at least that's what it felt like—and then jump-started violently. He imagined himself pale with shock, his eyes bugging out. He felt his hair follicles tingle. What had they said while he'd been sitting there stunned? What had he missed? He forced himself to take a breath, clear his mind, concentrate. Because the only coalescing thought in his head was that she was here. In London. In this house.

He'd thought he would never see her again. Hadn't wanted to see her again.

But she was here.

'…when we weren't really expecting her,' Tina said.

Huh? What? What had he missed while his brain had turned to mush?

'You know what she's like,' Brand said.

What? What's she like? Aaron demanded silently.

'What do you mean, what she's like?' Tina asked, sounding affronted.

Bless you, Tina.

'Independent. Very,' Brand supplied. 'She's used to looking after herself. And she's been in scarier places. Somehow I think she'll make it home tonight just fine.'

'Yes, but what time? And she hasn't even told me how long she's staying. Mum and Dad are going to want a report. How can I get the goss if she runs away when she should be talking to me?'

Brand gave her a warning look. 'If you fuss, she *will* go.' He turned to Aaron, changing the subject. 'So, Aaron, when do you move in?'

'A week,' Aaron said, racking his brain for a way to get the conversation casually back to Ella. 'Is that all right? I mean, if your sister is here...' he looked back at Tina '...maybe Kiri and I should leave earlier.' He'd lost it, obviously, because as the words left his mouth he wanted to recall them. 'We can easily move to a hotel.' Nope. That wasn't working for him either.

He caught himself rubbing his chest, over his heart. Realised it wasn't the first time he'd thought of Ella and done that.

'No way—you're not going any earlier than you have to,' Tina said immediately, and Aaron did the mental equivalent of swooning with relief.

And that really hit home.

The problem wasn't that he didn't want to see Ella—it was that he did.

On his third trip downstairs that night, Aaron faced the fact that he was hovering. He hadn't really come down for a glass of water. Or a book. Or a midnight snack.

Barefoot, rumpled, and edgy, he had come down looking for Ella.

On his fourth trip he gave up any pretence and took a seat in the room that opened off the dimly lit hall—a library-cum-family room. From there he could hear the front door open and yet be hidden. He turned on only one lamp; she wouldn't even know he was there, if he chose the sensible option and stayed hidden when the moment came.

He was, quite simply, beside himself.

Aaron helped himself to a Scotch, neat, while he waited. His blood pressure must have been skyrocketing, because his heart had been thumping away at double speed all day.

And he had *excellent* blood pressure that *never* sky-rocketed.

He knew precisely how long he'd been waiting—an hour and thirteen minutes—when he heard it.

Key hitting the lock. Lock clicking. Door opening.

A step on the tiled floor. He took a deep breath. Tried—failed—to steady his nerves. Heard the door close. Then nothing. No footsteps. A long moment passed. And then another sound. Something slumping against the wall or the door or the floor.

Was she hurt? Had she fallen?

Another sound. A sort of hiccup that wasn't a hiccup. A hitched breath.

He got to his feet and walked slowly to the door. Pushed it open silently. How had he ever thought he might sit in here and *not* go to her? And then he saw her and almost gasped! He was so monumentally unprepared for the punch of lust that hit him as he peered out like a thief.

She was sitting on the floor. Back against the door, knees up with elbows on them, hands jammed against her mouth. He could have sworn she was crying but there were no tears.

He saw the complete stillness that came into her as she realised someone was there.

And then she looked up.

CHAPTER EIGHT

AARON WALKED SLOWLY towards Ella. She was wearing a dark green skirt that had fallen up her thighs. A crumpled white top with a drawstring neckline. Leather slide-on sandals. Her hair was in loose waves, long, hanging over her shoulders—he'd never seen it loose before.

He felt a tense throb of some emotion he couldn't name, didn't want to name, as he reached her. He stood looking down at her, dry-mouthed. 'Where have you been?' he asked.

'Why are you here?' she countered, the remembered huskiness of her voice scattering his thoughts for a moment.

The way her skirt was draping at the top of her thighs was driving him insane. *Concentrate.* 'Here? I've been staying here. I'm working here. In London, I mean. Brand's film.' He couldn't even swallow. 'Didn't they tell you?'

'No,' Ella said, sighing, and easily, gracefully, got to her feet. 'Well, that's just great. I guess you're going to expect me to move out now, so I don't corrupt Kiri—or you.'

'No. I don't want you to move out. We'll be leaving in a week, anyway.'

'Oh, that makes me feel *so* much better. I'm sure I can avoid doing anything too immoral for one lousy week.'

Her silky skirt had settled back where it was supposed

to be. It was short, so he could still see too much of her thighs. He jerked his gaze upwards and it collided with her breasts. He could make out the lace of her bra, some indistinguishable pale colour, under the white cotton of her top.

His skin had started to tighten and tingle, so he forced his eyes upwards again. Jammed his hands in his pockets as he caught the amused patience in her purple eyes.

'Why are you waiting up for me?' she asked.

He had no answer.

She sighed again—an exaggerated, world-weary sigh. 'What do you want, Aaron?'

'I want you,' he said. He couldn't quite believe he'd said it after everything that had gone on between them, but once it was out it seemed so easy. So clear. As though he hadn't spent agonising weeks telling himself she was the *last* thing he needed in his life and he'd been right to put the brakes on in Cambodia. 'I haven't stopped wanting you. Not for a second.'

Her eyebrows arched upwards. Even her eyebrows were sexy.

'I think we've been through this already, haven't we?' she asked softly, and started to move past him. 'One week—I'm sure you can resist me for that long, Sir Galahad.'

His hand shot out. He saw it move, faster than his brain was working. Watched his fingers grip her upper arm.

She turned to face him.

He didn't know what he intended to do next—but at least she wasn't looking amused any more.

She looked hard at him for a moment. And then she took his face between her hands and kissed him, fusing her mouth to his with forceful passion. She finished the kiss with one long lick against his mouth. Pulled back a tiny fraction, then seemed to change her mind and kissed him again. Pulled back. Stepped back. Looked him in the eye.

'Now what?' she asked, her breathing unsteady but her voice controlled. 'This is where you run away, isn't it? Because of Rebecca. Or Kiri. Or just because it's me.'

That strange other being still had control of him. It was the only explanation for the way he jerked her close, crushed his arms around her and kissed her. He broke the contact only for a second at a time. To breathe. He wished he didn't even have to stop for that. His hands were everywhere, couldn't settle. In her hair, on her back, gripping her bottom, running up her sides. And through it all he couldn't seem to stop kissing her.

He could hear her breathing labouring, like his. When his hands reached her breasts, felt the nipples jutting into his palms through two layers of clothing, he shuddered. He finally stopped kissing her, but kept his mouth on hers, still, reaching for control. 'Now what?' He repeated her question without moving his mouth from hers, after a brief struggle to remember what she'd asked. Kissed her again.

Ella wrapped her arms around his waist and he groaned. He looked down into her face. 'There doesn't seem to be much point in running away, because you're always there. So now, Ella, I get to have you.'

One long, fraught moment of limbo.

He didn't know what he'd do if she said no, he was so on fire for her.

But she didn't say no. She said, 'Okay. Let's be stupid, then, and get it done.'

Not exactly a passionate acquiescence, but he'd take it. Take her, any way he could get her.

He kissed her again, pulling her close, letting her feel how hard he was for her, wanting her to know. Both of his hands slipped into her hair. It was heavy, silky. Another time he would like to stroke his fingers through it, but not now. Now he was too desperate. He dragged fistfuls of it, using it to tilt her head back, anchoring her so he could kiss her harder still. 'Come upstairs,' he breathed against her mouth. 'Come with me.'

'All yours,' Ella said in that mocking way she had—but Aaron didn't care. He grabbed her hand and walked quickly to the staircase, pulling her up it at a furious pace.

'Which way to your room?' he asked.

Silently, she guided him to it.

The room next to his.

Fate.

The moment they were inside he was yanking her top up and over her head, fumbling with her skirt until it lay pool-like at her feet. The bedside lamp was on and he said a silent prayer of thanks because it meant he could see her. She stood before him in pale pink underwear so worn it was almost transparent, tossing her hair back over her shoulders. He swallowed. He wanted to rip her underwear to shreds to get to her. It was like a madness. Blood pounding through his veins, he stripped off his T-shirt and shoved his jeans and underwear off roughly.

She was watching him, following what he was doing as she kicked off her sandals. Aaron forced himself to stand still and let her see him. He hoped she liked what she saw.

Ella came towards him and circled his biceps with her hands—at least, partly; his biceps were too big for her to reach even halfway around. Aaron remembered that she liked tattoos. His tattooed armbands were broad and dark and intricately patterned—and, yes, she clearly did like what she saw. The tattoos had taken painful hours to complete and, watching her eyes light up as she touched them, he'd never been happier to have them. He hoped during the night she would see the more impressive tattoo on his back, but he couldn't imagine taking his eyes off her long enough to turn around.

He couldn't wait any longer to see her naked. He reached for her hips, and she obligingly released his arms and stepped closer. She let him push her panties down, stepped free of them when they hit the floor. Then she let him work the back fastening of her bra as she rested against him, compliant. As he wrestled with the bra, he could feel her against him, thigh to thigh, hip to hip. The tangle of soft hair against his erection had his heart bashing so hard and fast in his chest he thought he might have a coronary. Oh, he liked the feel of it. She was perfect. Natural and perfect. His hands were shaking so badly as he tried to undo her bra he thought he was going to have to tear it off, but it gave at last. Her breasts, the areoles swollen, nipples sharply erect, pressed into his chest as he wrenched the bra off. He was scared to look at her in case he couldn't stop himself falling on her like a ravening beast…but at the same time he was desperate to see her.

'Ella,' he said, his voice rough as he stepped back just enough to look. With one hand he touched her face. The other moved lower to the dark blonde hair at the apex of her thighs. He combed through it with trembling fingers. Lush and beautiful. He could feel the moisture seeping into it. Longed to taste it. Taste her. He dropped to his knees, kissed her there.

Aaron loved the hitch in her voice as his fingers and tongue continued to explore. 'I do want you, Aaron. Just so you know. Tonight, I do want you,' Ella said, and it was like a flare went off in his head. He got to his feet, dragged her into his arms, holding her close while his mouth dived on hers. He moved the few steps that would enable him to tumble her backwards onto the bed and come down on her.

The moment they hit the bed he had his hands on her thighs and was pushing her legs apart.

'Wait,' she said in his ear. 'Condoms. Bedside table. In the drawer.'

Somehow, Aaron managed to keep kissing her as he fumbled with the drawer, pulled it open and reached inside. His fingers mercifully closed on one quickly—thankfully they were loose in there.

He kissed her once more, long and luscious, before breaking to free the condom from its packaging. Kneeling between her thighs, he smoothed it on, and Ella raised herself on her elbows to watch. She looked irresistibly wicked, and as he finished the job he leaned forward to take one of her nipples in his mouth. She arched forward and gasped and he decided penetration could wait. She tasted divine. Exquisite. The texture of her was maddeningly good, the feel of her breasts as he held them in his hands heavy and firm. He could keep his mouth on her for hours, he thought, just to hear the sounds coming from her as his tongue circled, licked.

But Ella was shifting urgently beneath him, trying to position him with hands and thighs and the rest of her shuddering body. 'Inside,' she said, gasping. 'Come inside me. Now.'

With one thrust he buried himself in her, and then he couldn't seem to help himself. He pulled back and thrust deeply into her again. And again and again. He was kissing her mouth, her eyes, her neck as he drove into her over and over. The sound of her gasping cries urged him on until he felt her clench around him. She sucked in a breath, whooshed it out. Again. Once more. She was coming, tense and beautiful around him, and he'd never been so turned on in his life. He slid his arms under her on the bed, dragged her up against him and thrust his tongue inside her mouth. And with one last, hard push of his hips he came, hard and strong.

As the last waves of his climax receded, the fog of pure lust cleared from Aaron's head and he was suddenly and completely appalled.

Had he hurt her? Something primal had overtaken him, and he hadn't felt in control of himself. And he was *never, ever* out of control.

He kissed her, trying for gentleness but seemingly unable to achieve it even now, because the moment his mouth touched hers he was out of control again.

Aaron couldn't seem to steady his breathing. It was somehow beautiful to Ella to know that.

He sure liked kissing. Even now, after he'd exhausted both of them and could reasonably be expected to roll over and go to sleep, he was kissing her. In between those unsteady breaths of his. He seemed to have an obsession with her mouth. Nobody had ever kissed her quite like this before. It was sweet, and sexy as hell, to be kissed like he couldn't stop. It was getting her aroused again. She'd sneered at herself as she'd put those condoms in the drawer, but now all she could think was: did she have enough?

He shifted at last, rolling onto his back beside her. 'Sorry, I know I'm heavy. And you're so slender,' he said.

'It's just the—' She stopped. How did you describe quickly the way long hours, fatigue and illness sapped the calories out of you at breakneck speed? 'Nothing, really. I'm already gaining weight. It happens fast when I'm not working.'

'So you can lose it all over again the next time,' Aaron said, and Ella realised she didn't have to explain after all.

His eyes closed as he reached for her hand.

Okay, so now he'll go to sleep, Ella thought, and was

annoyed with herself for bringing him to her room. If they'd gone to his room she could have left whenever she wanted; but what did a woman say, do, to get a man to leave?

But Aaron, far from showing any signs of sleep, brought her hand to his mouth and rolled onto his side, facing her. He released her hand but then pulled her close so that her side was fitted against his front, and nuzzled his nose into the side of her neck. He slid one of his hands down over her belly and between her legs. 'Did I hurt you, Ella?'

Huh? 'Hurt me?'

'Yes. I was rough. I'm sorry.'

As he spoke his fingers were slipping gently against the delicate folds of her sex. It was like he was trying to soothe her. Her heart stumbled, just a little, as she realised what he was doing. And he was looking at her so seriously while he did it. He had the most remarkably beautiful eyes. And, of course, he was ridiculously well endowed, but she'd been so hot and ready for him it hadn't hurt. It had been more erotic than anything she could have dreamed.

How did she tell him that his fingers, now, weren't soothing? That what he was doing to her was gloriously *good*, but not soothing?

'No, Aaron, you— Ah...' She had to pause for a moment as the touch of his fingers became almost unbearable. 'I mean, no. I mean, you didn't hurt me.' She paused again. 'Aaron,' she said, almost breathless with desire, 'I suggest you go and get rid of that condom. And then hurry back and get another one.'

He frowned, understanding but wary. 'You're sure? I mean— Oh,' as her hands found him. 'I guess you're sure.' He swung his legs off the side of the bed and was about to stand but Ella, on her knees in an instant, embraced him from behind. Her mouth touched between his shoulder blades then he felt her tongue trace the pattern of the dragon inked across his back.

'I don't want to leave you,' he said huskily. 'Come with me.'

Ella, needing no second invitation, was out of the bed and heading for the en suite bathroom half a step behind him.

Ella trailed the fingers of one hand along his spine and snapped on the light with the fingers of her other. 'Oh, my, it's even better in the full light.'

Aaron discarded the condom and started to turn around. She imagined he thought he was going to take her in his arms.

'No, you don't. It's my turn,' Ella said.

She turned on the shower, drew Aaron in beside her, and as he reached for her again she shook her head, laughing, and dodged out of the way. 'I'm glad this is such a small shower cubicle,' she said throatily. 'Close. Tight.' She spun Aaron roughly to face the tiled wall, slammed him up against it and grabbed the cake of soap from its holder. Lathering her hands, his skin, she plastered herself against his back, moving her breasts sensually against his beautiful tattoo as she reached around to fondle him. 'I love the size of you,' she said, as his already impressive erection grew in her hands. 'I want to take you like this, from behind.'

'I think I'd take you any way I could get you,' Aaron said, groaning as she moved her hands between his legs. He was almost panting and Ella had never felt so beautiful, so powerful.

At last.

She could have this, at last.

As her hands slid, slipped, squeezed, Aaron rested his forehead against the shower wall and submitted.

* * *

Aaron watched as Ella slept. She'd fallen into sleep like a stone into the ocean.

No wonder. Aaron had been all over her from the moment they'd left the shower. Inexhaustible. He didn't think he'd understood the word lust until tonight. If he could have breathed her into his lungs, he would have.

He didn't know why he wanted her so badly. But even having had her three times, he couldn't get her close enough. She was in his blood. What a pathetic cliché. But true.

The bedside light was still on, so he could see her face. She looked serious in her sleep. Fretful. Aaron pulled her closer, kissed one of her wickedly arched eyebrows. He breathed in the scent of her hair. Looking at her was almost painful. The outrageous loveliness of her.

Sighing, he turned off the bedside light. It was past five in the morning and he should go back to his room, but he wanted to hold her.

He thought about their last meeting, in Cambodia. The horrible things they'd said to each other. They'd made a pact to forget they'd ever met. How had they gone from that to being here in bed now?

What had he been thinking when he'd left the library, when he'd seen her slumped against the front door with her fists jammed against her mouth?

On a mundane level, he'd thought she must have been drinking. Or maybe he'd hoped that, so he could pigeon-hole her back where he'd wanted to.

Oh, he had no doubt she regularly drank to excess—it fitted with the general wildness he sensed in her. But tonight she'd smelled only like that tantalising perfume. And her mouth had tasted like lime, not booze. It was obvious, really, when he pieced together what he knew about her, what he'd seen of her: she wouldn't let Tina see her out of control. She would be sober and serene and together in this house. The way her family expected her to be. The way she'd been described to him before he'd ever met her.

He thought about the day he'd held her as she'd cried over Bourey's death. And the other boy, Sann, whose death had been infinitely painful for her. Things she didn't want anyone to know.

She was so alone. She chose to be, so her fears and sorrows wouldn't hurt anyone else.

Aaron pulled her closer. She roused, smiled sleepily at him. 'You should go,' she said, but then she settled herself against him and closed her eyes, so he stayed exactly where he was.

Wondering how he could both have her and keep things simple.

CHAPTER NINE

ELLA ROLLED RESTLESSLY, absent-mindedly pulling Aaron's pillow close and breathing in the scent of him, wondering what time he'd left.

She didn't know what had come over her. She'd finally managed to get past second base—way past it, with a blistering home run. And it had been with her brother-in-law's friend under her sister's roof. Not that there had seemed to be much choice about it. It had felt like…well, like fate.

And Aaron wouldn't tell, she reassured herself.

She got out of bed, reached for her robe, and then just sat on the edge of the bed with the robe in her lap. She didn't want to go downstairs. Because downstairs meant reality. It meant Tina and Brand. And Aaron—not Lover Aaron but Friend-of-her-sister Aaron. Daddy Aaron.

She stood slowly and winced a little. It had been a very active night. A fabulous night. But she would have been relieved even if it had been the worst sex of her life instead of the best. Because she had needed it.

Yesterday she'd forced herself to think about Sann. Tina's pregnancy was an immutable fact, and Ella knew she had to come to terms with it; she couldn't run away every time a pang of envy hit her. So she had deliberately taken the memories out of mothballs and examined them one by one. A kind of desensitisation therapy.

But forcing the memories had been difficult. So when she'd come home to find Aaron there, sex with him had offered an escape. A talisman to keep her sad thoughts at bay, hopefully ward off the bad dreams.

She had been prepared to make a bargain with herself—sex and a nightmare-free night, in exchange for guilt and shame today.

And she did feel the guilt.

Just not the shame.

What did that mean?

Get it together, Ella. It was just a one-night stand. People do it all the time. Simple.

Except it was *not* simple. Because she hadn't managed it before. And she recalled—too vividly—Aaron walking towards her in the hallway, and how much she'd wanted him as their eyes had met. She was deluding herself if she thought she'd only been interested in a nightmare-free night. Oh, he had certainly materialised at a point when she'd been at her lowest ebb and open to temptation, but she had wanted him, wanted the spark, the flash of almost unbearable attraction that had been there in Cambodia.

But now what?

Nothing had really changed. All the reasons not to be together in Cambodia were still there. Kiri. Rebecca. Javier.

Definitely time to return to reality.

Ella tossed the robe aside and strode into the bathroom.

She looked at herself in the mirror. Her mouth looked swollen. Nothing she could do to hide that, except maybe dab a bit of foundation on it to minimise the rawness. She could see small bruises on her upper arms—easily covered. There were more bruises on her hips, but nobody would be seeing those. She sucked in a breath as more memories of the night filled her head. Aaron had been insatiable—and she had loved it. She had more than a few sore spots. And, no doubt, so did he. Like the teeth marks she'd left on his inner thigh.

Ella caught herself smiling. Aaron had called her a vampire, but he hadn't minded. He hadn't minded at all, if the passionate lovemaking that had followed had been any indication.

The smile slipped.

He would have come to his senses by now. Remembered that he didn't like her. Didn't want her near his son.

Time to store the memory and move on.

Tina checked the clock on the kitchen wall as Ella walked in. 'So lunch, not breakfast.'

'Oh, dear, am I going to have to punch a time clock whenever I come and go?'

'Oh, for heaven's sake!'

'Well, sorry, Tina, but really you're as bad as Mom. Just sit down and tell me stories about Brand as a doting father while I make us both something to eat.'

Ella forced herself to look at Tina's stomach as she edged past her sister. Bearable. She could do this.

Tina groaned as she levered herself onto a stool at the kitchen counter. 'I am so over the doting father thing. We've done the practice drive to the hospital seven times. And he's having food cravings. It's not funny, Ella!'

But Ella laughed anyway as she laid a variety of salad vegetables on a chopping board. 'Where is he now?'

'On the set, thank goodness. Which reminds me—I didn't tell you we have other guests.'

Ah. Control time. Ella busied herself pulling out drawers.

'What are you looking for?' Tina asked.

Ella kept her head down and pulled open another drawer. 'Knife.'

'Behind you, knife block on the counter,' Tina said, and Ella turned her back on her sister and took her time selecting a knife.

'Where was I?' Tina asked. 'Oh yes, Aaron. Aaron James and his son. You know them, of course.'

Indistinct mumble.

'Aaron is in Brand's movie,' Tina continued. 'That's why he's in London. They've been staying with us, but they're only here for another week.'

'Why's that?' Ella asked, desperately nonchalant, and started chopping as though her life depended on the precision of her knife action.

'Aaron was always intending to find a place of his own, and yesterday he did.'

'So…would it be easier if I moved out for the week? Because I have friends I was going to see and I—'

'What is wrong with you people? Everyone wants to move out. We've got enough room to house a baseball team! And, anyway, I need you to help me look after Kiri.'

Uh-oh. 'What? Why?'

'Kiri's nanny had some crisis and can't get here until next week. Aaron's due on set tomorrow so I volunteered. I told him it would be good practice. And Kiri is adorable.'

Ella's hand was a little unsteady so she put down the knife. Kiri. She would be looking after Kiri. Aaron wouldn't want that. 'But what about—? I mean, shouldn't he have stayed in Sydney? With his mother?' *Drugs, Ella, drugs.* 'Or—or…someone?'

Tina looked like she was weighing something up. 'The thing is—oh, I don't know if… Okay, look, this is completely confidential, Ella.'

Tina put up her hands at the look on Ella's face. 'Yes, I know you're a glued-shut clam. Aaron is just sensitive about it. Or Rebecca is, and he's respecting that. Rebecca is in rehab. Drugs. Apparently, she auditioned for a role in a new TV show while Aaron was in Cambodia, but didn't get it. The director told her if she didn't get things under control, she'd never work again.'

'That's…tough. How—how's Kiri coping with the separation?'

'Aaron does all the parenting, so it's not as big a deal as you'd think. He has sole custody. But that's not to say Rebecca doesn't see Kiri whenever she wants. It's just that the drugs have been a problem for some time.'

'Oh. *Sole* custody. Huh.' Ella scooped the chopped salad vegetables into a large bowl. 'But should he…Aaron… should he be here while she's there?'

'Well, they *are* divorced, although sometimes I wonder if Rebecca really believes that. But in any case, it's not a case of him shirking responsibility. Aaron found the clinic—in California, while he was over there auditioning for a new crime show—because Rebecca wanted to do it away from her home city where it might have leaked to the press. And he got her settled in over there, which pushed back filming here so it's all over the place, but what can you do? And of course he's paying, despite having settled a fortune on her during the divorce. He'll be back and forth with Kiri, who thinks it's a spa! But there are strict rules about visiting. Anyway, I hope it works, because Aaron needs to move on, and he won't until Rebecca gets her act together.' She slanted an uncomfortably speculative look at Ella.

'Don't even!' Ella said, interpreting without difficulty.

'Come on, Ella. He's totally, completely hot.'

Ella concentrated on drizzling dressing over the salad.

'Hot as Hades,' Tina said, tightening the thumbscrews. 'But also sweet as heaven. He is amazingly gentle with

Kiri. And with me, too. He took me for an ultrasound last week. I had a fall down the stairs and I was petrified.'

Ella hurried to her sister's side, hugged her. 'But everything's all right. You're fine, the baby's fine, right?'

'Yes, but Brand was filming, and I couldn't bring myself to call him. Because I'd already had one fall on the stairs, and he was furious because I was hurrying.'

'Well *stop* hurrying, Tina.' Tentatively, Ella reached and placed a hand on Tina's stomach. The baby kicked suddenly and Ella's hand jerked away—or would have, if Tina hadn't stopped it, flattened it where it was, kept it there. Tina looked at her sister, wonder and joy in her eyes, and Ella felt her painful envy do a quantum shift.

'So anyway, Aaron,' Tina said. 'He was home. Actually, he saw it happen. I don't know which of us was more upset. He must have cajoled and threatened and who knows what else to get the ultrasound arranged so quickly. He knew it was the only way I'd believe everything was all right. And he let me talk him into not calling Brand until we got the all clear and I was back home.' Tina smiled broadly. 'Unbelievably brave! Brand exploded about being kept in the dark, as Aaron knew he would, but Aaron took it all in his stride. He just let Brand wear himself out, and then took him out for a beer.'

Ella tried not to be charmed, but there was something lovely about the story. 'Well I'm here now to take care of you,' she said, navigating the lump in her throat.

'And I'm very glad.' Tina took Ella's left hand and placed it alongside the right one that was already pressed to her stomach. 'It really scared me, Ella. But I'm not telling you all this to worry you—and don't, whatever you do, tell Mum and Dad.'

'I wouldn't dream of it.'

'I just wanted you to know. I mean, you're my sister!

And a nurse. And…well, you're my sister. And I wanted to explain about Aaron. Don't disapprove of him because of Rebecca. He takes his responsibilities very seriously. He practically raised his three young sisters, you know, after his parents died, and he was only eighteen. They idolise him. So does Kiri. And so do I, now. He'll do the right thing by Rebecca, divorced or not, and—more importantly—the right thing by Kiri.'

Ella moved her hands as Tina reached past her to dig into the salad bowl and extract a sliver of carrot.

'You're going to need more than salad, Ella,' Tina said. 'You're like a twig.'

'Yes, yes, yes, I know.' Ella moved back into the food preparation area. 'I'll make some sandwiches.'

'Better make enough for Aaron and Kiri—they should be back any minute.'

For the barest moment Ella paused. Then she opened the fridge and rummaged inside it. 'Where are they?'

'The park. Aaron's teaching Kiri how to play cricket.'

'Ah,' Ella said meaninglessly, and started slapping various things between slices of bread like she was in a trance.

'Yeah, I think that's enough for the entire Australian and English cricket teams,' Tina said eventually.

'Oh. Sorry. Got carried away.'

Breathe, Ella ordered herself when she heard Aaron calling out to Tina from somewhere in the house as she was positioning the platter of sandwiches on the table.

'In the kitchen,' Tina called back.

Tina turned to Ella. 'And I guess you'll tell me later about last night. Probably not fit for children's ears, anyway.'

Ella froze, appalled. Tina *knew*?

'I mean, come on, your mouth,' Tina teased. 'Or are you going to tell me you got stung by a bee?'

'Who got stung by a bee?' Aaron asked, walking in.

CHAPTER TEN

'Oh, nobody,' Tina said airily.

But Aaron wasn't looking at Tina. He was looking at Ella.

And from the heat in his eyes Ella figured he was remembering last night in Technicolor detail. Ella felt her pulse kick in response. *Insane.*

'Nice to see you again, Ella,' he said.

Could Tina hear that caress in his voice? Ella frowned fiercely at him.

He winked at her. Winked!

'Kiri can't wait to see you,' he continued. 'He's got a present for you—he's just getting it.'

'Oh, that's— Oh.' She gave up the effort of conversation. She was out of her depth. Shouldn't Aaron be keeping Kiri *away* from her? Ella wondered if Aaron had taken a cricket ball to the head. They were deadly, cricket balls.

Ella was aware a phone was ringing. She noted, dimly, Tina speaking. Sensed Tina leaving the room.

And then Aaron was beside her, taking her hand, lifting it to his mouth, kissing it. The back, the palm. His tongue on her fingers.

'Stop,' she whispered, but the air seemed to have been sucked out of the room and she wasn't really sure the word had left her mouth.

Aaron touched one finger to her swollen bottom lip. 'I'm sorry. Is it sore?'

Ella knocked his hand away. 'What's gotten into you?'

The next moment she found herself pulled into Aaron's arms. 'I've got a solution,' he said, as though she would have *any* idea what he was talking about! Yep, cricket ball to the head.

'A solution for what?'

'You and me. It's based on the KISS principle.'

'The what?'

'KISS: keep it simple, stupid.'

'*Simple* would be to forget last night happened.'

Ella started to pull away, but he tightened his arms.

He rested his forehead on hers. 'Let me. Just for a moment.'

Somehow she found her arms around his waist, and she was just standing there, letting him hold her as though it were any everyday occurrence. *Uh-oh. Dangerous.*

'There's no solution needed for a one-night stand,' she said.

He released her, stepped back. 'I don't want a one-night stand.'

'Um—I think you're a little late to that party.'

'Why?'

'Because we've already had one.'

'So tonight will make it a two-night stand. And tomorrow night a three-night stand, and so on.'

'We agreed, in Cambodia—'

'Cambodia-shmodia.'

'Huh?'

'That was then. This is now.'

'Did you get hit in the head with a cricket ball?'

'What?'

'You're talking like you've got a head injury.'

'It's relief. It's making me light-headed. Because for the first time since Tina and Brand's wedding I know what I'm doing.'

'Well, I don't know what you're doing. I don't think I want to know. I mean, the *KISS* principle?'

'I want you. You want me. We get to have each other. Simple.'

'Um, *not* simple. Kiri? Rebecca? The fact you don't like me? That you don't even know me?'

'Kiri and Rebecca—they're for me to worry about, not you.'

'You're wrong. Tina wants me to help her look after Kiri. Surely you don't want that? Aren't you scared I'll corrupt him or something?'

'Ella, if I know one thing, it's that you would never do anything to hurt Kiri. I've always known it. What I said, in Cambodia…' He shrugged. 'I was being a moron. Projecting, you called it, and you were right. There. I'm denouncing myself.'

'I don't want to play happy families.'

'Neither do I. That's why your relationship with Kiri is separate from my relationship with Kiri, which is separate from my relationship with you. And before you throw Rebecca at me—it's the same deal. You don't even have a relationship with her, so that's purely my issue, not yours.'

'You said the R word. I don't want a relationship—and neither do you.'

Aaron took her hand and lifted it so that it rested on his chest, over his heart. 'Our relationship is going to be purely sexual. Casual sex, that's what you said you wanted. All you were interested in. Well, I can do casual sex.'

'You're not a casual kind of guy, Aaron,' she said.

He smiled, shrugged. 'I'll *make* myself that kind of guy. I said last night I would take you any way I could get you.

We're two adults seeking mutual satisfaction and nothing more. An emotion-free zone, which means we can keep it strictly between us—Tina and Brand don't need to know, it's none of Rebecca's business, and Kiri is…well, protected, because your relationship with him is nothing to do with your relationship with me. Simple. Agreed?'

Ella hesitated—not saying yes, but not the automatic 'no' she should be rapping out either. Before she could get her brain into gear, the kitchen door opened.

As Ella pulled her hand free from where, she'd just realised, it was still being held against Aaron's heart, Kiri ran in, saw her, stopped, ran again. Straight at her.

'Kiri, my darling,' she said, and picked him up.

She kissed his forehead. He hugged her, his arms tight around her neck, and didn't seem to want to let go. So she simply moved backwards, with him in her arms, until she felt a chair behind her legs and sat with him on her lap.

Kiri kissed her cheek and Ella's chest tightened dangerously. Kiri removed one arm from around Ella's neck and held out his hand to her. His fist was closed around something.

'What's this?' Ella asked.

Kiri opened his fingers to reveal an unremarkable rock. 'From the beach where you live,' he said. 'Monica.'

Ella smiled at him. 'You remembered?'

Kiri nodded and Ella hugged him close. Santa Monica. He'd been to Santa Monica, and remembered it was where she lived.

She felt a hand on her shoulder and looked up. Aaron was beside her, looking down at her, and she couldn't breathe.

The door opened and Tina breezed in. She paused—an

infinitesimal pause—as she took in Aaron's hand on Ella's shoulder, Kiri on her lap.

Aaron slowly removed his hand, but stayed where he was.

'So,' Tina said brightly, 'let's eat.'

Lunch was dreadful.

Kiri was at least normal, chattering away about Cambodia, about Disneyland, about Sydney, completely at ease.

But Tina was giving off enough gobsmacked vibes to freak Ella out completely.

And Aaron was high-beaming Ella across the table as though he could get her on board with the force of his eyes alone—and if they were really going to carry on a secret affair, he'd have to find his poker face pretty damned fast.

If? Was she really going the 'if' route? Not the 'no way' route?

Casual sex.

Could she do it? She'd liked having someone close to her last night. She'd felt alive in a way she hadn't for such a long time. And she hadn't had the dreaded nightmares with Aaron beside her. So. A chance to feel alive again. With no strings attached. No emotions, which she couldn't offer him anyway.

But, ironic though it was, Aaron James seemed to have the ability to make her want to clean up her act. Maybe it was the way he was with Kiri, or that he cared so much about an ex-wife who clearly made his life a misery, or his general tendency to turn into Sir Galahad at regular intervals and save damsels in distress—his sisters, ex-wife, Tina, her.

Whatever the reason, if she wanted to rehabilitate her self-image, was an affair the way to start? Every time she'd let a guy pick her up, determined to do it, just do it and move on, she'd hated herself. Now that she'd gone the whole nine yards, wouldn't she end up hating herself even more? Especially if it became a regular arrangement?

'I'll clear up,' Tina said, when lunch couldn't be stretched out any more.

'Ella and I can manage,' Aaron said quickly.

'No, *Ella and I* can manage,' Tina insisted. She stood and arched her back, grimaced.

Ella got to her feet. 'You should rest,' she told her sister. 'And you...' with an almost fierce look at Aaron '...should get Kiri into bed for a nap. He's sleepy.' She started gathering empty plates.

Aaron looked like he was about to argue so Ella simply turned her back on him and took an armload of plates to the sink. She stayed there, clattering away, refusing to look up, willing him to leave.

And then, at last, Tina spoke. 'The coast is clear. You can come up for air.'

Ella raised her head cautiously and waited for the inevitable.

'What's going on?' Tina asked simply.

'If you mean between me and Aaron, nothing.'

'Of course I mean you and Aaron. He's gaga. It's so obvious.'

'He's not *gaga*.'

'Oh, I beg to differ.'

'We just... We just got to know each other in Cambodia. I called in to check on Kiri a few times when he was ill with dengue fever and Aaron was out in the field, so he's...grateful. I guess.'

Tina snorted out a laugh. 'If that's gratitude, I'd like to

get me a piece of it. I'm going to remind Brand tonight just how grateful he is that he met me.'

Ella had stayed out as long as public transport allowed but Aaron was nevertheless waiting for her when she got back, leaning against the library door.

No reprieve.

She'd three-quarters expected this, though, so she had a plan.

She would be *that* Ella—the cool, calm, untouchable one—so he knew exactly what he'd get if he pursued this insanity that she couldn't quite bring herself to reject. With luck, he would run a mile away from her, the way he'd run in Cambodia, and spare them both the heartache she feared would be inevitable if they went down this path.

If not…well, they'd see.

'Are you going to wait up for me every night?' she asked, in the amused tone that had infuriated him in the past.

'I can wait in your bed if you prefer.'

The wind having effectively been taken out of her sails, Ella headed slowly up the stairs without another word. Aaron followed her into her room, reached for her.

'Wait,' she said, stepping back. 'You really want to do this?'

'Yes.'

'One hundred per cent sure?'

'Yes.'

She sighed. 'It's going to end in tears, you know.'

'I'll take my chances.'

Another sigh. 'Okay, then—but, first, ground rules.'

He nodded, deadly serious.

'No PDAs,' she said. 'If this is casual sex, it stays in

my bedroom—or your bedroom. No touchy-feely stuff beyond bed. And *absolutely* nothing in front of Tina or Brand or Kiri.'

'Agreed.'

'When one or the other of us decides the arrangement is over there will be no questions, no comments, no recriminations, no clinging. I will let you go as easily as that…' she clicked her fingers '…if you're the one ending things. And I expect you to do the same.'

He narrowed his eyes. 'Agreed.'

'No prying into my private life.'

He looked at her.

'Agreed?' she asked impatiently.

'I don't know what "prying" means to you—you're supersensitive about things other people consider normal conversation, and I don't want you taking a machete to my head if I ask what any reasonable person would think is an innocuous question.'

'If you think I'm unreasonable, why do you want to go down this path?'

He smiled, a smile that held the promise of hot, steamy sex. 'Oh, I think you know why, Ella.'

She was blushing again.

'What about if I agree that you are under no obligation to tell me anything that makes you uncomfortable?' he asked.

She digested that. 'Fair enough. Agreed. And ditto for you.'

'No need. You can ask me anything you want, and I'll answer you.'

That threw her, but she nodded. 'But I won't ask. Any conditions from your side?'

'One. Monogamy. Nobody else, while you're sleeping with me.'

'Agreed,' she said, but she tinkled out a little laugh to suggest she thought that was quaint. 'Anything else?'

'No. So take off your clothes.'

CHAPTER ELEVEN

'I DO LIKE a masterful man,' Ella said. And then she reached for the hem of her dress.

But Aaron stopped her. 'I've changed my mind,' he said. 'Come here.'

Ella stepped towards him, her eyebrows raised in that practised, disdainful way that seemed to aggravate him.

When she reached him, he took the neckline of her cotton dress in his hands, and ripped the dress down the front.

A surprised 'Oh…' whooshed out of her. There went the practised disdain.

She looked up at him. His face was stark as he dragged her bra down her arms, imprisoning her with the straps, and bent his head to her breasts. He sucked one nipple, hard, into his mouth, and she gasped. Moved to the other. He eased back to look into her eyes as he pushed her tattered dress almost casually over her hips until it dropped to the floor. 'I'll buy you another,' he said.

She couldn't speak, couldn't raise her defensive shield of indifference. Could only wait and watch. Her arms were still trapped, and he made no move to free them. Instead, he brought his hands up to cup her breasts, thumbs smoothing across her nipples, and then lowered his mouth again.

How much time had passed—a minute? Ten? Longer? He wouldn't let her move, just kept up that steady pressure, hands and lips, until she was almost weeping with pleasure. Ella was desperate to touch him, but every time she tried to reach around to unhook her bra and free herself, he stymied her.

At last he stepped back, examined her with one long, lascivious look from her head to her toes. Then his hands went to the front of her panties and she felt, heard, the fine cotton tear. 'I'll replace those too,' he said softly, and then her breath shuddered out, rough and choppy, as one of his hands reached between her legs. Within moments she was shuddering as the pleasure tore through her like a monsoon. Hot, wet, wild.

He spun her, unhooking her bra with a swift efficiency that seemed to scorn his earlier languorous attention to her body. With the same speed, he stripped off his own clothes. Then his hands were on her again, arousing her, preparing her, as he backed the two of them towards the bed.

He fell onto the bed, on his back, and dragged her on top of him. 'Here, let me.' His voice was hoarse and urgent as he positioned her over him, moving her legs so that they fell on either side of his and thrusting blindly towards her centre.

'Wait,' she said.

It took only moments for her to raise herself, straddling him with her knees on each side of his straining body. She reached over him, grabbed a condom from the drawer. She ripped the package open with her teeth, slid the sheath onto him with slow, steady movements. Smoothing it as he jumped against her hand. And then she took him inside her with one undulating swirl of her hips. Stilled, keeping him there, not letting him move, deep inside her.

'No,' she said, as he started to buck upwards against her. 'Let me.' And, rising and falling in smooth, steady waves, she tightened herself around him until he gasped her name. Clutching her hips, he jammed her down on top of him and exploded.

Ella, following him into ecstasy, collapsed on top of him. She stayed there, spent, as his hands threaded through her hair, stroking and sliding.

She wanted to stay like that all night, with Aaron inside her, his hands in her hair, his mouth close enough to kiss.

Except that he hadn't kissed her. Not once.

For some reason, she didn't like that.

It's just casual sex, she reminded herself.

On that thought, she disengaged herself from his body and got off the bed. Pulling her hair back over her shoulders, she smiled serenely down at him. 'Excellent, thank you,' she said. 'But there's no need for you to stay. I'll see you tomorrow night.'

Tina had assorted chores to do the next day, so she left Kiri in Ella's sole company.

Ella had taken him to the park to practise catching the cricket ball. Was that the hardest, unkindest ball in international sport? Ella thought so, as she looked at her bruised shin.

So for the afternoon she'd chosen a more intellectual pursuit—painting. It was a challenge to keep Kiri's paint set in the vicinity of the special child-sized activity table Tina had moved into the library for him, but they'd accomplished it.

As assorted paintings, laid out across every available surface, were drying, she and Kiri curled up together in one of the massive leather chairs, where she entertained him by letting him play with her cellphone.

She was laughing at Kiri's attempt at an emoticon-only text message when Aaron walked in.

'Shouldn't you be on set?' she asked, sitting up straighter.

'I'm on a break so thought I'd come back to the house. What happened to your leg?'

'Cricket-ball injury. That's a sport I am never going to figure out.' She gestured around the room. 'Check out Kiri's paintings while you're here. Which one's for Dad, Kiri?'

Kiri scrambled out of the chair. 'Two of them. Here's Mum…' He was pointing out a painting of a black-haired woman in an orange dress. 'And here's Ella.' In her nursing uniform.

Ella felt her stomach drop with a heavy thud. Just what the man needed; his ex-wife and his current lover, as depicted by his son, who knew nothing of the tension in either relationship.

But Aaron was smiling like it was the most wonderful gift in the world. 'Fabbo. One day, when you're famous, these are going to be worth a fortune.'

Kiri giggled, and then went to perch back with Ella. 'Ella's teaching me the phone,' he confided. 'I called Tina.'

'You're not international roaming, are you?' Aaron asked. 'That will cost you a fortune.'

Ella shrugged, not having the heart to deny Kiri. 'They're only short calls.' She smiled at Kiri as she scrolled through her contact list.

'See, Kiri, there's Dad's number. If you hit this, it will call him. Yes, perfect.'

Aaron's phone rang, and he dutifully answered it and had a moment's conversation with Kiri.

And then Aaron tossed metaphorical hands in the air. He asked Ella for her phone number, punched it into his contact list, then handed his phone to Kiri, showed him the entry and let him call her.

She and Kiri chatted for a while, as though they were on opposite sides of the world instead of sitting together.

Then Kiri looked pleadingly at his father. 'Dad, can I have a phone?'

Aaron laughed. 'Who do you need to call, mate?' he asked.

'You. Mum. Tina. Jenny. And Ella.'

'Well, calling Ella might be tricky,' Aaron explained, and lifted Kiri into his arms. 'Because we'll never know where in the world she is. And we don't want to wake her up at midnight!'

An excellent reminder, Ella thought, of the transience of their current arrangement—because at some point in the near future she would indeed be somewhere else in the world, far away from Aaron and Kiri.

When Aaron took his leave a short while later, she felt ill at ease.

It had been a strange interlude. Why had he even come? Maybe he didn't trust her with Kiri after all, and was checking up on her.

But it hadn't felt like that. In fact, he'd seemed delighted at her obviously close relationship with Kiri. And not at all freaked out at having a painting of her presented to him as a gift, which must have been awkward.

Knowing how much Aaron adored Kiri, and how keen he'd been to keep the two parts of this London life separate, well, it didn't make sense.

And Ella didn't like it.

Ella spent the next three days in a kind of hellish heaven.

Taking care of Kiri during the day and spending her nights with Aaron.

She adored her time with Kiri. She took him to Madame Tussaud's and to see the changing of the guard at Buckingham Palace, toy shopping for the baby, and for him. In the process, falling a little more in love with him every day.

She longed for her nights with Aaron. The pleasure that made her want to sigh and scream, the roughness and gentleness, the speed and languor, and everything in between.

But the arrangement was playing havoc with her emotions. Kiri's innocent stories about his father were making her feel altogether too soppy about a casual sex partner. And there were moments during the steamy nights when she and Aaron seemed to forget their agreed roles, becoming almost like real parents having the whole family chat.

Minus the kissing.

An omission that should have reassured her that this was just sex…but didn't.

And then, after five consecutive nights of lovemaking, Ella opened the morning paper and the sordidness of her current situation was thrown into sudden, sharp relief.

Only one half-column of words, not even a photo. But, still, the wreck of her life came crashing back.

It was an article about Javier, full of platitudes from various authorities with no actual news of his fate. But it felt like an omen, and it savaged Ella's conscience. Because she realised that since being with Aaron, not only had she been free of nightmares but she hadn't had any thoughts about Javier either.

So when Aaron came to her room that night, carrying a bag, she pleaded a migraine, knowing she looked ill enough for him to believe her.

'Can I get you anything?' he asked, concern creasing his forehead as he dumped the bag carelessly on her bed.

She forced a strained smile. 'Hey, I'm a nurse, remember?'

He nodded, and then completely disarmed her by drawing her against him and just holding her. 'Sleep well, angel,' he said, and left her.

Angel?

That was going to have to be nipped in the bud.

She approached the bag with some trepidation. Pulled out a raspberry-coloured dress that even she could see was something special, and a bra and panties set in a matching shade that was really too beautiful to wear. The replacements for the things Aaron had ripped off her, obviously—although, strictly speaking, he didn't owe her a bra.

She stared at them, spread on the bed, and tried to shrug off the sense of doom that gripped her.

Aaron was dragged out of a deep slumber by a kind of screeching wail, abruptly cut off.

He sat up, perfectly still, perfectly silent, and listened. Nothing.

He shook his head to clear it.

Nothing. Imagination.

So—back to sleep. He gave his pillow a thump and lay back down.

Sat back up. Nope—something was wrong. He could feel it.

He got out of bed, padded out of the room, shirtless and in his shorts.

He opened the door to Kiri's room opposite and peered in. He was sleeping soundly.

So…Ella? He opened the door to her room quietly.

She was lying perfectly still, her eyes wide and staring, her hands jammed against her mouth.

He didn't think. Just slid into bed beside her, took her in his arms and arranged her limbs for maximum sleeping comfort.

She said nothing, but she didn't kick him away, which had to be a good sign.

'Just to be clear,' he said, 'I'm not asking questions. So don't even think of telling me to leave.'

She looked at him for one heartbeat, two, three. Then she closed her eyes, and eventually he felt her ease into sleep.

It wasn't going to be easy to not ask at some point. He'd better wear his thermal underwear to ward off the frostbite during that moment. Hmm. Oddly enough, it didn't daunt him. He snuggled her a little closer, kissed the top of her head. *One day, Ella, I'll know it all.*

Damn Aaron James.

It was his fault she was in a dingy hotel room that wasn't big enough to swing a rodent in, let alone a cat.

Not that she hadn't slept in an array of substandard places over the years, though none had ever cost her a staggering hundred and twenty pounds per night.

He'd had to come into her room last night when she'd been at her most vulnerable. And sneaked out this morning without waking her, without having the decency to talk about it so she could slap him down.

So here she was. Hiding out. Staying away until she could find the best way to end things with him. Because things were just not quite casual enough to make this arrangement work.

Aaron was moving house tomorrow. That should signal the end of their liaison. She shouldn't have let Aaron persuade her in the first place. Because look where it had landed her. She was confused about Aaron, guilt-stricken about Javier, miserable about everything—and in a shoebox-sized room that was costing her a bomb.

Ella sighed heavily, and sat dispiritedly on the bed. It was kind of slippery, as if the mattress protector was plastic. She popped into the bathroom to splash some water on her face and the *eau de* public toilet aroma jammed into her nostrils.

Well, that settled one thing: she might have to sleep here, but she wasn't going to breathe in that smell until she had to. She was going out for the evening.

In fact, for this one night she was going to rediscover the excesses she'd left behind in Cambodia. And when she was sozzled enough, she would return to face the room.

She would *not* run headlong to Tina's and one last night with Aaron.

Which was how Ella found herself playing pool with Harry, Neal and Jerome; three gorgeous, safely gay guys.

She was hot. Sweaty. Dishevelled. A little bit drunk.

Just how you wanted to look for a surprise visit from your lover.

Because that was definitely Aaron James, entering the pub just as she hit the white ball so awkwardly it jumped off the table.

Aaron James, who was standing there, glaring at her.

Fate. It really wasn't working for her.

CHAPTER TWELVE

HE'D BEEN WORKING his way through the pubs in the vicinity of Tina and Brand's because he'd known Ella wasn't staying with friends, as she'd told Tina, and he suspected she wouldn't stray too far, given Tina's advanced pregnancy. So it wasn't exactly fate that he'd found her, because this was the seventh pub he'd tried. But it sure felt like it.

He should go, leave her to it. She didn't *have* to see him every night. Didn't have to get his permission to stay out all night. Didn't have to explain why she was laughing over a pool table with three handsome men.

Except that she kind of *did* have to.

And it would have been stupid to search through the pubs of Mayfair for her and then turn tail the moment he found her.

She was wearing a skin-tight black skirt that would give a corpse a wet dream. A clingy silver singlet top just covering those perfect breasts. Black high heels—that was a first, and a very sexy one. Her hair was piled on her head, who knew how it was staying up there? In fact, not all of it was. Her messy hair made him think of having her in bed.

Aaron watched as she bounced the white ball off the table. As all four of them chortled. He seethed as the blond guy kissed her. Felt murderous as the other two hugged her, one each side.

She knew he was here. He'd seen the flare in her eyes, the infinitesimal toss of her head as she'd directed her eyes away.

Oh no you don't, Ella. Oh, no. You. Don't.

Ella decided the best thing to do was carry on with her evening as though she hadn't seen Aaron standing on the other side of the pub with his hands fisted at his sides like he was trying not to punch something. She was not going to be made to feel guilty about this.

The guys started hunting in their pockets for beer money. Ella dug into her handbag. 'Don't think so,' she said mournfully, as she scrabbled around inside. And then her eyes widened. 'Hang on,' she said, and triumphantly drew a ten-pound note from the depths, along with one old mint and a paper clip.

'Hooray!' Jerome exclaimed with great enthusiasm. 'Off you go, my girl—to the bar.'

'Or maybe not.'

The voice came from behind Ella but she knew to whom it belonged. That accent.

She'd known he would come to her. Had expected it. Was she happy about it? Yes, unbelievably, given she'd intended to avoid him tonight, she was happy. *A bad sign.*

She looked over her shoulder at him. 'Hello, Aaron.'

'You and pool tables, what's up with that?' Aaron asked mildly. He tucked a strand of loose hair behind one of Ella's ears. 'Run out of money, sweetheart?'

'Yes,' she said, looking at him carefully as she turned fully towards him. He wasn't giving off *sweetheart* vibes. Aaron dug into his jeans pocket, pulled out a fifty-pound note and handed it to her.

'Are you going to introduce me to your friends?' he

asked, as she stared at the cash as though she couldn't believe she was holding it.

'Huh?' she said eloquently.

'Your friends?' he prompted.

Ella looked around as though she'd forgotten their existence. Pulled herself together as she noted her three new drinking buddies gazing at her with avid interest.

'Oh. Yes,' she said, and hastily performed the introductions.

'And do you really want another drink, or shall we hand that money over to the guys and head off?'

Ella was torn.

'Ella? Are we staying or going?' Aaron asked, steel in his voice.

She *should* tell him to go to hell. But she found she didn't want to fight with Aaron. Not here. Didn't want to fight with him, period.

'I guess we're going,' she said. 'So here you go, boys, thanks for buying my drinks all night and I hope this covers it.' She smiled at them. 'I had a brilliant time. And remember what I said about LA. If you're ever there…'

Assorted hugs and kisses later, Ella did her slow walk out of the pub.

'You're not fooling me with the slow walk, Ella,' Aaron said as they reached the footpath.

She stopped. Turned to him. 'I don't know what you m—'

He pulled her into his arms sharply, shocking that sentence right out of her head.

He moved to kiss her but Ella put her hands up, pushing against his chest. 'You don't kiss me any more.'

'Is that so?' Aaron asked. Purely rhetorical—she had no time to answer as he planted his mouth on hers like a heat-seeking missile hitting its target. His hands went to her bottom and he pulled her against him, pelvis to pelvis.

Ella gasped as he released her, and her fingers came up to touch her mouth. 'Why are you so angry with me?'

Aaron looked down at her, unapologetic. 'Because you left me.'

Ella couldn't help herself—she touched his cheek.

She went to pull her hand away but Aaron caught it, held it against his face. 'And because I'm jealous,' he said.

'Jealous?'

Aaron nodded towards the pub.

Ella was stunned. 'But they're gay.'

He didn't miss a beat. 'I don't care if they're eunuchs. Because it's not sex I'm talking about. We're monogamous, you and I, and I trust you with that.'

That certainty shook her. She swallowed hard. 'Then what?'

'It's the whole deal. Being with you. In the moment. In public. *That* smile. That's what I'm talking about.'

That smile? Huh? 'We're in the moment in public now,' she said. 'Which I hope you don't regret.' She tilted her head towards a small group of women as she tugged her hand free. They were staring at Aaron as they walked past. 'I think they know you. I keep forgetting you're a celebrity.'

'I don't care.'

'You're *supposed* to care. Just sex, on the quiet—no scandal. Look, let's be honest. It's not working out, this casual sex thing.'

'No, it's not.'

She couldn't think straight for a moment. Because he'd agreed with her. Which meant it was over. Just what she'd wanted.

'Right,' she said. And then, because she still couldn't think straight, 'Right.'

'We're going to have to renegotiate.'

'There doesn't seem to be much point to that, or much to negotiate *with*,' Ella said, as her brain finally engaged. 'Given you're moving out tomorrow, let's just call it quits.'

Aaron pursed his lips. 'Um—no.'

'No?'

'No.'

'Remember our agreement? No questions, no—'

'I don't give a toss about our agreement. We are not going to go our separate ways because you decided to click your fingers on a public street.'

'See? I told you it's not working. The casual sex deal meant no messy endings. And you're making it messy.'

'But it's not casual, is it, Ella? And I don't want to let you go.'

Her heart did that stuttering thing. She forced herself to ignore it. 'You knew there couldn't be anything except sex. And it will be too hard to keep even that going once we're living in different places.' Swallow. 'And I—I have an extra complication.'

'Which is?' he asked flatly.

'I have—I have…someone.'

'Look at me, Ella.'

She faced him squarely, threw back her head, eyes glittering with defiance.

'No, you don't,' Aaron said.

'Oh, for goodness' sake, I do! I do, I do!'

'If you had someone, you couldn't be with me the way you have been.'

She gasped. He couldn't have hurt her more if he'd stabbed her.

Because he was right.

How could she love Javier if she could pour herself into sex with Aaron in the no-holds-barred way that had become their signature? It had never happened before—only drunken fumbling that she'd run away from every single time. The antithesis of what she did with Aaron.

Aaron was looking at her with almost savage intensity. 'We need to settle this, and not here. Come with me.'

'Where are we going?'

'I don't know—a hotel.'

She laughed, but there was no softness in it. 'I have a hotel room. It stinks like a public toilet and has a plastic mattress protector. That sounds about right. Let's go there. And don't flinch like that.'

'I think we can do better than that, Ella.'

Ella wanted to scream. But she also wanted to cry. And instead of doing either, she was goading him, making everything ugly and tawdry, turning it into the one-night stand it should have always been. 'All right, then. Let's "settle" this,' she said. 'One last time. I'm up for it. You can use my body any way you want, and I will show you there is nothing romantic about an orgasm—it's just technique.'

'Is that so?'

'Let's find out. But if I'm going to play the mistress, I warn you now that I'm going to want access to the mini-bar.'

'Any way I can get you, Ella,' he said, unperturbed. 'You can devour everything in the mini-bar, order everything off the room-service menu, steal the fluffy robe, take the towels—anything you want.'

'I've always wanted to steal the fluffy robe,' Ella said, and took his arm.

CHAPTER THIRTEEN

AARON HAILED A cab and asked to be taken to the closest five-star hotel. On the way, he called to check on Kiri and let Jenny, who'd arrived in the early evening, know he wouldn't be home that night.

Ella waited through the call, clearly still furious with him. Well, too damned bad.

Aaron hastily secured them a room for the night and as they headed for the hotel elevator, he drew Ella close to him, holding her rigid hand. He breathed in the slightly stale pub scent of her. But he couldn't have cared less whether she came to him straight from the shower or after running a marathon through the city sewers.

The elevator doors opened and then they were inside. Alone. The second the doors closed, he was kissing her, sliding his hands under her top. One hand moved up to cover her breast, moulding it to his palm, teasing the nipple to maddening hardness with unsteady fingers. He'd thought she might push him away but, no, she kissed him back, straining against him. He broke the kiss, his breath coming fast and hard now, and bent his mouth to her shoulder, biting her there.

The elevator stopped and they broke apart, staring at each other. Without a word, Aaron grabbed her hand and pulled her quickly out and along the corridor. His hands were shaking so much he almost couldn't work the door mechanism to their suite. And then they were inside and Aaron reached for her again. Wordless. Driven. Desperate.

But so was Ella.

She yanked his T-shirt up his chest and over his head. 'Ah,' she breathed, as her hands went to his hips and she pulled him toward her. She put her mouth on one of his nipples and held tight to his hips as he bucked against her.

'Ella,' he groaned, hands moving restlessly to try to hold onto her as her tongue flicked out. 'Let me touch you.'

'Not yet,' she said, and moved her mouth to his other nipple. As she did so, she started to undo the button fly of his jeans.

He groaned again but couldn't speak as her hands slid inside his underwear.

'Do you like me to touch you like this?' she asked.

'You know I— Ahh, Ella, you're killing me.'

Laughing throatily, Ella stepped back, started to undress.

'Hurry up,' she said, as he stood watching as she wriggled out of her skirt.

It was all the encouragement Aaron needed. In record time, he'd stripped.

Ella, naked except for her high heels, turned to drape her clothes over the back of a handily positioned chair. Aaron came up behind her and caught her against his chest. His arms circled her, hands reaching for her breasts.

She dropped her clothes and leaned back against him, thrusting her breasts into his hands. She moaned as he kissed the side of her neck, gasped as one questing hand dived between her thighs.

'Oh, you're good at this,' Ella said, as she felt her orgasm start to build.

'You can still talk,' Aaron said against her ear. 'So not good enough.'

With that, he bent her forward at the waist until she was clinging to the chair, and thrust inside her. His hands were on her hips as he continued to move inside her, pulling all the way out after each thrust before slamming into her again.

The feel of her bottom against him, the intoxicating sounds of her pleasure as she orgasmed, clenching around him until he thought he'd faint from desire, the exquisite friction of his movements in and out of her built together until the blood was roaring in his head and demanding he take her harder, harder, harder.

Ella. This was Ella.

His.

Ella slumped against Aaron. After that explosive orgasm, he'd turned her around to face him, kissed her for the longest time, and now he was holding her with every bit of gentleness his lovemaking had lacked.

What she'd meant to do was give him a clinical experience. Instead, she'd drenched herself in soul-deep, emotionally fraught lust. Her anger was gone. And the bitterness. She felt purged, almost. Which wasn't the way it was supposed to be.

Nothing had changed. Nothing that could open the way for her to have what she wanted with a clear conscience. Sex couldn't cure things. Even phenomenal sex. Life couldn't be that simple.

Javier was still out there, the uncertainty of his fate tying her to him. Aaron still had a problematic ex-wife and a little boy whose inevitable loss, when they went their separate ways, would devastate her.

'Did I hurt you?' he asked, kissing the top of her head.

'This really is a regular post-coital question of yours, isn't it?'

'No. It's just that I've only ever lost control with you.'

There was a lump in her throat. 'Well, stop asking,' she said, when she trusted herself to speak. 'You didn't hurt me.' *Not in that way.*

'I didn't even think about a condom,' Aaron said.

Ella shrugged restlessly, eased out of his arms. 'I know. I wasn't thinking straight either. And me a nurse.'

'I'm sorry.'

'Me too, but it's done. Not that it's really the point, but I'm on the Pill. So if that worries you, at least—'

'No. No—I'm not worried about that. At least, not for myself. I wish I *could* have a child with you, Ella. Not to replace Sann but for you.'

That lump was in her throat again. She turned away. 'Complicating as all hell, though, pregnancy, for casual sex partners,' she said, trying for light and airy and not quite making it. She remembered ordering him to never say Sann's name again. But it didn't hurt to hear the name now. Not from him.

Aaron—what an unlikely confidant. The only one who knew her pain.

She cleared her throat, 'But now, do you think we could actually move out of this hallway? And where are those fluffy robes?'

Aaron obligingly guided Ella into the lounge area of the suite. He fetched a robe for each of them, and watched as Ella belted hers on, then sat on the sofa to remove her shoes.

He came to sit beside her, slipped an arm around her shoulders and drew her back against him so that her head was against his shoulder.

'You know, don't you, that I'm not a nice person?' she said.

'No, I don't know that. I've watched you work. Seen how much you care. The way you are with Kiri. I know how protective you are of your family. I know you wanted to adopt an orphan from Cambodia, and I've seen what the grief of that did to you. These things don't add up to "not nice".'

'I've been jealous of my sister, of the baby. That's not nice.'

'It doesn't look to me like Tina's had her eyes scratched out,' Aaron said calmly.

'Well, I'm over it now,' she admitted. 'But it took some soul searching.'

'I'm thinking soul searching is a bit of a hobby of yours.'

'And I— Over the past year I've done things. Things I'm not proud of.'

'You've had a lot to deal with. Cut yourself some slack, Ella.'

'You stopped kissing me.'

'And you think that was some kind of judgement?' He broke off, laughed softly. 'That was a defence mechanism. That's all.'

'What?'

'Casual sex? Just sex—no kissing, because kissing is not casual.'

'Oh.'

They stayed sitting in silence, his arm around her, for a long moment.

Now what? Ella wondered.

But then Aaron broke the silence. 'So tell me, Ella, about the "someone". The someone I know you don't have. The someone I think you once *had*. Past tense. Right?'

'Had *and* have.'

'Hmm, I'm going to need a little more.'

'His name is Javier. He's a doctor. Spanish. He was kidnapped in Somalia.' *Whew.* 'There was an article in the paper this morning.' She looked up at him briefly. 'Hence my need to go a little off the rails tonight.'

Aaron nodded, saying nothing. And somehow it was easy to relax against him and continue. Aaron, her confidant. 'We were in love. Very newly in love, so new that nobody else knew about it, which was a blessing the way things turned out, because I couldn't have borne the questions, the sympathy.' Pause. 'I should have been with him that day. It was my twenty-fifth birthday, two years ago. I was supposed to be in the jeep with him.'

Long pause. She could almost hear her own pulse. 'You've got no idea how awful it was. The conditions. The soul-sapping struggle to provide healthcare to people who desperately needed it. Because even before you think about treating illnesses like malaria and TB and pneumonia and HIV, you know that the drought, the violence, the poverty, the poor harvests have made malnutrition a force that simply can't be reckoned with. The kids are starving. Sometimes walking hundreds of kilometres just to drop dead in front of you. And ten thousand people a day are dying.

'And your colleagues are being kidnapped or even murdered, and armed opposition groups make it almost impossible to reach people in need, even though everyone *knows* the suffering, and even hiring a vehicle to get to people is a tense negotiation with clans in constant conflict, and the very people who are providing the tiny bit of security you can get are okay with the deaths and the kidnappings.'

She stopped again. 'Sorry I'm so emotional.' She shook her head. 'No, I'm not sorry. It needs emotion. When you're resuscitating a one-year-old girl, and there is a tiny boy next to her so frail that only a stethoscope over his heart tells you he's alive, and two more critically ill children are waiting behind you, why *not* get emotional?'

His hand was in her hair, stroking, soothing. 'Go on, Ella. I'm here.'

'Anyway. Javier and I were heading to one of the refugee camps in Kenya. But I got malaria and I couldn't go. So I'm here and he's somewhere. Alive, dead, injured, safe? I don't know.' Ella drew in a shuddering breath. 'And I feel guilty, about having a normal life while he's lost. And guilty that I can be with you like this when I should be waiting for him. And just plain guilty. I'm a wreck.'

'Ah, Ella.' He eased her out from under his arm and turned her to face him. 'I'd tell you it's not your fault, that you have a right to go on with your life, that anyone who loved you would want that for you, that you wouldn't want Javier to be trapped in the past if your situations were reversed; but that's not going to set you free, is it?' He ran his fingers down her cheek. 'You have to be ready to let it go.'

'The thing is I don't know what he'd want me to do, or what he'd do in my place.'

'That says something, doesn't it? You were only twenty-five, and in a very new relationship. If you're really going to keep a candle burning in the window for the rest of your life, I'm going to have to find the guy and make sure he's worth it, and I don't really want to do that. Somalia is scary!'

Ella smiled. 'You really do have that heroic thing going on, don't you? I think you *would* go there if you thought it would help me.'

'Nah. It's not heroic, it's self-interest. Memories can bring on rose-tinted-glasses syndrome. Which, in this case, makes it really hard for a mere actor to measure up to a Spanish doctor kidnapped while saving lives in Africa. Even with the malaria documentary under my belt, I'm coming in a poor second.' He kissed her forehead. 'But it's just possible, in a real flesh-and-blood contest, I could edge past him. Unless he happens to be devastatingly attractive as well.'

'As a matter of fact…' Ella trailed off with a laugh.

'Well, that sucks. Maybe I *won't* go and find him after all.'

'Yeah, well, Somalia really *is* scary, so I wouldn't let you go. I wouldn't like to lose you too.' Ella resettled her head on his shoulder. 'Okay—now you know all the salient bits about my past. So, let's talk about you. You said I could ask you anything, and you'd answer.'

'Ask away.'

'I'll start with something easy. Tina told me you raised your sisters after your parents died.'

'Easy? Ha! It was like a brother-sister version of *The Taming of the Shrew*, but in triplicate.'

Ella smiled. 'And you love them very much.'

'Oh, yes. Lucinda, Gabriella and Nicola. My parents were killed in a boating accident when I was eighteen. The girls were fifteen, twelve and ten. I was old enough to look after them, so I did. End of story, really. Two of them are married with kids now, one is married to her job—she's an actuary but she looks like a fashion designer—and all of them are happy.'

'It can't have been easy.'

'We had some nail-biting moments over the years, no doubt about it. But I won't go into the scary boyfriend stories or the fights over schoolwork and curfews. We just belonged together. Simple.'

Pause. And then, 'Is it okay to ask about Rebecca? Like, how you met?'

'Sure. I met her through Brand. The way I meet all my women.'

Ella pinched his thigh.

'All right, not *all* of them,' he amended, laughing. 'Let me give you the abridged version. We met at one of Brand's parties. He was living in Los Angeles back then and I was over there, trying to make the big time— unsuccessfully. Rebecca was doing the same, equally unsuccessfully.'

'So you drowned your sorrows together?'

'Something like that. We were an item in pretty short order. Happily ever after. For a while at least.'

'What went wrong?'

'Nothing. That's what I thought, anyway.' He sighed. 'But looking back, it was all about work. When we returned to Australia I started getting steady jobs. We adopted Kiri and everything seemed fine. But I got more work. Better work. And more work. Making a fortune, no worries. But Rebecca's career stalled. She wasn't happy, and I was too busy to notice. Until it was too late. She started doing a few outrageous things to get publicity in the mistaken belief it would help things along. And before I knew it, it was party, party, party. Drugs. Booze. More drugs. I know Tina told you about the rehab. Well, Rebecca's been to rehab before. Twice.' He shrugged. 'I'm praying this time it will work. This place, it's called Trust, it really seems good.'

'Oh, Trust—I know it, and it is good. She's in safe hands there.'

'Thanks, Ella.'

Ella brought his hand to her lips and kissed it. 'So I guess you've been trying to make up for being too busy to notice when things started to go wrong.'

'That's about the sum of it.'

'Am I going to do the "not your fault" routine?'

Aaron touched her hair. 'No. I'm as bad as you are when it comes to guilt, I think.'

'And Kiri? Why adopt? And why do you have full custody?'

'The adoption? We'd always planned to adopt a child in need and that just happened to come before trying for our own. The custody thing? Well, no matter what's between Rebecca and me, she wants only the best for Kiri, and she recognised that that was living with me, because although she likes to pretend she's in control, she knows she's not.'

She touched his hand. 'You love her. Rebecca.'

'Yes, I do,' Aaron said. 'But it's no longer *that* love. I care about her, as a friend and as the mother of my son.'

'It sounds very mature.'

'Hmm, well, don't be thinking it's all sugar plums and fairy cakes, far from it. She likes to get what she wants.' He laughed. 'I suppose we all do, if it comes to that. But when she needs something, she tends to forget we're divorced and she's not above a bit of manipulation. That can make it hard for us to move on.'

'She wouldn't like it? The fact that I'm here with you.'

'Probably not,' he admitted. 'Unless she had someone first.'

'So you won't tell her.'

'That depends, Ella. On whether we're sticking to our initial arrangement.'

Silence.

Ella wasn't ready to face that.

She got to her feet, headed for the mini-bar and started looking through the contents. 'So,' she said, moving various bottles around without any real interest, 'getting back to the important stuff. Condoms. Or the lack of them. Pregnancy we've covered. But I can also reassure you that I was checked before I left Cambodia and am disease-free.

It's something I do regularly, because of my work with AIDS patients.'

'Me too, disease-free, I mean. I've been an avid fan of the condom for a long, long time.'

She turned. 'But weren't you and Rebecca starting to try for…?'

'Trying for a baby? No. For the last year we weren't trying *anything*. You see, along with the drugs came other problems—new experiences Rebecca wanted, such as sex with a variety of men. Including two of my friends. *Ex*-friends,' he clarified. 'I could forgive her for that. I *did* forgive her, knowing what was going on with her. But I couldn't…well, I just couldn't after that.'

'I don't know what to say to that.'

'Not much *to* say. I did try to keep my marriage together, because commitments are important to me. But some things just…change.'

Ella thought about that. What a lovely thing to accept. *Some things just change.*

'Anyway, enough gloom.' He walked over to her, gave her a quick, hard kiss. 'Come and have a bath with me.'

Aaron grabbed the scented crystals beside the deep bath and threw them in as the tub filled. Then he lifted her in his arms and kissed her as he stepped into the water, settled. Kept kissing her until the bath was full. He took the soap from her and washed her, kissing, touching, until she was gasping for air. But he wouldn't take her. Not this time. 'Condoms, so you don't have to wonder,' he said, by way of explanation.

'I have some in my bag,' she said, shivering with desire.

'Monogamy, remember?' Aaron said. 'I don't think roaming around London with a bag full of condoms fits the principle.'

'Just handbag history—like the expired bus tickets in there. I wasn't going to use them.'

'It's okay, Ella. I know that. Somehow, I really do know that.' He got to his feet, streaming water, but before he could leave the tub Ella got to her knees. 'Not yet,' she said, and looked up at him as she took him in her mouth.

The next morning Aaron ordered a veritable banquet for breakfast.

He was whistling as he opened the door, as the food was laid out in the living room. The robe he'd purchased for Ella was in its neat drawstring bag, positioned on one of the chairs.

He'd left Ella in bed with the television remote control, and was halfway to the bedroom to fetch her for their lovers' feast, mid-whistle, when he heard it. A sound between a choke and a gasp.

'Ella, what is it?' he asked, hurrying into the room.

She was pale. Deathly so. Like the life had drained out of her. She looked up at him, and then, like she couldn't help herself, back at the television.

There was a man being interviewed. A gaunt man. Beautiful—not handsome, beautiful.

'It's him,' Ella said.

CHAPTER FOURTEEN

'Him?' Aaron asked. But he knew.

The news moved onto the next item and it was like a signal had been transmitted directly to Ella's brain.

She got out of bed. 'I have to go,' she said. But then she simply stood there, shivering.

'Go where?'

'Africa.'

'You can't go anywhere in that state, and certainly not Africa.'

'Don't tell me what to do,' she said, and started dressing. It took her less than a minute.

'Ella, you have to talk to me.'

'I did enough talking last night.'

'For God's sake Ella, I—'

'No,' she cried, and then raced to her bag. She looked up, wild-eyed. 'Money. I don't have money for a cab.'

'Calm down, Ella. I'll take you where you need to go.'

'I don't want you to take me anywhere. I want—I want—' She stopped, looked at him, then burst into tears.

Aaron tried to take her in his arms but she wrenched away from him, turned aside to hide her face and walked to the window. She cried as she looked out at the world. Cried as though her soul was shattering.

And just watching her, helpless, Aaron felt his life start to disintegrate.

Gradually, her sobs subsided. She stood leaning her forehead against the window.

Aaron came up behind her, touched her gently on the shoulder. She stiffened but didn't pull away.

'You're going to him,' he said.

'Of course.'

'You're still in love with him, then.'

Pause. And then, 'I have to be. And I have to go.' She turned to face him. 'I know I already owe you money but will you lend me enough for a cab?'

'You don't owe me anything, Ella.'

Aaron grabbed her by her upper arms and drew her forward. 'I'll wait for you to sort this out, Ella. I'll be here, waiting.'

'I don't deserve for anyone to wait for me,' she said, and her voice was colourless. 'Because *I* didn't wait. I *should* have been waiting for him. I *intended* to wait for him. But I didn't. Instead I—I was…' A breath shuddered in. Out. 'I can't stand it. I have to go. Now. I have to go.'

'All right.' Aaron grabbed his jeans and pulled out a handful of notes. 'Take this. And here…' He grabbed the hotel notepad and pen from beside the phone and scribbled a few lines. 'It's my address in London. We'll be there from today. And this…' he dashed another line on the paper '…is the phone number for the house. You've already got my mobile number. Whatever you need, Ella, whenever.'

'Thank you,' Ella said, and raced from the room without another word or glance.

Aaron looked at the sumptuous breakfast, at the robe he'd bought for Ella just because she'd joked about wanting to steal one. She hadn't seen it, wouldn't have taken it if she had.

Javier was back. And that was that.

And then, two days later, Rebecca disappeared from rehab in the company of a fellow addict, a film producer, and he knew he was going to have to fly to LA at some point to bail her out of some heinous situation.

Yep. That really was that.

Ella felt weird, being with Javier, even after a week together.

He was the same and yet not the same.

Every time she broached the subject of the past two years he closed the discussion down. He simply thought they would pick up exactly where they'd left off, as though those two years had never happened, but Ella couldn't get her head into the same space.

She couldn't bear to sleep with him, for one thing.

She told *him* it was to give them a chance to get to know each other again. She told *herself* it was because she'd been stupid enough to forget the condom with Aaron—that meant she had to wait and see, because things *did* go wrong with the Pill.

But, really, she just didn't want to.

She tried, desperately, to remember what it had been like, that one time with Javier, but the only images that formed were of Aaron.

So it would have been disloyal somehow. To Javier, who didn't deserve for her to be thinking about another man. And, bizarrely, to Aaron, who was now effectively out of her life.

Ella sighed and got out of bed in her tiny hotel room. Padded into the bathroom and looked in the cabinet mirror. What did Aaron see that made him fall on her like he was starving for the taste of her? She was beautiful, she'd been told that often enough to believe it, but had never thought it important. Until now. Because maybe Aaron wouldn't have wanted her so much if she'd looked different.

Was it shallow to be glad that something as insignificant as the shape of her mouth made Aaron kiss her as though it was the only thing in the world he needed?

Ella gave herself a mental shake. She had to stop thinking about Aaron. Javier was her future. Javier, who'd been returned to her, like a miracle.

Today, they would fly to London so she could introduce Javier to Tina, who'd had the Javier story thrown at her like a dart as Ella had packed her bags. He would be there with her for the baby's birth. Even her parents would be coming in a month, to meet their grandchild…and the strange man who'd been kept a secret from them. And wouldn't *that* be interesting, after her mother's blistering phone soliloquy on the subject of Ella keeping her in the dark?

Out of control, the whole thing. A runaway train, speeding her into an alien future.

Ella closed her eyes.

Did I hurt you? Aaron's voice whispered through her memory.

Yes, she answered silently. *Yes, you did.*

Heathrow was bedlam, but Ella almost dreaded exiting the airport.

She was so nervous.

About introducing Javier to Tina and Brand.

And about the inevitable meeting between Javier and Aaron.

Javier, she'd discovered, was the jealous type. Not the cute, huggable kind of jealous Aaron had been that night outside the pub in Mayfair. Sort of *scary* jealous. The prospect of him and Aaron in the same room was enough to make her break into a cold sweat.

She welcomed the flash of cameras as they emerged from Customs. Javier was whisked away for a quick photo op, and she was glad. It meant she would have a moment to herself.

Or not.

Because, groan-inducingly, Aaron was there, waiting for her. In his T-shirt and jeans. Looking desperately unhappy.

He strode forward. 'Tina sent me instead of a limo. Sorry. I tried to get out of it, but nobody's allowed to say no to her at the moment, she's been so worried about you.'

'Everyone must hate me.'

'Nobody hates you, Ella. Everyone just wants things to work out.'

Ella could feel one of those awful blushes racing up her neck. 'I'm sorry. For running out like that, I mean. I should have explained, I should have—'

'Ella, don't. I know you. I know what you went through. I know why you had to go. I should have just stood aside. Please don't cry.'

Ella blinked hard, managed to gain her composure. 'You always seem to know. I wish… Oh, he's coming.'

Javier, unsmiling, put his arm around Ella the moment he reached them.

Aaron held out his hand, just as unsmiling.

It was like an old cowboy movie, trigger fingers at the ready, Ella thought, a little hysterically.

'Javier,' Aaron said. His hand was still out, ignored.

Ella took Javier's elbow. 'Javier, this is a friend of Tina and Brand's. And mine. Aaron James. He's very kindly giving us a ride.' Ugh, was that a *wheedle* in her voice? Disgusting.

'I'm pleased to meet you,' Javier said solemnly, at last taking Aaron's proffered hand for a single jerking shake.

Aaron gave him a narrow-eyed look. There was a small uncomfortable pause and then, taking their baggage cart, Aaron said, 'Follow me.'

Javier held Ella back for a moment. 'I don't like the way he looks at you,' he said.

Ella gritted her teeth. This was the fifth time in a week Javier had taken exception to the way a man had looked at her. She would have loved to tell him to get over it, but this particular time he had a right to be suspicious.

Aaron looked over his shoulder, no doubt wondering what was keeping them.

Looking straight ahead, Ella took Javier's arm and followed Aaron.

It was always going to be an uncomfortable drive, but this was ridiculous.

Aaron was fuming, relegated to the role of chauffer.

Javier spoke only to Ella, and only in Spanish.

Charming!

Ella answered him in English, but the agonised looks he was catching in the rear-view mirror told Aaron she knew her Spaniard was behaving like a jackass.

Okay—so maybe jackass was his word, not Ella's, but he stood by it. *Nice choice, Ella.*

It was a relief to pull up at the house. After he helped hoist their luggage out of the boot, Aaron drew Ella a little aside. 'Ella, so you know, Tina's insisting I come to dinner tonight,' he said softly.

'That…that's fine,' Ella said, glancing nervously at Javier, who was giving her a very dark look as he picked up their bags. With a poor attempt at a smile Ella hurried back to Javier, took his arm and ushered him quickly into the house.

Aaron sighed, wondered why he'd even bothered warning her about him being at dinner. However prepared any of them were, when you parcelled it all up—Ella's uncharacteristically submissive demeanour, Javier's haughty unfriendliness, the prospect of witnessing the reunited lovebirds cooing at each other all evening, and his own desire to do some kind of violence to Javier that would ruin at least one perfect cheekbone—dinner was going to be a fiasco of epic proportions.

Aaron had been braced ever since he'd got to Tina's, but he still couldn't help the way his eyes darted to the door of the living room when it opened for the final two guests.

Ella looked like a deer caught in the headlights. She was wearing a dress. Dark grey. Silky. Simple. Classy. She was wearing her black high heels. He wanted to run his hands up her legs. He could drool at any moment.

Their eyes met for one sharp, tense moment and she blushed.

Javier said something and Aaron shifted his gaze.

Javier was everything Aaron wasn't. It was more pronounced tonight than it had been at the airport. Javier was elegant and sophisticated. Stylish in that way Europeans seemed to manage so effortlessly. Javier's hair was jet black, lying against his perfect skull in well-behaved waves. His eyes were equally black—dramatically moody. He was dressed in black pants and a pale pinkish-purple shirt that not many men could carry off.

And since when had Aaron ever noticed, let alone cared about, what other men were wearing?

He tore his eyes away, took a bracing sip of his Scotch.

Hellos were said. A drink pressed into Javier's hand, another into Ella's. Tina kissed Javier on the cheek. Javier touched Tina's ringlets as though entranced.

Tina laughed. 'A curse, this hair. Only Brand likes it.'

Javier smiled. 'Not only Brand. I like it too. Lively hair.'

Tina laughed again, shaking her head until her curls danced a little.

Great, Aaron thought. Javier was going to be adored by Ella's sister. Just great.

Brand, who was standing beside him, made a disgusted sound and rolled his eyes. He'd always known Brand was an excellent judge of character.

Tina was saying something about the need to fatten Ella up.

'It's her work,' Javier said, pulling Ella very close. 'She worked too hard in Cambodia.'

'Getting any information out of Ella about her work is like pulling teeth, but Aaron told us a little about the conditions there.'

Javier looked straight at Aaron. Hostile.

Not that he could work out the whole backstory of Aaron's obsession with Ella from one glancing look.

Could he?

'And what were *you* doing, Aaron? In Cambodia?' Javier's voice was perfectly polite, and chilling.

'I was filming a documentary on malaria.' *And fantasising about your girlfriend.*

Tina was starting to take on a little of Ella's deer-in-the-headlights look. Sensing the undercurrents, no doubt. 'So, Javier,' Tina said, 'are you able to share with us a little about…about…your experience?'

Javier smiled at her, but to Aaron it looked almost dismissive.

'I was not badly treated,' Javier said. 'Just not free. But not, perhaps, a subject for tonight. Tonight is a celebration, you see. Ella and I…' He stopped, smiled again, drew Ella nearer.

How much closer could he *get* her, anyway? Aaron

wondered furiously as he watched Ella. But she wouldn't meet his eyes. Wouldn't meet anyone's eyes.

'Ella and I would like to share our news,' Javier said, and raised Ella's hand to kiss the palm. 'Ella has done me the honour of accepting my proposal of marriage.'

Aaron caught the sparkle on Ella's finger, and turning away, swallowed the rest of his Scotch in one swig.

Aaron hadn't come looking for Ella.

Didn't want to be alone with her. Not now. When he felt so raw.

And yet there she was, in the kitchen, straightening up after putting something in the fridge.

And there he was. In the kitchen. Forgetting why.

He must have made some sound because she straightened. Turned. The fridge door swung closed behind her.

For a moment Aaron couldn't breathe.

'How are you, Aaron?' she asked quietly.

'Fine.' The word sounded as though it had been bounced into an airless room.

'And Kiri?'

'Fine. He misses you.'

He saw her swallow. She said nothing. Well, what did he expect her to say?

Aaron took a step closer to her. 'There were no consequences? I mean as a…a result of—'

'I know what you mean. I told you I was on the Pill. But just in case, I'm waiting…' Stop. Another swallow. 'I mean, I'm not doing anything… I'm not…with…' She drew an audible breath. 'Until I know.'

'That's good,' Aaron said, miraculously understanding. 'I mean, is it good? Yes, I guess it's good. I guess it's…' Nope. He couldn't finish that.

Silence.

Ella was turning the engagement ring round and round on her finger. 'How's Rebecca? Rehab? How's it going?'

'It's not. She left early; with a drug-addicted film producer. Never anything mundane for Rebecca.'

'Oh, I'm so sorry.'

He rubbed a hand behind his neck. 'Just one thing. I told her about you, about us. In case…'

Ella was fidgeting—which he'd never seen her do. Playing with the damned ring. 'Does that mean…? Does everyone know about us?' she asked.

'No. Nobody else. And Rebecca isn't talking—except to her publicist, who's working out how to go public with the film producer.'

'It's just…Javier's the jealous type. I don't want him to… You know what I mean.'

'I'll fix it so nothing rebounds on you, I promise. And I guess there's nothing to say, anyway. You're engaged.'

Another awful silence.

Aaron took one step closer. 'Have you picked a date? For the wedding?'

'No. Not yet.'

'Why are you doing it, Ella?'

She held out her hands. Imploring. 'How could I say no? How could I refuse him anything after what he's been through?'

He had a few pithy answers for that—but found he couldn't voice them, not when she looked so tormented. 'I'm glad you're not sleeping with him,' he said instead.

He took one more step, close enough now to take her hands, hold them. 'And I know that's unworthy, Ella, but I've discovered I'm not good at giving in gracefully.'

'This is not doing us any good, Aaron.' Ella tried to pull her hands free, but Aaron held on. 'Let me go. If you don't, I don't know how I'll bear it.'

He pulled her hands against his chest, held them there. 'Ella, we need to talk.'

'We are talking.'

'Not here, not like this.'

'I can't. I need to get back in there.' She pulled her hands free. '*Please*, Aaron. It's very difficult just now. Please.'

'*Porque estas tardano tanto?*'

Both Aaron and Ella turned towards the doorway, where a frowning Javier was standing.

'I'm coming now,' she said in English, and walked out of the room, pausing just outside the kitchen door to wait for Javier to join her.

'*Andante, te seguire pronto,*' he said.

Ella looked at Aaron quickly, nervously, then as quickly away. 'All right,' she said.

Javier moved further into the kitchen. He looked Aaron over and seemed to find nothing there to worry about if his slight sneer was anything to go by.

'You know Ella well.' Statement, not question.

'Yes. I do.'

'You watch her.'

The comment surprised Aaron; he'd been conscious of *not* looking at her all night. 'Do I?'

'I can understand. She is beautiful.'

Aaron was silent.

Javier smiled, but it wasn't a friendly smile. 'She is beautiful, and she is mine.'

'If she's yours, what's your problem?'

'I just want it to be clear. So, I think you were bringing the cheese? I'm here to help.'

Cheese. Of course. He had offered to go to the kitchen and get the cheese.

When the two men returned to the dining room, Ella smiled blindingly at her fiancé—the mouth-only version, ha!—put her hand over Javier's when he paused by her chair and touched her shoulder, then moved her chair a smidgeon closer to his when he sat beside her.

Ella's hand kept disappearing under the table and Aaron guessed she was giving Javier's thigh an intermittent pat. Probably reassuring him that she was not remotely attracted to the brooding thug at the other end of the table who now, perversely, couldn't seem to keep his eyes off her.

Which word was stronger—disaster or catastrophe?

Because he was designating this dinner party a catastrophic disaster or a disastrous catastrophe—whichever was worse.

CHAPTER FIFTEEN

WHEN ELLA'S CELLPHONE trilled the next morning and Aaron's name flashed, she felt a wash of emotion that was a weird hybrid of joy and anxiety.

'Hello? Ella?'

Ella gasped. *Not* Aaron. 'Kiri! Is everything all right?'

'Where are you, Ella?'

'I'm at Tina's darling, why?'

'We're going to see Mum, and I want to say goodbye. But Dad says you're too busy.'

'Where's Dad?'

'Filming.' Giggle. 'He forgot his phone.'

Her heart swelled with longing. 'When do you leave, Kiri?'

'Soon.'

Which was kid-speak for any time. Tomorrow. Next week. An hour.

Ella bit her lip, thinking. Aaron was on set so the coast was clear. Javier was out, and he didn't have to know. The apartment was within walking distance. Could she do this? See Kiri once more? 'What about if I come over now?' Ella found herself asking.

'Yes!' Kiri said, excited. 'I painted you a picture. Of you and me.'

'Well, I have to see that!' she exclaimed. 'I'll be there soon.'

* * *

It didn't take long for Aaron to realise he'd left his phone at home. He felt guilty that he'd be late to the set, because Brand had to head to York in the afternoon to check out locations for an evening shoot, and the schedule was already tight, but he just had to turn back for it. After Kiri's dengue fever episode Aaron liked to be instantly contactable at all times.

Aaron raced into the apartment. 'Jenny?' He called out, and hurried into the living room. 'I forgot my phone, so—' He broke off, and his heart leapt so savagely he couldn't catch his breath.

Ella. Here.

She was sitting with Jenny and Kiri, one of Kiri's paintings in her hands, but she seemed to be holding her breath as her beautiful violet eyes rose to his and stuck there.

Jenny, looking from one to the other of them, murmured something about Kiri needing something. She took Kiri by the hand, led him from the room.

Ella shrugged awkwardly. 'Sorry,' she said, putting down the painting and getting to her feet. 'But he called and I... He said you were leaving?'

'We are—in a few days. Rebecca overdosed. I've got to make sure she's okay.'

'Oh, Aaron.'

'But there's a bright side. It scared her. She's heading back to Trust.'

'That's good. Great.'

'And I'm going to meet Scott too.'

'Scott?'

'The film producer. He's with her. Thank heavens he seems to be on track. She says it's serious between them, and I need to think about what that means for Kiri.'

He could smell her. His heart was aching. He couldn't

seem to stop his hand moving up to rub his chest, not that it ever made a difference to the pain.

'We're going to move to LA once the film is done,' he said. 'To support her. I had an audition there a while back, and I've got a callback, so hopefully...'

'That's great.' Ella smiled—that infuriating smile that didn't reach her eyes. She picked up her bag, preparing to leave. 'I'll be moving, too. Spain.'

'Not LA?'

She shook her head vehemently. 'Not LA. So maybe this time fate will do the right thing and keep us out of each other's way, huh?'

She laughed, but Aaron had never felt less like laughing, and her own dwindled away until she was staring at him, equally silent.

Aaron watched her closely. 'So, we're going to stand here, are we, Ella, and smile and laugh and pretend we don't mean anything to each other? Because I don't think I can do it.'

Her eyes widened. 'Don't,' she said. 'You and Rebecca and Kiri have a long path ahead of you. You need to concentrate on that.'

'And you have to concentrate on martyring yourself, is that it?'

'Stop it, Aaron. Loyalty is not martyrdom. I *owe* Javier this.'

'Two years apart, and then suddenly you get engaged? What do we even know about him?'

'*We* don't need to know anything. Only I do.'

'I told you I'd be waiting for you. And then—'

'Waiting for what? Don't throw Rebecca's new man in my teeth as though that's supposed to make a difference. You've just told me you're following her to America. Where does that leave me? Where?'

He crossed the floor to her. 'I *hoped* in LA. Close to me. Where we could work it out.'

'Oh, spare me. I'd just be carrying two loads of guilt— leaving Javier when he needs me, and being your bit on the side. Well, I'm not doing it.' She paced. One step. Two. Three. Back. 'I knew this would happen. Keep it simple, you said. Casual. And then you proceeded to make it anything but. I tried to make you leave me alone. Sydney, Cambodia, London—every time. Why couldn't you? Why?'

'Because.' *Oh, great answer. Who wouldn't buy that?*

She looked, rightly, incredulous. 'That's an answer?' She turned away, tearing her hands through her hair as though her head was aching.

'All right, I'll tell you why. Because I'm in love with you.'

She spun back to face him. Her mouth formed a silent 'O'. She seemed incapable of speech.

'It's true,' Aaron said, and felt a sense of wonder himself. 'I couldn't leave you alone, because I loved you. I *love* you.'

'I don't want you to.'

'You don't get to dictate to me on this, Ella. If I could have dictated *myself* out of it, I would have. Because, I can assure you, it's not something I wanted either.'

She backed away a step. 'It's just proximity. Because I'm here. And I threw myself at you.'

He laughed harshly. 'Except that I've been lugging it around since Cambodia.' It was true. True! Since *Cambodia*. Why hadn't he realised it before? 'And I'm the one who was doing the throwing,' he continued. 'Always, always me. You were the one running. And I'll tell you this: it's a pain in the butt. *You're* a pain in the butt most of the

time, with your bad-girl routine and your secrets. But...'
he shook his head '...I love you.'

'Well, stop it. This is a mess. We're a mess. Just as
predicted.' Her breath hitched. 'And I—' She broke off,
rubbed her hands over her face again. 'This is so frustrat-
ing. Why do we do this to each other? Why can't we ever
have a normal discussion?'

'I think it's because I love you, Ella.'

'Stop saying that.'

'And I think it's because you don't want to hear it, so
you prefer to fight.'

She did that thing where she got herself together, visibly changing from distraught to pale and blank and cool.
'Remember what I said about Disneyland? That it's a blast
as long as you remember it isn't real? Let's just say we've
had too many turns on the teacups. Your head will stop
spinning soon.'

'No, it won't, Ella. My head will still be spinning. My
heart will still be aching. And I will still be in love with
you.'

She looked at him coldly. 'Then just be happy I'm refusing to help you mess up your life.'

CHAPTER SIXTEEN

ELLA HAD AN uncomfortable night.

Aaron loved her. *Loved* her.

But it didn't change anything. Because with Brand stuck in York and Tina needing a distraction from her constant back pains, it was *Javier* who took her and her sister out for dinner. It was *Javier* stopping outside Ella's bedroom door when they got home, kissing her, urging her with that sharp, impatient edge to his voice, *'Let me in, Ella. It's time, Ella. Why not, Ella?'*

Why not, Ella? Because Aaron loved her. How was she supposed to sleep with anyone else, knowing that?

It was a relief when Javier left the house after breakfast the next morning, so she didn't have to feel the heavy weight of his dark eyes on her, silently accusing her, questioning her, beseeching her.

Tina was restless, and irritable, and uncomfortable. Demanding a cappuccino from a particular café, which Ella took herself off to buy and bring back so Tina didn't have to get out of her nightgown. Ella hoped Brand's train was on time. She had a nervous feeling Tina's persistent backache meant the baby was preparing to introduce itself to its parents, and Tina would make Brand's life hell if he missed even a second of her labour.

The thought made her laugh as she walked into the

house, takeaway coffee in hand. It always amused her to think of Brand—for whom the term alpha male could have been coined—as putty in her sister's hands. Because that's what—

The coffee cup slipped through Ella's fingers. 'Tina!' she cried, and ran towards her sister's crumpled form at the foot of the stairs.

Tina groaned.

Ella closed her eyes, silently thanking every deity she could think of. And then she crouched beside her sister. 'How many times do you have to fall down the stairs before you learn that you do *not* hurry when you're about to give birth?' Ella demanded. 'Brand is going to maim everyone in sight if anything happens to you.'

'It was only the last couple of stairs. I was feeling so awful, and I'm having those horrible Braxton-Hicks things, and I thought I'd go back to bed. So shut up, Ella, and just help me up.'

'Let me check you out first,' Ella said, but Tina was already struggling to her feet—only to slump back down again with a sharp cry.

'I can't get up, Ella. I think I sprained my ankle. And I...' She stopped, and her eyes widened as she looked down at herself, at the floor beneath her. 'Ella!'

She sounded scared. And Ella, seeing the puddle pooling around her sister, understood. Tina's waters had broken.

'But Brand's not here,' Tina wailed, and then she gasped and grabbed Ella's hand. A long, keening moan slipped out between her clenched teeth. 'Oh, no, oh, no,' she whimpered, as her hand loosened after a long moment. 'Ella, I can't do this without Brand. I promised him I wouldn't. He's going to kill me.'

Ella gave a shaky laugh. 'Tina, my darling, the only

way he's going to kill you is by kissing you to death. Now, there will be ages to go, but if you're okay to stay there for a moment, I'll go and call the hospital and tell them we're coming in. And I'll call Aaron—he's on standby to drive you to the hospital, right?'

'Okay. Good. No!' Tina grabbed Ella's hand again and held on so tightly Ella wondered if her phalanges were about to snapped in two. Instinctively, she timed the hold. Counting down, counting, counting.

Seventy seconds. The contractions were coming close together. *Uh-oh.*

Tina let go, took a shaky breath.

'Right,' Ella said again, super-calm despite a finger of unease trailing a line down her spine. 'I have to let you go, okay? Just for a moment, to call the hospital.'

Tina, white-faced, nodded. 'And Brand. You have to call Brand. Oh, what's the time? He told me this morning he was trying for an earlier train.'

'I'll try. Just wait, okay?'

Ella raced for the phone and let the private hospital where Ella and Brand had chosen to deliver their baby know they were on their way in. She tried to call Brand but got his voicemail. Assuming he was out of range, she opted not to leave a message; if he got a message about Tina going into labour the moment he switched on his phone, he'd likely hijack the train and make the driver go faster!

She came haring back to Tina, who was in the throes of another contraction—*way* too soon. She allowed both her hands to be grabbed, the knuckles crunched, for the duration, but said, 'Try not to hold your breath, Tina. Just breathe, nice and deep and slow.'

Tina gave her a look that promised her a slow death, but she gave it a gasping try. At the end of the contraction Tina looked up at her. 'Did you get Brand?'

'He must be out of range, Tina. But I'm sure he'll be here soon.'

Tina started to cry, and Ella hugged her. 'Shh,' she said, kissing the top of Tina's head. 'Everything's going to be fine. But we need to get you off these hard tiles and clean you up, and I still need to call Aaron— Oh, hang on, someone's at the door.'

Praying it would be someone useful, Ella raced to the door, tugged it open. Aaron—in the process of knocking again—almost fell inside, and slipped on the spilled coffee. 'Whoa,' he said.

'Thank goodness!' Ella said, and dragged him further into the hall.

'Before you say anything, Ella, I'm not stalking you. I promised Brand I'd look in on Tina, so—' He broke off. 'What's happening?'

'It's Tina, she's in full-on labour!' Ella whispered.

At the same time Tina threw out a wobbly, wailing, 'I know, it *suuuucks*,' from the floor at the base of the stairs.

Ella gave Aaron a warning look. 'It does not suck,' she said, all brisk and professional. 'Because the hospital is expecting us and Aaron is going to get the car and Brand is going to arrive, and everything is going to go according to plan.' She smiled brightly at Tina as she hurried back to her—just in time to take her sister's hands as a scream, followed by a string of graphic curses, tore from Tina's throat.

When the contraction finally stopped, Tina was incoherent, so Ella quickly pulled Aaron aside. 'We're not going to make it to the hospital,' she told him.

'What's wrong?' he asked, sharp and serious.

'Her contractions are too close together, they're too intense, and they're lasting too long. I'm thinking precipitous labour.'

'That sounds bad! *Is* that bad?'

'Well, it's fast, and it's going to be very painful.'

'But if we get her into the car straight away?'

Ella was shaking her head before he'd finished. 'No, the way things are heading, we'll be delivering the baby by the side of the road, and that's *not* happening with this baby. I'm calling an ambulance, but childbirth isn't the highest condition on the triage list. So I'm going to get ready here, just in case. And I'm going to need you to help me.'

Aaron looked completely appalled, but he nodded. 'Just tell me what to do.'

'She's twisted her ankle so—'

A scream from Tina interrupted her. Another contraction.

Ella hurried back to her sister, Aaron beside her. Ella gripped her sister's hand, uttering useless, placating nothings, until the contraction passed. Then she brushed Tina's sweat-damp hair off her face. 'Right, darling, we're not taking any chances with an Aussie driving in London. I'm calling an ambulance instead, and then we're going to make you comfortable while we wait for it to get here, okay?'

Tina nodded, white with stress and pain and terror.

'Aaron's going to stay with you while I'm gone—just for a minute, okay?'

'Okay,' Tina said, sounding pitiful.

Ella drew Aaron aside again. 'Just keep her calm. Encourage her to breathe, deep and slow, deep and slow, but get ready for some screaming.'

'I can take it,' he said.

Tina, eyes glazed, wasted no time in grabbing Aaron's hand as he dropped beside her, squeezing tightly through another fierce contraction. Ella waited, roughly timing through a scream, scream, scream, to the whimper and slump. Ninety seconds.

'Hello, Hercules!' Aaron said admiringly. 'I need to get me some of whatever it is you're eating, bruiser.'

As Ella raced for the phone, she heard Tina give a strangled laugh. She gave another silent prayer of thanks, for Aaron's arrival. Aaron would look after her sister in every way possible—her health, her spirits, her dignity. What more could you ask for at a time like this?

Three calls later, the ambulance, Tina's private obstetrician and another fruitless try for Brand, and she raced up the stairs as another agonising contraction ripped through her sister, with Aaron encouraging her to scream her lungs out if that's what she felt like doing. Not exactly keeping her calm, but Ella had the felling Aaron had the right of it. If Tina wanted to scream her way through, let her!

Ella grabbed an armload of sheets, towels and blankets. She added a fresh nightgown. She then picked up several pairs of sterile surgical gloves from her ever-ready supply, a bandage for Tina's ankle, scissors, rubbing alcohol and an assortment of cotton wool and gauze pads. She winced as she heard Tina's wailing cry as another contraction hit her.

She juggled the goods into a semi-manageable pile in her arms and descended the stairs again. Halfway down, when Tina was silent again, she heard Aaron say, 'You know, Tina, women have been giving birth for thousands of years—and *you're* the one who gets to have Ella personally presiding over the action. How cool is that?'

'Very cool,' Tina gasped out, and met Ella's eyes as she arrived at the bottom of the stairs. 'Very, very cool.' She mouthed, 'I love you,' at Ella, and Ella almost cried.

'Love you too,' she mouthed back. And then she took a deep breath and hurried into the library. She shifted the couch so she had room to stand at the end of it, then quickly put down a thick layer of towels, covered them with a sheet, spread more towels where Tina's hips and thighs would go. She propped cushions, stacking more towels close by, and prepared blankets for when they'd be needed. Over the sounds of her sister screaming, she quickly used the rubbing alcohol to clean the surface of Kiri's activity table, then laid out on it everything else she'd brought from upstairs.

By the time she was back at the stairs, Tina was lying on her side, half on Aaron, abusing him for not massaging her in the right spot.

Aaron, accepting the abuse with equanimity, merely looked up at Ella and asked, 'Ready?'

'Ready,' Ella said.

'Tina,' he said, 'I'm going to lift you now, okay?'

Tina, distressed and almost incoherent, shook her head. 'I'm too messy. Look! I can walk. Or hop. Arm. Just your arm.'

'Tina, when did you start being such a girl?' he asked. 'Get over it and put your arms around my neck.' And then he effortlessly gathered Tina close and lifted her. He carried her into the library, oblivious to the amniotic fluid soaking his T-shirt and jeans.

'Can you balance her while I get her changed?' Ella asked.

'Sure, if you promise not to tell Brand I saw her naked,' Aaron said, and that gave Tina a much-needed laugh—quickly choked off as another contraction hit her.

Somehow, Ella and Aaron managed to get her stripped, freshly nightgowned and settled on the couch.

Ella stroked Tina's sodden hair off her face again. 'Shall I tie your hair back?' she asked,

'Yes, it's really annoying me.'

Ella whipped the elastic from her own hair and bundled Tina's heavy mass of ringlets into a ponytail high on her head. 'And now,' she said, 'I'm going to go and wash my hands, while Aaron waits with you.'

Five minutes later she was back. 'Tina, I need to check how dilated you are, okay?'

Tina cast a look in Aaron's direction.

Ella smiled, understanding. 'While I do that, Aaron is going to go and get me an ice pack for your ankle.' She looked quickly at Aaron. 'And I need some string or twine—I think I saw some in the kitchen drawer. And I need bowls and a plastic bag. Oh, and warm water, but you can get that next trip.'

'On it,' he said, and bolted from the room as Tina went mindless with another contraction, her painful, guttural cries making Ella wish she could take the pain for her.

'Ella. Ambulance. Not…going…to get…here,' Tina gasped as the contraction eased.

'I don't think so, darling,' Ella said 'My niece or nephew seems particularly impatient. Like you, always in a damned hurry.'

'Okay, so let's get onto the important question,' Tina panted out. 'Do you…th-think Brand…is going to be upset…when he finds out I'm in love…with Aaron?'

Ella forced a laugh as she snapped on her sterile gloves, marvelling that her sister could crack a joke at such a time—her precious, amazing sister! 'I think Brand is going to be in love with Aaron himself once all this is over,' Ella said, and searched her head for a distraction. 'So, names. I'm thinking Boadicea, Thorberta and Nathene for a girl. Burford, Lindberg and Ogelsby for a boy. Nice, huh?'

But Tina's strained chuckle was cut off by another moaning scream. 'Ella, Ella, I need to push.'

'Just hang on, hang on, darling. Try to breathe through it.'

'Breathe? Don't be so stupid, Ella. I need to push!'

Tina was sprawled, spread-eagled, with one leg off the

couch. Ella positioned herself between her sister's thighs as Tina pushed, pushed hard. She lifted the sheet she'd draped over her sister's legs and, as soon as the contraction eased, inserted her fingers to find—

Oh, no. 'Tina, darling, I can feel the baby's head,' she said.

'What? What?' Tina panted.

'The baby's well and truly on the way. I think we can assume all those back pains you had yesterday weren't back pains, they were labour pains, so…'

But Tina was having another contraction, so Ella shut up, caught her sister as she surged up off the couch, held her and let her yell.

'You were saying?' Tina asked weakly, as she sagged back limply. But almost immediately another contraction hit her, and Ella held onto her again and simply breathed, hoping to calm her.

'I'm going to kill Brand. Kill him!' Tina screamed.

Aaron, coming back into the room loaded up with everything Ella had asked for, said, 'Let me do it for you.'

Tina's laugh turned into another screech, and then it was roller-coaster time.

The contractions had Tina in their vicious grip and wouldn't let her go. She was sweating gallons, and Aaron stayed by her side, hanging onto her hand when she needed it, wiping her brow, occasionally leaning over to wipe Ella's too.

Ella had gloved up again, and this time when Tina said she had to push she told Tina to go ahead, because nothing was going to slow this baby down.

All modesty had fled. Tina just wanted the baby out, even if Aaron had to reach in and yank it through the birth canal—which Aaron pronounced himself ready to do, only to be punched and to be told not to be such an idiot.

Ella was staring between her sister's legs. 'The head is crowning,' she said, very calmly. 'Not long now.'

The house phone was ringing. Then Ella's. Then Aaron's. All were ignored.

More contractions. 'Now push, Tina, push now.'

Phones ringing again. One after the other. Once again ignored.

Another contraction. Pushing, pushing, panting, pushing. Tina was shaking. 'Here comes the baby's head,' Ella said. 'Try to stop pushing now, Tina. Stop, the head is here. It's here, Tina.' Ella checked quickly to ensure there was no cord wrapped around the baby's neck. Breathed a sigh of relief. 'Beautiful. Oh, Tina, so beautiful.'

Aaron was holding a weeping Tina's hand, whispering encouragement, kissing her forehead, tears in his eyes, while Ella was supporting the baby's head.

Phones. Ignored.

'One more push and it will all be over,' Ella said, as the baby's head rotated to one side as though it knew what it was doing. And then one shoulder emerged, and the other, and the baby shot into Ella's hands like a bullet. Ella was crying, Tina was crying, Aaron was crying.

'It's a girl,' Ella announced, and, supporting the tiny baby's head and neck carefully, she tilted her to enable any fluids to drain from her nose and mouth.

The baby, eyes wide open like she was completely outraged, gave a strong, angry cry, and Ella quickly checked that she was pink right down to her extremities, her limbs were strong and flexed and that basically she was alert and perfect and gorgeous. Tina held out her arms, and Ella laid the baby on her mother's chest.

Ella checked the wall clock as she took off her gloves. Forty-five minutes from the time she'd spilled that coffee in the hall to the birth of her niece. Incredible! 'Aaron, just pull Tina's nightgown down a little, off her shoulders. Tina, that will let you be skin to skin with the baby. It will help release oxytocin in your body, which will make the placenta slip out faster.'

Judging by the delirious look on Tina's face, Aaron could have done anything just then and she wouldn't have known it. As Aaron adjusted Tina's nightdress, Ella drew a blanket up over the baby's back, making sure Tina, who was shivering, was covered too.

'What can I do next?' Aaron asked, looking at the blood soaking the towels underneath Tina.

'The blood's nothing to worry about, Aaron.'

He passed a shaking hand over his eyes. 'Thank goodness.'

'There is just the placenta to go, if you can pass me that bowl,' she said.

'And then do we get to cut the cord?' Aaron asked.

We. Such a little word, but it made Ella want to kiss him. 'When it's stopped pulsing, if the ambulance isn't here.' She ran a tired hand across her forehead. 'But first—the phones, Aaron. I'll bet it was Brand. Can you—?'

But Aaron didn't have to do anything, because Brand erupted into the room, wild-eyed, followed by two paramedics. 'What the hell—?' he started, and then came to a dead stop. His mouth dropped open as he stared at Tina. Then he rushed forward, fell to his knees on the floor beside the couch. 'Tina?' He sounded awed and shaken. 'How did this happen?'

Teary, exhausted, but smiling, Tina reached out a hand, and touched his cheek. Ella and Aaron shared a look as Brand grabbed Tina's hand, pressed a kiss to the palm—just a simple kiss and yet it was so intimate.

One of the paramedics came over to confer with Ella, who quickly provided details of the morning's drama.

And then Ella realised she and Aaron were *de trop*.

The baby was being checked; the placenta would be delivered and bagged; Tina would be taken care of. Brand was cooing at his wife and daughter.

With a smile at Aaron Ella inclined her head towards the door, and the two of them left the library. The stood in the hall, looking at each other. And then Aaron said, 'I never did get the warm water.'

Ella started to laugh.

'And where the hell did I put the ice pack?' he asked.

And then they were both laughing. They laughed, laughed, laughed, as Aaron—covered in dried amniotic fluid—pulled Ella—covered in blood—into his arms. He buried his face in her loose hair. They clung together for a long moment, before drawing apart slowly.

Euphoric, shaken, exhausted, they stared at each other. Ella's heart was aching, her breath jammed in her throat with a lurching, desperate need to touch him. To huddle against him and weep and sigh and just *have*.

Brand broke the spell, exploding out of the library with the same energy with which he'd entered it. 'I cut the cord,' he announced proudly.

Next moment, he was grabbing Ella, hugging her. Ella could feel him shaking. 'I love you,' he whispered in her ear.

'I love you too, Brand,' Ella whispered back, and kissed his cheek. 'And your beautiful wife, and your adorable baby girl.'

'Audrey Ella McIntyre—that's her name,' he said. And then he freed one arm and reached for Aaron, dragged him in. 'Mate,' he said. Just one word, but it said everything, because in it was joy and love and excitement and gratitude.

'Do we get to smoke a cigar now?' Aaron joked, and was dragged closer still.

'You're an uncle now—no smoking,' Brand said, in a suspiciously husky voice.

Then Tina and the baby were being wheeled out of the library, and Brand, laughing maniacally, was off like an arrow as he followed his wife and daughter out of the house.

Aaron cocked an eyebrow at Ella. 'So, can I clean up that spilled coffee over there and make you a new one?' he asked.

He was very conscious of the butterflies swooping in his gut, now he was alone with her.

Butterflies? Did a grown man even *get* butterflies?

He *never* got butterflies.

Ella looked at him, biting her bottom lip. Was she going to say no?

'It wasn't my coffee. It was Tina's.'

'So I *can't* make you one?'

'Yes, yes, of course you can,' she said, but she looked nervous. 'I'll clean the spill later, though.' She took a deep breath. 'Right now, I really, really do need coffee. Just as soon as I wash myself up.'

Aaron did what he could to clean himself up, then made his way to the kitchen. He wondered what kind of conversation they could have after delivering a baby together. And after yesterday's conversation, when he'd told her he loved her.

So, Ella, how's it going? Decided you love me yet?

His smile twisted. Maybe not.

Aaron realised he was standing there in a trance, looking at her while he rubbed his hand over his heart. He hated it that he did that when he looked at her, whenever he even *thought* of her. His T-shirts were all going to start showing wear and tear in that one spot.

He busied himself with boiling water, setting out cups, spooning instant coffee. Ella came in and took a seat at the kitchen counter.

Aaron handed her a mug. 'So, Ella, do you need…do you need…anything? From me? Now? Do you need…' *Me? Me, me, me? Do you need me, Ella?* 'Um…anything?'

'No. It's just…'

Just her voice. Her husky Yankee voice was enough to make him melt. 'Just?'

'I can't believe I was jealous—of my own sister, of this baby. Because now…' She stopped, shook her head. 'It's just so perfect. Isn't it? Perfect!'

'Yes it's perfect, so take off the hair shirt for a while, Ella, hmm?' He reached over, touched her hair, just once. 'Funny, isn't it? Brand had every specialist in Europe on speed dial, and all it took was you.'

'I was so scared,' she said, and he heard the steadying breath she dragged in. 'I don't know what I would have done if you weren't here.'

'Nobody would have known you were scared. You're just amazing, Ella. But, hey, if you want to fall apart now it's all over, here I am,' he said. 'You can cry all over me.'

Ella looked at him and smiled—that glorious smile, with her mouth and her eyes and her heart and her soul.

That smile.

It told him that, regardless of what they wanted or didn't want, they were connected.

It was fate.

'Oh, Aaron,' she said.

He thought she would say more, but then, outside the room, there was a quick burst of Spanish.

'I'd better go,' Ella said, and leaving her coffee, untouched, on the counter, she rushed from the kitchen.

Hmm. Fate had a lousy sense of timing, all things considered.

When Aaron and Kiri walked into Tina's hospital room that night, Ella was there, holding the sleeping baby.

Her eyes lit up when she saw him and his heart felt like it was doing a triple back somersault with a full twist. He caught himself doing that hand-rubbing thing over it again and had a bad feeling it wasn't a habit he was going to kick any time soon.

'Hello, Kiri,' she said. 'Aaron.' She looked kind of shy. It was entrancing. 'Recovered from today's high drama, then?'

'Yes,' he said. Not exactly a scintillating conversationalist tonight, but after the intimacy they'd shared at Audrey's birth—even though they'd been so focused on Tina they'd barely spoken to each other through the experience—he found himself tongue-tied. He was just so in love with her. He wondered how he hadn't seen his obsession with her for what it was sooner.

Love. If he'd admitted it to himself in Cambodia, they'd be married and she'd be pregnant by now; although, after today, how he'd actually *live* through Ella in labour he didn't know, and nobody would have the power to keep her from him—not even her.

'Ah, Kiri, my favourite boy,' Tina said. 'Did you come to see me or Audrey?'

'You *and* Audrey,' Kiri said, approaching the bed. His eyes were huge, staring at the baby.

'Smooth talker,' Tina said, laughing. 'Ella, let Kiri see her properly.'

Ella settled herself in the chair next to Tina's bed and beckoned Kiri closer.

When Kiri was beside her he asked, 'Can I touch her?'

'Yes,' Ella said. 'In fact…' She shot Tina a questioning look and waited for Tina to nod. 'You can hold her. But you'll have to sit very still in this chair. Can you do that?'

'Give Tina the picture first, mate,' Aaron told him, and Kiri handed it to his father without taking his eyes off the baby.

Aaron laughed as he presented it to Tina. 'I think we know where his priorities lie, Tina, and they're not with you or me—or even Ella, who used to be his favourite up until two minutes ago.'

Ella settled Audrey on Kiri's lap and positioned his arm so that it was firmly under her head. 'She doesn't have a strong neck yet, so you need to be careful that you hold her head like this. All right?'

Kiri nodded. Audrey didn't fret, just accepted this little boy who was holding her as though it was the biggest adventure of his life. Then Kiri leaned his face down to the baby and softly kissed her forehead.

Ella looked at Aaron. Aaron looked at Ella. Aaron reckoned an outsider could have mistaken them for the parents of both children.

Tina cleared her throat. 'Ella,' Tina said, 'why don't you take those flowers from Aaron?'

'Sure,' Ella said, and there was relief in her voice. 'I'll go and cajole another vase out of the nursing staff.'

Aaron perched on the edge of Tina's bed, watching Kiri with the baby.

'I'm so grateful, Aaron, for what you did today,' Tina said.

'I didn't do anything.'

'You kept me calm, you rubbed my aching back, you

let me squeeze your fingers, you took more verbal abuse than any man should have to.' Slight pause. 'And you gave my sister strength, just by being there.'

Aaron shook his head. 'Ella didn't need me, Tina.'

Tina looked at him, like he was a puzzle. 'Men really are stupid, aren't they?' she asked. 'Look, Aaron, now that you've seen my lady bits being stretched to oblivion, I feel I know you well enough to be blunt with you. So I'm just going to come right out and ask you: what are you going to do about Ella?'

Aaron jerked so suddenly his leg slipped off the bed. 'I—I— She—'

'Yes, you're as articulate on the subject as she is. Look— you're divorced. Can you make like you really, really mean that, Aaron? And then get my sister away from that man.'

'I thought you liked him?'

'And that's what's stopping you, is it? The way you think I feel?'

'Ella doesn't feel that way about me.'

She fixed him with an incredulous stare. 'Don't be an imbecile. She won't *admit* to feeling that way about you while you've got a wounded animal to look after. Apologies to Rebecca, but you get the picture.'

'She won't leave Javier.'

Tina gave an exaggerated sigh. 'Stupid and so damned *aggravating*. All right, then, forget Ella. Stay in your rut, juggling all your balls and making sure none of them accidentally hits another while they're in the air, and let Javier have her. Because she will marry him, you know. She has a greater capacity for pity than Mother Teresa ever did. Oh, well, at least they'll have good-looking kids.' She turned to Kiri. 'Kiri, sweetheart, I think Daddy wants a turn. You come and tell me about this lovely painting.'

Aaron took that to mean she couldn't bear to speak to him.

He lifted Audrey out of Kiri's arms and stood there, staring down at the newborn and rocking her in his arms. And wondering...

Ella smiled at him as she came back into the room. 'Got a vase,' she announced, and positioned it, flowers already arranged, on the window ledge.

'I think Audrey's smiling at me,' Aaron said.

'If she is, Brand will beat you to a pulp,' Tina said, sounding like she was relishing the thought.

Ouch. 'All right, maybe she's not smiling,' he said. Her tiny mouth opened and closed a few times. 'Is that what you'd call gurgling, maybe?'

Ella laughed. 'No,' she said.

'Hmm. Man, she smells good,' he said after a moment.

'Yes. Babies always smell delicious.' She made a last adjustment to the flowers and then held out her arms for Audrey. 'Time for her to go back to bed,' she said. Aaron gently laid the baby in her arms so she could place her in her bassinette.

Oh, Lord, he thought as that mesmerising scent of Ella's hit his nostrils. She smelled more delicious than a thousand babies.

'Where's Javier tonight?' Tina asked, all innocence.

'He's out with some of his friends. There's a new medical mission in Ethiopia and...' She shrugged.

Tina raised her eyebrows. The picture of disapproval. 'So he's going back to Africa. Would that be before or after you're married, Ella?'

'I don't know, Tina. I guess he'll tell me when he tells me.'

A snort from the bed. 'Very wifely of you, waiting to be told. But not very Ella.'

'It's not like that.'

Another snort.

Aaron judged it time to step into the breach. 'I have something to talk to Ella about.' he said to Tina. 'Can we leave Kiri with you for a few minutes?'

Tina gave him a beaming smile. 'Go. Please. Go.'

'I guess we'll go, then,' Ella said dryly.

Ella and Aaron paused outside the room. And then Ella burst out laughing. 'Is it hormones, or did I miss something?'

'You missed something. I don't know how to break this to you, but I don't think she's crazy about your fiancé.'

'Oh, I know that. Subtle, she isn't.'

'What happened?'

'Just a vibe, I think.' She looked hesitant. 'Do you think we can grab that coffee, without launching World War Three across the table?'

'I'm game if you are. I'll try to keep it at skirmish level rather than a heavy mortar attack.'

'Then I'll keep my grenade pins just half-pulled. Cafeteria, then? The coffee will be awful, but—'

'Cafeteria,' he agreed.

Ella wondered what the hell she was doing.

In a cafeteria, with Aaron, on purpose. Aaron, whose last attempt at drinking a cup of coffee with her had ended with her running to Javier. Aaron, whom she'd basically ordered not to love her.

'So what's the vibe?' Aaron asked, sliding a cup of coffee across the table to her.

Her mind went momentarily blank.

'Javier, Tina?' Aaron prompted. 'The vibe?'

'Oh. Well.' She stalled, taking a sip of coffee. 'She says he's too controlling.'

'Is she right?'

'He…' Another sip of coffee.

'What's wrong, Ella?'

'Huh?'

'If you can take two sips of that coffee and not make an icky face, then you're not tasting it. Which means you're distracted. So, what's wrong?'

What was *wrong* was having this conversation with Aaron. But somehow, bizarrely, it was *right* too.

'Javier is…different,' she started, hesitantly. 'From what I remember, I mean.'

Aaron leaned back in his chair. 'And we're not talking good different.'

It wasn't a question, but Ella answered anyway. 'I think, no. But I don't really know yet. He won't talk about what happened. It makes it…hard.'

She watched as he absorbed that. His fists had clenched. And there was something in his eyes that urged caution.

'Go on,' he said.

She shook her head. 'This is a bad idea, talking to you about this. After…well, after—'

'After I declared my undying love and you threw it back in my face?'

'Yes, definitely a mistake.' She started to get to her feet.

He reached across the table, gripped her wrist. 'Sorry, Ella. If I promise to not let my skyrocketing testosterone get in the way, will you tell me?'

She relaxed into her seat. Nodded. Then she licked her lips, nervous. 'I told you he's the jealous type. Well, he *really* is.'

'You mean, of me?'

'Oh, yes. Even the thought of you helping me today with the baby? Well, let's just say it didn't go down well.'

'But that's insane.'

'And it's not just that. Not just you. He's jealous of everyone. Every man I talk to. Every man who looks at me.'

'Frankly, he's an insecure dirtbag.'

That surprised a laugh out of her. 'That's your testosterone not getting in the way, is it?'

'But he really *is* a dirtbag. Jealous of me? I get it. Because I want you. You know it. I know it. Tina and Brand know it. Tinkerbelle the neighbour's Chihuahua knows it. But, Ella, he does realise you're Hollywood-gorgeous, doesn't he? Every heterosexual man on the planet would take a second look at you. Come on! He's going to be living in hell if he can't cope with that—or he's going to make *you* live in hell because you won't be able to stop it. If he knew you, he'd trust you. So you're basically telling me he doesn't know you.'

Coffee. Sip. Ghastly. Okay, tasting the coffee was a good sign. 'You're so sure you know me that well?'

'I know that much about you. In fact, I'm wishing you were a little *less* faithful the way things are panning out. So, we're back to him being a dirtbag.'

'I haven't exactly been the poster girl for virtue, though, have I?'

'People do all kinds of things to get through tough times. They drink. They play pool with strange men.' Smile. 'They have sex with hunky Australian television stars.' Bigger smile. 'So what? Last time I looked, it wasn't the twelfth century. Nobody expects a twenty-seven-year-old woman to be a virgin, or to enter a convent to wait until her man rises from the dead.' He took her hand. 'Here's the sales pitch for me, just in case you ever end up interested: I wouldn't care if you'd had sex with a thousand men before me, Ella.'

She wanted to both smile and cry, but did neither. 'It wasn't like that, ever. In fact—'

He cut her off with a sharp, 'Hey, stop.'

'Stop?'

'Yes, stop. Don't tell me. And it's not because I'm squeamish either. Or *jealou*s. It's just none of my business. As long as it was *before*. Now, after? Well, that's another story.'

'But it wasn't before, was it?' she said. 'It was after. I had the option of waiting for him and I didn't. I was with you.'

'You are *not* serious, Ella! He was missing for two years; maybe dead. And in my book you *were* waiting. You certainly weren't living.' He squeezed her hand. 'You're not really going all hair shirt on me, are you?'

'I don't think you're the right person to be lecturing me on excessive conscience, Mr Married-Not-Married.' Her shoulders slumped. 'I wish he was more like...' She cleared her throat. 'Nothing.'

'It's "not married". *Not* married. Just to be clear, in case that's what's stopping you from leaving him and throwing yourself at me.' Pause. 'And it's not nothing, I think.'

She smiled. 'It's just...well, you're very different from Javier. And I think he *would* care that I'd been with you. And I think...' Pause, swallow. 'I think I have to tell him. Don't you?'

He let go of her hand, sat back abruptly. 'How did we end up here? One minute we're talking about your sister's excellent intuition when it comes to fiancés and the next you're getting ready to throw yourself on your sword and confess something that's *none of his business*. Shall I say that again? *None of his business.*'

'But what if he finds out? *After* we're married?'

'Who's going to tell him?' Then Aaron seemed to catch himself. He shook his head, bemused. 'I can't believe I'm saying this! If it sounds like I'm talking you into marrying him, don't listen to me.'

'It just seems dishonest. Knowing how he feels about other men even looking at me, telling him is the honourable thing to do.' She looked Aaron straight in the eye. 'It's what you would do, isn't it?'

'I'd break up with him. That's what I'd do.'

'Be serious.'

'I am. Serious as a sudden home birth.'

'You told Rebecca about us.'

'Rebecca and I are divorced, remember?'

'And when you found out about Rebecca being unfaithful, you forgave her.'

He sighed. 'It's not the same, Ella. It's not as simple as admitting you've been unfaithful—although in your case I'll dispute that to my dying day—and getting a blessing in return for being honest.'

'*You'd* forgive me.'

'As far as I'm concerned, there's nothing to forgive. But that's me. If he's the jealous type, and controlling…' He paused, seemed to be weighing his words. 'Who knows how he'll react?'

She looked at her watch. 'Anyway, we'd better get back to Tina. It's late and you need to get Kiri home.'

They left the cafeteria and walked in silence back to Tina's room.

'Thank you for listening,' she said, stopping him just outside. 'You know, don't you, that I've never been able to talk to anyone the way I talk to you? I *don't* talk to anyone like this. Only you. Do you know how much it means to me to have this?'

She reached up, cupped his cheek, and he pressed his hand over hers.

'You don't need to do this, Ella,' he said.

She removed her hand. 'I do,' she insisted. 'And I have to believe he'll forgive me.'

He blew out a breath. 'He will, if he's not a complete idiot. And, for the record, I'd forgive you anything shy of genocide.' He pursed his lips. 'Nah—I'd forgive you that as well.' He frowned down at her. 'And if he *is* a complete idiot, you've got my number. I told you I loved you and I meant it. And I told you I'd wait for you. I will, Ella.'

His hand was over his heart, rubbing. Ella, noticing it, frowned. 'Are you all right?'

'What?' He looked down, stopped the movement straight away. She was surprised to see a slight flush stain his cheekbones. 'Oh, yes,' he said.

Long pause. 'It's hopeless for us, you know that, Aaron.'

'No, I don't,' he answered. 'And I hope you realise I'm in deep trouble with your sister. She thinks I'm out here convincing you to run away with me.'

'You don't want that, Aaron. Not really. Rebecca needs you. Kiri needs Rebecca. And Javier needs me. That's our lives.'

'You left out who you need, Ella. And who I need. I don't accept that our lives are about what everyone *except* us needs. If you could be a little less martyr-like about it—'

'I am not a martyr.'

'Maybe not all the time, but you're in training. Inconveniently, right after meeting me.' He took her hands in his, forestalling any more protestations. 'Anyway, just don't get married too soon. Make sure you get to know the man a little better first.'

'Ella?'

They broke apart and Ella whirled in the direction of Javier's voice.

Ella hurried towards Javier. 'I'm glad you made it.'

He made no move to touch her. 'Are you?' he asked, keeping his flashing black eyes trained on Aaron, who nodded at him and stayed exactly where he was.

Like he was on sentry duty.

Ella was torn between wanting to thump Aaron and wanting to kiss him. Here he was, protecting her from her fiancé in case Javier didn't like what he'd seen—when, really, what was there to like about it? Seeing your future wife holding another man's hands and gazing at him.

There was going to be an argument. And it wasn't going to be pleasant. But not here.

'Yes, I am,' Ella said, determinedly cheerful. 'Visiting hours are over but they're not too strict. Let's go and see Audrey. She looks just like Tina.' She looked at Aaron. 'Doesn't she?'

'Yes,' Aaron agreed. 'It was good to see you, Ella. I'll just pop in for a moment to say goodbye and collect Kiri, then leave you to it.' With what Ella could only describe as a warning look at Javier, Aaron walked into Tina's room, saying, 'Kiri, time to make tracks.'

Ella started to follow Aaron in but Javier stopped her with a hard grip on her arm. 'First, I think you had better tell me what is going on with you and him,' he said.

'Not in a hospital corridor.' Ella eased her arm free. 'Now, come in and see my sister. See the baby. Then we'll go home. And we'll talk.'

Javier didn't touch her on the way home. Didn't speak to her. Didn't look at her.

Ella dreaded the impending argument. But she longed for it too. Because they had to deal with everything—their pasts, their fears, their insecurities, their hopes—before they took another step towards marriage.

Having Aaron to talk to had made her realise she should never have kept her grief locked in for so long. Being able to talk to someone, confide in someone would have eased two long years of heartache.

So now she was going to talk to *this* man. She was preparing to share her life with him, and she couldn't do that without sharing how the past two years had changed her. And if Javier wouldn't confide in her in return, tell her how he'd stayed sane during two years of captivity... well, she didn't know what she'd do. Because she needed that knowledge. The insight. The trust.

They entered the house, went to Javier's room.

'So talk,' he said, and closed the door.

'I—I guess I should start with—'

'Start with what is going on with Aaron James. Why was he holding your hands?'

Ella stayed calm. 'He was comforting me. That's all.'

'Comforting you *why*?'

Still calm. But she licked her lips. 'Because I had just made a difficult decision.'

'What decision? And why were you with him when you made it? Why not me?'

Okay, not so calm. 'I was with him because the decision concerns you.'

His eyes narrowed. He said nothing. Just waited.

'To explain, I need to go back. To when you were kidnapped, and I tried so hard to find out what happened to you, and nobody could—or would—tell me anything. I wasn't a wife, I wasn't a sister. Nobody knew I was even a girlfriend. I'm not sure anyone would have helped me anyway. Because nobody knew anything. All I could do was wait. And wait. And…wait.'

He hadn't moved a muscle.

'It does something to you, the waiting,' she said, drowning. 'And I know you must know what I mean, because you were waiting too.'

'This is about you, Ella, not me.'

'But you never talk about it. You never—'

'You. Not me,' he rapped out.

She jumped. 'Right. Yes. Well…I—I—'

'Waited for me,' he finished for her, and it was more of a taunt than a statement.

'Yes, I did.'

'And you kept waiting, and waiting, and waiting.'

'Y-yes.'

'Until Aaron James came along.'

She sucked in a breath. Sudden. 'No. At least, yes but… no.'

He looked at her. Utterly, utterly cold. 'Yes but no?'

The snap in his voice had her stomach rioting.

'You slept with Aaron James. Just say it.'

She jumped, jolted. 'I thought you were dead.'

He had started pacing the room. 'You wished I was.'

'No!' she cried. 'Never, ever, ever.' She felt like she was running at a brick wall. It wouldn't yield; only she could. Or try, at least. 'It's over between me and Aaron. He is no threat to you.'

Javier stopped, looked at her, incredulous. 'No threat to me? No *threat*?'

'I will be living in Barcelona, with you. He will be on the other side of the world.'

He shoved her against the wall. 'He is your sister's friend. He will be there, always.' He punched his fist into the wall beside her head. 'You have been denying me what you gave *him*. You introduced him to me. You made a fool of me.'

Ella stayed ultra-still, scared to move. 'I wanted to tell you. I am telling you. Now.'

'Now!' He looked into her face. He was only just holding his fury in check. 'Two years I survived, to come back and learn that you have slept around.'

'Don't say that,' Ella said.

'How do I know that you weren't sleeping with who knows how many men from the moment I was gone? We'd only known each other a few weeks when you slept with me. A woman like you would sleep with anyone. That's what I think you have spent the last two years doing. Now, just admit it, Ella.'

Ella thought of all the things she had planned to tell him tonight. The confession about Aaron, yes, but also about Sann, about her life in despairing limbo. And this is what it had come down to. 'No,' she said quietly. 'I will not admit to that.'

He raised his hand as if to hit her.

Her eyes blazed. 'If you touch me, I will make you sorry you're not still in Somalia,' she said.

'No, I won't hit you,' he said. 'You're not worth it, Ella.'

It took all of Ella's courage to turn from Javier. To walk slowly out of the room, not run, as his curses continued to rain on her.

She sat in her bedroom, shaking. She could hear drawers and cupboard doors slamming. Curses. Wheels on the floor—his bag. There was a pause outside her door. She imagined him coming in...

She held her breath, realised she was trembling like a leaf.

Then another inarticulate curse. Footsteps going down the stairs.

Out of her life.

Even three floors up she heard the front door slam.

'Some things just change,' she whispered to herself, and remembered Aaron saying exactly that to her.

She'd thought it would be comforting to accept that.

Instead, it made her cry.

CHAPTER SEVENTEEN

ELLA? ELLA PICK up. It's me.

Hellooo? Ella? Why didn't you return my call?

Ella, pick up! Come on, pick up!

Yeah, three messages were probably enough, Aaron decided, catching himself before he could leave a fourth.

He contemplated calling Brand to do some back-door sleuthing—but pictured his lifeless body sporting a variety of blunt and sharp force injuries should Ella get wind of that, and opted to spend the night tossing and turning instead as he wondered how the confession had gone. Whether Javier and Ella were in bed, burying the infidelity hatchet in a lusty bout of lovemaking.

No!

He would *not* imagine that.

He would, instead, plan what he would say, how he would act, tomorrow, when he made a last-ditch effort to woo Ella, regardless of what had happened between her sheets tonight.

And screw the best-buddy routine the two of them had enacted at the hospital; he should have whisked her off into the night instead of letting her saunter off with the darkly brooding doctor.

Anyway, enough dwelling on what he should have done. More important was the future.

So, back to what he was going to say to Ella.

And it was suddenly so clear! Why did it have to be three o'clock in the morning when he realised that keeping things simple was not about compartmentalising things to death? Ella in one corner, Rebecca in another, Kiri in a third. Him in the fourth, sashaying back and forth between them. Tina had put it best—he was juggling balls to make sure they didn't ever connect.

Dumb, dumb, dumb.

Because who wanted to juggle for eternity? It was exhausting. You had to stop some time and hold all the balls together in your hands, if you didn't want your arms to fall off.

Yep, it was crystal clear at three o'clock.

He was getting quite poetic.

And perhaps a little maudlin. Because he couldn't help revisiting every stupid argument he and Ella had ever had, wishing he could go back and fix every single one of them to get the right ending.

How arrogant he'd been, to insist they couldn't have a relationship because of his complicated life. Who *didn't* have a complicated life? Ella's was worthy of its own miniseries! All he'd managed to do was give Ella every argument she'd ever need to keep him at arm's length for the rest of their natural lives.

And she knew how to use them.

One. What was good for Rebecca. Well, if Rebecca knew she was the main obstacle to his relationship with Ella, she'd laugh herself sick.

Two. What was good for Kiri. As if being around Ella could ever be bad for him!

Three. His own initial disapproval of her. Short-lived

it may have been, but Ella had turned out to be an expert at hurling that at his head.

He wanted to slap himself in the head when he thought back to how he'd made Ella feel like she wasn't good enough to be near his son. Except that he couldn't hit himself hard enough; he'd need some kind of mediaeval mace with all the spiky protuberances to do his self-disgust justice.

Just how was he going to fix the situation?

He could do better. He *would* do better. He would be sane, articulate, charming, passionate, clever. He would convince her that she belonged with him.

Tomorrow he would prove that love was really simple. Just being in it and grabbing it when it hits you and making your life fit around it, not it fit around your life. *Very* simple.

What time was a decent time to arrive at Brand's, given Tina and Audrey were coming home from the hospital? Just after lunch? That seemed good timing. For a sane, reasonable man who was insanely, unreasonably in love with a woman who held all the cards.

He found that he was rubbing his chest over his heart again.

Man, he hated that.

One look in the mirror the next day had Ella raiding Tina's store of make-up.

She couldn't look like one of the undead for Tina's return from the hospital.

And she would have to handle the news of her break-up with Javier carefully, with no mention of last night's awful showdown, if she didn't want Tina packing the electrical wires and blowtorch in a backpack and going off to hunt Javier down.

But she would, at last, tell her sister everything about the past two years, including what had happened with Sann. She would let her into her pain and grief the way she should have done all along.

And then she would go back to Los Angeles. And she would tell her parents.

And then it would be time for her to move on, and make new memories.

No guilt, no shame.

'She's not here, Aaron.'

Aaron heard the words come out of Brand's mouth but couldn't quite compute.

'Not here?' His eyes widened. 'Then where is she? *How* is she?'

'If it's the break-up with Javier you're talking about, she's fine. I'd go so far as to say she's relieved.'

Aaron felt a wave of intense happiness, until the look on Brand's face registered. 'So when will she be back?' he asked.

And then Brand put his arm around Aaron's shoulder, steered him into the library.

Not promising.

Brand poured Scotch into a glass, held it out for Aaron. 'Her flight home took off about half an hour ago,' he said.

Aaron took the glass, almost mechanically sipped.

Brand walked over to his desk, plucked a small envelope off it, handed it to Aaron.

Aaron.
I think we've all had enough upheavals for a while so let's not add any more drama. Good luck with Rebecca. And hug Kiri for me.
Ella

He looked up and caught Brand's eye.

'That's it?' he demanded.

'That's it.'

He reread the note.

'Yeah, screw that,' he said. 'When do we wrap up filming?'

'Four weeks.'

'Then that's how long she's got before I go after her.'

'Princess Tina will be pleased,' Brand said, and slapped him on the shoulder.

CHAPTER EIGHTEEN

ELLA WASN'T HOME.

Aaron almost laughed as he recalled the way he'd played this scene out in his head. He would knock on the door of her apartment. She would open the door, stare at him, smile that dazzling smile—the one that had her heart and soul in it—and then she would leap into his arms and kiss him. She would tell him she loved him, that she couldn't live without him. That she'd been waiting for him.

Very satisfactory.

Except that she wasn't home.

The only romance he'd had so far had involved charming Ella's young gay doorman into letting him into the building.

Well, he'd told Ella more than once he would wait for her. And here he was, waiting.

It had been four weeks. Enough time for Ella to miss him desperately. Enough time for him to get all the elements in place to counteract Ella's martyrish inclinations: Rebecca was doing brilliantly at Trust; her new love affair was steaming ahead and Aaron liked the guy; custody arrangements had been sorted; and Aaron had even managed to nab that lead role in the LA-based detective series he'd auditioned for.

Fate was lining up for him at last.

Now he just had to pray that Ella wasn't about to head off to the Congo or float herself down the Amazon, and life would be perfect.

If he could just get her to say three little words.

He didn't really know if she could say those words. Or feel them.

He heard the elevator, and scrambled to his feet. He'd done this four times already—all false alarms—but, hey, he wasn't about to be found by the love of his life sitting on the floor.

Then he saw her. She was wearing the dress he'd bought her in London. That *had* to be a sign.

He felt those blasted butterflies again. Actually, forget butterflies; these were more like bats. Humongous bats.

He knew the moment she saw him. The hitch in her stride. Then the slow, gliding tread towards him.

'Well,' Ella said inadequately, with the smile that didn't reach her eyes.

All Aaron's optimism dropped through his gut to the floor. 'Don't,' he said. 'Don't smile like that. Not like that. Not now.'

'I don't—'

'And don't say you don't know what I mean. Because you do. Aren't you happy to see me, Ella?'

He heard her suck in a breath. And then she said, 'Is everything…? Is everything okay? Rebecca…'

'In rehab. Taking control. Doing great. But even if her life were off the rails, I'd still be here, Ella. What I would have told you, if you hadn't left London when you did, was that I was going to make things work for us come hell or high water. No matter what was happening with anyone else. Rebecca, Kiri, your family, even Javier—I'd still want you with me. All right, to be honest, I still want to damage one of Javier's cheekbones, so having him in our lives might take a little work.'

'Javier just couldn't forgive. Couldn't even accept. And I realised either he'd changed or I never really knew him. But if you'd seen him, so heroic and caring and brilliant in Somalia, you—'

'Yeah, yeah, don't expect me to get all misty-eyed over his good doctor deeds, Ella. And he had nothing to forgive. I don't want to talk about him. I don't care about him. I only care about you.'

He stepped closer to her. 'I don't know what I'll do if I can't have you. You and I, we're supposed to be together. Can't you feel it? We've learned, both of us, that life isn't about hanging on the sidelines, waiting for things to get better. Or worse. Waiting for fate to come and toss a grenade or a bouquet or a wet fish. I'll catch every grenade, Ella, and I'll still love you. I'll navigate any difficulty to have you.'

She blinked hard. Again. 'Oh.'

'I'll follow you to Sierra Leone or Chad or Somalia or Laos.'

She shook her head. 'It's good old America for a long time to come, so you'll have to think of something else.'

'Hmm. So, what about…?' He held up his hands. They were shaking. 'What about this? Nobody else has ever made me shake just because they were near me, Ella.'

'Are you sure? Are you really sure, Aaron?'

He waved his hands at her. 'Look at them! Like a leaf in a gale.'

'I don't mean— I mean I don't want you to regret me. I don't want to become one more responsibility to bear. And you know, better than most, I've hardly been a saint, so I'd understand—'

'Stop talking like that!' He started undoing his shirt.

'What about Kiri? How will Rebecca take it?'

'Kiri loves you, and as for Rebecca—was I just talking about not caring? But if it will get you over the line, I swear I'll get her blessing in writing. My sisters—they've posted an embarrassing video on YouTube begging you to take me—wait until you see it. And I've already gone and—'

'What are you doing?' she asked, seeming to notice at last that he was removing his shirt. 'I'm not— I don't— I— Oh!'

'Do you like it?'

Ella came forward, put her hands on his chest. He'd had her name tattooed across his chest. Her name. Bold and beautiful.

And something else.

Dropping from the A over his left pectoral muscle was a gold ring that looked like it was entering his skin where his heart was, anchoring her name there. Her fingers traced it. 'Oh, Aaron. Yes, I like it.'

'I'll ink my whole body for you Ella, if you want.'

'No, just this,' she said. 'It looks…permanent.' She put her head on one side, querying him. 'Is it?'

'The things I'll do to get a green card,' Aaron quipped, and then gathered her in, held her against his chest, tilted her face up to his. 'Yes, it's permanent. And so are you. Are you ready, Ella, my darling? You know I want you. You know I'm obsessed, besotted, madly and wildly in love with you. Tell me you feel the same. Tell me you're ready. Come on, Ella. Say it. Say it.'

'I love you. And, yes,' she breathed. And then she smiled and her face lit up like the sun. Bright and gold and glowing. His smile. Just for him. 'I'm ready.'

He closed his eyes. Breathed in. Out. Opened his eyes. 'Then let's get inside. I want to have my way with you— No, wait! I want you to have your way with me. Hang on, I want— Oh, Ella, just open the door.'

* * * * *

MILLS & BOON®

Why shop at millsandboon.co.uk?

Each year, thousands of romance readers find their perfect read at millsandboon.co.uk. That's because we're passionate about bringing you the very best romantic fiction. Here are some of the advantages of shopping at www.millsandboon.co.uk:

* **Get new books first**—you'll be able to buy your favourite books one month before they hit the shops

* **Get exclusive discounts**—you'll also be able to buy our specially created monthly collections, with up to 50% off the RRP

* **Find your favourite authors**—latest news, interviews and new releases for all your favourite authors and series on our website, plus ideas for what to try next

* **Join in**—once you've bought your favourite books, don't forget to register with us to rate, review and join in the discussions

Visit **www.millsandboon.co.uk**
for all this and more today!